This Is It, Boys: Damn You, Jackson!

This Is It, Boys: Damn You, Jackson!

The Boys of Uncle Sam Series

J. Allen Clary

ABSOLUTELY AMAZING eBOOKS

Published by Whiz Bang LLC, 926 Truman Avenue, Key West, Florida 33040, USA.

For information contact:
Publisher@AbsolutelyAmazingEbooks.com

ISBN-13: 978-1945772504 (Absolutely Amazing Ebooks)
ISBN-10: 1945772506

The Boys of Uncle Sam Books by J. Allen Clary

Here We Go Again, Boys

This Is It, Boys: Damn You, Jackson!

Introduction

I dedicate this story to my father, First Lieutenant Raymond Darwin "Buck" Clary, a veteran of WWII who fought across France and Belgium, all the way through Germany's capitulation. After the surrender, he stayed in Germany for another 5 months until he was discharged, October 1945.

Landing on the beaches of Normandy 7 days after a successful invasion, he fought in many battles during the chase across France. He fought in the hedgerows of Normandy, St. Lo, the Battle of the Bulge, Aachen, and many of the battles in between. He was also an outstanding father. He is still my greatest hero.

After experiencing the Ardennes fighting, my father hated snow, so in 1953, he moved his family from Newark, Ohio to Tampa, Florida. Around 1956, he went to work for a 3-store chain of furniture warehouses called Maas Brothers. He started on the docks loading and unloading furniture from tractor, trailers, and counting inventory. The bottom rung of the ladder. When he retired from Maas Brothers thirty years later, he was on the Board of Managers for all 38 stores, and he had accomplished his milestones despite the fact that he hated his job, and he always had a smile on his face. Always. My father is my greatest hero. Thank you, dad, for sticking up for us.

- J. Allen Clary

Chapter 1

The attack began on the 19th of February, 1943. Bad leadership and the inexperience of American troops resulted in a tactical victory for the Germans. On the opposite side of the battle line, the Americans were handed their butts on a platter by one of the foremost panzer commanders in the German Army, Field Marshal Erwin Rommel.

The Kasserine attack started out well but ran into some problems when friction arose between Rommel and the commander of the 5th Panzer Army. Some units were withheld from the battle, and orders were ignored. The commander of the 5th Panzer Army deliberately failed to support the attack because of his own agenda, and by the 24th of February, the Germans were retreating back to their start positions. Lack of a unified co-operation between the two forces doomed the attack to failure.

Two weeks after the battle, Colonel Martin's battalion was bivouacked in the desert, just inside the Algerian border, about ten miles southwest of the Tunisian town of Feriana. Reinforcements hadn't arrived yet, so Division dumped the wounded battalion in a quiet, out of the way sector to lick its wounds and await much needed replacements. The battalion had been hit hard by the German onslaught.

Staff Sergeant Alfred Brooks was soaked in sweat and was just leaving Battalion headquarters. Everywhere he looked there was nothing but dust, dried out scrub brush, eye-burning sunlight, and sun-baked dirt. "Damn, it's hot!"

Former platoon sergeant, PFC Alex Sims, was walking beside Sergeant Brooks when he replied, "Al, if we were knee deep in snow, you'd still complain about it being hot."

Turning his head, Baker Company's finest shooter looked at Sims and said, "This oven-baked, crap-hole Division stuck us in doesn't bother you?"

His friend's expression was absolutely neutral when he replied, "I don't think about it. Besides, I'm shorter than you, so I'm farther away from the sun than you are."

Sergeant Brooks quickly came to a two-step halt. Folding his arms across his chest, he gazed at his friend for a moment before he said, "Really, Alex? You think three inches is going to make that big of a difference? Now I know why you lost your stripes. You keep thinking that way, and you'll be officer material in no time. At least, you won't have to worry about sewing new stripes on your shirt."

"Oh, come on, Al, no need to get hostile. I'm not that bad." Then he shook his head. "We sure took a beating at Kasserine, didn't we?"

"Yeah. We got our butts spanked that's for sure." An unexpected pause ensued while Brooks stared at his friend, watching his friend's expression change. "What are you smiling about, Alex?" Still smiling, Sims turned and walked towards his canvas-covered barracks. Replying over his shoulder, he said, "Replacements, Al. They're due in today. Remember?"

"Oh, yeah, that's right. Damn! It would have to be today. I hope we don't get any more idiots like that Spencer guy. That bonehead was a real screwball. I hear he's in supply, now. Hey! Where do you think you're going? Get back here, PFC."

"Have fun, Al. Your job now. I lost my stripes, and you got the platoon. Remember?"

"Sergeant Brooks?"

Staff Sergeant Brooks turned to face in the direction of the voice. "Yes, sir."

"The colonel wants to see you."

"Thank you, sir," he replied, and then he turned to look at his retreating friend. "Come on, Alex. Maybe Colonel Martin has a mission for us. Anything is better than waiting for reinforcements to arrive."

The walk to battalion headquarters didn't take long, nor did the mission briefing. The two men stood somewhat at attention in front of the colonel, waiting to receive their orders. They didn't have long to wait. "Stand at ease, men. Sergeant Brooks, I need you to go out on a recon mission tonight. I want some prisoners. Preferably able to talk when you get them back."

"Yes, sir," replied Brooks. Recalling his last outing, he had to struggle hard not to laugh and derail the briefing. "Sorry about the last grab, Colonel. Corporal Cane got a little trigger-happy when one of the prisoners pulled a short-gun out of his sleeve. Do you want me to leave him behind this time, sir?"

"No, Sergeant. I think you're going to need Corporal Cane on this one."

An immediate change in the colonel's expression put Sergeant Brooks on the alert, but only for a couple seconds. An approving nod followed the change of expression, along with a verbal confirmation. "Your request is now official, effective immediately. Good luck, Sergeant Brooks."

A quick thank you, sir, yes sir, and an even quicker salute ended their stay, and the two men left Colonel Martin's headquarters to go pick the troops for the upcoming mission. When they arrived back in the company area, they found six boyish, mostly man-sized boys, standing around as though lost. They didn't look eighteen to Sergeant Brooks; they looked more like sixteen.

"What can I do for you?" he asked.

A skinny beanpole resembling a kid stepped forward. "We're looking for Sergeant Brooks."

Sergeant Brooks let out a short chuckle before he answered. "Well, you've found him."

The beanpole was still smiling when he cheerfully said, "Private Timothy Jackson, reporting, sir. Lieutenant Jacobs sent us over. We're your new replacements."

Staring down at the beanpole in uniform, Brooks couldn't believe what he heard. *Great, they send us kids instead of men.* Not knowing what else to think, he immediately fell back on his training. *Well, that's the army for you.* The saying was age-old, but it sure made situations sound less complicated.

Lieutenant Jacobs walked up to Sergeant Brooks, interrupting his thoughts. "Colonel Martin wants you to take one of the new guys with you when you go."

"Yes, sir, Lieutenant... Damn!"

Lieutenant Jacobs shook his head somewhat sympathetically before he said, “Look at it this way, Sergeant Brooks; at least, you get to pick who goes.”

Somewhat perplexed, Sergeant Brooks removed his helmet and wiped his brow while he silently gazed at his platoon leader for a moment. After putting his helmet back on, he nodded slowly and said, “Thank you, sir. I really appreciate that.”

Brooks spent the rest of the day watching his new replacements, wondering how many were still going to be around after the next go-round with the Germans. Still thinking about his choice, and still not completely satisfied with his decision, he turned and asked, “Alex, who is that skinny kid? The kid wearing the butt-pack? What was his name again?”

He was still arguing with himself about an hour before sundown, when he finally made up his mind. “Alex, hunt down that Jackson kid and have him report to me ASAP. Also, you better tell Cane he’s on point tonight before he gets too inebriated to walk. Oh, and grab Baker while you’re at. His German speaking talent might come in handy tonight.”

Thirty minutes after the squad was called together, Sergeant Brooks had his map spread out on the hood of a burned-out jeep, his favorite briefing room. “Pay attention guys. Our route will take us near the town of Feriana. Just beyond that town are the Germans, exactly where we’re going. Now tighten it up and listen.”

~ ~ ~

The squad moved cross-country through rugged, hilly, hard-dirt terrain that rapidly cooled down to almost cold. Crawling to the crest of a small rise, Sergeant Brooks paused while he scanned the area for a couple of minutes, searching for anyone silhouetted against the skyline before moving closer to the town. “I don’t see anything, Dan. What do you think?”

“I say we go, Al. An extra pair of eyes are always useful. You see what I see. Nothing appears to be out there.”

The late evening was peaceful and quiet where the squad was hunkering down. Only the distant flashes of war, lighting up the nighttime horizon and the long-distance crack and boom of artillery going off, unraveled the peaceful scene, revealing its false setting. Then there was the occasional sudden eruption of battle when small Allied recon units ran into small German hunting parties looking for the Allied recon units.

The sound of voices carried across the sand, but Sergeant Brooks couldn't tell whose they were. Crawling back behind the rise, he led his men on towards the town, swinging wide right and hoping to avoid any unexpected revelations. He was determined to be the trigger of surprise, not its aftermath.

Coming up to a much larger rise situated about a mile northeast of Feriana, Corporal Cane signaled, and the squad immediately went to ground. Sergeant Brooks waited about ten minutes before Cane appeared out of the shadows, slinking towards him.

"Kraut machine gun on top of that rise. Looks wide open, Al. Not a good target in my book."

Sergeant Brooks whispered back. "Let's scootch in a little closer to that small ledge, so you and Baker can sneak up the side and find out what Fritz is talking about. All right people. Walk softly, and no talking. Corporal Cane, lead us to the promised sand."

After a quiet scamper to the rocky shelf Brooks had pointed out, the squad was hunkered down, waiting for Cane and Baker to return from their foray. About fifteen minutes into their wait, Sergeant Brooks received a tap on his shoulder. Turning, he discovered the tapper was the beanpole looking kid from Arizona, and he said. "Someone's coming, Sarge."

Staring down at the kid, Brooks was about to tell Jackson he was nuts. He was about to say, "I don't hear anything, Private," when he heard something. Turning to his right, he watched Cane and Baker walk into view, along the base of the thirty-foot rise of rock and sand, instead of coming down the way they went up. Somewhat taken aback, Brooks took a second look at the beanpole of a kid who was too skinny to fill out the uniform he was wearing.

The rise was actually a large chunk of rock with age-old, wind-blown sand, and rocky debris forming up the gently sloping sides, along with the dead undergrowth that had tried to make a stab at life and failed.

Using hand signals, Corporal Cane indicated that there were three Germans on the top of the ridge manning a machine gun: a gunner, an assistant gunner, and a rifleman. The latter was used to ward off flanking movements and snatch-and-grabs. Not the ideal situation for seizing prisoners. Brooks stared at Cane while he tried to come up with a plan. *How do we grab these guys without getting shot? We need to bring back live prisoners, not dead ones.* The situation wasn't the most desirable setting to be in, and it had him wondering.

The five men were gathered at the base of the rise at the seven o'clock position to their enemy's left. The top of the lone hill was hard, rocky ground, with wind-blown sand resting up against the stems of scrub brush and whatever else halted its progress. Dry, rocky, runoff gullies added another danger: the unwanted crunch of rock and sand, caused by an unbalanced step.

To reach the machine gun from the rear required a sixty-foot sneak without cover. Coming up behind the enemy with that much distance between them would be very dangerous at best, so the risk far outweighed the reward in this situation. Sergeant Brooks recognized this certainty and called a quick conference. "We're going to have to look elsewhere for our snatch and grab. It's just too risky to try and take these guys." He felt a tap on his shoulder and turned to his left, and there was Private Jackson, ready to tap again. "I want to see the enemy, Sarge."

Jackson had never seen the enemy before, so he wanted to see if the Germans were really the ring-tailed monsters he was hearing about. Sergeant Brooks had a smile on his face when he issued his order. "You three stay here. I'll take skinny-ass and show him what the enemy looks like. If we're lucky, maybe he won't piss in his boots."

Turning, the squad leader led off around the lone rise to the rear of the German position. When he arrived directly behind the enemy, he turned to whisper to Jackson, but the kid was nowhere to be seen. Trying to find him, Brooks searched around, but couldn't see him anywhere. *Where in the hell did that boy disappear to*?

Taking one last look around, he started backtracking to where the rest of the squad was waiting and caught a shadow of movement coming from the top of the rise to his right. Turning to look up, his heart instantly skipped a beat, and he immediately raised his rifle to his shoulder. He was about to let loose with three rapid shots; his finger was already squeezing the trigger. Abruptly, he stopped and raised his eyes from his rifle sights, a somewhat incredulous look on his face; the enemy had their hands in the air. When they had moved below the crest of the hill, he spotted another silhouette that appeared to be following the surrendered enemy; it was Private Jackson.

Sergeant Brooks was stunned. *How did that skinny little kid pull this off*? He didn't say a word; he couldn't. He was in absolute shock over what he was staring at. When Jackson stopped the three Germans in front of him at the base of the rise, he still had no idea what to say, but he knew what to do.

Still a bit bewildered, Brooks quickly took out the cord he had brought along and tied the prisoners' hands, and then he placed part of a sock in each man's mouth. Next were the gags and then the blindfolds, and during all that effort, he still had no idea what to think beyond *how did that skinny-ass kid pull this off*? Still in shock, he still hadn't said anything to Jackson yet.

Corporal Cane spotted the enemy before Sims and Baker and brought up his rifle, ready to fire until he saw Brooks and Jackson following behind. He was also shocked. "Ho, will you look at this? Prisoners on our first try. What time is it? If we head back now, we'll still have two hours of drinking time left. What do you say, Al?" Nobody else spoke. Sergeant Brooks pointed off to the west, and the five men, plus the prisoners, headed back to headquarters. Several times he started to say something to Jackson, but each time, he failed. He ended his attempts with a disbelieving shake of his head, instead. After walking for an hour, Corporal Cane asked him what happened.

"I have no idea, Dan," replied Brooks. "When we got behind the Germans, I turned to caution the kid, but he wasn't there. I looked around, and when I couldn't find him, I thought maybe he got cold feet and headed back to you guys, so I headed back. I caught a movement off to my right, and I see these three Germans coming down the hill with Jackson following them. I have no idea how he pulled it off."

Chapter 2

Sergeant Brooks entered Colonel Martin's office and stood at attention. "I have your prisoners outside, sir."

"Good job, Sergeant Brooks." Somewhat astonished after the words hit home, Colonel Martin did a double-take and immediately looked at his wall clock. "I take it you didn't run into any problems? That was quick."

"No, sir. No problem at all. Corporal Cane heard the prisoners talking on top of a hill, and Jackson went up and captured them. The Krauts were manning an MG42."

Colonel Martin looked at Sergeant Brooks for a moment, not sure if he heard correctly. "You just went up and grabbed a Kraut machine gun crew, and no one got hurt? That was it?"

Standing more than several inches taller, at 6-1, Brooks smiled down at his commanding officer and said, "No, sir, Colonel. Jackson went up and captured the Germans, and no one got hurt. We were still down at the bottom of the hill, sir."

Colonel Martin stared at his sergeant for a moment, wondering if he was pulling something on him. "Really, Sergeant? No bullshit? Just one rooky private captured an entire machine gun crew, out in the open, and no blood was spilled?"

"You got it, sir. Jackson just went up to the top of that hill and brought the Krauts down. All three of them. They're outside if you want to see them. Will that be all, sir?"

"Yes, Sergeant. You can go now." Saluting, Sergeant Brooks turned and left the room.

Colonel Martin was still somewhat skeptical about the report until he walked out onto his private balcony and looked down. "Well, I'll be damned. Major! Bring me the files on the new replacements assigned to Baker Company, first platoon."

Sergeant Brooks was still amazed at the happenings earlier that evening. That is, until he spotted Jackson. Then the steam started pouring out. "What in the hell were you thinking about when you pulled that little stunt, Private? You could've gotten us all killed with your stupid antics! I ought to shove your ass in the stockade for that. What in the hell's wrong with you?"

"I'm sorry, Sarge," said Jackson. "The Germans were too busy talking to hear me coming up behind them. It was real easy."

Sergeant Brooks just glared at Jackson for a moment before he said, "Don't you ever jeopardize my squad's life like that again. Do you understand me, Private?"

Terrified, Jackson swallowed hard before he replied. "Yes, sir, Sergeant Brooks!"

Brooks glared down at Jackson for a couple of seconds before he took a deep breath and blasted the kid for calling him sir. His heated deliverance had the private cringing inside the entire time he was getting chewed-out until, without warning, the sergeant's tirade ended with his final words; "Now, get out of my sight before I *do* put you in the stockade!"

Jackson's retreat was immediate. He turned and took off running so fast that his platoon sergeant was on the verge of laughing. The skinny kid from Arizona didn't want to spend the war in a stockade, so he took off running for the nearest tent. His plan was to get out of sight quickly. Seconds after achieving his goal, he noticed Private Lemons leaning up against a shot-up jeep and wandered over.

Sam was eager to hear what happened and why Sergeant Brooks was so hot around the collar. When he asked, Jackson told him everything. "Damn," he blurted out. "No wonder he was pissed." Sam was also excited and wanted to hear more about Jackson's exploits, so he goaded his friend into telling him all about it.

The next day, Sergeant Brooks was telling Lieutenant Jacobs about the previous night's mission. Jacobs listened to what his platoon sergeant was saying until he arrived at the part about Jackson. That episode really threw him for a loop. "Well, I'll be damned. Private Jackson just snuck up on three Germans and captured them, just like that?"

Brooks was nodding and smiling when he replied, "Yes, sir, he did. Out in the open, I might add. I still find it hard to believe, sir. We might have us a good man if he can stay alive long enough to learn something."

"Then you might want to take him along again," said the lieutenant.

"Take him along where, sir?" asked Brooks.

"Colonel Martin wants you to go out and grab some more prisoners tonight."

Sergeant Brooks didn't know what to say at first. Then he asked that all-important question. "Can I get drunk first, sir?"

Lieutenant Jacobs unsuccessfully tried to keep from laughing. "Not this time Sergeant. Follow me and I'll show you on the map where you're going."

After a two-minute walk, the lieutenant and Sergeant Brooks were staring at a map pinned to a wall in Lieutenant Jacob's adobe quarters. "Here's the place. It's a town just northeast of Feriana called The ... lepte, The ... le ... ah shit. I can't pronounce the name of that place without my tongue cramping up."

"Close enough for Army work, sir," answered Brooks. Then he took a closer look at the map. "It's farther than Feriana, sir. We're going to need a little more time to snatch our grab and get back before sunrise. This mission might turn into a two-night venture, Lieutenant."

"I know, Sergeant Brooks, and I took that into consideration. I have your favorite limo standing by, ready to transport you and your squad north to Dernia. From there, you'll travel on foot. Your limo should be waiting at Dernia for your return. Are there any more questions?"

"Yes, sir," he replied. "Is my favorite limo equipped with tracks this time, sir?"

"Yes, Sergeant Brooks. It also comes equipped with a big 50 cal., so don't piss off the driver on this run."

Smiling, Sergeant Brooks answered. "Hopefully, this driver won't get us stuck. See you on the flip side, sir."

"Good luck, Sergeant Brooks. I'll see you when you get back."

With a yes, sir, and a salute, Brooks was off to pick his men once again. "Jackson!" he yelled. "Get over here!"

"Yes, sir, Sarge!"

Seconds later, Jackson was standing in front of Sergeant Brooks and was on the receiving end of a glare that wilted all others. "Sir? Do you see any butter bars, crow wings, or stars on my collar? You call me sir again, and I'm going to turn you upside down, and bounce your head off the ground a couple of times. Now get your gear; we're going out again. And while you're at it, inform Corporal Cane, PFC Baker, and PFC Sims that I want to see them by that burned-out jeep in fifteen minutes."

"Yes, sir, Sarge!" And off he went. It was hard to tell if the spring in Jackson's step was from excitement or because he was shaking so bad from the chewing out he just received that he couldn't keep his feet on the ground. *Crap on the ground. That was intense.*

Fifteen minutes after their summons, the men Sergeant Brooks had requested were waiting at the jeep when he arrived. "We have another grab to make tonight, and it looks like an all-nighter. We leave at 2000 hours. We'll meet back here at 1930 hours, and I'll brief you then. Find a hole and get some sleep while you can. That's all for now."

Jackson found Lemons in the mess line and told him what was going on. "Damn. I wish I was going," he said. "I'd really like to go on this one."

Jackson chuckled at his friend's disappointed expression before he answered Sam's not so subtle inquiry. "I would ask Sergeant Brooks, but as hot as he was a little while ago, I'm afraid to push it. There will be other patrols. I'm sure you'll go on one of those."

At 1930 hours, the five men were standing by the burned-out jeep, listening to Sergeant Brooks. Their platoon sergeant was beaming brightly when he told his men they were going to have to climb a six-hundred-foot hill. "This ought to take away the hangovers. All that fresh air and exercise, the exotic plant life, and sucking in all that dust and crap. I can't find a better way to clear a hangover. Now gather round."

No one said a word. The men just stared at Sergeant Brooks, trying to figure out if he were fooling around, but he didn't give the squad anymore time to think about his words. "We'll cut across here and head north until we get behind this circled town. There's an unidentified Kraut headquarters located where we're supposed to do our snatch and grab. Colonel Martin wants it identified." Then he tossed something at PFC Sims. His conniving scheme with the colonel had paid off. Sims' rise in rank came as a complete surprise to him.

"Have these on your shoulders before we head out, *Corporal* Sims, or I'll rip your sleeves off, and you'll never get to wear them. Evidently, somebody upstairs thinks you're worth it, but for the life of me, I can't figure out who would think that way."

~ ~ ~

At 2000 hours, the five men were on their way to the drop off point. The halftrack they were traveling in slowly ground its way through the rocky, hilly, countryside. To the men bouncing around in the back, it seemed like an inch at a time, but the halftrack was actually making pretty good time. A little over an hour later, they were dropped off and on their way north towards their towering climb.

The night was dark where the squad was walking, but not dark enough to keep them from seeing where they were going. About three hundred feet up the slope, Corporal Cane discovered a footpath that ran in the same general direction the squad needed to take later on, so Brooks decided to use it to avoid the remaining climb. While the squad was moving along the path, Jackson moved up next to Brooks. "I hear voices, Sarge."

Brooks signaled for the men to stop and cocked his head to listen. After a moment or so he turned towards Jackson. "You're nuts, Private." Then he heard the voices.

Looking around quickly, he spotted some rocks down below the trace. "Behind those rocks. Now," he whispered. Within seconds, the squad was scattered about, hiding and waiting among the rocks. A minute or so went by, and then they watched while three locals leading two camels walked along the narrow dirt trail, passing the squad and heading west. Following a few paces behind the camels was an eight-man squad of German soldiers.

The path itself was barely wide enough for the camels to pass in a column, so anybody coming from the opposite direction would have to move down off the trail to let them pass. Brooks waited about fifteen minutes before he and his men scrambled back up to the path to resume their eastward journey.

Pulling on his right ear, Brooks was deep in thought, wondering about Jackson. *How did he hear those voices before anybody else?* Puzzled, he continued to ponder the question while he stared out at the terrain. *He was walking in the middle of the squad, and still he heard them before we did. Maybe I should put him on point? No, he's too green. But still. He did hear those voices before anyone else.* The thought was a puzzler, and it wouldn't leave him alone.

The men of 1st squad were looking down the side of the hill towards the direction of Feriana. They had to be very quiet for the next couple of miles until they could put the town behind them. Sound carries at night, so the fear of being discovered by the Germans was very real.

Without warning, Private Jackson tapped Corporal Sims on the shoulder and whispered, "I think someone's coming, Corporal."

Corporal Sims immediately tapped Brooks on the shoulder and said, "The beanpole says someone's coming down the path."

Sergeant Brooks didn't hesitate. He ordered his men down the side of the hill, and then the squad hit the ground. There were no rocks where the five men had to go, so the scrambling warriors had to rely on the shadows to hide them this time. A couple of seconds after they quit moving around, Sergeant Brooks heard the sound of thumping boots walking along the path. Squeezing as close to the ground as they could, Brooks and his men held their collective breath, hoping the enemy patrol wouldn't notice the last of the dust filtering down to the ground.

Ten men made up the patrol, and they were heading west. The Germans were talking in whispered voices, so PFC Baker was unable to hear what they were saying. After waiting for about twenty minutes, Sergeant Brooks ordered his men back to the path, but this time Jackson was out front, on point. After what had happened over the last forty minutes, that perplexing thought he had bouncing around in his head quickly turned into action. *Green as he is, that kid seems to be able to hear things a lot sooner than the rest of us.*

Ten minutes later, he felt a tap on his shoulder and jumped, startled at the sudden rap on the shoulder. "Sarge, there's another patrol heading this way."

"Damn! How close are they?" he asked.

"Another two or three steps and they'll be here," replied Jackson.

Sergeant Brooks abruptly stopped and turned to stare sharply at Jackson for a couple of seconds before he gave the order to climb downhill and hug the ground. *Damn smartass kid.* The dust had barely settled before the Germans were heard coming down the path. Eight men were in the patrol this time, and they weren't talking, but the squad could definitely hear them scuffing up the path as they walked.

Three patrols in the same hour? The Germans must be up to something.

The squad was again holding their breaths and praying they wouldn't be discovered. Watching his enemy closely, Sergeant Brooks heard one of the Germans say something, and almost immediately, he thought he heard PFC Baker whisper something that sounded like "Duck," just before the German patrol stopped. Sergeant Brooks looked over at Corporal Cane, and whispered, "What's with all the Kraut patrols? Did you kick them in the ass again?"

Corporal Cane smiled and shrugged his shoulders. Without warning, one of the Germans turned towards his left and started peeing down the side of the hill, right where Brooks and his men were hiding. When the enemy warrior was finished, the patrol started on again.

As soon as the Germans were out of hearing, Sergeant Brooks whispered a quiet prayer, "*Damn*," and then he scrambled up the side of the hill with his men following. Even moving along the path, he was still whispering his quiet prayer, "*Damn Krauts*." He continued to whisper the prayer under his breath until Corporal Cane couldn't stand it any longer.

"What's wrong?"

The man wearing wet and dusty, olive green apparel shot a quick glance at Corporal Cane and then started swearing all over again. "That damn Nazi bastard pissed all over me. That's what's wrong!"

A short moment of silence passed, and then he heard someone snicker. The snickerer turned out to be PFC Baker, who was grinning from ear to ear when he said, "I told you to duck."

Sergeant Brooks stopped the squad and faced towards PFC Baker. Then Jackson started snickering. Brooks didn't look as though his funny bone was impressed. "Next one I hear laughing or tries to crack a joke will spend the next month cleaning out latrines. Do I make myself clear?" Silence followed the intense statement the boss-man had just made, but the grins never left their faces.

Only thirty minutes went by before Jackson once again reported that another German patrol was heading their way. Once more, Sergeant Brooks moved his men down the side of the hill, but this time there were rocks to hide behind. While the squad crouched behind the rocks, they watched the German patrol pass by, and Brooks came to a conclusion. *This path is too well used.* "Jackson, head down the hill and take it slow. No rock slides, people."

The descent down the hill was slow going because of noise discipline. Brooks didn't want any sounds from loose rocks falling, so the men had to go *really* slow. When they reached the bottom, they moved northeast in order to come up on the town from the south. After about an hour, Sergeant Brooks called a halt. During their break, he studied his map for a few minutes. The time was almost 2330 hours, and they were beginning to run out of it. Again, he thought the prisoner grab was a bad idea.

"Hey, Sarge."

Brooks about jumped out of his skin. "What the hell is it, Jackson?"

Everyone could see by his expression and his sudden words that he was startled by Jackson's completely unexpected call to him. "There's a German halftrack up ahead about a hundred yards or so. There's only five Germans that I could see. Maybe we can grab one of them."

"How?"

"Four of them are asleep, Sarge. We can grab the one who's awake, gag him, and then get the other four."

Sergeant Brooks looked at Jackson to see if he was serious or just joking. "You're not fooling around. You're serious about doing this?"

"Yeah, Sarge. I know I can do it," whispered Jackson.

Hesitating, Brooks stared at Jackson for a moment or two before he asked, "What's the cover look like around the track?"

"There's some rocks about twenty feet away that we can hide behind, and there's a small orchard we can use to get to the rocks."

"Show me," asked Brooks. Turning, he spoke to the rest of the short-squad. "You guys find some cover and wait for us here. We'll be back in about twenty minutes or so." Immediately following the order, the two men turned and headed for the small oasis.

After a quiet scamper, the two men were hiding in the orchard, staring out at the scene. Sergeant Brooks could barely see the halftrack and the guard walking a perimeter patrol. After studying the situation for about ten minutes, he turned to Jackson and said, "Those rocks look a bit on the small side. You really think you can use them for cover?"

Jackson nodded before he replied. "No sweat, Sarge. Piece of cake."

Sergeant Brooks glanced over at Jackson, and a somewhat comical expression crossed his face. "Yeah, beanpole. Maybe you're right. Just don't turn sideways, you might blow away."

Sergeant Brooks couldn't see the other four Germans and said as much to Jackson. "They're on the other side of the halftrack," he answered. "I saw them lying on the ground while I was under it."

Brooks just stared at Jackson, absolutely expressionless. "You what?" he whispered. "You were under the track?"

When Jackson nodded, Sergeant Brooks didn't know what to think. With his scout's words still ringing in his head, he kept watching the enemy walk his beat around the camp.

Amazed, he studied Private Jackson for a moment longer before he said, "Go back and bring the rest of the squad forward while I stay here and keep an eye on these guys."

Shortly after their summons, the five men were hunkered down together, studying the situation and watching Sergeant Brooks. They were having their own confab. "You really think he's going to send the kid in?"

"Yeah, two packs worth."

"Two packs of cigarettes?"

"Yeah, Baker. What's the matter? Momma got your purse strings tied too tight?"

"I don't smoke, Corporal Cane," said Baker. "What else you got...?"

"Can you take out that guard walking around the track?"

" Huh? What? What guard? What are you talking about, Al?"

"What are you talking about, Corporal Cane? I'm trying to question the kid."

"I'm trying to place a bet, and you're asking me if I can take out a guard. I can't do both, so which do I do?"

Sergeant Brooks stared at Corporal Cane for a few seconds before he asked his own question. "What does the winner get? Maybe I might be interested in this bet you're rigging."

"Two packs of smokes," replied Cane.

"I don't smoke, Corporal Cane."

"Shut up, Baker, I'm talking to a potential sucker. I'll get back to you in a minute. Well, Al? Are you interested?"

"What's the bet?"

"Yes or no."

"Yes or no what?"

"That's the bet, Al. You bet yes or no."

The platoon sergeant's smile was more of a warning. "Watch out, Baker. You're about to be had." Then he turned back to Jackson. "Can you take out that guard walking around the track?"

Jackson again nodded.

Sergeant Brooks looked towards Corporal Cane for a couple of blinks and then back to Jackson. "Are there any Germans nearby?" he asked.

"No, Sarge. None that I could find."

"You went looking for more? Damn, beanpole! You were only gone ten minutes!"

Jackson felt like he was being scolded, so he was *crap on the ground* scared to death when he answered. "Yes, sir."

Absolutely dumbfounded, Sergeant Brooks looked down at Jackson. "I swear you little beanpole. If you call me, sir, one more time, I'm going to yank you up by your ankle and bounce your head off the ground." Then he turned his attention back to Corporal Cane. "Okay, Dan, what's the bet. I want to know what I'm betting on."

"I thought you were briefing the kid?"

"What's the bet, Dan?"

Corporal Cane looked at Sergeant Brooks for a moment before he said, "If I tell you what the bet is then there is no bet. You have a fifty-fifty chance to win, so; pick or choose."

Sergeant Brooks again thought about the situation. He was definitely nervous about trying to take all five Germans, prisoner. "We're facing five, Jackson. If we're discovered before we can disarm them, then we might end up as dead meat on a stick. Definitely not something I'm looking forward to."

While Sergeant Brooks struggled with his decision, PFC Baker started whispering to Jackson.

"All right, Dan," said Brooks. "Two packs and drinks all night on the loser. What do you say?"

Baker and Jackson were still conversing until Sergeant Brooks turned to the two men and interrupted. "When you two honeymooners are through talking, I would like to say something."

The two men stopped talking and turned to hear what Brooks had to say.

"Well, Dan? What is it?"

Corporal Cane didn't answer right away. Instead, he stared at Sergeant Brooks for a long few seconds before he shook his head and said, "You figured it out, you lump of mud. Well, Baker, I guess Al and me won't drink on you when we get back. Definitely a shame. I was really looking forward to a drinking night on your pocket." Turning, Corporal Cane calmly nodded to his platoon sergeant and said, "Ready when you are."

Chapter 3

After the one-sided conversation was over, the squad watched while Jackson pulled a fourteen-inch hunting knife from out of his butt-pack and strapped it across his chest. Leaning his rifle up against a tree, he took off his leggings and combat boots, got down on his knees, sat on his heels, closed his eyes, and for about thirty seconds, was motionless. When he was through, he plopped to the ground and began rolling back and forth in the sand until his uniform was dirt-stained, almost the color of the terrain. Then he nodded to himself, took a deep breath, and proceeded to slither his way to the edge of the orchard.

Private Jackson watched the guard slowly walk around the short perimeter, stopping occasionally to search the area. The four soldiers he spotted earlier were still sound asleep; he could hear them snoring softly.

When the sentry reached the front of the track, he faced away from Jackson. Immediately, the private took off in a low scamper to the rocks, dropped to the ground, and waited until his enemy had gone around the camp perimeter again. When the guard stopped at the front of the track again, Jackson quickly and silently scampered to the passenger side of the track and crawled underneath it.

Not sure why, but alert, nonetheless, the guard cautiously worked his way past the driver's door, to the back of the track, searching the ground on his way. Step by step, he carefully crept around the rear of track and then to the passenger side. When he moved past the rear tracks, Jackson crawled out from under the vehicle on the driver's side and quietly slithered his way behind the sentry until the guard was on the passenger side again.

Momentarily startled, the sentry stopped. He was looking down at scuffmarks in the sand, Jackson's scuffmarks. Warily, the guard bent down lower before cautiously edging back from the track until he noticed a bare footprint squarely between his own retreating steps. Absolutely bewildered, all he could do at the moment was stare down at the baffling sight. Then Jackson went into action.

Jumping onto the back of his surprised enemy, he quickly wrapped his left arm around his adversary's throat. At the same time, he wrapped his legs around the soldier's waist, and squeezed tightly, further restricting the German's ability to breathe and maneuver. Jackson's fourteen-inch blade came next. He waved it under his enemy's right eye before he could yell for help and whispered something. Immediately, the struggling German surrendered and silently went to ground, spread-eagle. In an instant, the scout was sitting on his enemy's back with the point of his knife below the man's right eye again.

The squad had been so absorbed in watching Jackson that it took a few seconds before they realized that he was waiting on them to do their part. Sergeant Brooks waved his men on, and they quickly and quietly closed in on the track and the sleeping enemy.

Cane, Brooks, and Sims silently moved to a position about four feet behind the snoring troops, and there they crouched, grinning greatly. The private's idea of a joke was about to spring forth. As soon as everyone was in position, Baker started shouting at the Germans in their own language. Almost immediately, they jumped to their feet and snapped to attention, thinking they were in trouble for some reason, and all the while, the fog of sleep reigned supreme over the bewildered men.

Not fully awake yet, the befuddled warriors needed a moment to figure out what was going on. What was going on, however, didn't dawn on them until after they felt the poke of rifle barrels in the middle of their backs. Turning their heads, the four captives found themselves staring at three Americans showing off their pearly-whites. They were absolutely floored. Their next surprise was when PFC Baker silently walked out of the shadows, and viola, they noticed that Baker was also an American, one who spoke their language. The surprise was breath-deflating to the enemy.

Sergeant Brooks stood gazing at his five prisoners, absolutely astonished. Then he turned to face Jackson and asked, "Where in the hell did you learn how to do that?"

"I've been sneaking around and doing this kind of thing all of my life, Sarge," he answered. I have three older sisters and they wouldn't leave me alone. I had to enlist in the Army just to get away from them. They were always trying to dress me up in girl's clothes when I was growing up because they thought I looked cute in them."

Astonished, all Brooks could do at the moment was pull on his right ear and stare down at the 17 year-old private. Then he turned his attention to PFC Baker. "Can you drive this thing?"

"I think so," replied Baker.

Nodding, Sergeant Brooks gave the order. "Then get to it, PFC." The squad now had five German prisoners on their hands.

The halftrack they captured was a Sd.Kfz. 251, open roofed vehicle, with an MG34 mounted on it. After spending several minutes figuring a few things out, PFC Baker finally got it running. Within minutes, they were heading home.

Baker drove, with Brooks sitting in the passenger seat. Corporal Cane manned the machine gun, while Private Jackson and Corporal Sims kept the prisoners covered. Not long after they departed the area, the men and their uniforms were covered with a custard-colored dust as fine as talcum powder.

After thirty minutes of choking on dust, they turned south in order to pass below Feriana. When they had the town to their northeast, they swung back to the northwest. Sergeant Brooks wanted to reach Dernia before daybreak. Once again time was getting tight.

Just short of 0400 hours, he and Baker spotted a German soldier, shouting and waving his arms, calling for the track to halt, so Baker let off on the gas pedal. "What's he want?" asked Brooks.

Holding back a laugh, Baker turned and said, "I think they want a ride back to their unit. You want me to stop?" Brooks didn't answer. In fact, when he heard Corporal Cane pulling the bolt back on the machine gun, all he had time for was a quick glance at Baker, followed immediately by an, "Ahh shit," before Cane opened up with the MG34.

Jackson and Sims grabbed the prisoners and immediately shoved them to the floor of the halftrack. With Jackson guarding the prisoners, Corporal Sims opened up, while Brooks and Baker joined the fray, firing from the cab.

The vehicle had no windows, only visor slits to fire out of, so the two front seat riders did what they could, relying on Cane and Sims to do the most damage to the enemy. When Sims ran out of ammo he quickly swapped rifles with Jackson and then continued firing. Jackson's big-ass knife kept the prisoners terrified and hugging the bed of the track during the whole skirmish.

Not knowing that one of their own vehicles was about to fire on them, the German squad had wondered onto the dirt road with their weapons hanging loosely in their hands, looking for a ride back to headquarters. They stayed confused throughout the fight, and it was a costly confusion. The little battle ended just a few short minutes after it started, when the last of the Germans were finally killed. Corporal Cane was nicked in the shoulder, but nothing serious. Nobody else was hurt. After their little hair-raiser, Sergeant Brooks decided to ride in the back with the other three men.

Just outside of Dernia, Brooks called a halt, and sent Private Jackson on ahead to warn the waiting halftrack that friendlies were driving the captured track. He gave Jackson fifteen minutes; then he was going in.

Fifteen minutes, on the dot, the commandeered halftrack rumbled into view. Warily watching the captured vehicle, the man fingering the trigger on the powerful fifty cal., kept his machine gun pointed at the German halftrack until he saw Sergeant Brooks jump down from the track and wave to him; then the grins appeared. Shortly after the backslapping, the American halftrack took the lead while Brooks and his men followed in their newly acquired ride. The sun was just starting to rise when they pulled up in front of battalion headquarters with five German prisoners, and one captured, halftrack. The five Americans were exhausted, but very proud of their accomplishments.

After Brooks and his men departed the vehicle they dismounted the prisoners. Marching them into battalion headquarters, the men of 1st squad were standing tall when they handed their prisoners over to the officer of the day. The captives were still blindfolded, and their hands were still tied behind their backs, so there was really no concern that they would try to escape. However, Brooks and squad still hung around until the boss man arrived.

Colonel Martin was somewhat surprised to find a German halftrack parked out in front of his headquarters. He was even more surprised to find five German prisoners sitting on the floor inside, clogging up the already cluttered isles. He looked at Sergeant Brooks and then back at the five prisoners. "I take it you had no problems again?"

Smiling, Sergeant Brooks answered. "Not from the enemy, sir."

A couple of minutes later, five men entered the colonel's office, and each carried a chair. After arranging the chairs in front of his desk, the five men quickly left the room when they received a thank you from their boss. Turning his attention back to the squad the colonel said, "Grab a seat, gentlemen."

"Yes, sir. Thank you, sir."

Colonel Martin stared at the men seated before him for a few seconds before he reached into one of his desk drawers. Abruptly, an unopened bottle of Jack Daniels appeared in his right hand while his left gathered enough coffee cups to fill the need. Then he popped the cork and poured a shot into each cup, as he handed the cups to Sergeant Brooks and his men. Smiling deeply, Colonel Martin raised his cup and said, "A toast gentlemen. To Tennessee! Makers of the best sour mash whiskey in all the world!" And then, as if it were an afterthought, he nodded approvingly, winked, and finished the toast ... "and to a job well done!"

Almost as one they downed their drinks. Jackson didn't drink, so when he swallowed his shot, he choked over it for a good five minutes, with tears rolling down his cheeks. Then, the debriefing began.

The session lasted about an hour and a half. Shortly after it ended, Colonel Martin was on the horn, talking with Division. Within a few days, the brass hats were discussing Colonel Martin's request.

Over the next couple of weeks, Sergeant Brooks was busy training his new replacements to his way of doing things. He went over everything, from hand signals to teamwork and suppression. He also had the new replacements firing on a makeshift shooting range. During target practice, Sergeant Brooks discovered another of Jackson's hidden talents: he out shot everybody in the company, including, Staff Sergeant Brooks, the pride of Baker Company.

The shooting match between the two men began first with 100-yard targets. From there, the distance rose in 50-yard increments almost as quickly as the betting until the two shooters were stymied at 400 yards. "Hey, Al. The pot is at 300 bucks. When are you going to serve that puppy up for breakfast?"

After going shot-for-shot with his platoon sergeant for almost an hour, Jackson finally put eight shots in a row in the black center from a range of about 400 yards. Jackson's choice of weapon was his M1 Garand. Sergeant Brooks also chose his favorite weapon, his own, personalized, 1903 Springfield, bolt-action rifle.

When Jackson put all eight of his shots in the center circle, Sergeant Brooks shook his head and said, "Damn, beanpole. I hate to see what you can do with a scope. You've got some good eyes." Sergeant Brooks quit shooting when his sixth round missed its mark. There was nothing left to say. Somewhat disgusted with himself, Corporal Cane just rubbed his head and said, "I should have bet on the kid. I lost twenty bucks betting on you."

Laughing, Sergeant Brooks slapped his friend on the shoulder and said, "You should have bet on the kid, Dan; I did. I just took in seventy-five dollars."

"What? You bet on that beanpole? You took my twenty dollars? Damn it, Al. I should've known you'd try and turn nothing into profit."

Three days after the shooting match, Sergeant Brooks received orders for another prisoner grab. This time, though, he took Lemons and Avery with him. The squad returned the next day without bringing back any prisoners. They had traveled over ten miles, but never ran into a single enemy; German or Italian. They had just disappeared.

Chapter 4

Sergeant Brooks was not a happy soldier. He had been informed by Colonel Martin that instead of the five men he'd chosen earlier, he was to take an entire squad. This change meant that he had to take six rookies behind enemy lines. *What a load of crap*, he thought. *Damn*!

Orders were to sneak through the German lines, head northeast towards the enemy controlled town of Mateur, snoop around a bit, and then head south to Medjez El Bab. When that spy session was over, they were to head northeast towards Tunis. They were to get as close to Tunis as they could and snoop around without getting caught; how close they got was left up to Sergeant Brooks. Once the squad had gathered all the intel described in the mission-briefing, they were to head southwest, learning everything they could about the German defenses on their way back to Allied lines.

What Colonel Martin wanted to know, Sergeant Brooks had no problem with. However, he knew they were in for a rough ride after the sudden addition of more troops. *An entire squad*? That thought had Brooks shaking his head. "Sir, that's too many men for what you want. It's a lot harder to hide twelve men than it is five, sir." But what sergeant can win an argument with a colonel?

When that thought was dismissed, Sergeant Brooks glanced at his watch. "Well, sir, it's almost 1900 hours. I guess I'd better gather the men who are going and get them all briefed about the mission."

~ ~ ~

Sometime around 2130 hours, the squad left on their mission. Their secondary mission was to map out any hidden German 88 sites they came across; at least those they found. German 88's can open up a tank faster than a pair of sharp scissors cutting through paper. Even from a distance of two thousand yards, the weapon was deadly accurate.

Rommel used his 88's in the ambush role during his tenure in North Africa and lured many a British tank unit into a tanker's nightmare. He was very successful using this tactic.

The 88's began their career as an air defense and artillery piece. As it so happened, the gun turned out to be one of the best anti-tank weapons the Germans produced. Rommel discovered this hidden talent during the invasion of France back in May, 1940, when he tried to force a crossing of the Meuse River without tank support. The French counterattacked the bridgehead, compelling him to call up his 88mm anti-aircraft batteries for help. That particular day began their career as deadly tank killers. The 88mm anti-aircraft gun was a highly versatile piece of equipment.

Using the terrain as much as possible to hide their movements, the squad cautiously made their way northeast. Private Jackson was leading the way, about sixty yards out in front. Coming up to a slight rise, he lowered himself to the ground and crawled up to the crest to look out into the distance for the enemy.

Every time Jackson stopped, Sergeant Brooks signaled, and the squad went to ground. Looking back in the direction they had just come from, Brooks shook his head, amazed at how quickly they had passed through the enemy's lines. *Damn*, he thought. *That was too easy*. He could see the outpost they had bypassed earlier, silhouetted off in the distance, yet it seemed like it had only been a minute or so since they spotted it. That adventure, though, was already twenty minutes into their past. Then he looked over at Jackson.

Crawling back below the rise, Jackson scampered back to Sergeant Brooks, and said, "Sarge, there's plenty of Germans in a slit trench up ahead. If we sneak quietly enough, we might be able to bag the whole lot."

Sergeant Brooks looked at Jackson for a few seconds, cocked his head a little to the right, and whispered. "Are you insane, beanpole? How are we going to care for a bunch of POW's and accomplish our mission at the same time?"

"We can hit them on the way back, Sarge. Bag some Germans at the tail end of our recon to cap off our success."

Jackson's expression was hard to discern. It was a cross between youthful excitement and devil prepare. Sergeant Brooks didn't like to looks of either one.

Gazing at some small hills, off to their left, Brooks turned to Jackson and said, "You see those shadows out there? I want you to find out if the Germans are hiding in them. Just snoop around and get back safely."

While Jackson moved off to the left, Sergeant Brooks moved his men behind the rise from which the scout had just departed. Inching forward, Brooks peered over the crest to see where the enemy was, but all that he could see were dark shadows. "Damn, Alex," he whispered. "That kid's got some good eyes." The two men could hear the friendly artillery going off in the distance, and they were glad that command had called off the strikes in their area.

Sergeant Brooks was waiting back down below the crest of the rise when Jackson returned. "The Germans have an 88 tucked in between those dunes, and there's a tent set up behind it. I think they have a radio in that tent. If you let me have PFC Baker, we can go back and find out what they're talking about. What do you think, Sarge?"

Sergeant Brooks looked at the skinny kid from Arizona for a moment or two, and then he turned his gaze to PFC Baker...thinking...and then he turned his gaze back to Private Jackson. Still staring at the two men, he said, "Oh brother, hell is about rise. Okay, okay, but don't take any chances. And while you're at it, get a head count if you can. PFC Baker, stay on his ass even when he pisses. Don't let him out of your sight for any reason."

Baker nodded the affirmative. "No problem, Sarge. I think this might be fun to watch."

The two men returned about forty minutes later and reported to Sergeant Brooks. "What did you find out?" Brooks asked.

His excitement apparent, Private Jackson eagerly whispered his report. "Only five Germans are manning the 88, but about forty yards to the right of the tent is a machine gun position. If we silence the machine gunners, we might be able to catch the Germans unaware inside their tent."

As if on cue, PFC Baker gave his report. "The Germans have some maps in the tent that they were looking at. They were discussing where our main assault will be coming from. I think those maps could be useful to us if we can get our hands on them."

"What's going on?" asked Brooks. "Are you two ganging up on me? This isn't the mission."

Leaning closer to his platoon sergeant, PFC Baker whispered urgently. "What if those maps have artillery positions penciled in, Sarge? They might give us an advantage the Germans don't know about. They might even have the location of their 88's scrawled in on the maps."

Brooks fixed his gaze on the two men, and their expressions didn't change. He also noticed that neither one appeared ready to back down, nor did they drop their stare when he shifted his weight.

Taking a quick moment to search his surroundings, Brooks turned his attention back to the two men, and they were still staring intently at him. "You are ganging up on me, you little bugs. All right, you win," he said. "We'll take out the machine gun position first, and then we'll hit the tent. You'd better be right about those maps, or I swear, I'll nail your hides to the wall." And then he shook his head. *I don't believe this kid.*

"Listen up, people. Cane, Decker, and Jackson will take out the machine gun. The rest of you will help me take the tent. No shooting if you can help it. The minute we start shooting the Krauts will be down our throats in no time."

Nine men headed towards the tent while the other three headed for the machine gun. Sergeant Brooks gave the three men ten minutes to take out the machine gun, then he would hit the tent.

When the ten minutes were up, he and his men quietly entered the tent. Without firing a shot, they captured a captain, two lieutenants, a corporal, and a private. The look on their enemy's faces when they entered the tent was at first utter disbelief and open-mouth astonishment. Then the reality of the situation, and the shock of being captured behind their own lines hit the five German warriors all at once.

Baker walked quickly over to a cluttered, makeshift table made from stacked up wooden crates and began studying the maps. Then his eyes lit up. Immediately, he gave the maps to Sergeant Brooks. "This ought to help out our artillery." Seconds later, Jackson poked his face in the tent and reported, "Company coming, Sarge. They could be the rest of the 88 crew."

Brooks didn't hesitate. "Let's go, gentlemen."

In seconds, the tent was evacuated, and Brooks was leading his men north, past the silent machine gun position, and into the shadows of the night. However, the squad didn't get very far before they heard angry shouts after the Germans discovered the dead machine gun crew. The enemy hadn't yet discovered that they were also missing three officers and two enlisted men, and just thirty yards away were the escaping perpetrators.

To keep the prisoners quiet, Jackson put the point of his fourteen-inch knife underneath their captain's chin. The largeness of the knife and where the point was resting were the perfect enticements for the prisoners to keep quiet while the squad silently moved north, deeper behind German lines.

After traveling north for about twenty minutes, Sergeant Brooks led his squad west, back towards Allied lines. The prisoners were acting up, giving the squad a hard time, so he separated the five prisoners and placed two of his men to guard each prisoner. Jackson came up with the idea of holding a knife blade to the side of their necks. As the Germans walked, the knife bit into their necks from the impact of their strides. After a few minutes of walking and with blood dribbling down their necks, the prisoners, deciding not to chance a miss step and end up with a knife in their throats, gave up completely.

Approaching the outpost they had bypassed earlier, Brooks decided to eliminate it before they continued on. There was nothing in front of the squad now, except for Allies, so if they took out the position, they could head home standing up.

Corporal Cane immediately volunteered for the chore. However, instead of doing it quietly, he tossed a grenade at the machine gun position, and with a loud boom, the outpost was eliminated. After removing his helmet, Brooks scratched his head for a moment before he said, "That was amazing, Dan. Next time why don't you try using some comp B. Maybe you can eliminate the hill at the same time."

~ ~ ~

Sometime around 0400 hours, Brooks and his men were challenged by an American squad out on roving patrol. Once 1st squad's identity was ascertained, they were escorted to a captain, who in turn got on the horn with Colonel Martin's headquarters to verify that Sergeant Brooks was actually who he said he was. After the inquiry was completed, Brooks led his men to battalion HQ to report their preliminary findings. They still had the rest of their mission to complete.

Colonel Martin was in his office piecing together the little tidbits of information gathered by three different squads. When Sergeant Brooks and entourage arrived at battalion headquarters, Sergeant Duncan ushered them into the colonel's office. After Brooks, his men, and the five blindfolded prisoners entered the colonel's office, the sergeant shut the door. Colonel Martin was sitting down at his desk, completely focused on his intel reports until he heard his door close.

Slowly looking up from his reports, the colonel first glanced at his sergeant and then his wall-mounted, mission calendar because Sergeant Brooks was back from his recon days too soon. When he noticed the captured officers, he immediately stood up, surprise written all over his face. He was so taken aback that all he could do for the moment was stare at the smirk on his sergeant's face. "What do you want me to do with these guys, sir?" Pulling at his ear, Brooks handed the maps over to the colonel and said, "These maps were what we were after, sir. The prisoners just came along for the ride."

Colonel Martin stared at Sergeant Brooks for a few seconds before turning his gaze to the squad, but he had no words to say. Still in shock, he glanced over the first map, and his eyes almost popped out of his head. After looking over the other two maps, he quickly reached down, opened a drawer, pulled out his bottle of Jack, and again poured drinks for everybody, except Jackson; he received a bottle of Coca Cola instead.

After the drinks were finished, Sergeant Brooks placed his cup on the chair he had been sitting on earlier and said, "Thank you for the drinks, sir. If we're finished here, I'd like to give the men a four-hour break before we head out again. Playing nursemaid to the prisoners kind of wore them out, sir."

Colonel Martin was tapping the captured maps against his other hand, eager to hand them over to Division. "That sounds good, Al. Carry on." As Brooks was leaving the colonel's office, Colonel Martin called for his halftrack and an MP escort to take care of the prisoners. When the prisoners were on their way to interrogation, he quickly jumped into his staff car and headed straight for Division headquarters with the maps shoved inside his shirt and hidden from view.

Sometime around 2000 hours, 1st squad was on the move again. Sergeant Brooks had decided that this time he would lead the squad northeast towards Beja. "All right, people, listen up. Make sure nothing rattles. If I can hear you, so can the Krauts. The colonel wants to know what the Germans are up to, so we're going deep behind enemy lines. Put three extra bandoliers of ammo and an extra canteen of water in your pack and make sure you wrap the canteen in a towel to help hide the sloshing. You new guys, pay attention and keep your mouths shut. Watch and learn. Jackson, you're on point. Corporal Cane, cover the right." Abruptly, he paused and then looked at his newly appointed permanent pathfinder. "You know where you're going, right, Jackson?"

The grin on the scout's face gave Sergeant Brooks his answer. His expression also told Brooks what he was in for. "You really like doing this shit, don't you?"

Private Jackson's expression never wavered, nor did he say a word. He just nodded the affirmative, too scared to say anything, fearing he might jeopardize his new position as point scout.

~ ~ ~

Jackson was on point with Lemons bringing up the rear. The men were moving in columns of two instead of being strung out because Brooks wanted to keep an eye on the new guys. The terrain was rough and rocky, with small ridges and crevices that were abundantly dotted with scrub brush, which helped hide the squad's movement.

Without warning, Private Jackson appeared out of nowhere and again took Sergeant Brooks by surprise. "What is it, Jackson?" hissed Brooks.

"Germans up ahead of us, Sarge. If we move around to the left a little bit, we can go right by them," he whispered.

Sergeant Brooks looked at him for a few seconds and then nodded. "All right, Jackson. Lead the way."

Pointing, the Arizona scout turned west and said, "This way, Sarge. If we stay in this line of shadows, the Germans can't see us too well."

"How many men?" whispered Brooks.

"About ten, I think." replied Jackson.

"Okay, beanpole, move out."

Chapter 5

After several hours of slinking around behind German lines, Sergeant Brooks finally called a halt. The squad had left the enemy position far behind and had gone around a couple of towns the enemy was occupying. The stars were out in dazzling fashion on their first night, and the sight was amazing. Using what light the stars gave off, Sergeant Brooks made little notes on his map to keep track of their journey through enemy territory. That was his mission. To spy and record.

"Hey, Al, shh. You hear that? Someone's talking."

"Yeah, Dan, I hear it. It sounds like the voice is getting closer. Where the hell is Jackson?"

Three breaths later, Sergeant Brooks felt a tap on his shoulder and almost jumped out of his skin. The tapper was Jackson, and he had his finger across his lips. Then he pointed to the ground and trailed his finger to a shallow depression, hidden in shadows. He didn't look around to see if anyone was following, he quickly dropped to the ground and quietly low-crawled into the depression. Immediately following, just a half a reach behind, was the rest of the squad.

Hunkering down, everyone in the shadows was hoping the enemy would pass them by. But the situation didn't turn out as everyone had hoped.

The depression the squad was hiding in was an old, shallow, slit trench, about twenty yards below a gently sloping grade. Dug into the ledge the squad was occupying, it was almost completely filled with wind-blown sand. Beyond the trench, the terrain still went downhill for another sixty feet.

Private Brown unintentionally dislodged a baseball size rock, and it went tumbling down the hill, rattling its way across a path five German soldiers were walking along. Immediately, the veterans of the famed Afrika Corps looked up in the direction the rock had come from, but all they could see were shadows and the darker shadows of the bigger rocks.

They stood where they were, whispering back and forth for a couple of breaths until one of the men issued out a string of orders. It appeared to Sergeant Brooks as though the enemy had decided to investigate what caused the disturbance.

Inching their way up the side of the hill, the German soldiers spread out, five men, using the shadows and terrain to help mask their advance.

"The Germans are serious about coming up here, so get ready. Don't open up until I start firing. Damn," whispered Brooks. "Now, everybody will know we're here."

The Germans were getting close. The squad could hear their heavy breathing as they navigated the soft hillside terrain; struggling and crunching their way up the incline. When Brooks had gauged them within dead-to-rights range, he signaled to his men to open fire, stood up, and a crescendo of death ripped into the German squad. Still hidden in the shadows on the ledge, twelve weapons opened fire on the Germans climbing up the hillside, and the attack was a brutal, killing surprise. Even though the German troops were ready to fire, they were still caught unaware. A shadow abruptly stood up, and then the whole ledge erupted with weapons' fire. Only two errant shots were fired by the enemy, but they missed by a wide margin. Within seconds, the skirmish was over.

For a couple of moments, the ledge the squad had fired from lit up for all to see. When the shooting was over, the Americans hit the ground and rapidly low-crawled east away from the scene. They had barely moved a few yards from their previous position when the shadows on the ledge they had just vacated was hit by machine gun fire. Machine gun bullets slammed into the ledge and then ricocheted all over the place, leaving lines of tracers aimlessly screaming and whistling off into the distance. If not for the cover of night, Brooks and his men could have been chewed up pretty badly.

The Americans could hear the Germans shouting from a distance. Then the machine gun firing ceased, but the shouting didn't stop. "Damn," whispered Brooks, "we've stirred up a hornet nest. Let's get the hell out of here. Jackson, sneak us clear."

"Yes, sir, Sergeant Brooks."

After the men had crawled another forty yards, they stood up, and crouching over, ran sprint-to-cover for another ten minutes before slowing down to catch their wind. "All right. Who farted?" whispered Brooks. "You weren't supposed to be moving around so that means somebody had to have farted to start that damn rock rolling down the hill."

Private Brown sheepishly answered. "Sorry, Sarge. My leg twitched. I couldn't help it." Brooks looked over at Brown and said, "Next time, be more careful. You almost got us all killed." Then he turned to Jackson. "Get on point, and get us the hell out of here."

~ ~ ~

The squad was spread out, crouching down and using the scrub brush for cover while they waited for Private Jackson to return from his scouting foray. He had heard voices, so Brooks had sent him out to investigate. "Sarge?"

Thirty heartbeats all in one breath and a stare hardy enough to wilt a cactus greeted Jackson. "Damn you, Jackson," said Brooks. "What did I tell you about sneaking up on me like that?" Immediately, Sergeant Brooks stopped whispering and just stared at the scout for a few seconds before he asked, "How did you find me? We didn't hit cover until after you left."

"You breathe funny, Sarge. Put a blindfold on me and I'll pick you out every time. I've never heard anyone breathe like you."

Sergeant Brooks stared at Jackson for a couple of more seconds, not sure if he should believe what he heard. "Scout out the area to the north. If it's clear, we'll head in that direction. The Krauts are still confused, so that gives us a few minutes. We can't hang around for long, so make it quick."

Quick was about twenty minutes later, and Sergeant Brooks was beginning to worry. Looking southwest, he could hear the Germans searching the ledge and the immediate area. Off to the south, the sinister noise of vehicles cranking up was equally disturbing. *Damn, where is....* Before he could finish his thought, Sergeant Brooks abruptly turned to his left just in time to spot Jackson slinking out of a shadow where he was signaling a direction. He pointed northeast. Immediately, Brooks signaled, and the squad stood up and followed the veteran sergeant, who in turn, and without hesitation, followed a seventeen-year-old kid, Private Timothy Jackson, into the heart of the German defense.

On the second day, sometime around 0100 hours, the Americans ran into another large concentration of enemy troops. The larger encampments were difficult to get past because of the numerous patrols they could afford to send out. Of course, Jackson, with his ability to see and hear things that nobody else in the squad could, except for maybe Private Lemons, was a huge asset to Brooks and the squad. Lately, however, Private Lemons was forced to keep his head down as if searching for something on the ground. Most of the time, what he was actually doing was hiding his smile, and trying desperately not to burst out laughing. On this occasion, the beanpole was hiding in a shadow and Sergeant Brooks was about to walk right over him.

Brooks was barely one step from a shadow cast by a large stand of cactus when out of that shadow, another shadow slowly stood up, and Sergeant Brooks almost dumped a load. Then the steam came pouring out. "Why do you keep doing that to me?"

"Doing what, Sarge?"

"Sneaking up on me like you just did," whispered Brooks.

Jackson's hushed response had ambush ringing all through it. "I didn't sneak up on you, Sarge. You snuck up on me. I was just sitting in the shadows, napping." Instantly, the snickers spread through the squad as rapidly as a raging river.

"Can it, you guys. What's up, Jackson?" Brooks asked. That was all he could think to say; he was still shaking inside. He was also trying desperately to ignore what his scout had said, and he was having an even tougher time trying not to burst out laughing.

"There's a village just over that set of ridges. It sits in a small valley sort of, but it's filled with Germans and tanks. It looks like the Germans are covering a pretty large area to me."

"How long will it take you to scout it out?"

"About two hours, I think."

"Okay, do it. We'll stay here while you're gone."

As soon as Private Jackson disappeared from sight, Sergeant Brooks moved his men a little higher up the hill to hide behind some rocks until Jackson returned.

Jackson took off towards the ridges he had pointed out to Sergeant Brooks, and just before he topped out, he dropped to the ground and crawled to the edge to check out the scene below. He noticed some faint lights glowing near the village and figured the lights were probably from the Germans. He spent the next thirty minutes watching the area before deciding to come at the village from the east.

He had left his M1 Garand with Lemons because it was too bulky for what he needed to do. When he got back headquarters, he promised himself that he was going to check into getting an M1 carbine. It was lighter and much easier to handle, perfect for the kind of scouting forays he was sent out on. After forty minutes of scampering, he arrived at the east side of the village and hunkered down about one-hundred yards from the scattering of structures.

Hmm, lots of tents and transport. There must be at least a company of infantry camped here. The lights coming from some of the tents had him wondering out loud. "Why would they be using lights at night?" There was a tent off by itself, so he headed for it. Moving cautiously, he sneaked around it until he was facing the entrance, about sixty feet away. The lights were dimmed, but they could still be seen from the air.

He was peering into the tent when he watched an officer come around the side and enter. He couldn't get any closer without moving into the light, so he continued to watch from where he was hunkered down.

Moving away from the tent a couple of minutes later, he slithered his way northwest to see how far the enemy was stretched out around the village. Very quickly, he discovered that he had come upon a much larger concentration of troops than he had first believed. *Crap on the ground. This encampment is going to take a long time to get around. A lot longer than two hours.*

After more than four-hours of scouting around the camp, Jackson arrived back to where he left the squad and reported to Sergeant Brooks. "Sarge, the Germans are scattered over a one-mile area. They take up almost the entire valley."

"Can we get around the Krauts by going north?"

The scout nodded and said, "We can if we do some climbing."

"What about the other side? Can we get around them going east?" asked Brooks.

"No, Sarge. There's a lot more Germans to the east."

Thinking about the situation for a minute, Brooks made his decision. "Listen up, men. Corporal Cane you take Private Lemons, PFC Baker, and two of the new guys, I'll keep the rest of the squad with me. Follow Lemons up, and when you reach the top, spread out and cover us. We'll cover your backs while you climb until we see you're in position. Then we'll start up."

Corporal Cane immediately nodded the affirmative. "All right. You heard the man. Hanky, Stony, on me. Private Lemons, you lead the way, and try not to drop any rocks on us." Then Corporal Cane turned. "See you at the top, Al."

Sergeant Brooks nodded and said, "You got it, Dan." Then as an afterthought. "What do you calculate the odds are that we're going to make it through this mission?"

Smiling, Corporal Cane answepred. "One-in-ten we make it."

"With or without Jackson?"

"One-in-twenty without Jackson. Watch your back, Al. That last step is a doozey."

After pulling on his ear for a moment, Sergeant Brooks quietly said, "Enjoy the climb, Dan. I think you're going to like this adventure."

Two hours and a lot of under-breath swearing later, twelve sucking-air warriors found themselves atop their goal. Squatting on their knees, their butts resting on their heels, and with their hands on their hips, they were just absolutely winded. "Damn, Al," said Corporal Cane. "That was a tough climb. Man, I hate climbing."

Taking off his helmet, Brooks reached into his backpack and pulled out a small towel to wipe the sweat from his head. When he put his helmet back on, he turned to Corporal Cane and said, "I do believe ..." but before he could finish his thought the beanpole in uniform interrupted him.

"Hey, Sarge, are we staying here?"

Sergeant Brooks wasn't sure he had heard correctly, so he glanced to his left, and there was Jackson, standing in-place and waiting for an answer. "Are you ready to head down now?" Brooks asked.

"Yeah, Sarge. Let's go."

Sergeant Brooks continued to stare at Jackson for a few seconds before he responded. "Beanpole, don't say another word. Just go sit beside Corporal Cane so he can clamp you to the ground."

While everyone was slowly recuperating from the climb, Sergeant Brooks was pulling on his ear while he thought about their current situation. Contemplating deeply, Brooks was gazing absentmindedly at his scout. Private Jackson was sitting beside Corporal Cane, not moving a muscle. While Brooks stared at him, a sudden inspiration came to mind. "Jackson, get over here."

"Yeah, Sarge?"

"Get on down to the bottom and find us a place to hole-up until nightfall. The sun is due to arrive in another couple of hours, so you don't have much time left to look. I'll give you an hour. Then we're climbing down."

The squad took forty minutes to climb down the rocky ridge. Corporal Sims was the first to reach level ground, and there was Jackson, standing twenty feet away. He was pointing at a large shadow about a hundred yards from where the two men were standing. "I found a cave in that small canyon. It's not much, but it will hide us during the day. Where's Sergeant Brooks?"

Abrupt swearing told Jackson where Sergeant Brooks was, and then a cascade of dust, dirt, and fist size rocks came tumbling down, followed by a dust-covered sergeant. "Damn, I hate the desert."

Chapter 6

Jackson woke up with the sun and went over to Lemons to wake him up. Sam was already awake, but he hadn't stirred yet. The two men scouted out the canyon, first with their eyes before venturing out of the cave. Leaving the cave and canyon behind, the two scouts headed east for about twenty minutes until Jackson abruptly dropped to the ground, followed immediately by Private Lemons.

Lying down in a little depression, the two scouts watched the dust clouds forming as enemy vehicles started moving southwest. They noticed a lot of dust clouds, but nothing was heading their way, so they went back to the cave to get out of the sun. The early morning was already, baking hot.

The rest of the squad woke up around 1230 hours, but stayed inside the cave while they waited for the sun to go down. Several aircraft flew by overhead, traveling east with their engines straining. More aircraft flew by, and a small air war began. The roar of the exerting engines and the firing of the aircraft had the cave dwellers captivated the whole duration, and then the attack was over. The rest of the day, however, went by so slowly it was almost maddening. With nothing else to do, the men fell asleep again until Sergeant Brooks woke them up an hour before the sun went down.

The squad was just leaving the canyon when, out of nowhere, tiny puffs of black smoke erupted high in the sky to the southeast. Then came the tracer rounds from the 20 and 40mm anti-aircraft batteries. Everything the Germans could throw at their attackers followed next, and moments later, the sounds of the explosions were heard. Immediately, the squad recognized what the flak batteries were firing at. British and American planes were liberally pounding the hell out of the German positions.

Explosions and fires abruptly erupted where the planes were attacking, and plumes of smoke were seen rising into the air. One of the attacking planes burst into flames and showered flaming debris on the enemy that had just shot it down. In less than twenty minutes, the attack was over, but the planes left behind several fires and many clouds of oily smoke rising over the German positions. Further to the southeast, the enemy was being pounded just as hard. The Allies were attacking the enemy from the air every day, softening up their defenses before the main assault. While the planes were on the ground, re-fueling and re-loading, the artillery took over the job of reducing the enemy positions.

An hour after sundown, Jackson headed due east with the rest of the squad following. The hope was they were far enough behind the enemy not to run into any more large troop concentrations for a while. Heading due east also had the squad moving straight towards Tunis. Sergeant Brooks, however, had no intention of getting close to Tunis. “Jackson, when we reach this ridge, turn south and head for Sidi Bouzid. Once we reach the town, we can head for home.” Everyone in the squad stood up taller when they heard him utter those words.

The terrain the squad was moving through began to change. The land became less rugged, more open, and easier to traverse the further east they traveled. Around 0030 hours on the third day, while Sergeant Brooks was meandering through his thoughts, he caught a slight movement out of the corner of his eye. Before he could react, however, Jackson came into view, seemingly out of nowhere, and, yet again, startled Brooks. “What is it this time, Private?”

“There’s an armor column heading our way, Sarge. I can hear the tracks squeaking.”

“I don’t hear anything,” said Brooks.

“You will if we don’t move out of here fast,” replied Jackson. “There’s also infantry following the tanks. We have about one minute to clear the area before they come up over that rise.”

“Damn! And we’re out in the open! Let’s go,” ordered Brooks. Immediately, the squad took off running north, moving as fast as their worn-out legs could carry them. They managed to run about 200 yards before they crapped-out behind a small rise of mostly sand and dry grass. Breathing deeply, the men lay exhausted, listening to the approaching vehicles and gasping for air. "Damn you, beanpole. Shut up and sit down."

"I didn't say anything, Sarge." The scout continued to gaze at Sergeant Brooks, and then a slow smile spread across his face. "Not bad for a sergeant. You ran 200 yards in less than a minute." Before Sergeant Brooks could figure out what Jackson said, he was unexpectedly interrupted.

Sudden and violent gunfire hit the German armor column 1st squad was hiding from, and immediately tracer rounds were seeking out the lead tank. Then bam, the lead tank went up in flames. Immediately following the first blast, another violent burst of shooting erupted on the column's left, lighting up the desert night. One after another, the third and fifth tank in the column burst into flames, and then the rear tank exploded.

At the onset of the attack, hell ripped through the surprised column in the form of hundreds of shrieking thirty and fifty caliber tracer rounds, and all the invisible rounds in between the tracers, spreading death and destruction through the surprised column before anyone had a chance to fire back. Chaos, panic, and the shock of sudden violence had the Germans in an uncontrolled uproar. Whoosh! A red flare rose up into the night sky, and the attack was over. Heard above all the din of chaos and explosions was the straining roar of engines racing south, away from the burning tanks.

Damn ... but before Brooks could finish his thought, the German armor column opened up with their main guns, shooting blindly at the retreating attackers, all the while, pushing pedal to the metal in hot pursuit, chasing after the attacking force. Brooks didn't hesitate. "Jackson, head north. Let's go, people! Now, before the Krauts come looking in this direction."

Immediately, Brooks and squad moved north as fast as they could step off, and they were stepping off rather quickly. The area around the burning tanks was lit up brightly, so they were beating feet to clear the area. Then the onboard tank ammo began exploding. Gun turrets blew thirty to forty feet into the air before crashing back down to the ground.

Anything and everything blown away from the tanks turned into deadly shrapnel, shredding what troops were caught in the open. What infantry had deployed to attack were left moaning on the ground after the second round of explosions, but there were no further attacks on the column.

The Germans had discovered that moving their forces at night was more economical and less hazardous, and the Allies were trying to put a stop to that line of thinking.

This is fast becoming a bad idea, thought Brooks. "Did anyone see who was doing the shooting? The Krauts will be out for blood after this one."

Moving the squad north for about thirty minutes, Sergeant Brooks changed direction and led his men east. He had no idea where they were at the moment. He only knew that they were off course and behind schedule, and necessity was dictating what they did next. They had to find a place to hide before the sun came up, or they would be in some serious trouble.

Jackson went out searching for a hiding place, but he was having a difficult time finding anything. The only concealment that he could find was an old ruin that didn't have a roof. In fact, there were no doors or windows, only holes and the partially standing walls. Just something to hide behind, so the men did exactly that.

The walls of the ruins were made of sunbaked mud brick, so Corporal Cane was able to cut a small hole through one of the walls. He had a fairly good view of the area in front of him and of the enemy soldiers and vehicles moving off in the distance. Turning to his squad leader he said, "Al, you better hope the Krauts don't come this way. There're a lot of Germans out there."

Brooks winked at Corporal Cane and said, "Good. Maybe the Krauts will surround us, then we'll really have them by the nose."

The Germans had slowed down their daylight movements because of the increasing air attacks. Brooks and his men were rudely awakened from one of those attacks. It seemed as though everybody in the German army was shooting at the attacking planes, and men were running all over the place, hunting for cover. Three Germans were running towards the ruins the Americans were hiding in, so Brooks told his men to get ready. "Hold your fire. Maybe the Brits will kill them before they reach us."

Several halftracks were already on fire, and a couple of tanks were belching black smoke. One tank made a hissing noise followed immediately by a sudden gush of flames coming out of the open hatches, brewing up nicely, while another tank exploded, sending the turret about fifteen feet into the air. Allied planes were strafing and bombing the Germans, and to Brooks and company, the scene was a sight to behold.

The three Germans running for the ruins never made it. A British fighter caught them in the open and chewed them up about twenty yards from the ruins. The pilot didn't release the trigger fast enough when he passed over the American position and ended up ripping a large, vertical, chunk out of the wall, forcing the Americans to split up.

The whole area was a mess. Dead and wounded Germans lay on the ground where they had fallen, and plenty of burning vehicles were all around. Some of those exploding vehicles sent columns of black smoke, skywards. The broken remains of what had once been a thriving armor attack group was scattered all over the ground. The current state of affairs had the squad trapped in the ruins until the sun went down. Not a good predicament to be in. The situation forced a very long and anxious day on the squad.

A medic and six soldiers carrying three stretchers went over to the three men lying dead on the ground. The medic looked the men over and determined that they were indeed dead, so he instructed the stretcher bearers to load the men up on the stretchers and take them over to the row of dead men already laid out on the ground about a hundred yards from the ruins. While the stretcher bearers carried the dead away, the medic walked towards the ruins to see if there were any dead or wounded behind the walls.

When he walked around the left side of the damaged structure he was temporarily out of sight of his buddies. Instantly, he was seized by a couple of Americans and rudely yanked to the ground. A skinny kid in uniform had a very large, man-sized knife, and he poked it under the medic's right eye, while another American tied his hands. The skinny kid had his finger over his lips to indicate silence. When the medic's hands were tied, Sergeant Brooks shoved a dirty rag into his mouth.

Low voiced, Jackson asked, "What do we do with him now?"

"We keep him with us until we leave. Then we leave him here," said Brooks.

Quickly interrupting the conversation, Corporal Cane said, "I have a better idea. Why don't we just kill him and be done with it?"

"Because we don't kill medics," said Brooks. "They are non-combatants, and they save people's lives. We will do it my way, Corporal. Do you understand?"

"He's the enemy, Sarge," replied Cane, "but if you don't want us killing medics then we won't."

The prisoner tried to talk, but because of the gag, he was unable to. Jackson put his knife up against the medic's throat and then removed the gag. "Thank you for not killing me," said the German. "I will not give away your position, just don't put that awful tasting rag back in my mouth." Looking at the surprised expressions on the American's faces he smiled and said, "I went to medical school in America."

"Well, I'll be damned," said Brooks. "We're educating our enemies so they can come back and kill us. That makes real good sense." Then the sergeant threw out a little surprise of his own. "If you give your word that you won't try anything I'll leave the gag out, but your hands will remain tied. Do you agree?" Sergeant Brooks received a reciprocal surprise. "I give you my word," answered the medic.

An hour after the medic had been captured, his buddies were out looking for him. Nobody had noticed the ruins, yet, but that wishful dream didn't last long. A couple of enemy soldiers were already walking towards the ruins, just to make sure their friend wasn't there. About thirty yards from the bombed-out structure, the two men were surprised to see their friend emerge from the ruins, a bit crumpled, but unharmed.

Smiling, the medic explained that he had crawled behind the ruins to take a break and fell asleep. "I was so tired," he said, "that I don't even remember falling asleep." The three men headed back to their assembly area, to wait around until moving off to a different location.

"Well, now. Aren't you glad that we didn't kill him?"

"What if he decides to tell someone about us?" asked Jackson.

"He won't," said Brooks. "If he was going to do that, this place would already be hip deep with Germans. Besides, there is nothing that we can do about the situation now, so get some rest. The sun won't go down for another six hours."

Twenty minutes into their rest, the Americans heard the whine of engines coming to life. Brooks looked along the edge of the vertical crevasse the British fighter had created in the wall, and watched the Germans prepare to leave. While he was watching, he noticed a soldier with a red cross on his left arm. He was a bit surprised when the man raised his hand and waved at the ruins. Then, he watched the man climb into the passenger side of a truck, and immediately, the truck raced after the German armor column heading north. Thirty minutes after the last vehicle disappeared out of sight, Brooks got his men ready to travel. "Jackson, take a look around to make sure the Krauts didn't leave anything or anyone behind."

Jackson came back about twenty minutes later. "Sarge, the Germans left a fresh water well intact. It's just behind that burned-out building."

"Any Germans lurking about?"

"No, sir. We're all alone."

Exasperated, Sergeant Brooks glared down at Jackson for a few seconds before he pushed his helmet to the back of his head to wipe his brow. Then he said, "If you call me, sir, one more time, I'm going to hand you over to the Germans. Hell, I might even pay the bastards to take you just to get you out of my hair. Now, you little beanpole, lead us to that well."

As soon as all of the canteens were filled, the squad headed south. They were a third of the way through their mission, and so far, they had been lucky. Very lucky. An hour into their travels, Jackson spotted a dust cloud off in the distance, so Brooks immediately started looking around for some place to hide just in case the dust cloud turned into Germans.

Off to the squad's left, just east of their current position, was a hill that stretched for about a half a mile from east to west before it made a dogleg to the south, running parallel with the squad's line of travel, about a hundred yards east of where Brooks and his men were walking. It was on the dogleg that the squad found cover. It was excellent ground cover, but the squad was completely exposed from the air.

They waited for over an hour before they saw the first vehicle. It was an armored car with what looked like a 20mm cannon, and it was moving north. Trailing about ten minutes behind the armored car were several tanks and then some halftracks, followed by five trucks straining through the shifting sand.

Brooks had decided to head out before the sun went down, and now they were stuck behind some hill until either the enemy left, or the sun finally went down. Somewhere around 1630 hours, on their third day, Sergeant Brooks noticed a startling sight. "Look at that, Dan? Every German unit we've come across over the last couple of days has been heading north. You think they're retreating?"

"Could be, Al. I mean look at us? We're such a terrifying sight."

Sergeant Brooks stared at Corporal Cane for a few seconds before he said, "You may be right, Dan. We sure scared the hell out of that unarmed medic." Turning his attention to Jackson, Brooks said, "When the Germans are gone, scout out the area south of us and find out what's going on."

Because of the situation, Jackson wasn't able to head south until sometime around 1700 hours. The Americans were still in the flat area, but they could see more mountains off in the distance to the southeast. Jackson ran into three more enemy columns before he decided to return to the squad. On his way back, he noticed several more dust clouds heading his way.

The scout took about two and a half hours to complete his scouting foray. He reported to Sergeant Brooks about the dust clouds he had seen. He also found out from Sergeant Brooks that the three columns that he had seen earlier had already passed by the squad. "The Germans are retreating," said Brooks. "Something bad must have happened to them down south. We'll wait here until the sun goes down, and then we'll head out."

The artillery never seemed to stop. When it quit in one area, it started up in another area. While listening to the artillery fire, the squad watched one of the dust clouds turn into the enemy just as the sun was going down. The German troops looked worn out and beat up, and they appeared to be retreating. Hundreds of infantry were walking, trying to keep pace with the vehicles. Every space on the moving vehicles was taken up by the wounded, and still, a lot of walking wounded were trudging north. They were an exhausted group of warriors.

"Look at them, Al. This lot looks beat to shit. Hitler's vaunted Afrika Korps. Ha! Put in the right commanders, and we kick the enemy's ass until they look like these guys; all used up."

Corporal Cane was staring at the retreating Germans when he said, "Hell, they look like we did a few sorry months ago. We've changed the game, Al. Now, it's our turn, and we won't quit until we're walking all over their graves."

"Wow, Dan," said Brooks "How motivating. I think if the folks back home heard you, they would flock to the polls and immediately vote you in as President. I'm sure that if the Germans heard your words, they'd throw ole Hitler out of office and put you in his place, no doubt, inspired as much as I am."

Disgusted, Corporal Cane stared out at the enemy for a moment before he turned to Brooks and said, "Go shit in your hat, Al. Herman Goring is next in line. You know that." When their bantering ended, they turned their attention back to the retreating Germans.

Brooks had no idea how many columns were headed his way, but it didn't much matter. The squad had to get on with their mission and get back to headquarters with what intel they had gathered. “Another hour and we can move out,” whispered Brooks.

The sun had fallen before the last of the enemy passed by the squad’s position, so the time to move out was at hand. At 2100 hours, the squad started out again. They were heading southeast along the same route their enemy was using on their way north. The distance they still had to travel, appeared to be about five or ten miles, but once they reached the mountains, they would have good cover.

~ ~ ~

Sergeant Brooks was looking at a shadow that didn’t appear to be natural and soon discovered that it wasn’t; it was Jackson. Once again, he was startled by the scout. Even though he had seen the shadow, he was still startled when he got close to it because the shadow abruptly spoke to him.

“Damn you, Jackson. What is it now?” whispered Brooks.

“The Germans are coming up on our left Sarge, and there are more about fifty yards to our right. I believe they’re advance scout squads, checking out the area before the main bunch arrives.”

“How many are there?” asked Brooks.

“About ten on the left and about six on the right,” replied Jackson.

“Will they pass us by if we stay right here?”

“I don’t know, Sarge. They’re doing a pretty good job of checking out the area, so I wouldn’t trust that idea.”

“Which group will get to us first?”

Jackson thought about the question for a moment before he answered. “I think the squad on the right will reach us first, Sarge.”

“How long have we got before they get here?”

“I’d say maybe ten minutes at the most.”

“How far back do you think the main bunch is?”

“Oh, maybe about a half a mile or so,” replied the scout.

“Damn, beanpole. How do you sneak around out there without getting caught?” Turning his attention back to the squad, he issued his order. “Okay. Let’s put the Germans on our right to our left. If we have to fight it out, let’s get the six

Krauts first, then move off about thirty yards or so, and maybe the second bunch will miss us. If not, we'll be in a position to hit them hard before they can get any help. After that, we run like hell. We'll also need to find us some cover to fight from." Turning back to Jackson, Brooks said, "Find us some cover positions that we can fall back to, about thirty yards apart. I want three or four positions just in case the Krauts give us too much trouble."

Each position that Jackson had located was twenty to thirty yards apart and to their right, and heading in a northerly direction from their current position. The shadows the fallback positions were in provided them with additional concealment, but not protection.

The squad was ready and waiting as the enemy approached their position. Jackson spotted them first, and then Baker saw them. The enemy scouts were checking out every hole or crevasse large enough to hide in, but they were not expecting any trouble because they were still in German held territory.

Baker started moaning and caught the attention of one of the Germans. "Who is that?" asked one of the enemy scouts. The other five had stopped and were waiting, rifles at the ready. In German, Baker replied, saying that he was wounded.

"What unit are you from?" asked an enemy scout.

Baker remembered the unit that the medic had said he was from and blurted out the unit designation. "We were attacked by Tommy (British) aircraft. I'm all shot up." The corporal in charge had heard something about that attack so he called his companions over to help.

The enemy warriors relaxed their attention and walked up to the bomb crater their wounded comrade was supposedly lying in and soon discovered that they had been duped. Twelve bodies stood up, where only one wounded comrade was supposed to be, and let loose with a hail of bullets. The volume of rifle fire from the squad tore into the six enemy scouts and ripped them apart. The Americans immediately hit the ground and started low-crawling to their next position, while the other German squad opened up on their enemy's previous position from about sixty yards away.

The second squad rushed towards the American's last known position, laying down a suppressing fire while they scrambled for position. Crouching over and spread out, they quickly scurried forward, rapidly closing in on their enemy's position. Finally in place, the German squad attacked, rushing the American position from three different sides, expecting to come into contact with someone, but they found no one there.

The men of first squad continued to hold their fire until their enemy was starkly outlined against the sky, and then they let loose with everything they had. Seconds later, they disengaged and moved towards their third position, and upon arriving, they again held their fire.

What was left of the remaining German troops decided against continuing the battle and moved back to a safe position; help from the main column was now on its way. Brooks heard the vehicles approaching and decided that it was time to run like hell, so he and his men quietly took off and melted into the desert landscape.

Chapter 7

Jackson was out in front, looking for cover and concealment from the enemy. The time had finally arrived for a break to figure out their current location. With all of the constant changes in course, they had no time to pinpoint where they were. Brooks knew they were somewhere in Tunisia and heading west, but that was about all he knew.

The men immediately dropped to the ground with a grateful sigh and relaxed, except for Jackson; he quickly took off again. He never seemed to slow down or stop. He was like a windup toy that never needed winding.

"Has anybody seen, Jackson?" asked Brooks.

"What's up, Sarge?"

Sergeant Brooks almost jumped out of his pants. "Damn you, Jackson. Where the hell have you been?"

"I've been snooping around, Sarge. I think we're behind the main German lines. If we continue to head in the direction we're going, we'll run right smack-dab into a big bunch of them. They're dug in and spread out pretty wide."

Quickly, Jackson knelt down and drew in the sand what he had scouted. Sergeant Brooks looked at the diagram drawn in the sand and started asking him questions about the Germans' positions. When the two men were done with their question and answer session, Brooks moved off by himself for a minute or two to ponder the situation before turning to face the squad. "The Krauts are digging in, people. If we don't clear the area quickly, we'll be on the receiving end of our own artillery. We're done here. Jackson, get us around this bunch, and then head us home. I think we've seen enough. Corporal Cane, cover the rear."

Twenty minutes later, both Jackson and Lemons were out in front with Corporal Cane still watching the rear. With a lot of German patrol activity going on around them, the Americans were forced to move, sprint-to-cover, until they were completely behind the main force.

First squad was moving cautiously in a north-northwesterly direction. Sneaking back towards Allied lines, they were having trouble slithering their way through the German defenses. Jackson had been roaming all over the area to the north and northwest in a kind of semicircle, trying to find safe-passage through the German lines. An hour into his scout, he found a small village off to the northeast about 200 yards to the right of the squad's line of march. He met the squad as they were coming abreast of the darkened village, and informed Sergeant Brooks about township.

"All right. Jackson, Lemons, you two clear out those rocks and then go fill the canteens. We'll wait here."

Twenty minutes went by before the two scouts reported back to Sergeant Brooks. Private Lemons gave the report. "The Germans have an 88 hidden in those rocks, but only two men are guarding it. There were signs of more, but the rest of the crew must be in that village. All we could locate were the two watching the gun."

Pulling on his ear, Brooks thought the situation over for a moment before he issued his order. "Okay. We'll take these two out and then try to spike the gun. Corporal Cane, I want you to take Jackson and Baker with you to take out those gunners and no shooting. Send Baker back when you've killed them. A silent kill, gentlemen. That's how it has to be," said Brooks. Baker returned a few minutes later and gave the all-clear, so Sergeant Brooks quickly moved the rest of the squad into the rocks and positioned them facing the village, while he tried to spike the gun.

Taking some of the sandbags from in front of the gun, Brooks emptied enough sand out to shove the sandbags up the barrel. Taking the sponge rod he pushed the bags as far up the barrel as he could without shoving out the muzzle block. With that chore completed, he ordered the dead to be removed and placed behind a large rock formation about sixty or seventy feet behind the gun.

Brooks didn't think that the Germans would be foolish enough to fire the gun without checking it first, but there was always that hope. Minutes later, the squad was heading towards the village, coming at it from the west. Sergeant

Brooks stopped the squad in the shadows and scrub brush about thirty yards from the cluster of structures and then sent Jackson, Baker, and Lemons in to find some water.

The three men found a well in the center of the village and immediately fanned out, searching for the enemy. Coming up to a small structure, Jackson heard raucous laughter inside, coming from more than just one man. Looking through one of the windows, he watched while five German soldiers, laughing harshly, brutally pushed a small man around the room until he fell to the floor, crying out in pain.

In the far corner of the room, he noticed a woman sitting on the floor with her knees drawn up to her chest and her arms wrapped around her legs, and she was crying. The woman had lumps and bruises on her face and arms, and her clothes were torn and dirty. *Crap on the ground. These goons must be the rest of that 88 gun crew.* Silently, Jackson moved back to where the squad was waiting and reported what was happening to Sergeant Brooks. While Brooks and Jackson were arguing over what to do about the situation, Corporal Cane spoke up. "That's your mom and dad in there, Al. What do you want us to do?"

Brooks and Jackson both stopped their little whispering argument, looked at Cane, and then they looked at each other. Immediately, Sergeant Brooks understood Jackson's expression, and with a sigh of resignation, he agreed to do something about the situation.

~ ~ ~

Sergeant Brooks positioned his men in the shadows, covering both sides of the doorway, and waited until Jackson returned; the scout had an idea. The five Germans inside had been drinking heavily, so they were a bit wobbly in all departments and had no idea their enemy was only a few feet away just beyond the door. The scout returned about twenty minutes later with a German uniform shirt and had Baker put it on.

The laughter had died out, and now the drunken soldiers were starting on the woman again. The woman's husband was lying on the floor unconscious as a result of being pushed into a wooden desk and hitting his head on it. When the squad was ready, Baker started yelling for the men inside to come out. "There is a problem with the gun, and I can't figure it out."

After several minutes, the men inside finally started filtering out to see what the problem was. As soon as the first German stepped into the night air, PFC Baker spoke up again. "The breach-block isn't locking. Maybe you can figure out what the problem is. Follow me."

The rest of the gun crew were about ten feet from the door when the men of 1st squad moved out of the shadows behind the Germans. Corporal Cane snickered, and the enemy gunners turned around only to find multiple American rifles pointing at them. Cautiously, they put their weapons on the ground and raised their hands above their heads. They were still drunk, but now, they were a lot more terrified than drunk.

Jackson went into the little house and helped the woman take care of her husband while Stone, Avery, and White filled up the canteens. The two people were surprised that the Americans were there, yet they were not ungrateful, a fact that had Jackson grinning from ear to ear.

"Ah, no, sir, thank you sir, but we can't take your goats. We have to move quietly, sir. No, really, sir. I don't know the first thing about goats."

Still grinning, Jackson quickly said goodbye when he received a nod from Private Stone. Once outside and with Stone, Avery, and White, the four men started running to catch up with the rest of the squad, who were busy marching the five Germans out of the village. When the squad was about a hundred yards from the village, Brooks called a halt and had Baker explain to the enemy what was about to happen to them.

"This is for those two defenseless people you were beating on, you bastards."

Then they were shot.

~ ~ ~

Around 0300 hours, on the fourth day, Jackson was sent out to find another hiding place for the squad. The only places that he found could be easily spotted from the air, but they really had no choice. At the present moment, the enemy on the ground posed the bigger threat to them, so they moved through the little valleys between the hills. They were running out of food, but for the time being, they still had plenty of water.

The sun was poking its head above the horizon, allowing the Americans to see what was around them. The terrain had a lot of hills and small, rocky mountains about two to six-hundred-feet high. There were so many of them close together that it was pretty easy to hide from ground units.

Peaking over the edge of one those hills, Jackson watched while his enemy put the last finishing touches to their defenses. The day was already baking hot, but the squad was now forced to stay where they were until the sun went down.

Puffs of black smoke abruptly appeared over the German positions Jackson was watching. A few seconds later, he heard the roar of airplanes as they dove and dropped their deadly packages on the enemy. For thirty minutes, the air attack continued to pound the Germans, and when the planes had left, the artillery opened up for over an hour, before the air attacks began again. To Jackson, it seemed like the entire front was under air and artillery attack.

The whole front had erupted with explosions and fire. The scout could hear the Germans firing, and it sounded as though they were firing every weapon they possessed. Tracer rounds were going every which way trying to kill their enemy. Jackson ran down the backside of the hill and met Sergeant Brooks who was coming up to see what was happening. Looking to the north, Brooks noticed the same thing happening there too. Looking to the south, he saw smoke rising, and lots of it. He was getting excited.

Forgetting where he was, Brooks shouted down to his men, “They’ve started the battle without us, boys.” As the day and the explosions wore on, the enemy began to retreat. Smoke, knocked out vehicles, and burning debris covered the battlefield. The Allied aircraft were following the enemy retreat and chewing them up. The whole squad was now on the rim of the hill, watching the battle and cheering the Allies on.

Off in the distance, 1st squad noticed Allied troops advancing towards the Germans. Thousands of troops and scores of vehicles, all moving forward, forced the enemy to fight as they withdrew. The Allied fighter planes had complete control of the air, so they were pounding the hell out of the Germans.

A group of Germans were heading towards the hill that the squad was hiding behind, so Brooks readied his men for battle. "Spread out and fire only after I fire. Corporal Cane, take three men over to that cluster of rocks and then hit the Krauts in flank when they reach that big one. Lock and load, gentlemen. We're about to earn our pay."

One of the British fighters that had flown over the hill had spotted the squad and thought they were the enemy, so the pilot strafed their position. Brooks frantically waved his arms, but the pilot paid no attention to him. The plane had missed its mark on its first try and was circling around for a second attempt when the pilot spotted some men scrambling up the hill.

Corporal Cane's detachment opened up on the Germans first, taking the enemy by surprise. When they turned to face the unexpected threat, the rest of the squad stood up and fired down on the enemy's exposed left, shredding the dying warriors almost as fast as they could pull the trigger.

The fighter pilot saw the two groups firing at each other and finally recognized the American uniforms dotting the reverse slope of the hill, so on his return pass, he fired at the men coming up the hill and watched the last of them fall. The men of 1st squad immediately stood up and pumped their weapons up and down in victory at the pilot and got a wiggle out of the airplane. However, Corporal Cane noticed another enemy formation, and they were running straight for the hill the Americans were occupying.

About thirty Germans were running for the hill, and most of them still carried their weapons. Brooks watched them quickly move towards the hill, in an attempt to hide from the Allied planes. When they reached the hill, the scattered dead caught a lieutenant's attention for just a quick moment. The direction the bodies were facing had him thinking, but then he remembered the fighter and completely dismissed his apprehension, unaware that an American infantry squad was hiding just beyond the crest of the hill.

The fighter plane came back for a strafing run on the enemy and joined 1st squad's attack on the Germans. When the pilot let go with his machine guns, the Americans popped up and added their spunk to the fight, firing on the Germans at the same time. Within seconds, only the men of 1st squad were still standing. Over sixty dead were left scattered on the east side of the hill. With a wave of his wings, the fighter pilot, now completely out of ammo, turned back to the west and flew for his airfield.

The pilots already knew about Brooks and where he was, so as long as they could, they tried to protect the squad as much as possible. After an hour of dodging bullets and fighting, the squad was finally out of ammo, water, and Germans. The only soldiers coming towards them now were Americans. "Hey, guys," shouted Brooks, "what took you so long? I thought my boys and me were going to have to whip the Germans all by ourselves!"

Yes, it was a happy reunion.

Chapter 8

The Allies launched their attack on the 22nd of April and by the end of the month had captured almost all of Tunisia. Rolling strong and unstoppable, the Allied juggernaut continued to pound on their enemy until the Axis power in Africa finally collapsed. On May 13th, the last of over 250,000 Axis troops surrendered, ending almost three years of exhausting and brutal warfare in North Africa. The time had arrived to get on with the business at hand, and that was to knock Italy out of the war.

On the 10th of July, the Allies invaded the island of Sicily. After six weeks of hard fighting, they were victorious, but the Axis armies fighting in Sicily had managed to evacuate most of their troops and equipment to Italy. They would fight another day.

The invasion of mainland Italy began on September 3, 1943. General Mark Clark, commanding the U.S. Fifth Army, was to land at Salerno while General Montgomery landed at Calabria and Taranto with the British Eight Army. Around the middle of September, the Salerno bridgehead was declared secure, and the Allies were on the move, up the boot of Italy.

The fight had been long and hard, but the war in North Africa was finally over. Standing by the ship's portside railing and looking out at the Mediterranean Sea, Sergeant Brooks had to wonder why they had been so lucky to survive the missions they were sent on. *If it hadn't of been for Jackson, Lemons, and Baker, we might not have fared so well.* Newly promoted Sergeant First Class Alfred Brooks turned to face freshly chevroned, buck sergeant, Daniel Cane. "Finally, we're leaving this sunbaked country behind. Now, I believe in miracles."

Sergeant Cane looked at his platoon sergeant and said, "We're not heading for Italy, so that leaves jolly old England. I guess we're going to invade France. This fight should be a snap."

"I wouldn't count on that, Dan," said Brooks. "We're fighting an enemy on their own ground, territory they have already fought and bled over. The Krauts know the lay of the land; we don't. No, Dan. It's not going to be a snap. This fight's going to be a brutal slugfest. We're going to have to beat the piss out of the Krauts to win this war."

Onboard ship, Jackson was a nervous wreck. He hated ships and large bodies of water, and he was seasick the whole time. Afraid of nothing the enemy could throw at him, he was a frozen-in-place, toilet-hugger his entire trip to England.

"Hey, Hanky. Did you see Jackson's face when he caught sight of England? You'd have thought he just won the jackpot he was so happy. Poor guy!"

"Yeah, Stony, I saw him. The kid looked kind of puny, didn't he? Hey, rumor has it that we'll be in England for a long time. Lots of training and lots of dames. Nobody knows when we're going to invade France, so I guess we'll be having a good ole time until they figure things out."

~ ~ ~

"It's June, 1943, and I'm here in jolly ole England. The weather's not too bad. It's been raining a bit off and on, but not a whole lot. For the most part, it's been nice. Training has been a little rough lately because of the time off we had before the training began. Running is the killer. The more we run, though, the less it hurts. That's all we're doing right now. We run, march in full field gear, then run some more, up and down hills and along roads. We're supposed to also go through small unit tactics; like teamwork and suppression, setting up ambushes, fire and maneuver. Just about everything that we did in Africa, but in England our extra training is just making us better at it. The air force is doing its job, pounding the Germans all over Europe and along the Atlantic Wall. Rumors are going around that we're going to invade France at the Pas de Calais, and that Normandy is going to be a diversionary attack. Everybody has their own ideas and their own guesses, but me? I don't care. I just want to do my job so we can win the war, and then go home. Gotta go. I will write more later.

We've been training for almost a year now and my men are getting tired of waiting. Let's go and get this thing over with so we can go home. Security has gotten very tight over the last few months, and it seems to be getting tougher all the time. It's May, 1944, now, and something is in the wind. I can feel it. Infantry training appears to be winding down, so I guess we've learned all we can. You probably won't receive this letter until after the war, and hopefully, I'll be the one delivering it to you.

Love you both, Alfred."

Chapter 9

Sergeant Brooks and squad were hunkered down just below the crest of a hedgerow, an enormous stretch of dirt embankment, bordering and almost completely enclosing sections of farm land, sometimes one to two acres in size, along with everything imaginable growing on it. Solid, centuries old, and hard packed, the embankment was reinforced by the roots of whatever was growing, like re-bar in concrete.

D-Day was a success, but now the push inland was in danger of stalling because of the hedgerows. The unexpected scope of the checkerboard terrain forced the Americans to clear out the hedgerows one by one. A tough job to do, for when a squad or a platoon had cleared out a hedgerow and then moved on to the next one, the Germans would re-occupy the one just recently cleaned out.

Private Lemons had moved around the right side of a hedgerow and was trying to find a well-camouflaged machine gun that had just shredded four men. The machine gun was tucked back into a corner, covering the only entrance leading to the interior of that particular hedgerow. Grenades didn't seem to be working, and so far, no one could figure out why. When someone tossed a grenade over the top of the embankment into the suspected corner, it would explode. The only way to prove the attack was successful was to try going past the entrance. Most of the time the German gunners mowed the poor souls down. Definitely a tough nut to crack, and the problem had Sergeant Brooks almost walking in circles.

Not long after the last explosion, Sergeant Brooks heard another grenade explode, and then a few minutes later, Private Lemons appeared. "Well?" asked Brooks.

"No, go, Sarge. I tried climbing up the backside to get a better angle and got shot at for my troubles. This nest is going to be a tough one to take out."

"Jackson, go with Lemons and see if you can kill that sniper when Sam starts climbing up the back side." When there was no response from his scout, Brooks turned to find out why and discovered that the beanpole had disappeared. "Damn," was all he could think to say.

Ten minutes went by before Sergeant Brooks spotted Jackson cautiously slinking out of the smoky haze. "The Germans dug this one deep into the base of the hedgerow, Sarge. They also piled dirt up in front to help shield against shrapnel. What we need is a Sherman."

"The Shermans are busy right now, Jackson, so it's up to us."

Abruptly, Jackson smiled. "I have an idea. Sam, follow me," he said. "You can be the bait. When the sniper makes his move, I'll try to get him before he gets you."

"Why me?" asked Sam.

"Because you're faster than I am," replied Jackson. "And besides, I'm a better shot than you are."

After a brief conversation with Sergeant Brooks, Jackson led Lemons to within a couple of feet of the opening of the hedgerow, and then he quickly slithered his way to the crest, overlooking the interior of the hedgerow and the shadowed corner. "Okay, Sam. Get ready."

"Wait a minute, Tim. What are we doing here? I thought we were going after a sniper?"

"Change of plans. The squad is already in position; we're just waiting on you."

"What am I supposed to do in this new plan of yours?"

Private Jackson was hiding in the brush growing on the hedgerow, so Sam couldn't see his smile. "Run inside the hedgerow and hit the ground. When the machine gun opens up, I'll kill the gunners before they can nail your Lakota ass to the turf."

"What if you miss?"

Private Jackson was still smiling when he replied. "If I miss, then you'll get a chance to feel what it's like to get shot by a machine gun."

Private Lemons looked up in the direction of Jackson's voice and shook his head. "I should have had enough of your ideas in North Africa, yet here I am again. Shit! This is getting old. When do I get to dangle *you* in front of the Germans?"

"Oh, shut up sour man and get ready to run." Instantly, the men of 1st squad were snickering quietly and shaking their heads. "Damn, beanpole," said Private Hanky. "One of these days you're gonna get poor Sam, shot."

From the opening of the hedgerow to where the machine gun was firing from was about fifty to sixty yards. Jackson gave the signal that he was ready, so Sam took a deep breath and darted out about thirty feet into the hedgerow and then hit the ground.

The machine gun opened up on Lemons just seconds after he hit the ground, but the rounds were hitting well short. Immediately the gunner walked the rounds up to where Lemons was hugging the ground, leaving Jackson only a few seconds to do what he planned before the Germans could shoot Sam full of holes.

Jackson immediately rose up and started shooting when the machine gun opened fire, and at the same time, 1st squad let loose with additional supporting fire. The scout was aiming just above the machine gun flashes, into the shadows where he thought the Germans might be hunching down over the machine gun sights. The enemy bullets were hitting only a few feet short of Private Lemons when they abruptly stopped flying. Sam immediately got up and ran back away from the opening.

While the squad continued to fire into the corner of the hedgerow, Jackson took off to his left to close on the enemy position. When he was close enough, he tossed a grenade into the position. When it exploded, he watched an MG42 machine gun go flying off to the left, twisted and bent, no longer serviceable, like the crew that was manning it.

"You sure took your damn sweet time," yelled Lemons. "That Kraut machine gun almost got me."

"No he didn't, Sam," said Jackson. "He was too busy trying to locate which blade of grass you were hiding behind; he was just guessing at where you were."

Private Lemons was looking at a bright and shiny new bullet scar on the right side of his helmet. "If you say so, Tim.

It sure sounded like a bullet hit my helmet. My ears are still ringing. I'd say that was a little more than guess work, don't you think?"

The sounds of war were everywhere, and they weren't stopping any time soon. The big thunderous guns of the Allied ships firing, the artillery boom and crash, the sharp crack of anti-tank and tank guns, and the snap-crackling of small arms fire gave testimony to the seriousness of what was transpiring. The Germans were putting up a deadly defensive battle throughout the hedgerows. Tanks without infantry support were sitting ducks in the hedgerow country, especially climbing over the top of one. That action left the soft underbelly of the tank exposed making it an easy kill. And then there were the deadly 81mm mortars. The Germans loved those nasty little infantry shredders.

The squad was still standing next to the defunct machine gun nest when bullets started whizzing by them. Immediately, they took off running towards the opposite corner, straight towards the shooters, with the intent of using the tall, northern embankment of the hedgerow they were occupying to hide behind. With an incentive, such as bullets churning up the ground around them, they covered the distance in no time, finally reaching the safety of the opposite corner. Brooks immediately turned to Jackson and said, "Find those Kraut bastards and then get back to me. Nothing else. Corporal Sims, take three men and cover the entrance, but stay out of grenade range."

The hedgerow that Brooks and his men were in was in a rectangular shape, about an acre in length and about a half an acre wide. The long edge of it went southeast to northwest. It was closed off at the southeastern end with a small, sixty-foot opening about a third of the way across the northern short-axis.

First squad was hunkered down in the northwest corner of the hedgerow, facing the back of the next hedgerow over. A ten-foot wide cart path separated this one from the next one over where the firing had come from. In most areas, these long and tall embankments gave the troops traversing the road network between the hedgerows, a sunken lane feeling.

Fighting a battle in a maze of tall embankments was a very terrifying and very nerve racking experience.

Brooks placed his men just below the crest of the ridge, facing where the firing had come from, to give Jackson support. The scout signaled that he was ready, so the squad opened fire all along the top of the adjacent embankment while Jackson sprinted to the southwest corner of the neighboring hedgerow. Once he reached the corner, the squad quit firing, but kept an eye out for any enemy heads popping up. Now it was all up to Jackson. All the Americans could do was wait for him to return.

Three Germans were firing on the Americans while they were standing by the deceased machine gun nest. The enemy had heard the fighting going on in the hedgerow to their south, but there wasn't much that they could do about it at the time. They were there to protect the machine gunners from flanking infantry attacks. Until those orders changed, they could do nothing.

While the fighting was going on between Brooks and the machine gun, the German corporal in charge changed those orders, and two of his men were ordered to climb to the crest of the hedgerow and see if they could help. It wasn't until the men of 1st squad started moving around that the Germans actually saw them. One of the two informed his corporal that there were Americans in the next hedgerow, so the corporal joined his men along the crest, and they started firing on the Americans until their enemy disappeared from sight. The corporal then moved back down to where the machine gun was positioned, leaving his two men to keep an eye peeled for the Americans.

A few minutes later, the Americans opened fire along the top of the hedgerow where their enemy was watching, forcing the Germans to duck below the crest to keep from being shot. That was when Jackson made his dash to the southwest corner of the hedgerow. After the firing stopped, the two enemy warriors took a peek over the top, but they were unable to see anything.

Jackson was halfway up the southwest corner of the hedgerow when he heard rattling noises caused by his adversaries. He now knew about where they were, so taking his time, he slithered his way towards them, moving as silently as a ghost.

Craning their necks, the two Germans tried to see over the edge without being shot, but neither man knew that Jackson was there. The Arizona scout took a bead on his closest enemy and fired three quick shots. Immediately shifting his aim, he fired on the other one before he could fire back and nailed him in the forehead.

The German corporal had been taken by surprise when the first shots were fired, but he quickly recovered and started firing at where he thought Jackson was. Bullets from his MP 40, submachine gun, kicked up the ground all along the top of the ridge, showering Jackson with leaves, dirt, and other debris. "Crap on the ground, this guy is pissed!"

Ducking low, and with bullets flying all around him, the Arizona beanpole beat a hasty retreat down the backside of the hedgerow to the narrow pathway bordering the hedgerows, and there he stood, in the shadows, shaking and trying to calm down his heart. A few blinks later, he was searching north along the path and curiously watched a bulky black shape move onto the path he was standing on. Almost immediately following the sighting, a big orange flame erupted from the black shape, followed by the explosion of the round some forty yards down the lane. *Crap on the ground. A German tank*! Before he had a chance to recover from his surprise, Jackson heard two more rounds go off at almost the same time, and he heard two different impact-reactions when the rounds hit their targets.

Quickly looking to the south, he watched a Sherman shudder to a stop with smoke and flame belching out of the open hatches before it was hit again. *Crap on the ground*! *I'd better get out of here*! Ducking, Jackson took off running and immediately headed back to the squad, with his boots digging in deep. *Crap on the ground. These guys mean business*!

The men of 1st squad, 1st platoon, Baker Company were waiting for something to happen. However, when something did happen, the event took them by surprise. They heard the cracks of an M1 carbine that Private Jackson had finally traded his M1 Garand for. A few seconds later, they heard the rattle of a German MP 40. Then, less than a minute later, 1st squad heard the heavy belch of a tank, followed by two more belches, and then silence. The symphony of deadly tank fire happened less than 250 feet from their position, yet they saw nothing. They only heard the action.

Humor, however, was rapidly taking the place of scared, concern. The men of 1st squad had front row seats as they watched Jackson sprinting towards them out of the smoky haze as fast as his legs could propel him. "Hey, beanpole," shouted Brooks. "Can you run any faster? The bullets are catching up."

Sergeant Brooks left the squad up on the ridge and was beaming from ear to ear while he headed down to talk to Jackson when the kid arrived. When the scout stopped in front of him, the poor Arizona beanpole was huffing and puffing, bent over with his hands on his knees, sucking in the air. "Very funny, Sarge," he said between gasps. "I didn't know there were any bullets following me until you told me. Crap on the ground, that was intense. There's a German tank at the other end..." Somewhat surprised, Private Jackson abruptly stopped talking and stared at Sergeant Brooks for a moment before he asked, "What are you looking for, Sarge?"

Brooks stopped looking along the ground and slowly turned to face Jackson. "Beanpole, where is the crap on the ground?"

Sergeant Brooks immediately lost his humor, and it was apparent through his expression, but the beanpole in uniform didn't get a chance to answer. The squad was only 15 feet away, so they heard everything, and very quickly, the snickers erupted. "Hey Sarge, watch out for the crap on the ground. You'll give us away from the smell if you step in it."

Still a bit agitated, Sergeant Brooks looked up at his men and said, "Corporal Sims! I'm sure the Germans would love you as a new hood ornament (an allied prisoner tied to the front of a German vehicle, an action that happened several times in the Caen sector) as much as I would love to give you to them. Might want to keep that in mind the next time you open your big mouth, or you'll be the one stepping in crap.

Somebody else care to comment? Beanpole said there was crap on the ground, so I looked. Anyone have a problem with that? Now, beanpole. What were you saying about tanks?"

Beanpole was still shaking inside from the agitated stare he received from Sergeant Brooks. "There's a German tank at the other end of that hedgerow, Sarge. It just knocked out a Sherman about 50 yards south of us."

Brooks immediately turned to look up at the men positioned along the crest of the hedgerow. "Corporal Sims, take Green, Todd, and White and go scrounge up a Bazooka and some rounds to knock out that German tank. There's probably Kraut infantry somewhere around because of that tank, so be careful. Don't let 'em ambush you." Then he turned back to beanpole. "What else did you find out on your little trip?"

Jackson was still jumping and twitching around inside from his recent encounters, so he was fidgeting in place, trying to calm down. "There are two machine guns, each well positioned to cover the other. One is in the southwest corner, and the other one is in the southeast corner, with at least two men by each gun. I know that one of them has an MP 40. What the rest of them are carrying, I have no idea."

"Can we lob grenades down on the machine gun positions? Damn it, beanpole. Will you stand still, you're making me nervous... Thank you."

Beanpole stopped moving upon request, but his lack of movement only lasted to the count of ten. "We can try," said Jackson. "But I think the Germans are going to have some men covering that area now that they know...we're...here. What are you doing, Sarge?"

Sergeant Brooks had calmly reached out during Jackson's report, put his hands on the scout's shoulders, and then forcefully pushed down until beanpole stopped moving. Then he grinned and said, "There! Now I don't feel so nervous. I guess we'll have to wait for the Bazooka to get here before we try anything else...What are you guys laughing about?"

Chapter 10

After a two-hour round trip, the four men made it back to the squad with a Bazooka and six rounds, followed by a squad of infantry. Sergeant Darwyn, the squad's commander, conversed with Brooks and Jackson for a few minutes before he ordered his men to move north up the cart path, but they didn't get very far.

Darwyn's squad had advanced only a few yards from the protection of the hedgerow they were previously occupying when they came under fire from hidden, German positions. Two Americans were dead, and another wounded before they made it back to the hedgerow Sergeant Brooks and his men had taken refuge in. Before they could catch their collective breaths, both squads heard the deep roar of diesel engines as a tank moved out of cover between the bordering hedgerows, intersecting the path Jackson had his encounter on. Only a couple of seconds passed before the tank opened up with everything it had, quick-firing down the path. Then, just as quickly, the tank slipped back into cover. Sergeant Darwyn's squad had already moved out of sight by the time the tank started firing.

"Jackson, as soon as it gets dark, I want you to take Lemons and two others and try to sneak up on that tank from the rear and knock it out. That gives you about an hour before sundown. Get some rest while you can. I have a feeling this is going to be a long night." Immediately, Private Jackson was smiling inside, waiting for that slow hour to pass.

Moving back up to where the rest of the squad was keeping an eye out for the enemy, Sergeant Brooks was wondering about the situation he was now faced with; how to position his men against a night infiltration attack. He had a hunch that the Germans might try to re-occupy their lost positions. If they were to succeed, a lot of Americans would die in the process.

He dug his men in along the base of the hedgerow, along the front, and along the two sides for cover against mortar and artillery fire. They had no more problems from the adjacent hedgerow to the north. It seemed as though the enemy in the neighboring hedgerow was content to be left alone for the time being.

PFC Baker and Private Brown went with Fox and Lemons to try and knock out the tank at the other end of the northern hedgerow. Only Jackson was excited about the incursion.

"Copy one, this is copy two. Glen Miller is a go. I repeat. Glen Miller is a go. Start the music at twenty-two."

"Confirmed, copy two. Music at twenty-two." Within three rounds, the mortar crews had their start range zeroed in. After receiving the much-needed status report, Sergeant Brooks prepared the four men for their move up the right side of the hedgerow.

At 2200 hours, the six mortars started their barrage. The bombardment was scheduled to last as long as it took the four men to scamper the eighty or ninety yards that was required, with the rounds hitting about twenty-five feet apart. The four men started out after the third salvo hit and moved forwards behind the exploding mortar rounds, quickly arriving at the intersecting path that the tank was on. Jackson took a quick peek to his left, around the corner of the hedgerow, and saw a shadow that was the tank; then he made a quick search of the area. "Wait here," he said, and then he was gone.

Baker, Lemons, and Brown stood absolutely baffled when Jackson left them, but no one said a word. A few minutes later, the scout appeared out of the shadows, but only Private Lemons was prepared for the ghost-like emergence. Together again, Jackson whispered softly. "The Germans had a couple of spotters covering that tank's rear. We almost walked into an ambush. Let's give it a minute or so, just to make sure we weren't seen. Sam, you know how to work that thing?"

Sam was smiling when he replied. "Yep. You put the rocket in the tube and wire it up. I pull the trigger and blow up the tank. Just remember to step aside, away from the back blast. As much as I'd like it to be, barbequed Apache isn't on the menu for tonight."

The German infantry had scattered when the mortar rounds started impacting, and they were still hunkered down in their holes when a Bazooka went off. A whoosh, a hissing charge to target, and then the rocket hit the tank. Immediately upon impact, a flaming explosion erupted, blowing the hatches open. Seconds later, another explosion rocked the tank, sending the turret and a gushing cloud of flame almost 30 feet into the air before the huge ball of flame evaporated into nothing.

"Shit-fire, did you see that, Tim? Damn, let's get out of here!" Quickly, the four men tried to leave the intersection quietly and head back to the squad, but that idea didn't work out so well. Sam was absolutely giddy with excitement. "How about that? First trigger pull and bam! Damn, Tim, who's the better shot now?"

"Quiet, Sam, you'll give us away to the Germans."

While en route, PFC Baker popped a green flare and the mortars began firing at the coordinates, which had begun the barrage, to clear any unwanted new arrivals. The mortar crews fired four rounds each and then stopped. Less than a minute later, Jackson and company passed through the still sifting dust, grinning greatly. Now it was time for accolades. "How about it, Sam. That's one Mark IV you won't have to worry about. That was some good shooting. Did you close your eyes before you squeezed the trigger? My mom does that when we're out hunting. The scary thing is, she hasn't missed yet."

~ ~ ~

Sergeant Brooks received a radio message while the four men were out killing the tank. The message was a short one, but it put a smile on his face just the same. "Well, what do you know, Alex? We finally get a break. Just think; hot food and a roof over our heads. We're to report back to Colonel Martin by 2330 hours."

"What's going on?"

"I don't know. Lieutenant Shane didn't say."

Corporal Sims' smile was tight. "Hmm. Colonel Martin, huh?"

"Yeah, Alex, you know; our commanding officer? He does still pull our strings. Why? What's with the concerned look on your face?"

"I don't know, Al. Pulling us out of combat like this reminds of North Africa. I bet we're about to do the same thing here."

Pausing for a moment, Sergeant Brooks pulled off his helmet to re-adjust the webbing inside of the helmet liner before he put his helmet back on and said, "What better way to butter us up than to stuff us with hot food before we leave? At least, it might get us out of this checkerboard fight."

"Yeah, well maybe," replied Sims. "I don't know what would be worse. Fighting here or being surrounded by Germans out there." Slinging his rifle over his shoulder, Corporal Sims slapped his friend on the shoulder and said, "Let's go get that hot food and think about what's worse afterwards. Everything looks different on a full stomach."

~ ~ ~

The time was around 2320 when Sergeant Brooks reported to Lieutenant Shane. "Colonel Martin has a mission for you and your squad, Sergeant Brooks. You'll be gone for quite a while, so you'll need to draw extra K's and ammo. Here's a list of what you'll be taking with you when you leave here. The rest you'll have to get after you meet up with a couple of guys from the French resistance. You'll rendezvous with them in three days."

"Resistance?" To say Sergeant Brooks was astonished was an understatement. He just stared at his recently acquired platoon leader and could think of nothing else to say. *Resistance*? *Damn*!

"Yes," replied Lieutenant Shane. "Colonel Martin will brief you and your men on the mission in about 30 minutes. That will be all, Sergeant Brooks."

The resistance? thought Brooks. *What in the hell is going on*?

Colonel Martin was sitting behind his desk in his new headquarters in an abandoned house near Colleville. When he was finished with his paperwork, he stood up, shook each man's hand, and thanked Sergeant Brooks and his men for their excellent work. Then he smiled and said, "Now, I have another mission for you and your squad, Sergeant Brooks. The French underground has reported that the Germans have a big gun camouflaged in the trees about ten or twelve miles from here, somewhere near a small village called Clervella."

Colonel Martin paused just long enough to tap his finger on the map where the village was located before he continued. "Headquarters seems to think it's the one that keeps hitting the beaches, annoying everyone trying to unload supplies and equipment. Although it hasn't really done that much damage, yet, Command still wants the gun knocked out anyway before the Germans can get it zeroed in on what's left of the Mulberrys. You've got the list of items you'll be taking with you on this mission, so if you need anything else, the French underground will have to provide it. I want that gun destroyed, Al. Split that barrel from muzzle to breach block. I've seen what you and your men can do, and that's why I picked your squad for this mission."

Sergeant Brooks stared at Colonel Martin, not sure of what to say in return. "Can I get drunk first? It seems like a long way to go on an empty stomach, sir."

Colonel Martin looked back at Sergeant Brooks for a long few seconds before he broke into a smile. Then he reached into his drawer and pulled out a half-full bottle of Jack Daniels. Looking back and forth from the bottle of Jack to the squad, his smile widened before he said, "You guys have been hitting this stuff pretty hard, lately. If this keeps up, I'm going to have to buy it by the case!"

Chapter 11

"Just like in North Africa."

"Shut up, Alex. I enjoyed that steak, so please, don't ruin the memory with an I told you so."

"I told you so."

"Thanks a lot, Corporal."

Sergeant Brooks and squad left Allied lines behind about an hour after sundown, heading south. The rain had started about twenty minutes into their journey, so the squad put on their ponchos, slogged their way through the fields and hedgerows, and quietly slipped past a confused enemy.

The men of 1st squad had a really tough job to do. Their mission had them slipping through the German lines and then going twelve miles into enemy held territory to destroy an enemy gun. The one good thing about this mission was they could hide in the small stands of trees that were dotting the countryside along the way. Providing, of course, that the enemy wasn't there first. That was the plan. Their line of march was dictated by the closest stands of trees along their route. Hide in the trees during the day, and travel only at night.

The twelve Americans sneaked through some tough veteran outfits. What was left of the German 352nd infantry division had dug-in west, south, and east of St. Lo. Elements of the 352nd manned some of the defenses covering Omaha Beach during the invasion. German misconceptions and false impressions of a German victory at Omaha Beach had brought about disastrous results when those veteran warriors were taken off the line. Then, of course, there were the panzer divisions; veterans of two different brands of warfare and quite possibly one or two SS panzer divisions. The Panzer Lehr Division was rumored to be somewhere near St. Lo, as was the 2nd SS Panzer Division Das Reich.

~ ~ ~

The rain was still coming down when the squad arrived at the outskirts of a small town not on Brooks' map. Not wanting anyone to know they were around, Brooks called for a short break while Jackson took a look around the place. Moving cross-country was about to get a lot tougher for the men now that the air force was grounded because of bad weather. The low cloud cover handed the enemy the perfect opportunity to come out of hiding and move supplies and reinforcements without fear of air attacks to where they were needed most.

Jackson reported to Sergeant Brooks that there were no Germans in the town. Despite the report, however, Brooks had decided to stay where they were for the time being. The men were about a half a mile northwest of the town in a thickly wooded area that offered good concealment.

Sergeant Brooks went over the plan again with his men to make sure everyone understood what was to happen just in case he was killed or captured. Then he handed Corporal Cane his sergeant's stripes and promotion orders, which now put him second in command of the mission. "Try not to lose your stripes again, Dan. Next time, you'll owe the colonel a case of Scotch to get them back."

Sergeant Cane took a serious ribbing from the men when they watched Sergeant Brooks hand him his stripes back. "Maybe next time you won't be so drunk you can't distinguish rank. That captain really got pissed after you broke his nose."

~ ~ ~

On day two, an hour after sundown found the men of 1st squad heading south once more. They were heading into the domain of the 3rd Fallschirmjager Division, a very worthy opponent with a do-or-die mentality, and a never-quit attitude. The 3rd Fallschirmjager Division was spread out over several miles, and Brooks had the unenviable task of trying to sneak his men past these very experienced soldiers. Thinking about where he was and where he had to be, he realized that accomplishing this mission was going to be one hell of a chore.

The squad was spread out in a loose wedge formation with the men about ten feet apart. Private Lemons watched the rear while Jackson was on point about 100 yards out. Corporal Sims covered the middle, between Jackson and the point of the wedge, which was Sergeant Brooks. Sims was the relay between the point man and the squad leader in case Brooks lost track of Jackson. All was pretty quiet so far. Their hope was that it would remain that way, but they were now in enemy held territory, and every step they took south took them closer and closer to death.

Twenty-three-hundred hours had just arrived when Jackson reported to Brooks. The squad had stopped in a field that was overgrown with wild flowers and waist high grass, so Brooks called a twenty-minute halt to give the men a rest. Jackson informed Brooks that they were coming up to a road intersection about a 100 yards further south. "All right, people, spread out and no talking. We wait here. Beanpole, take Lemons and scout out that intersection and everything around it just in case the Germans are watching it. And be careful."

The two scouts were spread out about 20 yards apart as they approached the intersection. When they came to the edge of the road, they spread out even further and then dropped to the ground and spent the next ten minutes listening to the night sounds. Not hearing anything from the field directly across the road, Jackson signaled for Sam to stay put while he went and scouted the field to his right.

Scampering to the other side of the roadway, Jackson hit the ground and immediately crawled to his ten o'clock, stopping to listen only after low-crawling another 15 yards. Straining to hear the un-natural, he waited about ten minutes before he silently scoured the field, searching for the enemy. Satisfied the field was empty of Germans, he crawled back to where he had left Sam. After signaling for Lemons to cross, the two men quickly spread out again before they moved towards the second road, just below the intersection.

One of the roads forming the intersection went from nine o'clock to three o'clock, while the road the two men were getting ready to cross went from seven o'clock to two o'clock.

Just as the two men were getting ready to cross the road, Jackson heard a noise off to his right and signaled Sam to stop. Turning to investigate, Jackson crawled to the edge of the field they were in and noticed a barn they hadn't seen earlier. Both scouts kept an eye on the barn and soon were reward for their patience. Ten minutes into their surveillance, dimly lit shapes were seen moving around in the loft. Several of them, in fact.

"Wait here, Sam."

Jackson moved to his right again and ended up in a clump of small trees. Using the trees for cover, he headed west through the evergreens and into another field with a hedge bordering the southern boundary of the acreage. Using the hedge for cover, he silently crawled past the loft door until he was facing the northeast side of the barn. Not seeing any windows, he scampered over to the side of the barn and slowly inched his way towards the back, stopping every now and then to listen for sounds of the enemy. Not hearing any, he continued to inch his way to the back of the barn until he reached the rear corner where he stopped again to listen.

Quickly scampering over to the adjacent corner, he paused again to listen. Nothing. After a few minutes, he still hadn't heard anything, so he stepped around the northwest corner and stood face to face with his enemy. The two men stared at each other for the count of three before they reacted.

The German had his rifle slung over his right shoulder. When he reached for it, Jackson swung his carbine up hard, butt first from his hip, and hit him on the bottom of his chin. Along with a loud clack of broken teeth and chin bone, Jackson knocked the German flat on his back, dazed, and unable to do anything. Grabbing his hunting knife, which was strapped across his chest, Jackson immediately rammed it into his enemy's heart before the soldier had a chance to gather his senses enough to warn his companions. Slinging his carbine across his back, the Arizona beanpole quickly grabbed the dead man and quietly carried him around behind the barn, where he laid him on the ground. Then as quick as a cat, he rushed to the corner of the barn to see if the little confrontation had been observed.

Watching for several minutes, he decided that his little battle had not been seen, so he headed for the window that was about five feet from the southwest corner of the barn. Peering through the window, he spotted four enemy soldiers lying on a thick carpet of hay covering the floor of the barn:

they were sound asleep. Searching the interior of the barn, he didn't see anybody else. *Hmm. The rest must still be in the loft.*

With that thought in mind, Jackson went back around the barn to the northeast side of the structure and moved to the southeast corner. Peering up at the loft, he tried to gauge where he had to be in order to lob the grenades just inside the loft opening. When he had everything all figured out to his satisfaction, he slung his carbine across his back again, grabbed two grenades, and pulled the pins. After another deep breath to fortify his courage, he stepped out and tossed the grenades one right after the other, just inside of the loft door. After the second grenade left his hand, he immediately bolted for a hedge only a few feet away. By the time he had hit the ground, the two grenades had gone off, one right after the other, causing the floor of the loft to collapse on the four sleeping soldiers, and killing everyone who was sleeping among the rafters.

Dust, bits of hay, and smoke came billowing out of the barn door, and less than a minute later, two of the four Germans came staggering out and were killed. Jackson had just killed the second man when a machine gun across the field from where Sam was waiting fired on him. Lemons saw where the firing was coming from and took a pot shot at the muzzle flash. For a few seconds, the machine gun quit firing. *Damn, I must have hit one.* Then it opened up again, but this time it was firing at Private Lemons.

Jackson got up and started running southeast to take the machine gun from the right before it chewed up his best friend. The distance was only about 200 feet to where he was heading, and he covered the distance pretty quickly. When he arrived at the stand of trees he was running for, he dropped behind a tree and opened up on the machine gun. Sam had been crawling back and forth along the hedge line, firing from different positions until Jackson started firing. Now the two scouts had the machine gun in a crossfire.

The small hamlet that was about a 100 yards from Sam's position was at his three o'clock. It also had a machine gun, but it didn't start firing at Lemons until Jackson got involved.

Now the two machine guns had Sam in their crossfire and the German gunners were chewing up the ground around him. The town also started spewing out German troops, about ten of them. They were running across a field, adjacent to the field that the first machine gun was firing from, the same field Brooks and the rest of the squad were hunkering down, in.

The enemy's plan was to out flank Lemons. They were about twenty feet from a road they had to cross when Brooks and his men popped up from out of the waist high grass and weeds. First squad had been silently moving towards the shooting when they spotted the Germans. The surprise was brutal. Hit in the flank from ambush, the Germans were cut to pieces. In a matter of seconds, the entire squad was dead.

When the two machine guns concentrated their fire on Lemons, Jackson took off running towards his five o'clock to draw fire away from Sam. The first machine gun had been so busy shooting at Lemons that the crew didn't see Jackson until he had almost reached another stand of trees; by then it was too late to do anything. With Jackson and Lemons firing on the first machine gun, the rest of 1st squad attacked the second gun. They had spotted the window the second machine gun was firing out of, so they laid down some covering fire and sent two men around to out flank it from the left. Without infantry support, the two machine guns didn't stand a chance. Just minutes after the infantry had been eliminated, the two machine gun positions fell silent.

"Let's get the hell out of here," ordered Brooks. "Lemons, you take the point, but no more than fifty yards out. Sims, I want you watching our ass. Move out. Jackson, you're with me. I want to know everything that happened and why it happened."

By the time Jackson had explained everything, the Americans had reached the first road they were to cross. There were no towns between them and the second road, so they only had to worry about running into the enemy.

When they arrived at their destination, they hung around for about twenty minutes, just long enough for Jackson to scout out the area. As soon as he returned, they crossed the road and headed due east, entering a forest just as the sun was beginning to rise. "Get what sleep you can, gentlemen, because tonight is going to be a tough one. We don't have much time left to meet the frogs, so we're going to have to travel without a break to reach Berigny in time. Jackson, you and Lemons take the first watch and stay out of trouble."

~ ~ ~

The squad moved out as the sun was going down. They were well rested, having slept all day long between watches. Yet, as spry as they felt, moving from field to field still took a lot of time. First of all, the fields had to be scouted to make sure there were no hidden Germans lurking in the bushes, and second, they had to avoid being spotted by the local inhabitants. The squad was heading into a long and tiring night.

~ ~ ~

Preoccupied at the moment, Sergeant Brooks was listening to the roar of the vehicles and the subdued voices of the enemy. Staring out at the shadows surrounding the squad's hiding place, he was taken by surprise when Private Lemons appeared out of nowhere. "There's a major road up ahead, and it's crawling with Germans. If we head east," said Lemons, "we'll run into a dry creek bed with lots of cover. We can wait 'em out from there."

Sergeant Brooks didn't hesitate. "Get us there, Sam." Immediately, the Americans slithered their way to the dry creek bed with Private Lemons leading the way. Once they were hidden under cover, Sergeant Brooks sent Jackson and Lemons to scout out the area and to keep an eye out on the Germans using the road. "Beanpole. No bullshit. You keep an eye on the Krauts and that's it. If I hear any shooting, I'm coming after you. Is that clear?"

Private Jackson nodded the affirmative and then gulped hard. "Yes, Sergeant Brooks. I hear you." However, Jackson and Lemons didn't stay gone for very long. "Sarge, the Germans have infantry combing the woods on both sides of the road, and they'll be here in about ten or fifteen minutes."

"How many?" asked Brooks. "Maybe we can hide in the shadows and wait for them to pass."

"I think, maybe a dozen or so." replied Jackson.

"Well, we can probably expect the same kind of patrolling, everywhere we go. I hear the resistance is hitting the Kraut convoys pretty hard these days, so they're probably just taking precautions against a frog attack. We have only two choices that I can see: fight or hide, and we don't have a lot of time to make that decision." Sergeant Brooks made another quick search of the area again, and then made his decision. "We stay here," he said. "Maybe the Krauts won't look in this neck of the woods."

Chapter 12

Private Lemons led the squad north and managed to gain some ground on the enemy troops searching the woods. An hour later, Sergeant Brooks was beginning to worry. Private Jackson hadn't reported back yet. He wasn't so much concerned about Jackson's safety as he was about what the little scout might do. That beanpole was such a sneak thief, and he was very good at it. At the same time, however, he was beginning to do an even better job at getting into spontaneous trouble all on his own.

Sergeant Brooks turned to Private Lemons and then paused for a couple of seconds before he asked, "What are you looking for, Sam? I need you to go find Jackson." Then, just as Brooks got the words out of his mouth, Jackson appeared out of the shadows about three feet from his platoon sergeant. Brooks jumped, and Private Lemons had to turn the other way, to keep from laughing out loud. "Damn you, Jackson. What did I tell you about sneaking up on me like that? And what the hell happened to you? What took you so long to get back?"

Private Jackson dropped six enemy bayonets at the feet of his platoon sergeant and smiled awkwardly. "There were only six," he said, "so we can go ahead and cross the road whenever you want." Sergeant Brooks just stared at Jackson for a few seconds. Then he looked down at the bayonets and then back at Jackson again. Astonished, all he could do was pull at his ear and mutter, "Unbelievable," before ordering his men to move out, heading south.

The woods the squad was traveling through continued on for another mile or so before the trees thinned out, and another road appeared. No enemy traffic was moving on it, so the men were able to cross it without any problems. An hour later, however, the situation began to change. The Americans were encountering more and more patrol activity the further south they went. Something had the Germans stirred up and searching.

Most of the activity was from motorized patrols running up and down the roads. However, there were some foot patrols as well, and they all appeared to be searching for something or someone. Coming up to a bombed-out farmhouse, Sergeant Brooks called a halt to let Lemons and Jackson check it out. "Don't draw any more attention to us than what you already have. Do you understand, beanpole? I wouldn't doubt the Krauts are out looking for us because of your antics. And remember, beanpole. If I hear any shooting I'm coming after you."

"Yes, sir," replied Jackson.

Brooks stared at the Arizona scout and had no idea what to say at first, so he pulled out a dirty, sweat-stained towel from his backpack and wiped his face. Then he took off his helmet and asked Cane, Baker, and Hanky for theirs. Stacking the helmets crossways, on top of each other, he sat on them while he pulled at his ear for a moment. Staring eye to eye with Jackson, he said, "You little rapscallion. I'm going to tie you in knots and bounce you all over France if you call me sir again. You get it right, or I'm going to drop-kick you all the way back to the States!" Then the middle helmet slid a little to the left when Brooks shifted his weight and then it squirted out like wet soap and Sergeant Brooks dropped down about a foot before he toppled sideways to the ground. Quiet snickers immediately erupted.

Only thirty minutes passed before Jackson and Lemons reported back. "We found a farmhouse, and it's empty, Sarge. As far as we could see, there are no Germans around. There's also a road just on the other side of the farmhouse, and about two hundred yards beyond the road is a large stand of trees. It looks like a good place to hide, Sarge."

Sergeant Brooks turned to the squad and said, "All right, people, let's go. Jackson, get us into those trees."

Sometime towards 2230 hours, the Americans reached their destination. An hour later, they stumbled across a clearing surrounded by trees. At the end of that clearing, they saw lights off in the distance. Staying just inside of the tree line, they slithered their way towards the lights and soon discovered a small Bavarian styled house, built on about an acre of land, and cleared right out of the middle of the trees.

Two dirt roads led from the house: one headed due south, and the other headed west. The house had a circular drive, and there were three enemy vehicles parked in front on the driveway, about sixty feet from the front door. Studying the house and the surrounding area, Sergeant Brooks pulled at his ear for a moment, and then he turned to his scouts. "Jackson, go find out what's going on with the Germans. I don't see any command markings or security troops roaming around, so this house can't be a Kraut headquarters. Sam, take Baker and check out those sheds. Be careful, you guys."

Jackson went around the entire house and didn't see a single German soldier anywhere, so he thought they must all be inside somewhere. Looking through one of the large front windows, he spotted several Germans sitting around a fireplace, sipping some kind of liquid, and being served by a very unhappy woman.

Moving to another window halfway around the house, he discovered eight more enemy soldiers sitting in what appeared to be a kitchen. Another fifteen minutes of searching around finally had him convinced that the eleven men he had discovered were the only enemy troops on the property. Immediately, he scampered back to give his report to Sergeant Brooks.

As soon as the men of 1st squad heard Jackson's report, they wanted to liberate the household from the Germans. Of course, Jackson's enthusiasm didn't help out at all. "It'll be a snap, Sarge. A piece of cake."

Still, as much as he tried, Brooks couldn't come up with a plausible reason not to make the attempt. With surprise on their side, there was a good chance they could pull the raid off, and this thought had Sergeant Brooks by the nose.

"Okay, here's how I figure it. The Krauts are relaxed, out in the middle of nowhere, uninvited, and drinking someone else's wine, so they won't be expecting trouble. They don't know we're here, so we shouldn't have a problem sneaking up on the bastards. What we need to do is hit both rooms at the same time and without any shooting. I'll take Sims, Decker, and Lemons with me. Sergeant Cane will take the rest of the squad. I'll take the officers, and the rest of you will take the kitchen full of Krauts. PFC Baker, you need to come up with a distraction that those Krauts in the kitchen will believe."

~ ~ ~

Leading from the front door was a long hallway that stretched about sixty feet until it ended at a swinging door that opened into the kitchen. On the right, about ten feet short of the kitchen door, was a set of wide double doors that opened outwards into the hallway, allowing entry into the living room, where the fireplace was located, and where the three German officers sat with their backs to the doors.

Brooks and six men quietly entered the front door and moved to the double doors. Three of them stayed with Brooks while the other three moved silently to the kitchen door. The four men were ready to enter the living room when the door closest to Brooks opened outward and a woman carrying a tray of empty wine glasses stepped into the hallway and closed the door behind her. Immediately, she was grabbed from behind and a hand closed upon her mouth to silence her.

Sergeant Brooks had grabbed the tray away from the woman to keep her from dropping it and, with barely a jingle from the wine glasses, put a finger up to his lips to signal quiet. He saw the surprised look on the woman's face, but he noticed no fear, just a glimmer of hope. An anxious hope. Immediately, he grinned at her and motioned for her to leave. When the hand was removed from around her mouth, she whispered to Sergeant Brooks in French-accented English. "There are more Germans in the kitchen. Please, don't let the Boche take my husband. He is with them in the kitchen. The Boche think my husband is in the resistance. I fear they are going to kill him."

The woman's expression, her body language, everything about her appeared calm, unruffled, proper, even with the SS sitting in her living room uninvited and drinking her wine. Yet there was still fear, and it showed in the way she rigidly clasped her hands. Sergeant Brooks stared down at the woman and winked. Then he nodded, held up eight fingers, and again motioned with his head for her to leave.

As soon as she cleared the house, Brooks held up his fingers and then counted off… one, two, three, and the four men quietly moved through the double doors. They were almost to the Germans before the officers turned around and froze, staring at four Americans and the rifles pointed at their heads. They didn't move or twitch. Only their eyes were moving, searching around, looking for more Americans.

With three men covering the captured officers, Sergeant Brooks tied their hands and then stuffed handkerchiefs into their mouths. Just as he was stuffing their mouths with handkerchiefs, they heard PFC Baker shouting out in German, and the three men by the kitchen door burst into the kitchen at the same time the rest of the squad waiting outside burst in through the back door.

The German troops in the kitchen were in the middle of eating when the Americans rushed through the two kitchen doors. They were so intent on eating, they were caught face-stuffed and greasy-handed from a freshly cooked goose. They were eating two-fisted with their rifles leaning up against the kitchen table, deep in their own territory. The situation was hopeless. With food still in their mouths, the Germans could do nothing but stare at the grinning Americans.

~ ~ ~

"Prisoners are all secured, Al."

"Good. Keep them quiet, Dan, while I figure out what to do." After a short pause, Sergeant Brooks turned to his two scouts and said, "Jackson, I want you and Lemons to scout out the road heading west, but don't go too far and then get right back." Immediately turning his attention back to Sergeant Cane, he said, "Load up the prisoners, Dan. I want to leave as soon as Sam and beanpole return."

When the two scouts reported back to Brooks that the coast was clear, Sergeant Brooks loaded up the squad and drove about three hundred yards west of the house, and stopped. The prisoners were dismounted from the vehicles, where they stood in place, blindfolded, with their backs to the vehicles, waiting for whatever came next. Brooks nodded, and the captives were very quickly rendered unconscious, put back into their vehicles, and driven out to the main road. Stopped in a column, Brooks ordered an evacuation, so the squad departed the vehicles and prepared to run like hell.

Immediately following the evacuation, a block of comp B with a grenade wired to it was tossed into each vehicle, and Cane, Decker, and Sims took off running after the squad. They didn't wait around to see the results of the explosions. Moving fast away from the scene, they cleared the area, praying all the while that the Germans would be slow to react.

Chapter 13

First squad entered Clervella from the east and slowly made their way towards the center of town. "Beanpole, see what you can find out. We'll wait here behind this building." Jackson nodded, took off behind the buildings, and soon disappeared from sight. Forty minutes into their wait, Jackson returned and reported back to Sergeant Brooks. "Nothing, Sarge. The town looks deserted."

"Are you sure?"

"Yeah, Sarge. I looked everywhere and I didn't see a single sole, not even a German."

"Damn," said Brooks. "Are we even in the right town?"

"Well, the sign says we are," replied Jackson. "I wonder where all of the people got off to?"

Brooks pulled at his ear, somewhat disgusted at the situation. "I guess we're just going to have to wait for a while and see what happens. Who knows? They might have all decided to go out for a walk."

About an hour or so before dusk, Jackson reported back to Sergeant Brooks. "I spotted a squad of Germans escorting some civilians, and they're heading right for us. They'll be here in about ten minutes."

"How many troops?"

"I counted ten," replied Jackson.

"Okay, people, spread out and be quiet. Our resistance guy might be one of those civilians."

There were only thirty people in the group, but according to the size of the town, there should be at least five times that many coming towards them. "Do we shoot the Germans?" asked Baker.

"No," replied Sergeant Brooks. "Leave them alone until we find out what's going on. Let's move back into that grove of trees and wait there."

The grove was about sixty yards from the town, and because of the direction the Germans were entering the town from, the buildings hid the Americans from view while they scurried towards the orchard. "Jackson, see if you and Baker can get close enough to find out what's happening to those civilians."

"You got it, Sarge." Quickly, the two Americans took off, heading for a church steeple, the tallest structure in town. They entered the church through the back door and as quietly as they could went up a creaking, wooden ladder, mounted up against one of the walls, through a trap door, and onto the bell tower floor. Looking out through the fancy railing, they watched the enemy herd the residents towards the church, shouting and waving their arms at their French captives. "Those are SS boys," hissed Jackson. "What do they want with these people?"

"Shut up, cowboy," whispered Baker. "I can't hear what they're saying."

"What did I tell you about calling me cowboy? Didn't I tell you that I was going to scalp your ass if you call me cowboy again?"

PFC Baker let out a quiet chuckle before he replied. "I'd like to see you try it, Jackson. I don't have any hair on my ass."

Absolutely dumbfounded and speechless, Jackson stared at Baker for almost a full minute and still couldn't think of anything say. PFC Baker, however, was on a roll. "Do you want to use my knife, or is yours good enough for the job?"

Jackson was still speechless, and then he wasn't. "I may not be able to scalp your ass because you have no hair there, but I can damn sure skin it."

The two men looked at each other and almost broke out laughing. With SS troops only thirty to forty feet below the bell tower, they were snickering.

"Ssh! Quiet," whispered Baker, "I think I heard the word, kill. Wait a minute, Jackson. Maybe I'll hear it again."

Time, however, didn't give PFC Baker a second opportunity. "Look, look, they're putting those civilians up against that wall! That loud mouth Kraut is telling them that if they don't turn over the murderers who are killing his soldiers, he's going to kill them all."

"Crap on the ground," whispered Jackson. "I'll take the loud mouth first, and you take the one standing next to him. On, three. Ready?"

"Sergeant Brooks isn't going to like this..."

"Look, Chuck, we just can't sit here and let those Krauts kill these people. Now get ready."

PFC Baker looked over at Private Jackson, just to make sure he was serious. The angered beanpole was already taking aim. "Damn! Sergeant Brooks isn't going to like us starting a minor war. Are you sure you want to do this?" Private Jackson didn't even flinch.

The two shots sounded almost as one, and the two targeted Germans hit the ground, dead. Two more died before the rest had time to react. Jackson started firing at those closest to the church, forcing them farther away from the church door, while Baker shot at the exposed troops still standing out in the open.

When the shots sounded, the death row civilians started screaming and running away in all different directions. The panicked scattering of people added additional chaos to the confusion and made it even more difficult for Jackson and Baker to kill the enemy without accidentally killing the residents. However, in less than a minute, the tiny square was empty of non-combatants, so the only people left in sight were the three remaining Germans, who were still actively fighting.

Two of them were trapped behind the town well, while the third was crouching behind a water barrel about ten yards from the well. After their initial shock was over, they realized that the shots were coming from the bell tower and started shooting at Jackson and Baker. A couple of minutes into the battle, a grenade went off near the well, and the two soldiers hiding behind it flew through the air and landed several feet away, dead. The man crouching behind the water barrel immediately stood up with his hands in the air shouting, "Make surrender! Make surrender!"

Jackson, however, wasn't waiting for Baker to translate. He emptied his magazine into the SS soldier, and when he was out of ammo, he continued to pull the trigger until PFC Baker gently pushed the barrel of the carbine down and out of line with the dead soldier.

"Hey, Tim, it's over. You can stop now. We won this one."

Jackson looked over at Baker's grinning face and was totally unprepared for PFC Baker's next words. "Hey, cowboy. It looks like the Indians won another one."

Jackson couldn't help grinning when he said; "I think I'll use your knife because it's not as sharp as mine. A dull blade will hurt more when I skin your ass." Then the two men looked at each other and asked the same question; "Who threw the grenade?"

"Beanpole, you and Baker get down here right now, and you had better have a damn good reason for starting this shindig."

The two Americans looked at each other before Jackson blurted out, "Quick, Chuck. Hide the knives so he can't skin us alive!"

The several minutes it took the two men to evacuate the church was on account of what was going to happen to them once they exited the church. "What the hell happened here, Baker?"

"Well, Sarge, it's like this," PFC Baker began to explain what happened.

Sergeant Brooks' response interrupted Baker's explanation. "Those Nazi bastards. Sergeant Cane, pick some men and drag these Krauts into the woods. Cover them up with leaves or whatever else you can find, and then get back here pronto."

While Baker was telling Brooks what had happened, the residents of Clervella were peering around corners and out of doorways at the strange uniformed soldiers. When they heard the Americans speaking, the citizens came pouring out into the little square, all talking at once, immediately forcing Brooks hold up his hands to quiet everybody down. Turning to Baker, he said, "Nobody speaks French here except the frogs, so find out if any of them speak German. Make sure you tell them we're not going to hurt them. Also, ask them if they know the guys we're supposed to meet here."

After what the citizens of Clervella had gone through, there was only one person willing enough to talk with Baker about the man the squad was looking for.

"His name is Henri, Sarge. He says that the men we're looking for are dead; they were killed two days ago by the same SS soldiers we killed today. He also says that the names of the men you were looking for were given to the SS by someone living in this village, so be careful when you talk to someone."

"Ask him about the gun. Find out if he knows where it's located?"

Baker turned back to Henri and asked him about the gun, but the man didn't know what he was talking about until Baker made a big circle with his arms and said the words "boom, boom, boom." Henri then got all excited and started talking in French until PFC Baker interrupted him and told him to speak in German. Henri turned his head to the right and spat on the ground, muttering some things, but the only word that Baker understood was Boche. Then the Frenchman started talking.

"Sarge, he says the gun was moved right after the five guys we were looking for were shot. The resistance guys were tortured, so the SS found out that the gun was going to be destroyed. According to Henri, the Germans moved it east, but he doesn't know where."

Brooks thought about what he had heard for a minute or so and then looked at Baker. "You better tell these people they'll have to leave town before the Germans come back and kill everyone here."

Very few words were needed to convince the people of Clervella to evacuate the town. The sight was sad to see. The residents had packed up what they could carry or put into carts and were leaving the only homes they had ever known. Looking at the scene, each member of the squad now understood, without a doubt, why they were fighting this war.

While Jackson was on his way up to the bell tower to keep an eye out for the Germans, Sergeant Cane and his men were returning after having dumped the dead troops in the orchard. The rest of the squad arrived back in Clervella just in time to watch the last of the citizens leaving their town and heading south.

"What gives, Sarge?"

"They're leaving, and so are we. The gun's been moved, and our resistance friends are dead, so get the squad ready to move out. We leave in five minutes."

Sergeant Cane got the men ready to leave and then went to speak with Sergeant Brooks. "What's up, Al?"

SNAFU, Dan, that's what's up. Command sent us out here to destroy a German gun, and the Krauts found out about it. Almost an entire town was wiped out because we didn't get here fast enough. Now we have to go back through German lines again, and without accomplishing our mission. Like I said, Dan. SNAFU."

"*GERMANS*! Coming in from the north," shouted Jackson. "Three trucks, and no mounted guns." Sergeant Brooks immediately looked up at the bell tower and then to where Jackson was pointing. He couldn't see what the scout was pointing at, but he could definitely hear the enemy vehicles approaching the town. "Get down from that bell tower. We're moving out now!" he shouted.

Running full out, the men immediately headed for a stand of trees that was located southwest of the town. They had to reach the trees before the Germans got to the town, or there might be a battle they had no chance of winning. Once they reached the trees, and with the sun going down, they could then change direction and head north.

The sprint to the woods was just under a mile. When they reached the trees, they were an exhausted group of runners, and collapsed to the ground, sucking in great gasps of air. Looking around, Sergeant Brooks took a count of his men and came up two short; Jackson and Baker.

"Has anybody seen Jackson or Baker?"

"The last time I saw Jackson, he was in the bell tower," replied Sergeant Cane. "I never saw Baker."

"Damn," hissed Brooks.

"Are we going to wait here until they catch up to us?" asked Cane.

"No," replied Sergeant Brooks. "They'll catch up to us when they can. We'll just keep moving as soon as we catch our breath."

After a five-minute breather, the squad was on the move again. This time, however, they were heading north, following the line of trees. Another hour had passed before Sergeant Brooks called a halt. They were far enough away now that the likelihood of being found by the Germans was almost next to nothing. The main reason, however, was to give Jackson and Baker a chance to catch up, provided the Germans didn't already have them.

~ ~ ~

"Why didn't you go with the rest of the squad?" asked Jackson.

"What, and leave my favorite cowboy behind? Not on your life. Besides, I've never seen an Indian skin an ass before," replied Baker.

Jackson immediately cracked up laughing at Baker's answer. "Keep it up white eyes, and you'll see it soon enough."

Turning serious, Baker looked at Jackson and said; "Okay, Tim, what's going on in that sneaky little mind of yours?"

Private Timothy Jackson just smiled. It was a wicked-looking smile that sent shivers down Baker's spine the minute he figured out what the scout had in mind. "You're going to get us killed, Tim. We're only two against a whole platoon. That's over forty men. Damn, Tim. You never fail me, do you? Whenever I'm with you something always happens! Shit!"

Slapping Baker on the shoulder, the scout's expression changed, turning more diabolical. "Not if we do the job right. Besides, I'm only going to kill two or three, just to show them what happens when they make an Indian mad."

"Great. Cochise is going on the warpath again. Don't you know those boys are hard-core fanatics? SS. Hitler's, elite? Do you think they're just going to sit around and let you kill them? Come on, redskin, come and kill me."

Jackson looked at Baker with an unpleasant look on his face. "Sir Charles. If you don't have the stomach for this, you can always leave."

"Fine. I think I will leave and good riddance. You're crazy!"

Two minutes later, however, PFC Baker was still squatting beside Jackson.

"Well?"

"Well, what?"

"I thought you were leaving?"

"I just figured I better hang around; you'll need someone to bury you."

"Okay then. You go ahead and stay here, but you better make sure you spell my name right on the headstone. It's beanpole with a capital B."

PFC Baker immediately pinched his nose until it hurt, trying desperately not to laugh. "You're really going to do this aren't you?"

"Yep."

"And there's no way I can talk you out of it?"

"Nope."

"Okay, Geronimo, then let's get the ball rolling."

Slapping Baker on the shoulder again, Jackson laid out his game plan. "We'll wait for them to calm down a bit before we start. Let them relax some. You know, lower their guard a little. Then we'll hit them and watch these SS coyotes lose their nerve. We'll show everybody that Hitler's SS aren't the supermen everyone thinks they are."

An hour after the sun went down, the enemy heard the first scream. It was a hideous, terrified, blood-curdling scream that got the attention of every German in the town. A few minutes later, they found their comrade lying on his back, his shirt open, revealing several knife wounds in his chest. He was dead. The enemy commander was deeply agitated. Staring around at his surroundings, he could only imagine who killed his soldier.

The SS officer in charge gave an order and four men picked up the dead man and took him off to be buried. Then he gave another order, and thirty plus men cocked their weapons and went on the hunt for the people responsible for the death of their comrade. After a forty-minute search of the town and the surrounding area, they came up empty handed.

They found nobody in the town, except for them. Sentries were posted throughout the village in pairs and were to be relieved every two hours, but unfortunately for one pair, they never saw their relief.

Thirty minutes after posting the sentries, the enemy heard another blood curdling scream, followed about a half a minute later by a second scream. When they found their comrades, the two men were lying side by side, in the same condition as the first one they found. Again, the enemy searched the town and the surrounding area, and again, they came up empty handed.

Three soldiers were dead, and there was no sign of the killers anywhere. An hour after the last two deaths, a platoon sergeant entered his platoon leader's command vehicle and found everyone inside, including his platoon leader, dead. The platoon leader's throat was slit, and poking out of his left breast pocket was a note written in German. It read; "*Sleep good Nazi dirt for death rules this night*."

After reading the note, the enemy NCO realized that to stay in town could mean their deaths, so he ordered his men back into their vehicles and left the town of Clervella in the same condition they had found it in when they first entered it; almost deserted, but very much dead.

Jackson and Baker had moved back into the bell tower a few minutes after the Germans had finished their last search. Beanpole had Baker write a note in German, and when he was finished, Baker handed the note to him and wished him good luck.

About forty minutes of anxious waiting went by before Baker heard someone coming up the ladder. Pulling out his bayonet, he prepared for battle. Three fearful eye blinks went by before Jackson's head and then his whole body appeared, climbing into the bell tower. "How did it go?" asked Baker.

"Watch and see," whispered Jackson. The two men didn't have to wait long. They saw the platoon sergeant enter his commander's command truck, and then the two men heard the shouting. After ten minutes of waiting, the two Americans watched, smiling greatly, while the last German vehicle left the town and disappeared into the night.

Chapter 14

The brief halt that Sergeant Brooks had called turned into an hour and then another hour, until he decided that they would stay the night where they were. He was worried about his two missing men, and everybody knew it. They were expecting any minute now to hear Sergeant Brooks swear because Jackson had sneaked up on him again. After several hours, however, the men began to lose hope. It appeared to the squad that maybe Jackson and Baker had been captured or killed by the Germans.

Midnight came and went, and finally, Sergeant Brooks could stand it no longer. “Let’s go people. Gear-up. We’re going back to Clervella to find those two heathens. Lemons, you take the point. Alex, you cover the rear. All right, people, move out. Sam, keep us in the trees as long as possible.”

Had Brooks been able to see in the dark, he would have noticed nine smiling faces. Each man knew that Brooks was beginning to think of Jackson as more than just a soldier, just like they did. Jackson was the youngest of the group, and he was the jokester that kept the smiles going, even in bad situations. The squad looked forward to the little scout’s antics, and they were always amazed when he pulled something off that they didn’t think was possible.

The Americans had been walking for almost an hour when out of the darkness they heard a shout in German. “Where is Baker when you need him?” muttered Brooks. Signaling his men to spread out, Brooks waited for the battle to begin, but it never started. Instead, he heard laughing, and then he heard, “Don’t shoot Baker, Sarge. He’s only the messenger.” and Sergeant Brooks almost jumped out of his skin, again.

“JACKSON! Where the hell have you two been? I ought to beat you two senseless, you little heathens. No. Better yet. Maybe I should turn you over to the Krauts and let them deal with you. Why didn’t you leave with the rest of the squad?”

About that time Baker, Lemons, and Cane walked up to a very agitated Sergeant Brooks. “Baker, I put you with Jackson to keep him out of trouble. Don’t make me regret that decision. I hope you’ll do a better job of it the next time. Now, what happened?”

Sergeant Brooks didn’t wait for PFC Baker to begin his report. He wanted to get moving immediately, so he issued out his orders. “Lemons, you and Cane take the point, and Jackson, you can cover the rear.”

Moving north again, Brooks listened to Baker explain what had happened after the squad had lit out of Clervella. Jackson knew Sergeant Brooks was a bit angry at him because he was bringing up the rear, his usual spot when he agitated his platoon sergeant. Jackson hated being in the rear, and Sergeant Brooks knew it. So did the squad, and they were snickering behind hand-covered mouths because of it. Again, the beanpole from Arizona was lighting up the faces of the men of 1st squad.

By the time the sun was coming up, the Americans were several miles northwest of Clervella, in a large wooded area. They could hear German artillery going off not too far away, which meant that they were getting close to the German rear areas. Almost two weeks had gone by since they had left on their mission. Although they didn’t get the opportunity to destroy the gun, their mission wasn’t a complete failure. By moving the gun, the Germans were no longer shelling the beaches with it. The bad side of that good news was still yet to come.

Everyone knew that within a day or so, they would once again be forced to sneak through enemy lines to reach friendly troops. The jaunt was not something they were looking forward to because, now, they would be sneaking through the lines of an entire German army instead of the smaller units they had sneaked through, on their way to Clervella.

~ ~ ~

The squad reached the northern edge of the forest they had been traveling through and stopped to look out at the terrain. Sergeant Brooks noticed that it was flat and open except for the occasional hedgerows. The hedgerows would offer some cover and concealment, but they would also be doing the same for the enemy.

The rain began just before dawn and continued its steady downpour throughout the morning and into the afternoon. By the time the sun had gone down, the rain had finally stopped, which left the ground soggy and slick, but dark clouds still remained overhead, a sure sign of more to come. "God does love the infantry," muttered Sergeant Brooks.

While the squad was eating their k-rats, the rain began again. Fifteen minutes after it started, the squad was on the move. Being that Sergeant Brooks was no longer agitated at Jackson, he was now where he loved to be, out front and leading the way, happier than a pig in slop. PFC Baker, however, was still in his platoon sergeant's doghouse, so he took Jackson's place at the rear of the squad, walking drag.

The first quarter of a mile provided the Americans with several hedgerows for cover. Thanks to the rain, they were almost invisible to anyone searching the same area. When they reached the third hedgerow, they found Jackson waiting for them, but there was no more cover for the next three-quarters of a mile.

Sergeant Brooks gave Jackson a five-minute head start before he ordered his men to move out. Stopping about fifty yards from a road they were heading for, Jackson and Lemons scouted out the avenue, in both directions for about a hundred yards. With the road clear in both directions, they crossed it and took cover behind a hedgerow. Jackson reported to Brooks about twenty minutes later and gave him another all clear, so the squad took off again, heading north.

The line of the hedgerows they were traveling beside was going in a northwest to southeastern direction, which was perfect for the Americans, especially in the rain. The route Brooks was taking would run them through the area of the 3rd Fallschirmjager positions again, but more to the west of their original route south to Clervella.

Calling for a halt to take a short break, Brooks stopped his men just outside of a small village, about twenty miles southeast of St. Lo. After a short confab, he sent Jackson and Baker to check the township to see if the place was occupied by the Germans. The woods they had stopped in extended south to north for about 100 yards, but were only about 60 or 70 yards deep, not a large stand, but enough to hide them.

After checking the town for Germans, the two men reported back to Sergeant Brooks that the town was clear of the enemy, so he went into the town with Jackson and Baker to see if they could get some food for their bellies and water for their canteens.

The Frenchman the three Americans walked up to had a mean look to his face, and his eyes looked a bit shifty. Jackson didn't like what he saw, and whispered to Sergeant Brooks how he felt. Brooks, knowing Jackson as well as he did, took the hint and decided not to trust the man, but because they were already in the village, he pulled out his canteen, and pointing to it, indicated that he wanted water, trying to distract suspicion away from his abrupt mistrust of the Frenchman.

Calling another man over, the Frenchman nodded to a second man, who appeared from one of the doorways, several buildings down. Walking up to Sergeant Brooks, he nodded, held out his hand and introduced himself. He didn't speak very good English, and his heavy accent didn't help much either. He dropped his hand when Brooks didn't respond in kind.

The Frenchman asked Brooks what he wanted, so Sergeant Brooks asked him for some food to eat and some water for their canteens. Meanwhile, the other Frenchman had quietly disappeared. Neither Sergeant Brooks nor PFC Baker had noticed that the man was gone, mostly because they were both absorbed in their efforts to make the villager they were talking to understand what they wanted.

Jackson, however, did notice the other man's disappearance, so he interrupted the Frenchman and asked, "Where did your friend go?" Sergeant Brooks and PFC Baker immediately looked around, and sure enough, the man was gone. Brooks took the safety off his rifle, pointed it at the Frenchman, and asked the same question, "Where'd he go?"

With a forced smile, the man explained. "I sent him to make sure the Germans weren't trying to sneak up on us. The

Boche SS are very sneaky. Why don't you wait here, and I go get food?"

Brooks turned to Jackson, but the beanpole was gone. *I hope that boy left to bring up the squad. This frog is more than a little south of sleazy*. Turning back to the Frenchman, Brooks' expression and attitude turned cold. "No, toad. We stay right here until your friend gets back. PFC Baker, plant one in this frog's head if he does anything more than stand in place."

"I think not." The voice was a little behind Sergeant Brooks and to his left. Brooks turned his head to face the voice and noticed that there were four men, one of them was the first Frenchman he had approached, and they all carried rifles. "Snuck away to learn how to speak English, did you?"

The man was sneering when he answered. "We will make a lot of money giving you to the Germans."

"Baker, shoot this bastard in the head if any of his friends make a move."

"Absolutely, Sarge." Baker took the safety off his M1 and pointed the muzzle of his rifle at the second Frenchman's temple, and then he smiled, but it wasn't a humorous smile.

Sergeant Brooks then turned to face the four men directly. "Are you sure you want to start something?"

Looking around nervously, the ringleader asked, "Where did the other man go?"

"Who? Jackson? He doesn't like cowards and traitors, so he left to go find a good place to shoot you from. You don't deserve to die a good death." What Sergeant Brooks said made the Frenchmen a little nervous, so they cast nervous glances at the shadows. "We have four guns, you have only two, and the Germans will be here soon. If you drop your guns now, you might live a little while longer."

Sergeant Brooks heard a vehicle approaching and figured that it was the Germans coming. "We're not dropping our weapons, and you won't live long enough to know what happened. You're the first son-of-a-bitch I'm gonna kill, so if you want to start something then do it. My friend and I are leaving right now."

The ringleader called Marcel didn't like what Brooks said, and he saw his money disappearing as the two Americans slowly backed away. The vehicle was almost to the little village, which bolstered the Frenchman's courage a little. Sergeant Brooks noticed Marcel's body tense up a little and knew that he was going to start something.

Three things happened in the space of two finger snaps. Marcel, seeing his profits going down the drain, raised his rifle and, expecting the other three to do the same, tried to kill Sergeant Brooks, but he was unsuccessful in his efforts. The squad had arrived just in time to participate in the little skirmish, turning the Frenchmen into holey Frenchmen, including the one Baker shot in the head. Then the German vehicle entered the town amid a hail of bullets, which resulted in the deaths of the driver, the assistant driver, and three of the Germans piling out of the back of the truck. Within seconds, the little square was empty of all combatants except the dead.

After a minute or two, the Germans poked their heads around corners, looking for the shooters before cautiously advancing towards the other side of the square, searching for the Americans. When they realized that the Americans were gone, one of the soldiers got on the radio and called in reinforcements, after which, they waited for help to arrive.

First squad had arrived at the edge of the town square and noticed the four armed Frenchmen facing Brooks and Baker. When they saw their friends slowly backing away, Cane readied the squad. When one of the Frenchmen raised his rifle to shoot, Sergeant Cane shouted and the whole squad fired as one, perforating the Frenchmen with many holes. Then they ran into the square just in time to see the German truck.

Immediately, they opened up on it and killed the driver and his partner, causing the truck to veer to the left and run into a building. The veering of the truck caught the Germans in the back by surprise, and they lost their balance while trying desperately to exit the truck in order to fight back. Three of them were killed before the Americans decided to vamoose out of there.

The squad reached the woods located about 150 yards southeast of the town in no time flat, and they were sucking air deeply to prove it. “Shit, Al. What the hell was that? Man, I hate to run.”

“They outnumber us by a lot, Dan. We can’t afford this fight. Not now. Let’s get the hell out of here.”

Sergeant Brooks knew the Germans were coming after them and only gave the men a five-minute breather before moving south. He knew the Germans would come after them because that was what he would do. The idea was to head south for a while, make a wide U, and then head north again to get around and behind the pursuing enemy. At least, that was the plan.

With the rain still coming down, it was going to be difficult for the Germans to find them, providing the squad got out of the area fast enough. After they had been traveling for about a half an hour, Sergeant Brooks changed direction, and headed west, forming the bottom of the wide U.

The men hadn’t slept in over 24 hours and were beginning to show it. They were getting clumsy walking over the uneven ground, and their alertness was lacking. The soft, steady sound of the rain hitting the ground was lolling their senses. Even Sergeant Brooks was having his problems.

Sometime around 0130 hours, Sergeant Brooks noticed what appeared to be a road. Upon further examination, he found that it was indeed a road, and that it went north and south for a ways. Moving his men back about a hundred yards from the road, he decided that now would be a good time to head north, so instead of crossing the road, the squad headed north.

An hour into their northern march, they came to a small patch of woods, and entering it from the south, they soon discovered that the northern edge was occupied by a German artillery battery. This discovery woke Sergeant Brooks and his men up in a big hurry. They had almost walked headlong into their enemy. They were a bit shocked at their stupidity and lack of alertness, but the mishap produced the needed effect on the men.

Brooks moved his men back to where they had run into the road an hour earlier and stumbled onto a tightly grown fruit orchard that was bordered by a hedgerow, something they had missed earlier while heading west.

"Pears, Sarge! Look at 'em all," said Baker.

"They're not quite ripe yet," said Brooks, but he too started pulling and eating the fruit. "Don't eat too much," he ordered. "You might get the runs. Jackson, I want you and Lemons to take a look around and see if we're close to any Germans. I would have thought that with these pears here, the Krauts wouldn't stray too far away."

Smiling, Jackson tossed a pear to Private Hanky and said, "Just you leave some for us. We haven't had any yet."

"Aw, don't worry, cowboy," said Baker. "It's a big orchard with plenty of fruit in it." The Americans were in hog heaven there in the orchard. They hadn't had any fresh fruit in months, and the Germans be damned was their thought at that moment.

Chapter 15

The SS captain stared at the dead men lining the side of the building. Five of his SS troops, and over in the square, five dead Frenchmen. “How many Americans were there, Sergeant?”

“I don’t know, Captain. I think maybe a squad; otherwise, they would have stayed to finish us off. They had the initiative, and surprise was on their side.”

“Assemble all of the villagers and hold them in the church. Find out as much as you can and then report your findings to me. I will be in that building over there.”

The building that the captain referred to was a large sprawling affair, and it was the largest structure in the town. It served as the town meeting hall and also doubled as the Mayor’s residence. The Mayor, however, was no longer living there, thanks to the SS captain. It was now the new headquarters for SS Captain Paul Schmidt, SS security, 4th district, France.

While his men were working on his new headquarters, the vehicles transporting the rest of his company were pulling into the town. When his new headquarters were finished according to his wishes, he ordered the citizens of the town removed from the church and herded into the town square. The round-up was a quick one. Once everyone was gathered in the square, he had the citizens interrogated thoroughly about what had happened earlier that evening. Two of the residents were shot for hesitating to answer his questions. After that episode, the captain was rewarded with the information he was seeking.

According to the last villager he had talked to, he found out that the Americans were the same troops that had killed some of his men in Clervella; the citizen’s name was Henri.

Now that he had the information he needed, he went to his headquarters and started studying his wall map. *The Americans must be trying to sneak back to their own lines, but where are they now? According to Sergeant Reiner, they left the town running east. This makes a lot of sense; the small stand of trees just east of the town will provide good cover. They could lose themselves in the trees, then head out in almost any direction they choose, and be gone in a matter of minutes.*

All Captain Schmidt had to do was figure out which direction they took after hitting the woods. If they were actually trying to get back to their lines, then the direction the Americans took was limited. His only recourse was to place his troops in a blocking position and wait. The perplexing problem he was facing was where to put his blocking forces.

"Which direction will you take, my American foe?"

He divided his forces up into four small combat groups. Each was led by a Puma armored car, mounting a 20mm cannon, and an MG34 machine gun. Attached to each group were two squads of SS troops, a radio halftrack, two MG42 machine gun crews, and two 81mm mortar crews. The force of troops and equipment allocated for hunting down only twelve American soldiers were large, but the Germans had a very big area to cover, and the Americans had already proved they were good at evading capture.

~ ~ ~

Henri was scared to death. He had been forced to go with Marcel when Clervella was evacuated by its citizens. Now, Marcel was dead, and so were nine others. Horrified, Henri stood in front of Captain Schmidt. The man had cold, merciless, scary eyes that held no compassion, no conscience. Schmidt had Henri terrified. The Frenchman wanted to live, and he felt ashamed for telling the SS captain about the Americans, but his fear had overridden any and all thoughts of being gallant and loyal to a group of strangers. He was not a warrior; he was just a simple farmer who wished to live.

The town looked deserted, but Henri knew it wasn't. There were over thirty SS troops scattered throughout the town, hidden from view and watching. He wanted to escape, to run as fast as he could to get away from this place, but he was too afraid to try, so he wished and planned, and hoped, that somewhere, somehow he would find the courage to leave.

~ ~ ~

Sergeant Brooks and his men were rudely forced awake by the sounds of tracks, squeaking and squealing, somewhere northwest of their position. Even though 0600 hours had arrived, the cloud cover and the drizzling rain kept the morning in dark, gray shadows.

The roaring of the vehicles really began to bother Sergeant Brooks. He didn't like what his instincts were telling him, so he turned the squad south and headed back to Clervella, hoping the move would confuse his enemy long enough for them to reach friendly troops. To make sure of his enemy's intentions, he sent Jackson and Baker out to keep track of the German's movements. If all was well and good, they were to meet up with the squad in the small stand of trees, located about three-quarters of a mile southwest of the town.

Jackson liked the idea; he always did when it called for sneaking around, but he didn't like the idea of having PFC Baker with him. It scared him to have somebody else with him because he feared that second person might get hurt or killed. In the end, though, he acquiesced to Sergeant Brooks, and Baker was then brought into the discussion. "You mean I have to play nursemaid to this cowboy again?"

~ ~ ~

The squad took all day and half the night to reach the western side of Clervella. By 0130 hours, they were safely hidden in the woods, almost a mile south of the town.

The next morning, about an hour after sunrise, the men of 1st squad, 1st platoon, Baker Company, slowly began to wake up. Sergeant Cane was the first one up, and then Private Lemons. Looking around, Sergeant Cane tried to locate his platoon sergeant, but he was nowhere to be found. The man seemed to have disappeared into thin air. Signaling to Lemons, Sergeant Cane indicated silence. Whispering softly, Cane asked, "Where's Sergeant Brooks?" In less than a minute, everyone in the squad had been quietly alerted and was now armed and ready, looking for Sergeant Brooks.

Sergeant Cane heard a snort and then snoring, but he couldn't find where it was coming from. Something made him look up, and there was Sergeant Brooks, cradled in the crook of a large branch about fifteen feet above the ground, peacefully snoozing away. Two finger snaps later, almost every man in the squad was standing under the branch Sergeant Brooks was perched on, looking up and trying to figure out some mischievous way in which they could wake up their rip-roaring sergeant.

"Sam," whispered Sergeant Cane. "Climb up there and push Al off that branch. We'll catch him before he hits the ground."

"Not, me," whispered Lemons. "He'll kill me."

"Hanky, you do it."

"Sorry, Sarge. I'm with Lemons. I don't want to die either."

"Avery, get up there and push him off."

"Not on your life, Sarge."

"Okay you chicken shits, I'll do it myself, but you had better make sure you catch him before he hits the ground."

Cane, only inches away from pushing Sergeant Brooks off the branch, looked down and mouthed the words, "Get ready to catch him," but the men were just standing there, looking up; hell, they weren't even ready to catch him.

Looking back up at Brooks, Cane found himself staring into the barrel of an M1 Garand. "I wouldn't do that if I were you, Dan." Sergeant Brooks wasn't smiling.

"Aw, hell, Al," said Cane, laughing. "Why'd you have to go and spoil everything?"

The squad watched as Brooks dropped to the ground, and he didn't look very happy. "All right, whose idea was it?"

"Mine," said Cane. "They were supposed to catch you before you hit the ground."

Sergeant Brooks didn't say another word; he just continued to look at the squad and Sergeant Cane. For almost two full minutes, the stern-faced platoon sergeant stared into the eyes of his men, not saying a word and watching his men fidget around wilting under his intense stare. Then, without warning, Brooks burst out laughing. "That was a good idea, Dan. Too bad you couldn't stay quiet long enough to carry it out."

Chapter 16

Private Lemons was out at the western edge of the forest when he noticed some movement. Slowly stepping back from the edge of the tree line, he ran back to report his sighting to Sergeant Brooks. In no time, the squad was in position and waiting, but nobody saw any movement anywhere. "Are you sure you saw something?"

"Yeah, Sarge. You see that corner of hedgerow pointing at us? That's where I saw the movement."

"What did it look like?"

"It looked like a man crouched over, running to the left."

When nothing happened after about twenty minutes had elapsed, Sergeant Brooks sent the squad back to camp, but kept Private Lemons with him, on watch. An hour later, Brooks was looking out along the edge of the forest line, studying the area Sam was concerned about when he was abruptly interrupted by a tap on his shoulder. However, he was already going to ground. "Sam, bring up the squad. Quickly now." Immediately Private Lemons rushed back to gather the men.

The Americans were deployed facing west. While half of them were looking out at the open area between the town and the edge of the woods to their left, the other half was keeping an eye on the approach to their left flank.

Soon, they heard somebody huffing and puffing, as though having run a long distance. Then, they spotted the source of that sound; it was PFC Baker. The men relaxed when they saw Baker, but they couldn't locate the beanpole.

A couple of minutes passed before Baker stumbled up to the squad and dropped to the ground, completely winded. "Holy shit, Baker. What in the hell happened to you? You smell like all of the cows in France shit on you for a week!"

"Where's Jackson?" asked Baker, who was absolutely winded. "I'm gonna kill that little heathen." The squad immediately figured out that the aroma emanating from

Baker was a direct result of something Jackson did to Baker, and they were right.

Brooks was trying really hard not to laugh at the man. He could almost picture what had happened to him. "Where's Jackson?" Brooks asked softly.

"I don't know," was the short reply. "He was running so fast he should have already been here by now."

"I see," said Brooks, shaking his head. "I see. Hmm. Well, when you catch your breath, get on down to the creek and get cleaned up. The Germans will damn sure smell you long before they see you."

Sergeant Brooks left Decker, Todd, and Brown to watch the perimeter, while the rest of the squad snickered all the way back to camp. While Brooks was on his way back to camp, he heard somebody giggling down by the creek and realized it was Baker. He didn't sound like he was disturbed anymore, so maybe Jackson's stunt was actually funny, now that he had some time to cool off.

A few minutes later, Baker came plodding into camp with his uniform shirt draped over his shoulder, dripping wet. Everybody in the squad was just dying to hear what happened, but Baker didn't say a word. He just walked over by the sterno-can fire and sat down. Then, he held out his shirt to the three-finger-sized flame to dry it, and not a word was said.

The silence lasted for several minutes until Sergeant Brooks inquired about the information the two men had gathered. PFC Baker told Brooks what the Germans had planned and where their forces were located. He also told Brooks about the type of forces one platoon had at their disposal.

"Armored cars? Machine guns, and mortars? Wow. They really mean business, don't they?" Then Sergeant Brooks asked the big question, "Why do you want to kill Jackson so badly?" Brooks was sitting down, with his back up against a tree, a few feet from the sterno flame and partly in the flickering shadows.

"I should have known from the way he was acting, that something was up, but I missed it. Again! The entire time we were out on this mission, he was always out front, so why was

I all of a sudden out front? Well, we were getting close to the trees he was heading for, and he kept hinting that he was hearing something. He's always hearing things before we do, you know that. Anyway, he suddenly whispers, "Germans," and then dives for the ground. So I did too. Right onto a pile of wet, stinking, cow shit. Tim gets up laughing and takes off running like a scalded rabbit, and that's when I knew I'd been had."

Nobody said a word. Nobody moved. That silence, however, lasted only for the count of ten before the squad lost control and burst out laughing, with Baker leading the charge. Tears were running down everybody's face from laughing so hard. Then, without warning, something flew through the air and landed in Baker's lap. It was a 3lb, burlap bag, full of French coffee beans. The men went silent. PFC Baker looked up in the direction of Sergeant Brooks and said, "Is this supposed to be an apology?"

Laughter broke out behind Brooks, and then Jackson walked out into the firelight, tears rolling down his face, too, from laughing so hard. In between spasms of laughter, he managed to blurt out his friend's favorite phrase; "When I'm with you something always happens!" The laughter from everyone was so hard and loud that they could almost hear it in Clervella. Of course, Baker and Jackson were laughing the hardest.

The smell of fresh ground coffee brewing over a wood fire set the juices flowing in everyone's mouth, especially for Sergeant First Class Alfred David Brooks. His taste buds were ready to revolt if they didn't get a taste of coffee; he was weaned on the stuff. The men hadn't had any coffee since they left headquarters in Colleville, and thanks to Jackson, they were definitely in downtown happyville.

"Krauts coming," whispered Decker. "A whole column of them pulling into town right now."

Brooks had forged the habit into his men of keeping their gear packed and ready to go, so that all they had to do was grab and leave. Now they knew why. "Head east. Take the route we mapped out earlier and go. Jackson get rid of that fire, and nobody pour out your coffee. Take it with you until we get far enough away to dump it or drink it."

In less than a minute, the squad was on the move. Jackson had dug a pit for the fire, and now was dumping the dirt back into the hole and covering the fire bed. Then he covered the dirt with leaves to hide the fire's location. As soon as he was finished hiding the fire, he started wiping out as much of their presence as he could before he started covering up the tracks the squad left behind on their way east.

Jackson watched from the tree-covered hill they had been staying on to see if the Germans were coming up to snoop around. He could hear small arms fire coming from the town and shook his head at the helplessness he felt. Taking one last look, he watched two halftracks and an armored car head his way. Time to go.

Jackson caught up with the others about forty minutes later and reported to Sergeant Brooks what he had seen. "Those Krauts are definitely the force Baker and I snuck up on. I recognized the numbers on that armored car."

"Baker said something blew up. Whatever happened really pissed those boys off," said Brooks. "Tell me exactly what went on?"

"I took some of the comp-B we were going to use on the gun and placed two chunks in a box of mortar rounds, in the back of an ammo track and two chunks under a radio track. Then I wired them to the starter of the ammo track. I really didn't think it would work, but it was worth a try."

"Where did you get the comp-B from, Private?" Jackson had a feeling he was going to get into some serious trouble when he gave his answer. Hesitating, he softly said, "From the pack that has the comp-B in it."

Sergeant Brooks felt like a father scolding his son for doing something wrong. The fact that he towered over Jackson enhanced that feeling.

All of a sudden, Jackson's words hit home and Baker's eyes opened wide. Forgetting who was talking to Jackson and what was going on, he interrupted Sergeant Brooks. "You wired two tracks? When did you do this?"

Smiling sheepishly, Jackson said, "While we were at that command tent and you were listening to the Germans. I snuck away when you moved behind that big log, but I was back in about fifteen minutes. You were still safe."

"Crap, cowboy! You left me surrounded by Germans! You almost got me killed again! Are you nuts?"

"Enough children. Damn! I feel like I'm running a kindergarten class the way you two are acting." Brooks stared down at Jackson for a moment before he said; "Next time you check with me before you grab something out of my pack. You got that?" An affirmative nod from Jackson was good enough for Sergeant Brooks. "All right, let's move out. We've squandered enough time here. Hell, the Krauts are probably closing in on us right now because of all the time we've wasted."

Chapter 17

The first light of a new dawn was approaching, so it was time to find a place to hole up for the upcoming day. The men of 1st squad hadn't seen any sign of the enemy since their explosive encounter almost two days prior. After searching his surroundings one last time, Brooks led his men towards a large dark shadow that he took for trees. After trudging non-stop from a very successful ambush they had laid on their enemy, it was time to take an all-day breather. Sergeant Brooks was still scratching his head at the unexpected help they received from a group of Frenchmen. They had distracted the enemy reinforcements sent to save the day, which allowed Brooks and his men time to finish up what they were doing and then escape.

The journey was a long and intense trip. The threat of capture or death kept the men of 1st squad on edge while they sneaked their way quietly towards the shadowed forest. Watching for the enemy, they stayed in the shadows as much as possible until they finally reached cover just in time for sunrise. They had just entered the trees when they were challenged in German. "Halt. If you move, we will open fire." Sergeant Brooks couldn't believe it. After all they had been through. After all the fights they were in and had survived, the escapes they had made despite the unfavorable odds, and how they had managed to emerge from all of those situations still in one piece. How stupid he felt to have walked right into a bad situation, just like a freshly minted lieutenant. "Baker, get up here!" shouted Brooks.

"Who the hell are you?" shouted someone in English.

"Sergeant First Class Alfred Brooks, 1st Special Tactical Force. Who are you?"

"What the hell is a Special Tactical Force?"

"That, mister, is classified," replied Sergeant Brooks.

"Don't move, Sergeant, I'll get back to you."

Sergeant Brooks could hear the whispered conversation, but he couldn't quite make out the words. Several minutes went by before the challenger called out to Brooks again. "Start walking towards us, Sergeant Brooks, but leave your men where they are."

"I'm not leaving my men anywhere. They are coming in with me, and if you don't like it, then you'll just have to shoot us."

Brooks heard a short laugh and then a reply. "Come on in, Al, but try not to scare the men too much. Seeing that ugly face of yours just might cause them to shoot at you."

"Lieutenant Shane? Is that you?"

"Captain Shane to you."

Sergeant Brooks chuckled and said, "Boy, was that a mistake, sir."

Turning, Brooks nodded to his men. "Let's go gentlemen. We've made it home."

Twenty yards later the squad was met by the newly minted Captain Jack Shane. "Welcome back, Sergeant Brooks."

"It's good to be back, sir."

First squad was in a daze, absolutely mind boggled that they were actually standing among friendly forces again. They had been on the move for almost a month, dodging Germans the whole time and thinking half the time, that they weren't going to make it back at all, but they did. The squad had made it back safely and with a whole skin, carrying only a few dents and dings to show for it. Now, the only thing they wanted was a week's worth of sleep; the donuts could wait.

Captain Shane led his men to a tent and gave each man in the squad a beer, including Jackson, who usually didn't drink anything alcoholic. Raising his beer, Captain Shane toasted Brooks and his men. "To a job well done, gentlemen."

A few minutes after they finished their beer, they heard jeeps pull up beside the tent. A nod from the captain told everyone it was time to go, so they stood up and waited. The order was not long in coming. "Okay everybody. It's time to see the colonel, so pile in and let's go."

The jeep ride was a thirty-minute drive to a former hotel where Colonel Martin had set up his new headquarters. It was a small affair, only twenty rooms, but it was the perfect fit for the special operation he was given command of while in North Africa. He had done so well there that the top brass had decided to keep the operation going once they had the Normandy beachhead secured. The command wasn't large, but the Special Tactical Force was a very effective unit that had less than 100 men, soldiers that went above and beyond on every mission. Some succeeded, and some failed. Sergeant Brooks and his men were the most successful unit in the organization. The unit consisted of volunteers only. Nobody knew about it except those who were asked to join, and so far, every man asked had joined. These were special men sent on special missions.

When the jeeps transporting the squad pulled up in front of the hotel, the first thing Sergeant Brooks noticed was a German halftrack painted OD green and sporting big white stars on the sides and on the top of the engine cover.

"What the hell is that Kraut track doing here?" asked Brooks.

Smiling, Captain Shane replied. "It's Colonel Martin's staff car.

"You're kidding. Right?"

"No, Al. Colonel Martin had it painted OD green, and stars put on it two weeks after you left for England. He says it's the symbol of the S.T.F., his baby. He went to war with headquarters to keep the command up and running, and he won. He's damn proud of you, Al. It's his reminder of what you and your squad did for him in North Africa. He has it washed twice a week."

"Well, I'll be damned," said Brooks.

Captain Shane let out a quick laugh before he continued. "Colonel Martin has been a royal pain in the ass these last couple of weeks because he thinks he sent you guys to your deaths. I haven't told him you're back yet, so be prepared."

"Prepared for what, sir?"

The men followed Captain Shane into the hotel and started for the colonel's office, but they were stopped by a sergeant. "You can't go in there, sir. He doesn't want to be disturbed."

Captain Shane, however, stopped the sergeant before he could block their path to the door. "Stand aside, Sergeant Duncan; he'll see these men right now."

Sergeant Duncan stopped, but he had a look of fear in his eyes. Colonel Martin had told him specifically that he was not to be disturbed, but Captain Shane was Colonel Martin's operation officer, which meant that the captain also had to be obeyed.

Colonel Martin looked up when his door opened, ready to blast out at Sergeant Duncan, but he was caught flat-footed and with his mouth open at the sight of Sergeant Brooks and his men. Sergeant Duncan began to apologize to the colonel for the intrusion, but he didn't get past the opening words. "Shut up, Carl, and bring in some chairs. Then go get something to eat for the next several hours. And close that door on your way out." Then he turned to face his sergeant.

"Al, I'm so glad you made it back. How did it go?"

"It didn't, sir. The mission was a bust. The men we were supposed to meet in Clervella were shot by the SS. The Germans got wind of our mission and moved the gun before we could destroy it."

"What the hell took you so long to get back?"

Sergeant Brooks looked at the colonel, and a good mad began to brew up. "Relax, Al, and calm down. I didn't mean it the way it sounded. Tell me what happened."

Within a few minutes, the office was filled with chairs and the exhausted men sat down.

The debriefing took over three hours. Each man had his turn to talk, and when they were finished, the colonel once again shouted for Sergeant Duncan. When the sergeant opened the door, he was ordered to bring in enough glasses for everyone in the room. "Why haven't you left yet, Carl?"

Sergeant Duncan smiled before he replied. "You needed these glasses, sir."

"Well, you brought them. Now, get the hell out of here and quit answering my yells."

"Yes, sir, Colonel."

Sergeant Brooks, however, wasn't quite ready for the confab to end yet. "Before we go any further Colonel, I want to bring up charges against Private Timothy Jackson. He disobeyed direct orders several times while we were out on this mission."

"It sounds serious, Sergeant Brooks. Are you sure about the charge?"

"Yes, Colonel. I'm sure. Can we talk somewhere private, sir?"

"Sergeant Duncan?"

Sergeant Duncan opened the door. "Yes, sir?"

"Get these men a long shot of whiskey."

"Yes, sir," replied Duncan.

Then beanpole spoke up. "Sir, I don't drink alcohol."

"Drink it, Private," said the colonel. "If what Sergeant Brooks says is true, you're gonna need it."

"Yes, sir," replied Jackson. His face was white as a ghost. The whole squad was stunned. *Jackson*? *Getting court martialed*? *What the hell's wrong with Sergeant Brooks*?

Twenty minutes passed by before Colonel Martin and Sergeant Brooks emerged from the small room they had entered for their private conversation. The squad was waiting to hear what was going on, but Sergeant Brooks didn't say a word; he just walked over to a chair and sat down, a stony expression on his face.

Colonel Martin moved behind his desk and stood of his chair. "PFC Jackson, front and center."

"I'm a private, sir."

"Really? Front and center now, Jackson."

"Yes, sir."

Beanpole stood before Colonel Martin, swaying back and forth. "Stand still, Jackson."

"I don't think he can, sir," replied Brooks. "He hasn't eaten anything since the day before, plus he has had a beer and that double shot of whiskey you ordered him to drink. I think he's drunk, sir."

"Well then," said Colonel Martin, "I think we ought to get this thing over with before he falls down, don't you think, Sergeant?"

"Yes, sir, I do."

Jackson was terrified. All he wanted to do was serve his country and make his family proud, but now he was being court martialed.

"PFC Jackson!"

"It's Private Jackson, sir."

"Shut up, beanpole. You're in enough trouble as it is."

Private Jackson was terrified.

"You have been charged with direct disobedience of orders on numerous occasions by your commanding NCO. Do you dispute these charges?"

Jackson gulped hard. "No, sir," replied a dispirited Jackson.

"You agree with everything Sergeant Brooks has told me?"

"Yes, sir," replied Jackson.

The squad was absolutely silent. Their little buddy was getting raked through the coals, railroaded by Sergeant Brooks. *What the hell is wrong with that man*?

"Then I have no alternative but to set your punishment as severely as possible," said Colonel Martin. "You are hereby promoted to the rank of PFC, and may God have mercy on your soul."

"*What*?"

The fog created by the alcohol had slowed down Jackson's mind a lot. It hadn't sunk in that this was all a ruse instigated by Sergeant Brooks. All those times he appeared out of nowhere, taking his platoon sergeant by surprise had finally caught up to him. The ultimate surprise. Hell, for a couple of seconds, even the squad had a hard time figuring out what was going on.

"Drinks all around," shouted the colonel. "Sergeant Duncan!"

The door opened once more. "Yes sir?"

"Get this man a Coke."

Smiling, Sergeant Duncan replied. "Yes sir!" *Damn I hate this job. I'm not out in the field dodging bullets.*

Sergeant Brooks was gazing down at Jackson when he said, "Well, what do you know, beanpole. It looks like I finally got the chance to sneak up on you this time."

Jackson was still feeling the terror from his unexpected surprise when he answered. Nodding, he acknowledged his platoon sergeant's ingenious prank. "Yeah, Sarge. I think you got me good."

Thirty minutes later, the men were led to the makeshift showers, and twenty minutes after the showers were turned off, they were snoring Dixieland blues in twelve-part harmony. The squad had made it back alive and in one piece.

The men of the 1st Special Tactical Force (Brooks and his men) were given a three-week leave in London, but that episode didn't turn out so well. One man was transferred out of the unit for causing too much trouble, while another man was busted down in rank because he tried to scalp the man causing the trouble.

Chapter 18

Ninety-six volunteers were assigned to the covert operations section of the Special Tactical Force. These men were sent out on infiltration missions that required small, elite units to accomplish, and they were good at what they did. Private Decker was no longer a part of the unit. Along with Jackson, he had been demoted to private because of fighting and for breaking the jaw of Major Thomas' driver. Sergeant Brooks had to find a replacement for Decker, but first, he had to take care of some business.

He wasn't about to let some major chew up Jackson for breakfast in front of the colonel. Wasn't Jackson's fault that the major's driver stuck his face between Decker and Jackson's fist. Remembering the incident, Brooks smiled to himself. *That was sweet. That driver never knew what hit him.* Decker saw the results of Jackson's punch and decided that he didn't want any part of beanpole anymore, so he stopped. Beanpole, however, didn't. The little scout had Decker pinned to the ground, and was ready to take care of business when the major walked outside. He saw Jackson getting ready to take a large sample of Decker's hair with a pocketknife and came to the rescue. Currently, they were standing in front of Colonel Martin, who was madder than hell that his breakfast was being disturbed by a snooping major.

"What's the problem, Major?"

"Two men are in the field hospital because of this man. One man has a busted head, and the other, my driver, has a broken jaw. This man," he said, pointing at Jackson, "tried to scalp, what was his name, Sergeant?"

"Decker, sir. PFC Decker."

"Yes, PFC Decker. This man tried to scalp PFC Decker with a pocket-knife, but I stopped him before he could do it."

Colonel Martin tried really hard not to laugh. With as serious an expression as he could muster, he looked at Jackson and asked, "Why did you try to lift that man's hair?"

And then he burst out laughing so hard he had tears rolling down his cheeks in seconds. For a minute or two, the colonel struggled hard to stop laughing, for the major didn't appear too happy about his behavior. In the meantime, Jackson was scared to death. Even Colonel Martin's laughing couldn't ease his mind.

When he received a nod from Colonel Martin, Jackson told his side of the event in question. "Decker doesn't like me, sir. He said he wanted to see what it was like to scalp someone. He said his grandfather was scalped by an Indian, so he figured he'd scalp me in return."

"Where did you get the knife from?"

"I took it away from Decker, sir, when he tried to use it on me."

Sergeant Brooks was biting his lip to keep from laughing, but lost control when the colonel started laughing again. Major Thomas stared at the two men laughing for a moment before he said, "What the hell's the matter with you two? This is serious. This man tried to scalp another man." But after looking at Private Jackson and remembering the lopsided size difference between the two men, Major Thomas also burst out laughing when he pictured the scene again.

"Sergeant Duncan!"

"Yes, sir, Colonel?"

"Bring me some clean glasses and a Coke, and put the do not disturb sign on the front door."

"Yes, sir," replied Sergeant Duncan.

Major Jake Thomas didn't like it when he was told that the information he requested was classified beyond his pay grade. Using the fight as an excuse, he was able to speak to their commanding officer, who was Colonel Martin. Two hours and several drinks later, Colonel Martin had a new executive officer. Major Thomas was now acting second in command of the Special Tactical Force. The position would become permanent once it was approved by higher command.

~ ~ ~

Going through training all over again was tough. The physical part wasn't all that bad, but the mental portion was really rough. It was boring and caused many a man in the squad to fall asleep, creating many hilarious episodes. Their classroom training went on for about a week. Thinking that their classroom instruction was over, the men of 1st squad decided to celebrate by going to one of the small drinking joints just down a little ways from the colonel's headquarters. They were caught by Captain Shane and sent back to headquarters before they could lift their first drink. They were also informed that they still had two more weeks of training to endure before they were completely finished.

The real bombshell hit when they were told that they would be going through jump school back in England. Nobody wanted to be dropped out of a perfectly good airplane behind enemy, lines, especially at night. "Crap on the ground," was Jackson's reaction to the news. The other members of the squad were a lot more, colorful with their choice of words.

The flight over the English Channel was uneventful and boring. Their landing was the same, but their boredom took a different turn when the men tried to depart the C-47 after landing. "Damn, Al, we're prisoners in our own camp. The least they could have done was stock this plane with beer, then I wouldn't mind being stuck here."

Sergeant Brooks stared at Sergeant Cane for a moment before he reached over flicked him on the nose with his finger, "Wake up, Dan. They did stock the plane. They stocked it with us first, so there wasn't any room left for the beer."

"Damn, Al," said Cane, "that hurt! Why the hell did you do that?"

Lightly slapping Cane on the side of his face, Brooks said, "Payback for trying to push me off of that tree limb a while back."

"Jesus, Al," but that was all he could say. Cane broke out laughing so hard, tears were streaming down his cheeks in seconds until his face turned red from choking on his chewing gum.

Thirty minutes after landing, Major Thomas pulled up beside the C-47 in a jeep, followed by a truck. The MP's standing watch then called out to Sergeant Brooks, informing him that he and his men could now leave the plane without getting shot.

The first week of training taught the men how to wear the parachute correctly, how to exit the airplane, and how to land without breaking any bones when they hit the ground. This area of their training was the part the entire squad liked. They were jumping out of a mockup, C-47 airplane, only two-feet off of the ground.

The second week, however, was a bit different. The reality of the situation began to sink in that they were actually going to jump out of an airplane. The squad's training was a bit more intense during this phase, so the men paid a lot closer attention to their instructors. They weren't going to jump out of airplanes for a living like the airborne boys did, but at the same time, if they didn't do it right the first time, they might not get past their first time.

The second week was the week the hair grew thick on their chests. That was the week they said they wouldn't jump no matter what. "I'd rather go up against a Kraut machine gun than jump out of an airplane at seven hundred feet. Especially traveling at over 100 mph. Hell, my arms and legs might fly off."

"Oh, come on, Hanky. Only your head will blow off. Your arms and legs aren't going anywhere."

"Shut up, Stony, or you'll give me nightmares."

After their first night jump, however, the men were pounding their chests, acting like old pros, nothing to it. Jackson was shaking like a leaf in the wind, and his heart was pounding, but he was wearing one hell of a grin.

The squad managed to make it through their second night jump, and that was all they were getting. Sergeant Cane sprained his ankle on that one, and then they found themselves flying back to France. Something had come up.

~ ~ ~

The bridal suite was the largest room the hotel had to offer. The big four-poster bed had been removed as well as all the mirrors on the walls and the ceiling. It was currently the briefing room for Colonel Martin. The aerial photographs as well as the still pictures the French were able to take were laid out on a table. Standing around the table in what appeared to be poses of boredom was an assortment of men looking down at a mockup of their next mission.

"The château is about ten miles south of Montmedy. It sits smack dab in the middle of over one thousand acres of thick forest. There are three roads leading to the château, but they're heavily guarded by SS troops."

"Why don't they just bomb the hell out of it, Colonel?" asked Brooks.

"We want to, but the French want Colonel von Pelt, plus the two Frenchmen. The French want to dish out their own brand justice for the three small villages that bastard razed to the ground. The two Frenchmen he's holding are supposed to be major players in the resistance. If they talk, a lot of people will die. We want to bomb the place into dust, just take out everything, but the French want their men back. That's your mission."

Pausing to wipe the sweat off of his face, Colonel Martin gazed at Sergeant Brooks and the men gathered as he waited for a reaction. Brooks' men just stood by the table looking at each other. "Doesn't look so tough to me. What do you think, Sarge?"

"The briefing isn't over yet, Alex. The Colonel hasn't reached the good part yet."

Staring at the squad, Colonel Martin didn't notice any concerned expressions. They acted as if they were in a classroom grouping together to solve a problem instead of preparing for a very dangerous mission. They didn't seem to be concerned at all about the dangerous part. Colonel Martin smiled and then he continued. "According to the French, the Germans have machine guns all over the place, plus they have dogs sniffing around everywhere."

Not sure if he heard correctly, Sergeant Brooks asked, "Dogs? Are you kidding, Colonel? If it's that hard to get to those guys, then why are you sending us, sir?"

"The French are asking for our help, Al, but that's not the main reason why you're going. The French asked for you and your men personally. They want you and your boys to rescue their two friends. Some Frenchy named Henri put up a pretty good fight and won his request."

"No sweat, sir. I met the man, but Colonel, that château is over a hundred miles behind German lines. If we parachute in, they'll know something's up. If we hoof it in, it'll take us at least, a week just to reach the château."

"Sergeant Brooks, what if I could transport you halfway there? That would make your job a little easier, wouldn't it?"

"Yes, sir, but Colonel...."

"But hell, Sergeant. That German halftrack sitting in front of this headquarters' building tells me exactly what you're capable of doing. You captured it on your second time out and with these same men."

"Colonel, I lost two good men. The replacements are unknown to me except for what I read in their files. Sergeant Cane sprained his ankle on our last jump, and PFC Decker, Private Decker got kicked out of the unit because of the crap he pulled. I don't know anything about Private Sharps or Sergeant Lucas."

"Aw come on, Al. They're both Rangers. You read that in their files. They volunteered for this unit. Hells bells, Sergeant. When they found out about you, they specifically asked to be assigned to your squad. I gave you the best, so what's the beef?"

"Colonel, do you have any more of that mule juice laying around? It has a mean bite to it, and I sure could use a stiff kick right about now. I knew that frog was trouble from the first time I laid eyes on him."

"Sergeant Duncan!"

"Yes, sir?"

"Send in Sergeant Lucas and add some 90 proof to the coffee."

"Yes, sir, Colonel."

"Sergeant Duncan."

"Yes, sir?"

"I won't need you for another hour, so why don't you go grab something to eat after you spike our coffee."

"Yes, sir." Sergeant Duncan was smiling when he left to go prepare the coffee. *Hell, this job really sucks. I'm not eating in the mud and rain.*

Chapter 19

The night wasn't as dark as Sergeant Brooks would have liked, but, at least, they were in the woods northeast of the château. Crouching under an umbrella of ponchos and using a flashlight, Sergeant Brooks and his men were studying the photos again. Once everyone had refreshed his memory of the layout, the light was turned off, and the ponchos were rolled up and put away. The squad stayed where they were for about twenty minutes, waiting for their eyes to readjust to the darkness before moving on.

"Everyone have their piss bottles?"

"Yeah, Sarge."

"Well, start pumping the stuff on then."

"Aw, come on, Sarge. Do we have to?"

Because of the dogs, Jackson thought of an idea on how to mask the human smell. Cow piss. He spent a lot of time selling the idea to Sergeant Brooks, but in the end, he won. Once that part was done, Jackson then had to figure out a way to apply it to the body. The problem was a perplexing one until, out of the blue, he remembered seeing a bottle of perfume with a squeeze ball on it, sitting on a store shelf. The two men then went to the colonel with their plan.

The idea was an instant success. The suggestion also had the colonel laughing so hard his sides hurt. He stopped laughing long enough to send Sergeant Duncan and three others out to scour the surrounding area for the perfume bottles. Within three hours, there were fifteen bottles sitting on the colonel's desk. The majority of them were confiscated from the GI's. Once that chore was taken care of, the hardest part had arrived. Gathering the piss without getting wounded.

The chore took poor Sergeant Duncan and his three companions many hours to collect the two gallons of cow piss estimated for the mission. It was such a riot to see them at work, trying to gather what they needed, but the four men weren't done yet. They still had to fill up all the perfume bottles with the stuff and then make sure the bottles didn't leak. When everything was in order, no leaks, and all of the bottles filled, Colonel Martin gave Sergeant Duncan and his three companions free access to the officer's showers and a week's leave in London. Smiling brightly, Sergeant Duncan muttered to himself. "This job sure beats the hell out of sleeping in a foxhole full of water."

The news about the piss bottles had spread like an out of control wildfire throughout the surrounding area. Pretty soon the entire S.T.F. Command was cracking jokes about the new Piss Brigade.

First squad had found a new weapon, and it was going to save Uncle Sam millions of dollars on ammo costs. It was going to revolutionize warfare on the modern battlefield. The weapon was pure genius. Soon, everyone in the European Theater of Operations would be clamoring to receive this new weapon, and it was simple to operate. Pull the trigger and piss on the Nazis.

Noses were wrinkling, and the comments were pouring out faster than a swollen river after a snowmelt. "Holy cow," said Corporal Sims. "Who pissed on your parade, Baker?"

"Aw, shut up, Alex."

"You're not getting pissed off, are you?" asked Corporal Sims. "If you get pissed off, then you're just going to have to put more on."

"You know the old saying, don't you, Hanky? It's better to be pissed off than pissed on."

"Oh, shut up, Stony," said Private Hanky. "You smell worse than limburger cheese."

"Can it children," said Brooks. "We have a war to fight, remember?"

"Damn, Sarge. Why'd you make us do this? Hell, the Germans will smell us long before they see us."

"Just about a minute ago, you guys were playing in this stuff, so what.... Damn you, Jackson. Stop sneaking up on me like that," whispered Brooks.

"You couldn't smell me, Sarge?" Immediately the snickers began.

"No, Private, I couldn't smell you. All I can smell is me. You do know that we're all going to kill you for this idea when we get back, don't you?" said Brooks.

Jackson was smiling when he replied. "Well, you'll just have to wait until the mission is over before you can do that. I found the château, Sarge. The area is swarming with Germans, but my idea worked. I was hiding in some bushes, and one of their dogs came up to the bush, took one whiff, snorted, and headed the other way. He definitely didn't like the smell."

"Well, neither do I," said Brooks. "Damn, this stuff stinks. How close did you get?"

"I was about sixty feet from the château."

Looking somewhat incredulous, Sergeant Brooks pushed his helmet to the back of his head and stared down at Jackson for moment before he said, "Damn, beanpole, you sure do beat all. How do you get away with that shit? How come the Germans can't see you?"

~ ~ ~

The squad was hunkered down about a hundred yards east of the château. "Sergeant Lucas," whispered Brooks, "what did you and Lemons find out?"

"We counted ten Krauts patrolling the rear of the château, and they have a dog with them. We found one machine gun position, but that was all. The Krauts are patrolling the back of the château pretty aggressively."

"Alex, what did you and White find out?"

Pointing at locations on an aerial photograph of the chateau, Corporal Sims began his report. "The Krauts have two dogs on the west side of the château, and there are two machine guns covering that side, here and here. Most of the Germans are about a hundred yards from the château, patrolling in these trees. They also have a dog between the château and the machine gun positions, but so far, they don't appear to be patrolling the front with dogs."

"Okay, gentlemen. We need to find a place to hide where the Germans won't find us, and we have a little over an hour before first light to get it done."

"Damn, Sarge. When are you going to take a bath?" whispered Corporal Sims.

"Shut up, Corporal," said Brooks. "The Germans are still looking for a hood ornament."

The squad had been moving carefully eastward until without warning they came to the edge of the forest and discovered a burned-out farmhouse. The only part of the structure left intact was the floor and a partial trap door that led to a small basement. "We'll stay here until we hit the château."

~ ~ ~

Sergeant Brooks was already regretting his decision to go on this mission. *How in the hell did I let Jackson talk me into this*? *I smell like half the cows in France pissed on me. The next thing you know, I'll start sprouting horns*!

"Hey Al, what the hell happened to you?"

"What are you talking about, Alex?"

"You have white and brown spots all over you, and you have horns poking out of your head."

Panic immediately seized Sergeant Brooks. Looking at his hands, he instantly spotted the brown spots, and then he grabbed the top of his head only to discover that he had indeed sprouted horns. "I'm gonna kill that Jackson!" screamed Sergeant Brooks. "I'm gonna ring that scrawny little neck of his!"

Sergeant Brooks woke up in a panic with sweat pouring down his face. Everyone else was still asleep. Looking around to make sure nobody was watching, he slowly put his hands on the top of his head and froze. "HORNS! DAMN THAT JACKSON!"

Staring around the pitch-black basement, Sergeant Brooks quickly realized that he had been dreaming, but now everyone was fully awake, trying to figure out why he was cussing out Jackson. Whispered questions flooded the platoon sergeant's ears as each man voiced his wonder at the sudden shouting. Tentatively, Sergeant Brooks reached a hand up to the top of his head, and then let out a big sigh of relief—no horns. He was really awake this time.

~ ~ ~

"Okay," whispered Brooks. "The first thing we need to do is get those Krauts away from the rear of the château and then keep them busy for a while. I think the rear of the château is our best way in."

"What do we do about the dogs, Sarge? We can't just kill them."

"What do you suggest we do with the dogs, Jackson?"

"Tie them to a tree or something," replied Jackson.

"Really, beanpole? We have to catch the dogs first before we can tie them to a tree. I guess the Krauts will just have to hold their fire until you get all the dogs tied up. That sound about right?"

The squad had been listening to the sounds of battle for the last two days, but now the fighting seemed to be getting closer and a little louder. They were hunkered down next a dirt road that led south behind the château. The men could hear vehicles moving about, close to the château, along with a lot of yelling. Moving to the edge of the clearing surrounding the small mansion, the men peered out. "Hey, what happened to the dogs?" asked Private Hanky.

Immediately, Jackson pointed towards a departing truck. "Look! They're in the back of that truck. See the kennels?"

Grinning, Sergeant Brooks shook his head and slapped Jackson on the shoulder before he said, "You know, beanpole. One of these days, lady luck is going to quit smiling down on you. I was going to make it your responsibility to tie up those dogs. That would have been fun to watch!" No one could keep a straight face.

Two trucks and a staff car were parked about twenty yards from the rear of the château. A German officer was standing beside the back door and giving orders to the men loading up the trucks.

"It looks like they're leaving, Sergeant Brooks."

"Yes, it does, Sergeant Lucas. It surely does," replied Brooks. "Baker, Jackson, see if you can get close enough to find out what's going on. Then get back to me pronto."

"You got it, Sarge." Smiling, Jackson turned to Corporal Baker and bowed. Using his best western drawl, he said, "Come on, Sir Charles. Let's go."

"Go shit in your hat, cowboy," replied Baker. "Damn! I can't believe I gotta play nursemaid to you again."

The two men circled the clearing until a small greenhouse blocked the view of the enemy moving in and out of the château. After a short hesitation, they ran quickly to the side of the greenhouse, which was about twenty yards from the parked vehicles. Jackson pulled out his knife and quietly dug away the wooden framework holding the glass in place and managed to remove several panes. Then they were inside, hunkered down under a workbench.

"Can you hear anything?" asked Jackson.

"Barely," replied Baker. "I'm only able to catch a word here and there."

"Come on, Sir Charles. Let's go around to the east side. You can probably hear better there."

"Why do you call me that?"

"Because you hate it, Chuck," said Jackson.

The two men made it to the east side of the château, where Baker edged closer to the corner, listening. "Wait here. I'll be back in a minute."

"Okay, cowboy," whispered Baker, "but don't do anything stupid."

Jackson just grinned. He returned about fifteen minutes later, and the two men quietly scampered back to the greenhouse. "What did you hear?" asked Jackson.

Baker was staring out of one of the dirty windows when he replied. "Our troops are ten miles east of Orleans and heading this way, so these guys are packing up everything they can carry and are heading to Belgium. They'll be leaving in about an hour. What did you find out?" asked Baker.

"These guys are it. There's nobody else here."

"Come on, cowboy. Let's get back to Sergeant Brooks."

"Why do you call me that?"

"Because you hate it, cowboy," whispered Baker.

The trip back to the squad didn't take long, and neither did their report. Sergeant Brooks took even less time to dislike what he heard. "How many Krauts did you locate?"

"I counted twenty, Sarge," replied Jackson. "Some of the windows were too dirty to see through, so there could have been more."

"How many frogs did you see?"

"All I spotted were the Germans. The Frenchies must still be under lock and key," replied Jackson.

"All right. This is how we do it. I'll keep Baker and Jackson with me. Sergeant Lucas, you take the rest of the men and slip around to the front. Wait until you hear us shooting, count to twenty, and then come in through the front door blasting. Wait until we fire before you move. And try not to kill that Kraut colonel if you can help it."

Sergeant Brooks continued to watch the Germans for a few minutes and noticed an eye opener. *This might work out just fine. Their weapons are slung across their backs.* Ten minutes went by before everyone was in position.

As soon as their colonel disappeared into the château, the three Germans standing watch beside the trucks decided to take a short walk and a break while they could. They were in the middle of turning to pee when they heard what sounded like a whispered shout.

"Now!" whispered Brooks. The three Americans stepped around the truck and opened fire on the preoccupied Germans. The shots resounded loudly in the château, echoing crazily off the walls and obstructing hearing. Colonel von Pelt yelled at his men to follow him, and the rest of his troops headed towards the back door, running and grabbing for their weapons.

Two of the Germans came rushing out onto the back porch before the rest could arrive, and ran into a hail of bullets before they could fire off a shot. Their momentum carried them rolling and bouncing down the steps, dead.

After the three enemy soldiers were killed, Brooks, Baker, and Jackson ran around the vehicles to cover the back door and heard the rest of the squad open up on the enemy from the front. The Germans were caught in a crossfire. The firing inside the château was so loud, no one could hear any more. The explosions from the guns firing echoed weirdly off the walls, more than tripling the sounds of the battle.

The enemy had been taken completely unprepared. Most of them had been carrying stuff looted from the mansion when the shooting started, and they were frantically trying to unsling their weapons while they ran to the back patio leading to the courtyard. It was then that Sergeant Lucas and the rest of the squad burst through the front door.

Several dead Germans were lying on the floor, and Brooks saw two of his men down, unmoving. Shouting at Jackson and Baker, he said, "Let's go," and the two men followed their platoon sergeant into the château, firing as they moved. Moments later, the battle was over.

They found Colonel von Pelt lying behind a couch, bleeding from several wounds. "Todd," shouted Brooks, "get over here." Not receiving an answer, he looked around for Private Hanky and saw him taking care of Private Stone. Stony had been shot twice, once through the shoulder and once through his left calf muscle.

"Baker, get over here and translate," shouted Brooks.

When Hanky was finished with Stone, he ran over to look at Colonel von Pelt to see if he could help the man, but there wasn't anything he could do to save the colonel's life. Ten minutes went by before Colonel von Pelt died, saluting Adolf Hitler without having said a single word. Brooks was greatly agitated.

"Stony's all right, Sarge, but he'll be out of the fight for a while. Sergeant Lucas didn't make it. He took a few to chest. He's dead, Sarge."

"Damn!"

Colonel von Pelt had been leading his men to the rear door when the bulk of the squad came through the front door, firing. Sergeant Lucas was the first man through the door and the first American the colonel fired at. The sergeant received three rounds to the chest and went down. Then the colonel fired at Private Stone, hitting him twice before the colonel was hit three times, knocking him out of the fight. The rest of the Germans fought hard, but when Brooks, Baker, and Jackson came through the back door, the Germans were caught in a crossfire, with their backs to the Americans. All of them were killed within a couple of minutes.

After checking the enemy dead, Sergeant Brooks called his men together.

"Grab Sergeant Lucas and carry him out back and bury him. Quickly now. Sims, move that staff car out of the way and then get that truck emptied out. The resistance guys were moved about half an hour ago. According to the corporal Baker interrogated, the Krauts in this area are heading for Belgium, and we're going after them. Quickly, gentlemen. Let's go. Hustle, hustle, hustle."

By the time the grave for Sergeant Lucas was dug, the truck had been emptied of its booty and was standing by, ready, its motor idling.

The men stood by the grave of their fallen comrade, saddened by his death. In the short time they knew him, they had discovered what kind of man Sergeant Lucas was and what kind of warrior he was. All of them were impressed by both the man and the warrior.

Sergeant Lucas' Thompson had been jammed into the ground, muzzle first, with one of his tags tied to the weapon. Sergeant Brooks put the other tag into his backpack, and then he placed the sergeant's helmet on the butt of his Thompson. Sending one last salute to the grave, the squad turned and sprinted for the truck.

"Okay, people, load up. The Krauts are about a half an hour in front of us, so let's get moving. Hanky, you stay here with Private Stone and take care of him. We'll meet you back here as quickly as we can. All right, Alex. Step on it."

Following the road northeast, the truck traveled at around 40 mph. They were moving as fast as Sergeant Brooks was willing to go. He wanted to sneak up on the Germans, not run into them. Twenty minutes into their journey, the squad came to a fork in the road. With brakes squealing, the truck came to skidding halt, spilling its passengers riding in the back, forward, and slamming them into a pile, up by the cab of the truck. "Damn, Corporal," shouted Stony. "This ain't no luxury liner, so take it easy on us!"

Brooks jumped out of the truck and immediately shouted for Jackson. "See if you can figure out which way they went."

Five minutes was all the time the Arizona beanpole needed to point the truck full of Americans in the right direction. In just minutes, they smelled the dust left behind by a passing vehicle. Somebody was traveling on the same road. A few minutes later, the dust was thicker, so they pulled off into the trees, stopped, and turned off the motor.

Off in the distance, the squad could hear voices, but no vehicle noises. "They've stopped," whispered Brooks. "Jackson, you and Lemons go find out what the Krauts are up to. While you're at, see if you can find those two Frenchmen for me." Immediately, the two scouts took off, heading for the enemy camp.

~ ~ ~

Moving silently through the trees, the two men were about thirty feet apart, quietly sneaking from shadow to shadow, bush to tree, vehicle to vehicle, but always in the shadows. A three-man patrol abruptly appeared out of nowhere, forcing the two scouts to melt into the deeper shadows and wait for the patrol to pass.

The encampment was large, close to 300 men. Most of them, however, were positioned west of the dirt road, waiting for an onrushing enemy. General Patton's boys were not far away.

"Sam, go back and tell Sergeant Brooks that it looks like the Germans are going to be here for a while. I'm going take a look around to see if I can find those Frenchmen. Tell him I'll be back in a couple of hours."

Shaking his head, Private Lemons replied. "He's not going to like that, Tim. Why do you keep provoking him like that?"

"He did say to find those Frenchies, didn't he, Sam?"

"Yeah. I guess you're right. I'll still bet my whole month's pay that he gets pissed at you anyway."

"Go on," whispered Jackson. "Get out of here and be careful."

Camouflage netting was going up to help conceal the vehicles along the edge of the trees, while the big tents were set up under the trees. The anti-tank weapons were unlimbered and placed in camouflaged positions, ready to wreak havoc on unsuspecting enemy vehicles. The Germans were digging in.

Chapter 20

Lying in the shadows, Jackson watched the Germans set up their tents in the trees. The moon was out, but it wasn't giving off much light where he was positioned. The moon was also in its final stages, and by next evening, there would be nothing but starlight.

The enemy didn't take long to set up their tents. While others were bustling about setting up camp, two civilians were led into one of the tents by two sentries and two officers. The two civilians were trussed up and blindfolded, so they had to be led. After the procession entered the tent, one soldier was stationed outside at the entrance of the tent, while the other stayed inside with the officers.

Jackson could hear the men talking, but couldn't understand what was being said because they were speaking French. The conversation went on in French for a couple of more minutes before he heard a voice rise in anger, followed by the unmistakable meaty smack of a fist colliding with someone's face. The impact was loud even outside of the tent where the Army scout was lying. *Crap on the ground! These guys are brutal.*

Jackson could see shapes of two men, apparently sitting down, with three others standing. The light in the tent was flickering from several lit candles, throwing distorted shadows back and forth across the tent sides. After the slap, only silence followed for a few seconds, and then the night turned even more brutal.

A big burley sergeant with gloved hands started pounding on the tallest of the two civilians until he was knocked to his knees, chair and all, and again only silence followed. At the moment, only the Germans were doing all the talking; nothing was being said by either of the two captives. The beatings and then the questions and then the beatings went on for about forty minutes until the two officers stormed out of the tent.

Jackson waited another ten minutes before he decided to head back to the squad and report to Sergeant Brooks.

~ ~ ~

His trek to the squad took him about thirty minutes, and now he was standing flat-footed, somewhat disgusted, and very much bewildered. “Hello, beanpole. Where the hell have you been?”

“How did you know it was me, Sarge?” he asked.

The disappointment of having been discovered by Sergeant Brooks was plain on beanpole’s face, and Brooks was grinning from ear to ear because of it. “I heard you coming a mile away.” He never let on that Private Lemons had warned him of Jackson’s approach.

“You heard me?” asked Jackson, absolutely shell-shocked.

“Yeah. I heard you all right. Now, what did you find out?”

Private Jackson was in a severe state of confusion, and bewildered was an understatement. “How did you hear me? You never heard me before?”

Sergeant Brooks shrugged his shoulders and smiled, his teeth gleaming in the starlight. “Are you going to tell me what you found out, you little sneak thief? Or, are you going to force me to beat it out of you?”

“But, Sarge, if you heard me, then the Germans can definitely hear me, and that could get us all killed.”

Brooks nodded before he answered. “Maybe now you'll think twice about sneaking up on me.” After hearing what Jackson had to say, however, Sergeant Brooks wasn’t smiling anymore. He was deep in thought, trying to come up with a solution to the difficult situation beanpole had just dropped into his lap.

He came up with a plan a few minutes later. The truck they had used earlier was a major part of his scheme. “Gentlemen, we have to push this truck down the road a ways and then move it into those trees out of sight. Lemons, you’re the lightest, so you’ll get in and steer it. There’s a slight incline about sixty yards back down the road. We’ll push it there, take a break, and then push like hell, using the incline to give us enough momentum to move it deep into the trees.”

"Then what, Sarge?"

"We wire the truck with a block of comp-B and blow it up."

"We don't have a detonator, so how do we set the stuff off? I don't like the idea of a block of comp-B, a hand grenade, and truck fuel being so close to my body. We need distance, Sarge."

"No sweat, Hanky. We use the truck battery. Beanpole, you still have that commo wire you took from the Krauts?"

"Yeah, Sarge, but it'll cost you another case of Cokes to get it." And then the snickers erupted.

"Beanpole, stay away from Sergeant Cane. It appears he's been a bad influence on you. I'll give you twelve. No more."

"Take it, beanpole," said Sims.

"No, Corporal. I think the whole case or nothing." Smiling brightly, Jackson looked at Sergeant Brooks and said, "I lied to you, Sarge. That 100 feet of commo wire I told you I stole from the Germans isn't 100 feet. I have close to 300 feet of it, and it's stashed away in my pack. How about that case of Coke now? Three hundred feet from the blast instead of spitting distance?" And now beanpole was grinning from ear to ear.

"Damn you, Jackson. Sam, keep beanpole away from Sergeant Cane, damn it, or the next thing we know, he'll be running this outfit. Crap on the ground, Jackson... Oh, all right. One case. Now get that wire."

Sims was having a really tough time keeping a straight face, as were the other men. Turning to face his platoon sergeant, he said in a matter of fact, tone, "Don't step in the crap on the ground, Sarge. You'll give us away from the smell if you step in it."

A moment of silence reigned until Sergeant Brooks pointed towards the château and said, "Shut up, Corporal Sims. The Germans are right over there, and I'm sure they're still looking for a hood ornament."

The idea was to blow up the truck hoping to draw enough Germans away from the tent to allow Lemons and Jackson to rescue the two Frenchmen. At least that was the plan. "Okay gentlemen. We go at 0000 hours (midnight). It's now 2130 hours, so that leaves us two and a half hours. Find a shady spot and get some sleep. I'll wake you at 2300."

While the men were heading off for the deeper shadows of the trees to rack-out, they were softly laughing at their platoon sergeant's comment.

~ ~ ~

The men were suddenly awakened by the sound of a vehicle starting up. Sergeant Brooks was the first to realize that the truck they heard starting up was their truck. "Jackson, go find out what's going on. It sounds like the Germans found our truck. Hanky, you pulled that battery, right?"

"Yeah, Sarge. It's right here."

"Damn. At least, something went right."

Thirty minutes later, Jackson returned and reported to Sergeant Brooks the bad news, the Germans had indeed found their truck. This news stood Brooks straight up, and now he had to come up with another plan.

"Sarge?"

"What is it, Jackson?"

Private Jackson took a deep breath before he spoke. "Why don't you let Baker, Lemons, and me go after the Frenchmen? After we free the Frenchmen, we can meet you guys back at the château."

"No," said Brooks. "It's too dangerous. Besides, you'll need a diversion, and our distraction just took off down the road to the enemy encampment."

Again, Jackson took a deep breath. "I'll be the diversion, Sarge. I'll go behind the Germans and start a ruckus. When they start coming after me, Lemons and Baker can free the Frenchmen."

Sergeant Brooks immediately shook his head and said, "You call that a plan? How do you know the Germans won't catch you?"

Beanpole beamed brightly before he answered. "If you can't see me Sarge, what makes you think those goons will? It'll be easy, Sarge. Alone, I know that anybody I hear will be the enemy. Trust me, Sarge, it'll be a piece of cake. Like a walk in the park."

Sergeant Brooks thought about Jackson's idea for a couple of moments before he spoke. "Listen up, beanpole. If you get caught I'm coming after you. Does that sound familiar?"

"Look, Sarge, I'm not going to get caught."

"Really? So how do you plan on not getting caught and getting the Frenchmen away from the Germans at the same time?"

Smiling, Jackson nodded towards Baker and Lemons. "Those two will get behind the tent the Frenchmen are in. There's a big tree behind the tent. They can hide in the shadows until the Germans leave. They cut a hole in the back end of the tent and drag the two Frenchmen into the shadows before they free them from the chairs. Then they get the hell out of Dodge and meet you where you want them to meet you. Everything else is up to me. Once you get the Frenchies, you guys can head for the château to pick up Hanky and Stone and then head for our lines. I'll catch up with you later."

"I don't like it, beanpole. It's too risky. I don't like gambling with the lives of my men, and the last time I checked, you're one of my men."

Immediately, Jackson snapped back at his platoon sergeant. "You got a better plan?"

Brooks stared hard at Private Jackson until beanpole dropped his gaze. "Sorry, Sarge. I guess I forgot my manners."

Brooks stared down at Jackson for a long few seconds, trying desperately not to crack up laughing at the kid's expression. Then he smiled and said, "No, beanpole. I don't have a better plan, so I guess we use yours."

Abruptly, the quiet night was again broken by the sounds of several engines cranking up. Within a couple of minutes, three vehicles left the German encampment, heading south along the dirt road in the direction of the château.

The Americans were about thirty yards inside the tree line bordering the dirt road, watching while one halftrack and two trucks, loaded with Germans, headed back towards the fork in the road. Sergeant Brooks took off his helmet and rubbed his head, disgusted at the sight. "Well, that tears it. Now, we're going to have to wait to see what the Krauts are up to before we can do what we need to do." Turning back towards Jackson, Sergeant Brooks discovered that the Arizona beanpole was gone, and angry steam clouds immediately began to form over his head.

While Sergeant Brooks was brewing up nice and angry, he moved his men deeper into the trees to await Jackson's return; now steam was trickling out his ears.

~ ~ ~

"Sarge!"

Brooks almost jumped out of his skin at the sound of Jackson's voice. "Damn you, Jackson. Make some noise when you come up behind me, or I just might mistake you for a rat and shoot you."

Beanpole was smiling when he asked his question. "Why didn't you hear me this time, Sarge?"

Sergeant Brooks, however, ignored Jackson's question. He was pissed. Really pissed. Beanpole's question immediately triggered the rest. "If you ever pull that stunt again, I will shoot you right between the eyes and call it desertion. We had this discussion one time before in North Africa, and I will not tolerate that kind of behavior from anyone in this squad. Do I make myself clear, Private Jackson?"

Jackson remembered their discussion in North Africa, and he felt now what he felt in North Africa, the queasy bite of fear in the pit of his stomach. He could only nod his reply. Brooks then asked, "Why did you leave?"

Jackson swallowed hard before he said, "I had to piss, Sarge," he squeaked. And then the snickers erupted, followed quickly by braced, raised hands, wriggling energetically.

Slowly, Sergeant Brooks turned to look at the rest of the squad absolutely astonished. Pulling at his ear, he stared at his men for a moment before he said, "I feel like I'm running a kindergarten for preschoolers. The way some of you guys act, a person would think you were children instead of soldiers."

About forty-five minutes after the three vehicles left the encampment, Sergeant Brooks was still trying to figure out what to do next. Private Jackson, still stinging from his chewing-out, was a bit hesitant about speaking to his squad leader. Sergeant Brooks, however, came up with an idea that broke the silence. "Beanpole, take Brown and Avery with you when you go. Leave them about forty yards from the tent in case you need extra help moving the frogs. What are you going to do to create a distraction?"

Jackson shrugged his shoulders and said, "I figured to lob a few grenades into a couple of their vehicles and start shooting. That should get their attention."

Sergeant Brooks immediately shook his head. "That idea should also get you killed, you little sneak-thief. If half that encampment starts shooting at you, they'll have you pinned down, and you won't be able to get away. I suggest you come up with a better distraction."

"Don't worry, Sarge," said Jackson. "I'll figure something out. When do you want to get things rolling?"

Sergeant Brooks let out a deep sigh. He didn't like the plan that Jackson came up with, but at the moment, he couldn't come up with anything better. "Okay, Private. Grab your men and get going. Remember. Leave Brown and Avery about forty yards from the tent and then get Baker and Lemons into position. Those Krauts at the fork might throw a wrench into the works. If the situation turns sour, we meet at that old Pz III wreck on the back side of the château. Good luck, beanpole." Nodding at the other three, he said, "Jase, Pete, Chuck, be careful and keep your heads down. I'll take the rest of the men, and if all goes well, we'll meet you at that old wreck, near the fork. Good luck, you guys."

~ ~ ~

Sergeant Brooks and squad made it to the wreck by the fork only to discover a platoon of Germans deploying to cover the split. Quietly, the Americans moved deeper into the trees about one hundred yards east of the junction. Again, he regretted taking on this mission. Everything that could have gone wrong seemed to have gone wrong. He could only wonder about what was going to happen next.

Jackson, Lemons, and Baker were kneeling low to the ground, in the shadow of a large, tall standing tree, about twenty feet behind the tent the Frenchmen were in. The Germans were beating on the two Frenchmen again, but they were no longer using their fists. Instead, they had switched to lengths of rubber hose. The meaty slap of the hose striking the captives was loud and brutal sounding.

Jackson was amazed at the inner strength of the two Frenchmen. The only sounds they made were grunts and groans of pain. Neither man let out a scream. Beanpole was so mesmerized by what he was witnessing that he forgot what he was supposed to do and just stood in the shadows with Baker and Lemons, watching the brutal scene taking place. The beatings stopped about twenty minutes later, leaving the enemy officers a bit frustrated with the lack of cooperation from their captives.

The prisoners themselves were bent over in their chairs as far as the ropes would allow. Besides the lieutenant holding onto the chairs, the ropes were the only thing keeping the Frenchmen from falling face first to the ground. Jackson was really beginning to dislike these vicious soldiers more and more.

The same burly German, who earlier was using his fists on the two captives before switching to a piece of hose, left the tent and then returned a few minutes later. He was carrying a bucket of water, hoping to revive the two unconscious Frenchmen. His effort, however, was useless. The two men were out cold and unresponsive. Disgusted, the two officers left the tent and headed towards a larger tent situated about sixty yards away.

The inside guard left the tent to go pee a couple minutes after the officers left, instructing the outside guard to watch the prisoners. The three Americans watched the proceedings until PFC Baker turned to Jackson. "He's leaving to pee!" Jackson immediately looked at Lemons and said, "Get ready to cut open the back of the tent as soon as I silence that guard."

Jackson slowly crept out of the shadow of the tree and moved towards the guard. Looking around to see if anybody was watching, he continued to creep towards the unsuspecting sentry until he felt a tug on the back of his shirt. Looking back, he saw Sam, who was motioning for the scout to follow him. At first, Jackson tried to ignore him, something Sam figured he would do, so he grabbed a handful beanpole's shirtsleeve and pulled him back into the shadow of the tree. "What are you doing, Sam?"

Private Lemons whispered back. "Chuck has an idea that might work even better."

~ ~ ~

The guard standing watch in front of the entrance to the tent suddenly felt something hit him in the back. Then he heard someone whispering, "Hey, come here and look at what I found behind the tent." The guard turned and whispered back. "Karl, is that you?"

"Yes, it's me. Come here and look at what I found behind the tent." The unsuspecting sentry moved towards the back of the tent thinking that his friend Karl had found something, not realizing that it wasn't even his friend's voice calling to him.

The area was dark in the shadow of the tree. Even the candles in the tent did nothing to take away the advantage of the shadows where Jackson crouched and waited for the guard to get closer. Four steps, and a soft exhale later, the short skirmish was over. The attack happened so quickly that the guard was dead before he had time to realize what was happening to him.

Jackson and Baker immediately picked up the dead man and carried him deeper into the shadows, leaving him leaning up against a tree, in the shadow of the tree. Rushing back to the tent, the two men were just in time to avert a disaster. Private Lemons was about to cut open the back of the tent when the other guard re-appeared. The big burly boy.

Walking towards the tent after completing his task, the second guard noticed immediately that his friend was not where he should be. "Paul, where are you?"

"Karl, I am behind the tent. Come see what I have found." PFC Baker reacted to the question without thinking more than, *it worked once, why not again*? And it worked.

Karl, thinking his friend Paul was behind the tent, did what he was told without hesitation, and he too, met the same end as his friend. Now it was time to cut open the back of the tent and rescue the two Frenchmen.

~ ~ ~

The interrogating officers were on their way to the tent when they noticed that the two guards were not at their posts. Upon further investigation, they discovered that their two captives had escaped, and their guards had been killed. Within minutes, the entire encampment was awake, and the search was on for the two escaped Frenchmen.

Even as far away as they were from the encampment, Sergeant Brooks and his men could hear the Germans shouting excitedly. The doors of hell had burst open, but he couldn't figure out why. Jackson's diversion never happened. There was no gunfire or grenades going off. Just out of the blue, the entire German encampment came alive. Then he heard the unmistakable crack of Jackson's M1 carbine off in the distance, followed by the deadly sound of German machine guns opening up. Again, he was confused. A tap on his shoulder brought him out of his thoughts. It was Corporal Sims. "Al, the Krauts are leaving the fork."

Sure enough, the Germans were scrambling into their vehicles, and within seconds, they were heading back towards their encampment. Sergeant Brooks was amazed. Everything seemed to be happening in reverse. Now, he was really worried about Private Jackson.

~ ~ ~

The unexpected, whispered alarm caught Sergeant Brooks by surprise. "Someone's coming up on our right."

"Yeah, I hear it, Alex." Then Brooks whispered to the rest of the squad. "Okay, people. Spread out and keep it quiet. Hold your fire until you hear my command."

Within seconds, the Americans were spread out, waiting for whoever was coming towards them. A few minutes later, the men of 1st squad heard labored breathing from what sounded like several people. Before they could get past their confused looks, the men of 1st squad heard Sam swear. "It's them," whispered Brooks. "Let's go get our boys and get the hell out here."

"What about Jackson, Sarge?"

Sergeant Brooks glanced at Private White. "He'll just have to do the best he can. There's nothing we can do to help him right now."

Brooks was starting to become angry again. They were surrounded by a small German army, and his men wanted to talk. "Shut up people and let's go. Alex, you take point."

The two captives were in pretty bad shape when they left the tent, so they were unable to stand up or walk on their own. They required help.

~ ~ ~

Private Lemons was out front leading the procession, with Baker as his danger relay. They were walking parallel to the dirt road just inside of the tree line, about a half a mile from the château when Private Lemons found Sergeant Brooks. Actually, Sergeant Brooks spotted him first and scared the hell out of the poor guy. "What are you guys doing out here?" whispered Brooks. "Trying to skip curfew again?"

Once the short reunion was over, Lemons gave an even shorter report. "There are a bunch of Germans chasing after Jackson, Sarge. The last I saw of him he was laughing and hightailing it northeast. Damn, that little man is crazy!"

"Did you see anything of Stone, and Hanky?" asked Brooks.

"No, Sarge. We didn't see either of them."

Brooks stared off in the direction of the shooting for a moment. Then he took a deep breath and exhaled slowly. Looking back at the two men he said, "Go back and check out the château and the area around it. Hopefully those two didn't get captured by the Germans. In the meantime, we'll wait here until we get the okay from you, but make it quick because we're running out of time."

Without saying a word, the two men immediately left, heading back to search for the two missing men.

With the squad no longer on the move, Sergeant Brooks decided to go and check up on his new guests. Walking over to where they were stretched out on the ground, he looked down at their faces. Even as swollen as their faces were, he was able to recognize one of the men. It was Jean, the same Frenchman who had helped him and his men out when they were being chased by an SS captain and his men.

"Hello, Jean. It looks like the Krauts finally caught you. How did they get you?"

Jean's face was so swollen that he couldn't smile without a lot of pain. His voice and his eyes, however, were able to take up the slack until an involuntary smile of exuberance began to appear shortly before the pain. "Hello, Sergeant Brooks. Was this rescue planned, or did we just get lucky?"

Sergeant Brooks was grinning when he said, "A little of both, I suppose. Your friend Henri raised such a fuss that General Larson heard about it, and now here we are. Your escape is where luck comes in." Immediately, Brooks raised his right fist and hissed, "Hit the ground, movement along the tree line." A shadow of movement had caught his eye, and then PFC Baker appeared, scampering along the edge of the trees. A few minutes later, he arrived. Whispering, Brooks asked. "Well, what's going on over there?"

"Sarge, we searched the whole area and the château and found no Germans anywhere."

"What about Stone and Hanky? Did you find them?"

"Not yet," said Baker.

"Well, keep looking until you find them. Search those trees over by that shed in case they took to them for cover. I'll take a couple of men and search that pump house and the trees behind it. Make it fast, people. The Germans are just around the bend."

Chapter 21

Jackson was somewhat surprised when the enemy found their dead comrades so quickly. He had been counting on a ten-minute head start before the Germans reacted, but the situation had changed. That ten-minute head start was also supposed to give Baker and friends the time they needed to get farther away before hell arrived. The whole camp was in an uproar, and most of the German troops were heading towards the squad. He had to think of something really quick, and the only option he came up with was to start shooting, so he did.

Jackson was about fifty yards behind the last tent when he opened fire. Shooting into one of the tents, he managed to hit an oil lamp, and because the lamp was still lit, it caught the tent on fire.

Immediately, the machine guns covering the rear of the camp opened up, spraying the woods with deadly weapons' fire. The thwack, thwack, thwack of the bullets hitting the trees and the tick, tick, tick of the bullets snapping through small branches and foliage forced Jackson to hit the ground. *Crap on the ground, that's a whole lot of bullets flying over my head.*

Lying flat on the ground, he looked around for an avenue of escape, while small branches and pieces of tree rained down on him, forcing him to duck involuntarily. *Well, I can't stay here, they'll get me for sure. Crap on the ground. This is intense.*

Shaking from the adrenalin rush and the death grip fear had on him, he slowly inched his way east as quickly as he could without giving himself away. The next few minutes was an extremely nerve-racking experience for beanpole. Low-crawling with hundreds of tracers, and all the invisible bullets in between searching blindly, impacting indiscriminately, and he was bouncing off the ground the whole time from shaking so much. He was scared to death, absolutely terrified. *Crap on the ground! That is a lot of bullets trying to kill me.* And during all this mayhem, he was crawling away from the château, away from his friends, and away from Allied lines.

He could still hear the shouting above the noise of the machine guns, but suddenly the machine guns stopped firing. Immediately, he began to worry. *The Germans must be coming after me. Why else would they stop firing? I guess they don't want to hit any of their own men by mistake. Damn. What a shame.*

Getting to his feet, but still bent over, Jackson moved away from the German encampment. He could see shadows moving through the darkness. After he had moved behind a big tree, he turned around facing the camp and again started shooting. This action incurred a reaction from the Germans, and they too started firing. The one advantage he had at the moment was that he could see his enemy, but all the Germans could see of Jackson were his muzzle flashes.

Going from tree to tree, he scampered to another large tree about forty yards to his rear, and then he opened up again, trying to draw the Germans away from the squad. So far, his ploy appeared to be working. Twenty minutes after the enemy had been alerted, Jackson had managed to draw most of them almost 200 yards northeast of the chateau. The Germans wanted their prisoners back. Their dogged determination to get them back allowed beanpole to fool them into chasing ghosts. The time had arrived for him to give the enemy the slip, so cautiously, he moved south, silently sneaking his way through a platoon of angry searchers.

~ ~ ~

"Come on, Sarge. Look. It's only a squad. We have the advantage of surprise on our side, and besides, if we don't plant those Krauts six feet under before they can leave, they'll take Pete and Dave with them, and we'll never see them again."

The section of woods that Sergeant Brooks and his men were hiding in was about thirty yards from the back courtyard of the château. The men of 1st squad could still hear the sporadic firing coming from the woods behind and east of the German encampment. They were worried about Jackson, but the fact that the firing was continuing meant that the scout was still alive and had not been caught or killed yet.

Sergeant Brooks watched the Germans carry their dead comrades and place them in the halftrack. It was an open-top vehicle with double rear doors that made it a little easier for the men to place the bodies of their slain troops in the back of the track. Pulling at his ear, Brooks gazed his enemy. He knew that Corporal Sims was correct. If the Germans left, they would never see Stone and Todd again. He just needed to come up with a plan. One that would involve no prisoners.

"Alex, take two men and move around to the right. I want you covering the right flank. Don't start shooting until after I do. Baker, you stay with me. Private Sharps, you take two men around the left and come in through that archway when the shooting starts. We'll hit them from three sides on my command. I'll give you guys ten minutes to get into position before I start shooting. Now move out."

"Where you going to be?"

Pointing at a small shed, Sergeant Brooks replied, "You see that clump of trees next to that pump house? That's where me and Baker will be."

"That's awful close to the Germans, Al. What if they spot you before we're ready?"

"Well then," he said, "I guess we'll have to start the war from there. Now, get going before I turn you over to the Krauts. Stay low, Alex."

The six men moved deeper into the trees and then started running bent over to get into their positions. Shortly after Brooks and Baker arrived at their location, they watched the last of the German dead being loaded onto the halftrack, while the rest of the enemy squad assembled at the rear of the track.

Abruptly, the volume of fire coming from Jackson's vicinity increased. The crack of Jackson's M1 carbine could be heard mixed in with the sounds of the German gunfire. The intensity of the shooting coming from Jackson's area concerned Sergeant Brooks, but the pause was short. There was nothing he could do to help Jackson's situation at the moment, so his main concern was focused solely on the engagement he was facing. He could not allow anything else to interfere with the outcome.

The château itself was in the center of the forest they were hiding in. The clearing where the château was located was about two acres in size. The right side of the château, as Sergeant Brooks was facing it, was about ninety feet from the trees, while the left side was about sixty to seventy feet from the tree line. The section of trees where Brooks and Baker were currently hiding in was about fifty feet from the halftrack, with a clear shot at the ten-man enemy squad.

Exasperated, Sergeant Brooks stared at his enemy. The Germans were about to leave the château. The squad itself was in formation facing Brooks and Baker, with their squad leader facing his men.

Brooks had given his men ten minutes to get into position before he opened the ball, but after watching his enemy for a few minutes, all indications were the Germans were about to leave before those ten minutes were up. He looked over at PFC Baker and issued his order. "I'll take the squad leader; you take the first man to his left. Hopefully the rest of the guys are in position. We fire on three. One, two, three."

The two men fired almost as one. The squad leader and the first man on the left dropped to the ground, dead. Immediately, Brooks and Baker quickly turned their sights on their next two targets. The Germans were taken completely by surprise, so they took a couple of seconds to react, allowing Brooks and Baker time to kill two more. Then Corporal Sims and his two men began firing on the surprised squad, and the Germans immediately gave ground, falling back behind the halftrack in order to re-group and fight back.

The enemy did exactly what Sergeant Brooks had planned for. They moved around to the opposite side of the halftrack to escape the weapons' fire. However, before they had a chance to do more than arrive, weapons' fire from Private Sharps and his two men, attacking through the archway, ripped into them, dropping all that remained to the ground, dead. The surprise attack was a perfectly executed action. In less than thirty seconds, the little battle was over, and ten German soldiers lay dead on the ground.

When the shooting started, Hanky and Stone had dropped to the marbled floor of the patio, leading to the courtyard to avoid getting shot. They were still lying face down when Brooks and Baker ran up to them. Private Sharps and his two men were the first to reach Hanky and Stone, and both privates were in a kind of shock from the unexpected attack.

Private Stone, his face already pale from his wounds, turned even whiter and almost choked over his words. “Damn, Sarge. Give a guy some warning next time.” Private Hanky, however, was still in shock over what had just happened and was unable to speak. The rest of the men stood staring off into the distance. Another burst of gunfire had them looking northeast, a sudden reminder that one of their own was still in trouble.

While Sergeant Brooks and his men were having a discussion, the two Frenchmen decided to try their luck at walking without help, and started moving towards their saviors. “Al, we’re done here,” said Sims, “so why don't we go and help Jackson out. He’d do the same for us.”

Sergeant Brooks looked at Corporal Sims for a few agonizing seconds before he answered. “No. We're not going to go help, Jackson. Right now, he thinks he's all by himself, so anything he hears or sees he knows is the enemy. If we go out there traipsing through the woods trying to help him out, and he hears or sees us, he might start shooting at us thinking we're the enemy. Or we might put his life in jeopardy. No. We're going to wait right here until he shows up.”

“Sarge,” whispered Baker. “The Frenchies are coming.” Sergeant Brooks looked back towards the trees where they had left the two Frenchmen, and sure enough, they were limping awkwardly towards him. He could see they were still having a difficult time walking, but at least they were walking now.

Sergeant Brooks smiled before he nodded and said, “Well, you helped us out of a bad situation a while back, and now we've done the same for you. I guess that makes us even.”

Jean stared intently at Brooks for a moment before he shook his head and said, “No, my friend, you are wrong. We did not save your life. We just made it easier for you to get back to your lines.

You saved our lives, so now we are indebted to you. Whatever you need, just ask for it."

Pulling at his ear, Brooks stared at the Frenchman before he said, "I like the sound of that, Jean, but I don't agree with you. You may not think that you saved our lives, but I know different. Without your help, we would've never made it back to our friends. Those Krauts were about to eat us for breakfast until you and your boys arrived. You don't owe us anything."

The two Frenchmen were still hurting, so they both sat down on the grass. Then Jean turned and looked up at Sergeant Brooks. "Who are the Germans shooting at?"

"They are shooting at Private Jackson," replied Sergeant Brooks. "Look, Jean. I would love to sit here and talk with you about anything you want to talk about, but right now, we're sitting out in the open and the enemy is just beyond that house. We need to head for cover. Gentlemen, get up off your butts and let's move into the trees. Let's go, people. Alex, help Hanky with Private Stone. The rest of you help these guys get under cover."

The squad had barely made it inside the trees when the sound of vehicles approaching paused their movement. Standing in the shadows cast by the trees, they watched while two truckloads of German infantry pulled in behind the château and stopped right behind the halftrack. Chuckling, Sergeant Brooks slapped one of his privates on the back and said, "Brown, did your leg twitch again?"

"No, Sarge. It must be the piss perfume we're wearing. The Krauts can probably smell us a mile away."

Chapter 22

Jackson waited, hiding in the shadows cast by a clump of bushes growing close to a large tree. He still had his M1 carbine, but he was running out of bullets. He only had one full magazine and what was left in his rifle. About forty rounds, total. He could hear the Germans whispering to each other, but, as before, he couldn't understand a word they were saying. Without warning, three Germans stopped about five feet from where Jackson was hiding in the shadows and the scout stopped breathing. The Germans were close enough, that if he reached out he could touch two of them.

He wanted to get up and run just like the rabbits did when he got too close to them. He realized, however, that if he did run, he would more than likely end up dead just like the rabbits. Almost immediately after that thought arrived in his mind, he envisioned himself running blindly through the trees with arms flailing, shouting "Ahhh," like some freaked-out character in a series of illustrations in a dime novel. He almost cracked up laughing. The sudden crack of a German rifle snapped him away from his illusion. As his laughter inside subsided, his feeling of panic disappeared as well.

Something soft and wet hit him in the face. Looking up, he realized that a light rain was falling. He had been so preoccupied with his present situation that he failed to notice that the clouds had covered the little sliver of moon, and very quickly, the trees went dangerously dark. He also realized that with the light rain falling, it would be harder to hear him when he moved through the woods. A devious smile formed on his face.

With a silent, "Hmm," it suddenly occurred to him that there were not as many Germans looking for him as there had been. Earlier, what had started out sounding like a herd of elephants was now just a soft rustling through the bushes. A much quieter search.

Jackson waited until the three enemy warriors had moved about thirty feet past him before he began his hunt. They were searching in small squads, from two to five men each. They were moving forward, spread out in an irregular skirmish line, searching for their escaped prisoners.

Leaving his carbine leaning up against a tree, Jackson stalked his enemy. The three men were spread out maybe fifteen feet apart, and they were paying very little attention to their rear. What was behind them was not a concern to the pursuing enemy squads because they had help coming up to cover their backs. That help, however, was busy at the moment chasing Sergeant Brooks and his squad, but the three German squads didn't know about that change in orders.

One of the men was lagging behind his friends, so he was Jackson's first target; he was barely ten feet away.

The soldier was a private and somewhat new to combat. He was a bit nervous, so he kept glancing back over his left shoulder. He was currently experiencing an uneasy feeling that was settling over him like a thick fog. *Damn this rain*, he thought. *Can't see or hear anything in this mess*.

Jackson studied the enemy trio for about forty steps. The straggler kept looking over his left shoulder, so Jackson moved up on the private's right. He was only a couple of feet behind his enemy when the German soldier abruptly stopped and turned to his right, discovering a little shadow that looked a bit odd only two feet away. At first, he didn't know what the shadow was. He was thinking that maybe it was a bush or something, but then the shadow moved.

Jackson had been waiting for the opportunity to strike, so when the man stopped and turned to face the shadow he was hiding in, the Arizona scout was ready and waiting.

Jackson's move was quick and sudden. With his left hand, he grabbed the soldier's rifle to keep him from using it to deflect the knife thrust. With his right hand, he thrust his knife as hard as he could upward through the soft area under the jaw. The sudden strike was so unexpected that the man quietly collapsed to the ground, dead, his rifle still gripped in Jackson's left hand. The attack had happened so quickly that the private never even had a chance to call out to his friends.

Jackson quickly withdrew his knife from the dead man, and moved a few feet away into the deeper shadows where he waited to see if he had been heard or seen. Nothing. The other two soldiers continued walking as if nothing had happened. Moving out of the shadows, Jackson went after his next two targets.

Reaching down, he picked up the dead man's rifle from where he had laid it on the ground and then his helmet. Replacing his own helmet with that of his enemy's, he nonchalantly moved up on the left side of his adversary. Not realizing what had just happened, the Germans mistook Jackson for their friend and only shot a quick glance in his direction as they continued to search for their elusive enemy. Jackson's expression was one of deadly intent.

A couple of minutes later, the German closest to Jackson turned to his left to say something to his companion, but his friend wasn't there. Coming to a three-step halt, he turned his head and searched the area for his comrade. A big mistake on his part.

Turning to his right, the man looked in the direction he had last seen his friend. He heard a sound and quickly turned to his left just in time to see a shadow coming right for him. By then, however, his reaction was too late. The beanpole had struck again, but this time, the conflict was heard. Jackson had rustled some bushes in his haste to close in on his enemy, so his kill wasn't quiet. The soldier had moved at the last second when he heard a noise, so instead of the clean, silent kill he was striving for, Jackson caught the German in the throat, causing him to choke on his own blood.

The last man on Jackson's list heard his comrade choking and realized that something was not right. Quickly turning, he immediately discovered that he was all alone, and that his nearest help was at least, a couple of minutes away. A blooded veteran of the eastern front, he moved quickly to the sound of the choking, ready for battle.

The rain was coming down even harder, worsening the already bad conditions. Without warning, a shadow moved, and the veteran of the Russian war forgot all about his dead friend. Firing at the shadow, he just missed Jackson's head by inches. Jackson heard the rifle fire and felt the bullet zing just past his head. Immediately turning to his right, he scampered hunched over for about twenty yards and then turned right again, before he ran for another twenty yards and dropped to the ground, quietly regaining his breath and waiting. About a minute or so later, his breathing under control, Jackson moved several feet to his right and entered the darker shadows to wait for his adversary.

After listening for a few minutes, Jackson heard footsteps approaching. He was unable to see anything, but he was still able to discern someone sloshing through the rain soaked forest. He could also hear shouting off in the distance on both sides of him, which meant that his hunt was about to become a lot more difficult in a few minutes.

After a couple of minutes of listening, Jackson was able to figure out where his enemy was. Turning west, he started gliding silently through the trees, moving towards the lone warrior, ghost-like and invisible.

The German was a sergeant and also a hunter. He knew what it meant to be silent in the woods. To make noise meant no food on the table, so he was moving as quietly as his experience would allow. His experience, though, was nothing compared to Jackson's.

The night was dark, and the rain was coming down hard, so visibility was very limited. The sergeant was standing only a couple of feet away from a large oak tree. The huge tree created deep shadows that had the veteran warrior spooked.

Looking off to his right for a second, he caught a sudden flash of movement over by the oak tree out of the corner of his left eye. As he raised his rifle to fire, he was abruptly attacked from behind and on his left. The sergeant barely had enough time to bring his rifle around to block his attacker's knife thrust. His first parry was successful, resulting in a loud thunk and ting as the knife struck the rifle stock and barrel at the same time. He tried to bring his rifle up to fire at his attacker, but his assailant was moving too fast for that action. His only choice was to continue blocking his attacker's knife thrusts until he had the opportunity to shoot him.

Jackson's only advantage was his speed and quickness. He had to stay close to the German in order to keep him from getting off a shot; he had to crowd him so he couldn't bring his rifle to bear. The beanpole kept attacking, thrusting with his knife and throwing punches as he tried to get through his enemy's defense in order to kill him.

The German was no slouch either. He had over four years of combat under his belt and had fought against the Belgians, the French, the British, and the Russians. Some of his fighting was close, hand-to-hand combat. He was a veteran of brutal warfare, so he knew what he was doing. But he had never fought against an enemy like Jackson before.

Everything was a blur of quickness. The only sounds from the battle were the clash of weapons when they collided, and the labored breathing of the two men as they fought to the death. There was no shouting, no swearing, and no threats being thrown around. That energy was needed elsewhere as each man struggled to be the victor.

Trying to plant his feet for better balance, the sergeant lost his footing and slipped on the wet, soggy ground, momentarily losing control of his rifle. Jackson's reaction was immediate. Quickly pushing the sergeant's rifle aside, the beanpole thrust his knife deep into his enemy's chest. A soft moan and a rush of escaping air were the only sounds the sergeant made as he fell to the ground. Quickly withdrawing his knife, Jackson thrust it into the man's heart, killing him before he could shout out.

The small battle was over, but it left Jackson shaking from the exertion and the rush of adrenaline. Turning north, he headed back to the tree he had leaned his rifle up against.

~ ~ ~

Private Jackson's quiet movement through the woods was akin to a barely discernible shadow sifting through the darkness. The rain was still coming down hard and the night was still black as pitch where he was walking. Now that he was alone again, he felt naked without his carbine, a situation he was trying to remedy as quickly as possible. He was still carrying his knife in his right hand, the only weapon he had available. Without warning, another German loomed in front of him, surprising both men. The Arizona scout was the first to react.

Jackson made the motion of throwing something at his enemy with his left hand, which in turn, caused the man to duck instinctively and momentarily lower his rifle. Reacting quickly, Jackson kicked at the man's rifle, knocking it out of his hands. Then he launched himself at the soldier. The struggle didn't last very long, only a few seconds, but it was long enough for the man to scream for help, realizing he was about to die. His scream was quickly cut off when Jackson's knife entered his heart, but the scream had caught the attention of the man's comrades.

Immediately, the silence of the woods was broken by the sound of gunfire. All the shots were directed in the vicinity of where the Germans heard one of their own screaming. Jackson was lucky that he was on the ground at the time the Germans fired. Had he been standing, he would have surely been hit. He didn't wait around, though. Knowing that the Germans were converging on where they thought the screams had come from, Jackson started crawling east as quickly and as quietly as he could.

The little scout didn't get very far before two Germans found their dead comrade. Looking around, Jackson found the darkest shadow and headed straight for it, hoping to lose himself in it. Now, he had to wait. To make any movement would only get him killed.

The Germans searched for Jackson for over thirty minutes before they decided that he was no longer in the area. What they didn't know was that they had stood within three feet of their prey at least a dozen times. Thinking that Jackson was heading north, back in the direction of their camp, the enemy moved north, searching for the elusive scout. After that move, there were no more Germans between Jackson and the château.

Jackson spent about forty minutes searching for his carbine, but he was still without his helmet. It wasn't where he left it when he went back for it. All he could do was shake his head and smile at the thought, *Sergeant Brooks is gonna kill me for losing my helmet.*

After retrieving his carbine, he waited in the shadows, spending a couple of minutes to listen, making sure that the Germans were indeed moving north before he began heading south towards the château. Once again, he was moving quietly through the trees, invisible, silently gliding through the woods like a wraith.

Chapter 23

Lemons spoke up first. "I'll go after him, Sarge."

"I'll go with you, Sam," said Sims.

Then Hanky spoke up. "Hell, we'll all go with you!" The entire squad was volunteering to go find Jackson, but Sergeant Brooks still wasn't convinced enough to agree. "This is mutiny you know. You can all be shot or hung for this, so you better think long and hard before you make this decision."

Corporal Sims chuckled and said, "Hell. Mutiny only happens in the Navy, Al. Don't you know that?"

Brooks placed his hand on Corporal Sims' shoulder before he cocked his head and said, "No, Alex, you're wrong. Mutiny isn't confined to only the Navy. They just have a richer history of it. It's used by all branches of the military, and the punishment is the same. Make up your minds, gentlemen."

"Let us find Jackson first," said Sharps. "Then you can shoot us or hang us afterwards."

Again, he looked at his men, but they weren't backing down. He could see it in their eyes. *If I give them a direct order, they will follow it, but I'll probably lose their trust and respect. Damn, beanpole. Where are you, boy*? Sighing deeply, he finally gave in. "If you promise to let me hang you *and* shoot you after we find Jackson, then I'll agree."

"Okay, Sarge. Let's go get him."

"Hold on a minute, Hanky. Do you even know where he is?"

No one said anything for a moment while they shuffled around trying to come up with an answer. Then, Hanky spoke up again. "He's that way, Sarge. Can I lead the charge?"

Sergeant Brooks gazed at Private Todd for a moment before he said, "What a cast of characters. White, you, Brown, and Hanky get the wounded heading north. I'll keep the rest of the squad with me to keep the Germans occupied for a few minutes. Then we'll head north and catch up with you. All right, gentlemen. Let's go."

The three men, along with the wounded started north. Sergeant Brooks, in the meantime, was to start a ruckus with the Germans, drawing them as far east as he could before he slipped past them and moved north to meet up with Private Hanky. What they didn't know was that Jackson had already arrived at the château and was scouting out the area, looking for an enemy that was currently chasing the rest of 1st squad.

~ ~ ~

"Baker, you stay with me. Private Sharps, you take two men and move to the right about thirty yards and don't bunch up. Alex, you take two men to the left about the same distance and wait for my command to open fire. Once the Krauts start firing back, be prepared to disengage and head east." He was about to say something else, but he was interrupted by the sudden crack of Jackson's carbine firing off in the distance. The shots sounded as though they were coming from the château.

Private Donald Sharps proudly wore the sleeve patch of the 5th Ranger Battalion. He had successfully stormed the beaches at Normandy where he received his first wound. He was a buck sergeant (just three stripes, no rocker) when he entered the field hospital. Right after he left the recovery tent, he received the news that his older brother Tap, with the 1st Ranger Battalion, had been killed in action in Italy, at a town called Cisterna. He took the news hard and proceeded to get drunk. An hour later, he lost his rank. He was demoted to private because he hit the wrong man. The fact that he had just found out that his brother had been killed in Italy didn't impress his superiors at all, so when he heard about the Special Tactical Force, he volunteered, taking Sergeant Lucas along with him.

Wow, will you look at this? thought Sharps. *I'm in command of a two-man squad about to deliberately attack a German force that outnumbers us almost 11 to 1.* He was smiling proudly. *Too bad I won't be able to tell anyone about it. Damn classified missions*! *Crap on the ground. That sucks*!

Private Sharps heard someone coming, and looked to his left, watching while Baker approached his position. Baker's whisper was short. "Count to sixty when you hear us fire and then open up. Not before." Baker quickly turned around and headed back to his position. When he arrived there, he noticed that Sergeant Brooks was smiling. He was about to say something to his platoon sergeant, but he was interrupted when Corporal Sims and his two men opened fire on the advancing enemy. Seconds later, Brooks and Baker opened up, and then the Germans cut loose, firing back at their attackers.

At first, only sporadic firing erupted from the Germans, but less than a minute later, their shooting intensified until everyone involved was laying down a withering fire, chopping up all kinds of vegetation, and sending different bits of debris flying in all directions. After the count of sixty, Private Sharps and his two men started firing, hitting the Germans in their left flank and disrupting their fire for a few seconds, just long enough for Brooks and Baker to scamper to their next position.

Although the Americans were hoping to kill some Germans, they weren't really trying all that hard because it was too dark to see much of anything. The squad's goal was to entice the Germans to keep coming until it was time to slip away to the north and meet up with Hanky.

The Americans continued firing at their enemy for another minute or so until Sergeant Brooks pulled out his forty-five and fired three shots. A couple of seconds later, he fired three more times. His shooting was the signal for the Americans to stop firing and start crawling to the east.

The Germans took a couple of minutes to figure out that the Americans had stopped firing, and then another minute or so to get their own troops to cease fire. The German commanders didn't realize that the .45 going off was a signal to disperse. They were used to flares signaling a dispersal order.

Captain Konitz was a bit puzzled by the actions of his enemy. He was thinking that he had finally caught up to the rescuers of the French resistance leaders. Judging by their condition when he had left the tent, he surmised that the well bludgeoned Frenchmen were holding up their rescuers because of their injuries, and this little firefight was part of a plan to slow his troops down, giving the wounded resistance members more time make their escape.

After a short five-minute meeting with his squad leaders. Captain Konitz redeployed his men again and started moving east towards the last known enemy positions, knowing full well that their enemy would not be there.

Currently, Captain Konitz was hunting the two escaped prisoners in a dark, rain soaked forest, in miserable weather, and he was being hindered in his search by an unknown enemy. What he couldn't understand was why his adversary was heading east, deeper into German held territory. It didn't make any sense to the captain unless his enemy was trying to slip past them to the south. If his enemy tried to go north, they would run into the platoon he had put in position to counter that action.

The Germans found the shell casings left by the Americans, but Captain Konitz was still not sure of whom he was fighting. Some of the equipment the French resistance was using was from the Americans, so he could be chasing French resistance fighters. Or they could be Americans. If they were Americans, then how did they get so far behind German lines undetected? He wondered at the unexpected puzzle.

~ ~ ~

Sergeant Brooks stopped his men about one hundred yards from their last position and set up new ones. Again, they were set up the same way. Sergeant Sharps and his two men were on the right again, with Corporal Sims on the left.

Brooks had just heard the story concerning Donald Sharps and felt that he had been unjustly treated, so he appointed Private Donald Sharps as acting sergeant until they returned to headquarters. Once they got back, he was convinced that when Colonel Martin heard the story, he would make sure that Private Sharps got his stripes back. The man had done an outstanding job, and Sergeant Brooks was ready to go to war for him.

“Sarge,” whispered Corporal Sims. “I think the Krauts are trying to outflank me. There's something moving around on our left.” Brooks thought about it for a minute before he said, “Okay, Alex. Go get Avery and White and get back here pronto.

Baker, go get Sharps and get them back here now." A few minutes later, the men were moving north. Time to give the Germans the slip.

The rain started to let up a bit, but visibility was still poor. The squad had left a few presents for the approaching Germans, hoping to slow them down even more. The Germans, sensing that their foe was close, moved cautiously towards where they thought their attackers were waiting. The night was too dark for them to see the commo wire stretched between the trees, so they were in for a very rude awakening.

The Germans took about ten minutes to arrive at the American positions. They were moving forward in a loose skirmish line when the first of six grenades exploded. Sharps was right. The results of his plan did indeed slow the enemy down. Considerably. Not only did the Germans have to watch out for their enemy, they also had to look out for more unexpected surprises their enemy might have left behind.

Six Germans were dead and five others had been wounded because of the grenade booby traps. Sergeant Sharps had thought of the idea and it worked out really well. First squad was still in a bad situation, but thanks to Sergeant Sharps, they currently had a much better chance of escaping a much disrupted enemy.

~ ~ ~

Twenty minutes into their break, Sims tapped his platoon leader on the shoulder and whispered, "The Germans are still moving east. I think we're clear of them for now. What do you think, Al?"

Sergeant Brooks looked over at Corporal Sims and noticed the expression on his face. Looking around, he noticed the same expression was on everyone else's face, so he stood up, threw his Lucky Strike cigarette to the ground, and then stretched mightily. When he was finished stretching, he looked back at Corporal Sims and said, "All right, gentlemen. Let's go find our lost lambs and get the hell out of here.

"What about Jackson, Sarge? Shouldn't we find him first?"

"Let's grab Lemons, first. We'll have a much easier time locating Jackson with Sam helping out."

The sun was just starting to poke its head above the horizon when they stumbled upon Private Lemons. They were soaked to the skin, and although the temperature wasn't really all that cold, they were starting to shiver. “Hey, Sarge,” whispered Lemons. “We’re over here!”

The reunion was a happy one, but short-lived. “How did you know it was us and not the Germans?” asked Brooks. The question was a puzzler until he noticed the beanpole-like expression on Sam’s face. “You still smell like cow piss, Sarge, and the wind is blowing right at us.” Private Lemons immediately wrinkled his nose and clamped it shut with his fingers. “Damn, you, guys. The smell of that piss is burning my nose. Go take a shower.” The effort was extremely hard for the squad, but they did manage to contain their laughter to only an occasional snicker. All Sergeant Brooks could do was shake his head. *Damn, another beanpole*.

“I was hoping the rain would wash this crap off, but I guess it didn't. We better get Jackson back before the Krauts kill him, so we can kill him for his little idea when we get back to headquarters.” The comment had everyone quietly laughing.

“Private Lemons. Sergeant Sharps. Get us to the dirt road. Private Todd, pick two men to carry the Frenchmen.”

“Sergeant Brooks, we do not need help any more. We can now walk faster than you can carry us. We do not wish to be a burden on your men anymore.”

“Are you sure about that, Jean?”

“Yes, Sergeant Brooks. I am very sure.”

“Okay, gentlemen. You heard the man. Move out.”

“What about Jackson?” asked Sims. “Are we going to look for him?”

Brooks nodded and said, “As soon as we get across the road, I'll send Sam after him. The rest of us will head towards the château.”

Chapter 24

The squad was in the process of crossing the dirt road when shooting erupted. Their first thought was that the Germans had found Jackson and were trying to kill him, but when the firing continued to intensify, they realized the possibility that Jackson might not be involved at all. Everyone was scratching his head over the confusing situation. "Who's doing the shooting, Sarge?"

"I don't know, Hanky. It's all German from what I can tell," said Brooks. "Maybe Jackson has the Krauts killing each other."

"Didn't he pull that trick on the Germans in North Africa?" asked Private Todd.

Gazing at Todd, Sergeant Brooks looked at him strangely before he said slowly, "Yeah, Hanky. Right before we hit Beja."

Looking off into the distance, Private Todd muttered, "Sounds like he's doing it again, Sarge."

No one else said a word. They were all looking in the direction of the shooting and wondering.

Gathering his men together about a hundred yards west of the dirt road, Brooks turned to Private Lemons. "Sam, go get Jackson. We'll meet you by that old shed east of the château. Be careful, Private. Don't get caught."

Private Lemons gave Sergeant Brooks a two-fingered salute and then disappeared from view in less than a minute. Although the sun was up, visibility was still poor because of the intense cloud cover and the rain. To Sam, this new adventure was the ultimate test of his abilities and his skills. If he failed this test, the results could be deadly for him. Like Jackson, he had given up his M1 Garand for the much lighter M1 carbine.

Moving through the forest as silent as a wisp of wind, Sam continued to head east towards the battle that had just ended. He knew that trying to find Jackson in all this mess was going to be extremely difficult. Knowing Jackson as well as he did, he also knew that the scout would try to hide his tracks. This search was going to take an awful long time. Forty minutes into his jaunt, Sam finally reached the scene of the battle.

He spent the next twenty minutes looking over the area, hoping to find some kind of a clue that Jackson had been there. He found plenty of small arms casings from enemy weapons, but no sign of American shell casings. A slowly spreading smile appeared on his face. From what he had ascertained, all the indications pointed to a satisfying fact. The Germans had been killing each other instead of Jackson. His smile deepened.

Private Lemons quickly moved south and soon discovered the body of an enemy soldier that his comrades had missed. He also discovered the tracks of his friend, so he circled the area, looking for additional sign. After a more thorough search, he found that his friend had moved further south, away from the battle. Jackson was still alive and kicking.

Private Lemons continued to follow his friend’s trail and quickly realized that Jackson was heading back towards the château. Sam’s excitement grew. Ten minutes after he started trailing the beanpole, he heard voices. He couldn't understand who the voices belonged to, but he knew the squad was almost a mile away to the southwest, so he figured the voices were the enemy. Moving west and a little south, he was trying to circle around behind them and continue tracking his friend.

Sam managed to get around behind the Germans twenty minutes later and discovered that it was a small squad. They had a one-burner camp stove going and were brewing something over the small flame. The aroma from whatever it was they were preparing wasn't very appealing to Sam’s nose. *Damn. What the hell are they doing? Are they cooking their socks?* He wanted to take a closer look at what smelled like month-old dirty socks, so he moved nearer. He was crouching down behind a tree about twenty feet from the enemy squad when, out of nowhere, he had this overwhelming feeling of being watched.

Looking around, he was unable to locate the cause of his uneasiness, so he stayed where he was, waiting for the feeling to pass, but it didn't. Now he was beginning to worry. Ever so carefully, he slowly and cautiously moved south, away from the Germans. He was about twenty or thirty yards south of the enemy squad when he decided to stop. The uneasiness just wouldn't leave him alone. He continued looking around, searching for whatever was bothering him, but he was unable to determine what was tormenting him.

He knew something was out there, but he couldn't figure out what it was, so he decided to move back further south, about another thirty yards or so. He could still hear the enemy talking, and was wondering why they were talking so loud. They were acting as if they were on a camping trip, not fighting a war.

Sam found a comfortable spot underneath an oak tree and listened for sounds that might indicate what was bothering him. Even as far away from the enemy as he was, he could still faintly hear them, but he couldn't distinguish any words.

Concentrating on the sounds of nature, he was trying to hear the unmistakable, unnatural sound that nature didn't make. He started cataloging in his mind the sounds he was hearing, like the sound the trees made when a slight breeze whistled through the branches and leaves. Or the noise the little rodents made as they scurried along the ground in their search for food or shelter. The steady plop, plop, plop of the raindrops as they hit the leaves on the ground, or the sounds the birds made when they flittered away from danger. Instantly, Sam froze. His sudden revelation was like a hard slap to the face.

When they flittered away from danger. What danger? His thoughts were wildly racing around in his head. *What are the birds seeing that I'm not? Where is the danger coming from?* Private Lemons slowly withdrew his bayonet from its scabbard. Bad news would appear in great abundance if he started shooting this close to his enemy. Drawing out his bayonet, he hoped the weapon would be enough.

Facing where the German squad was located, Private Lemons heard a soft rustling noise. Turning slightly to his right to face some bushes, he watched a little field mouse dash out of its hiding place and run for a large clump of bushes about three feet to his left. Sam was squatting on the balls of his feet when he saw the rodent. Abrupt chills went down his back at the same time he felt the urgent need to turn even further to his right. With his bayonet leading the way, he was already swinging his right arm at what he felt the danger was, even before his body had turned to face that danger. The sound of the two blades coming together was unmistakably loud in the forest.

When the German squad heard the collision of steel striking steel, their talking ended instantly. Grabbing their weapons, they turned towards the sound they had just heard, and quickly spread out, advancing south towards the disturbance. Then they heard Private Lemons shouting at Jackson. "*YOU JERK*!"

Sam had forgotten where he was because of the smile on beanpole's face. Just like two brothers arguing in the front yard, they both forgot they were in a war, but the unmistakable, clothe-ripping sound of an MG 42 firing and the bullets slashing at the foliage around them, reminded them both of where they were. Sam immediately dove at Jackson and tackled him to the ground just seconds before the searching machine gun fire cut into the tree they were standing beside.

The two Americans didn't hang around to discuss their situation. Immediately, they started crawling as quickly as they could, trying to outflank the Germans so they could get away, even while enemy bullets were ripping the foliage and the smaller trees apart, raining debris down on them.

Sam was agitated at Jackson more than just a little bit, and his expression drove that point home. Beanpole, on the other hand, was struggling greatly not to laugh at the expression on his friend's face, even with the bullets flying all around them, just barely missing them by inches. He felt that he had just pulled the best practical joke on Sam that he had ever done to this date. He could tell that Sam was still perturbed at him because he could still hear him muttering over and over again. "You jerk. You're a damn jerk. You know that, don't you? You shithead." Jackson, though, wasn't the only one who heard Sam talking.

To Jackson, it was a time of celebration, a moment to savor. As much as he wanted to stand up and shout, to let the world know what he had done to Sam, the bullets zinging overhead told him that now was not the time.

The two scouts heard the Germans shouting to each other and decided to change direction and head north. The enemy had also changed direction and was heading southeast, right for the disturbance, and still firing their weapons as they advanced.

The sudden change of direction by the two scouts quickly put them out of the direct line of their enemy's fire, which finally gave the two men a chance to circle around and get behind the Germans. After a few minutes of quiet scampering, the two scouts were somewhat behind their enemy and crouching down, waiting for the last of them to pass by completely. The Germans had quit firing, but they were still looking for the two Americans.

The two men could hear the enemy squad sloshing through the trees in front of them. While they were listening to the Germans trudging through the rain soaked, terrain, Jackson's eyes widened before he turned towards Sam and said, "If we can take out that MG 42, then the rest of those goons will be easier to kill. Without that machine gun, they only have their bolt-action rifles. We have these." Beanpole rattled his M1 carbine for effect. "You have any ammo? I'm empty."

After listening to Jackson explain his plan, Sam decided that he didn't like it and was ready to argue the point until Jackson raised his carbine to his shoulder as if to fire at the enemy. Fearing that Jackson was going to start shooting if he didn't comply, Sam handed the beanpole a fresh magazine without taking the time to think about what he was doing. Then he kicked at the ground after he realized that he had handed Jackson the only leverage he had to keep the Arizona scout under control. A magazine full of bullets.

Muttering to himself, Sam stood up and moved to where Jackson wanted him positioned. Within a few minutes, they were facing the backs of their enemy, about twenty yards behind them. With his right fist clinched, Jackson signaled, and Sam dropped to the ground.

His mouth dry, Jackson took a bead on the man carrying the MG42. Taking a deep breath, he slowly let it out while he squeezed the trigger. Before the sound of his first shot died out, he was firing on his second target, followed immediately by three more quick shots. In less than ten seconds, five Germans were knocked out of the fight. Then Sam opened up, killing three more, leaving only one man left alive. The last soldier started running back towards the château with Jackson hard on his heels. Battle had erupted so fast that the enemy didn't have time to react. Not one shot was fired by any of them.

Still sitting where he had been, Sam was shocked at the absolute deadliness of their ambush. He had no idea that Jackson's plan would work as well as it did. An entire German squad had just been wiped out, except for one man. Private Lemons had no doubt that Jackson would take care of him, and he was right.

Sam had barely moved about thirty yards south of his previous position when he saw Jackson trotting towards him. "Sam, let's go find Sergeant Brooks. There's a whole platoon of goons heading towards us from the château."

That was all Sam needed to hear. Within seconds, the two Americans were running towards Sergeant Brooks and the rest of the squad. What they didn't know was the German platoon at the château was under orders to hold the château, not to go chasing after anybody.

Captain Konitz and Sergeant Brooks both heard the two skirmishes and wondered what was happening. There was nothing Sergeant Brooks could do except pray that his two scouts weren't involved, but Captain Konitz could, and did, do something.

Two truckloads of enemy soldiers and one halftrack drove south on the dirt road towards the château. Unknowingly, they reached the location where Jackson and Lemons were about to cross and quickly squealed to a stop. The two Americans were still in the trees about twenty yards from the dirt road when the vehicles came to a halt. Surprised, Jackson looked at Sam and asked, "How did they know we were here, Sam?"

Before Sam could answer Jackson's question, they had another surprise. Ten SS soldiers came pouring out of the rear of the halftrack and lined up on the driver's side, staring straight at where Sam and Jackson were hiding. The two men froze where they were, crouching behind a large tree and hoping they hadn't been seen.

The SS troops stood by the halftrack for a couple of minutes until a shouted order started them moving into the trees, west of the dirt road, about 300 yards southeast of where 1st squad was waiting for Jackson and Lemons to return. The time was 0900 hours, and the rain was still coming down hard.

A couple of minutes after the SS troops entered the woods, the halftrack moved forward another twenty yards down the dirt lane before it pulled into the trees, off the road. Five Germans climbed out of the back of one of the trucks and followed the halftrack into the trees. "Look, Sam," said Jackson. "They must be there to guard the vehicles."

The two remaining trucks turned around and headed south down the road towards the château and disappeared into the distance. Jackson looked at Lemons, and there was a big grin on Arizona scout's face. Immediately, Sam whispered harshly at Jackson. "Oh, no you don't," but Jackson was already moving through the trees towards the halftrack and the unsuspecting enemy.

"No, Tim. You're going to get us killed. We need to get back to the squad, NOW."

"Ssh," whispered Jackson. "They'll hear you, Sam."

Six Germans were standing beside the halftrack now that the driver had gotten out of the vehicle. The two scouts were almost even with the halftrack and the six men, who were all standing on the driver's side of the halftrack, talking back and forth.

"Sam," whispered Jackson. "Give me a clip. I'm out of ammo."

Smiling, Private Lemons shook his head and said, "No, Tim. Not gonna happen. Not this time."

Jackson grabbed Sam's shirtsleeve and pulled him deeper into the woods. "Sam, they're going after the guys. We need to get those troops to head back this way. The distraction will buy us more time to find the squad and head back to our lines. The only way we can do that is to start a ruckus here, so that the Germans will be forced to come back and help their friends. Come on Sam. You know I'm right."

Shaking his head, Lemons took a deep breath and slowly let it out before he said, "What's game plan this time? I hope it doesn't involve running around naked." Jackson patted his friend on the shoulder and then explained his idea, but instead of the argument he had expected from Sam, he was surprised by the unexpected response. "Here, this ought to make you happy."

Smiling, Jackson said, "Thanks for the magazines. Give me a few minutes to get across the road. When you hear me open up, kill whatever I miss."

The plan was a simple one. Jackson was to come up behind the track on the west side of the road and start shooting. His shooting would force the Germans to stay on the driver's side of the halftrack where Sam would have them as helpless as a tied-up Turkey.

Jackson was in position about ten minutes after the SS troops had departed their halftrack and entered the woods. Signaling to Sam that he was ready, beanpole took aim and then let loose, firing rapidly at the talking enemy.

The Germans were still standing on the driver's side of the halftrack, towards the rear of the vehicle when Jackson started shooting. He had managed to kill two of them before they started moving towards the front of the halftrack, and out of his line of sight. Then Sam started shooting, and two more were dead. In a panic, the remaining two ran around to the passenger side of the halftrack only to run into Jackson's fire again, which ended the short little skirmish.

Quickly sliding under the vehicle, Jackson punched a couple of holes in the fuel tank and then waited for the fuel to leak all over the ground before he tossed a grenade under it and took off running. They ran about thirty feet before it exploded, sending a huge fireball high into the sky, followed by black oily smoke.

The shock from the exploding halftrack knocked both Americans to the ground, and the trees were peppered with pieces of the vehicle and the burning fuel, some of which landed on Jackson and caught his shirt on fire.

Quickly stripping off his burning shirt, Jackson beat it into the rain soaked ground, putting the fire out, but not before it had burned a basketball size hole in the back of his shirt and had blistered his back. Despite the recent, painful event, both men were grinning. As a result of the explosion, however, and despite their smiles, their ears were ringing, and it was hard to hear anything. After the shock of the explosion had worn off, they stood up and started running towards the squad as fast as they could, knowing that Hitler's SS were on their way back to their burning halftrack. The two men looked at each other and their grins were huge. "Notch up another victory for the Indians," said Lemons. "Crap on the ground. We're good!"

Chapter 25

The men of 1st squad kept looking at their platoon sergeant and hoping he would give the order to go searching for Jackson, but they knew that nothing would happen until Brooks was absolutely convinced of the need. He had too much confidence in Jackson's abilities to let his men railroad him into making a hasty decision that might get someone, or all of them killed.

Less than fifteen minutes after the Germans stopped firing, the men of 1st squad heard the crack of two M1 carbines firing rapidly for about twenty or thirty seconds and then silence. The sudden firing caused Brooks to start worrying all over again. Not only did he have Jackson and Lemons to worry about, he was also hearing vehicles heading south along the dirt road, and they were getting closer.

Great, thought Brooks. *They're coming after us again.* Twenty minutes passed before the squad heard the carbines speak again, followed a couple of minutes later by a huge explosion that immediately had the entire squad surrounding Sergeant Brooks and asking him all kinds of questions that he had no answers to. The main question was where were their two scouts, and who caused the explosion?

Sometime around mid-afternoon the rain stopped. The squad was still trying to figure out what had just happened when they heard the carbines open up again. This time the shots were much closer. The return fire from the Germans was sporadic because their targets were so elusive and hard to pin-down.

"Tim! We're too far north."

Jackson shook his head and said, "No, we're not, Sam. We're right where we need to be."

"Yes, we are," said Private Lemons. "The squad is due south of us, so we need to head south."

"No, Sam. We need to draw these goons as far away from the squad as we can. How much ammo do you have left?

"I have four magazines plus what's left in my carbine."

"Good. Give me two, I'm almost out."

Sam handed Jackson the two magazines he asked for and then asked, "What do we do now?"

"We go hunting."

Private Lemons let out a groan. "Okay, Tim. What do you have in mind this time?"

A few minutes later, the two scouts split up. Jackson stayed where he was while Sam moved into position about thirty yards south of his previous spot. Jackson could barely see Lemons and almost missed the signal Sam sent him when he was in position, waiting and ready. Taking a deep breath, Jackson fired a couple shots, hoping to lure the Germans in his direction, and his idea worked.

The German squad consisted of twelve men, and they were spread out in a skirmish line. Visibility was still poor because of the rain-induced haze, which gave the forest an unnatural appearance.

The Germans were closing in on Jackson's position, but they were unaware of where he was, and how close they were to him.

Jackson could see his enemy moving towards him, but from a distance of about forty yards, they were nothing more than dark, vague silhouettes moving through the trees.

The positions of the two scouts were currently about two hundred yards north of where the rest of 1st squad was waiting. The men were still gathered around Sergeant Brooks, and still asking questions. Pulling at his ear, Sergeant Brooks looked at his men for a moment before he nodded and said, "Okay, gentlemen, you win. Pack it up, we're moving out."

"Where are we going?" asked Baker.

Smiling, Brooks turned and said, "We're gonna find our two scouts, and then we're getting the hell out of here. Any more questions?"

Every man in the squad was thinking the same thing. It was about time. No more than a minute went by before they were moving out, heading north towards the sounds of the shooting. "Baker, you and Sergeant Sharps get out front and don't get shot. Flankers move out. Twenty yards, gentlemen. Keep us in sight.

First squad was currently about one hundred yards north of where they were when they heard Jackson fire the two shots. Corporal Sims whispered to Brooks. “Those shots were pretty damn close.”

“Yes, they were,” replied Brooks. Before he could send Corporal Sims after Baker and Sharps, PFC Baker appeared out of the mist.

“Sergeant Sharps thinks that Sam and beanpole are just up ahead of us. Also, there's a German patrol, about sixty yards from our two o'clock.”

Sergeant Brooks immediately signaled for his flankers to come in and then looked at Baker. “Where's Sergeant Sharps now?”

“He's moving east, trying to re-locate that Kraut patrol,” replied Baker.

“Okay, gentlemen. Let’s go rescue our scouts.”

Before departing, Brooks turned to the two Frenchmen and whispered, “Jean, you and your friend stay here with Private Stone. Don’t move from this spot. We’ll come back to get you.

“We can help you, Sergeant Brooks. Give us a gun, and we'll help you kill Germans.”

“No, Jean. My orders are to bring you back to headquarters alive, and that's exactly what I'm going to do. You and your friend just sit tight and don't move. We’ll be right back.” Then Brooks turned back to the squad. “Alex, take five men and hit the Germans from their right. I'll take the rest of the men and come up behind them. Don't do anything until you hear us firing, then open up with everything. And watch out you don't shoot one of us.”

Corporal Sims nodded and said, “I'll do my best, Al, but I won't give you any guarantees. In all this crap, I might mistake you for the enemy.”

Sergeant Brooks chuckled before he replied. “Thanks for the warning, Corporal. I’ll put on some more piss-perfume and approach downwind so you’ll mistake me for a lowly cow, strolling around in such fine weather.”

~ ~ ~

Jackson could see his enemy clearly. Cautiously he moved to the east, but he didn't go very far. He only moved about forty or fifty feet and then stopped. From where he was he was in a much better position to do a lot of damage to the enemy. *I hope Sam is ready*. Beanpole took a deep breath and slowly let it out while gently squeezing the trigger until the first shot sounded. Immediately following, he fired at his next three targets as rapidly as he could and noticed that two of them were definitely hit. He wasn't sure about his third target. Before he could fire another shot, however, he was forced to duck behind a tree from the hail of enemy bullets coming his way. Then Sam started shooting.

Within seconds, the enemy fire had split and some of it was shifted towards Sam, causing him to also duck behind a tree. The Germans were being hit from two different directions, and because of the surprise attack, they were confused. The enemy's inexperience, along with the sudden emergence of 1st squad, coming up behind them, made the outcome inevitable. In the meantime, just before the shooting started, Corporal Sims ran into Sergeant Sharps, and the sergeant was smiling. "You looking for something, Corporal?"

Corporal Sims immediately stopped in his tracks and stared at a three o'clock shadow, ready to dump a load. The abruptness of the voice immediately embedded a nauseating fear in the pit of his stomach. Then the shadow turned into a six-foot-one, U.S. Army Ranger, who was waiting for the corporal to stop swallowing long enough to answer back. After the shock of his surprise had dissipated somewhat, the corporal said, "Were supposed to wait here until Sergeant Brooks opens the ball, and then we hit the Krauts in the flank."

That was as far as the explanation went because Jackson had opened fire on the enemy. The Germans, Corporal Sims, and Sergeant Brooks were all taken by surprise when beanpole started shooting.

Sergeant Brooks felt a tug on his left shoulder followed by an intense burning sensation. He looked at his left shoulder and blood began to seep through his shirtsleeve, at the point of the shoulder. Amazed, he realized he'd just been hit.

Whoever was in front of the Germans had just shot him. He didn't slow down for even a second. Brooks hit the ground so fast that the dust didn't have time to rise after the impact. Then he heard another carbine opened up, and instantly, the only shooting he heard was coming from the Germans. After a short hesitation, he ordered his men to their feet and they advanced towards the shooting.

Jackson was still hugging the tree when he heard the deep throaty cough of a Thompson submachine gun open up on his left. Only two men in the squad carried a Thompson and one of them was dead. Now, the Germans were getting hit from just about every side, especially when Corporal Sims and his men entered the fray.

In less than a minute, the little skirmish was over, but the Americans continued to fire until everyone heard the cease-fire order. A breath-holding silence immediately followed and settled over the battlefield like a blanket. Then, determined faces peered cautiously around trees, searching for the enemy until they were convinced that none were left alive. Only smiles materialize out of the misty weather to greet the Americans.

After the firing had stopped, Jackson stood up and then Lemons. Both men recognized the sound of the Thompson firing and knew that the Rangers had come to their rescue, all one of them. All the men converged to where the German position was and witnessed just how deadly their attack had been. The Germans had been cut to pieces. The time had come to pick up the three walking wounded and get the hell out of Dodge.

"Hey, Sarge," shouted Jackson. "I hear more Germans coming towards us. We'd better get out of here fast."

Sergeant Brooks didn't need to be told twice. He could hear the Germans shouting at each other from somewhere to the north and knew he only had a few minutes' head start. "Let's go, people. The Krauts will be dead on our tails if we don't get out of here now. Sam, watch our rear. When you hear me signal, catch up. All right, people, move out."

Sergeant Brooks was walking with Private Jackson on their way to pick up the walking wounded. “Where were you when the shooting started?”

“I was north of the Germans and Sam was on their left. Why? What’s wrong?”

Sergeant Brooks looked down at beanpole, as stern-faced as he could manage without laughing. “Because, beanpole, whoever was facing the Germans, shot me in the shoulder.”

Jackson's expression and the paleness of his face caused Sergeant Brooks to start laughing.

Chapter 26

Since Patton's third Army broke out of the Saint Lo area, they had been on a rampage. The Germans were currently retreating all along their lines, heading east, back towards Germany. Most of the units retreating were just remnants of their former might, a power that had been decimated by the Allies during the opening stages of Operation Cobra. Forced to go on the defensive, the Germans were trying frantically to set up defensive positions on the east bank of Seine. The liberation of Paris not far behind.

Sergeant Brooks was now forced to sneak his men through these new German lines to reach the safety of Allied troops, and he was completely in the dark about the sudden turn of events.

"Sergeant Brooks? I'm sorry about your shoulder."

Patting his scout on the shoulder, Brooks looked down at Jackson and said, "It's all right, beanpole. My shoulder hurts only when I use it." This comment didn't make Jackson feel any better, despite the fact that Brooks was trying to joke around with him.

Alfred Brooks had a good sense of humor, but when he tried to crack a joke or joke around, most of the time, he was like a fish out of water. Elephants stood a better chance at learning ballet.

~ ~ ~

Private Lemons finally made it back from his scouting adventure sometime around 0330 hours. He brought back some entertaining news.

"What did you find out, Sam?" asked Brooks, who was completely unaware of Private Lemons' intentions.

Sam's expression was neutral when he winked at beanpole and he said, "It's dark this morning, and the ground is soaking wet. Other than that, sunrise is about four hours away."

Crap on the ground. Another damn beanpole. "That's an interesting report, Sam," said Brooks. "Any news on the enemy?"

Sam's expression was still neutral, despite the snickers. "Nope. The Germans behind us have called it quits. From what I've noticed, they have no idea where we disappeared to. Other than being behind German lines, I have no clue as to where the enemy is at this time."

Not another word followed. Sergeant Brooks stared at Lemons for a moment or two while he pulled at his ear. Then he said, "What a breath taking report, Private. Very enlightening. We'll be leaving in a couple of hours, so get some rest, Sam. I think you're going brain-dead."

~ ~ ~

The squad was tired. Very tired. So was Sergeant Brooks. Instead of leaving an hour before sunrise, he didn't wake up until the sunlight hit him directly in the eyes an hour *after* the sun had risen. And the entire squad heard how angry their platoon sergeant was because of his muttered words. Then Brooks winked at beanpole and said, "I guess for over sleeping I'll have to assign myself latrine duty for the next month."

"That was good, Sarge," said Jackson. "You're voice wasn't so monotone this time."

First squad was ready to move south. They were listening to the enemy vehicles, still moving up and down the road when the bottom dropped out of the peaceful day. Somebody had opened the doors of sudden hell, and it was loud. The sound of violent death was the unmistakable stutter of Browning, fifty caliber machine guns, and their firing brought the squad to an abrupt halt. They were all looking west.

Hearing the bark and roar of the big fifty's meant that an army of Americans was only a short distance away from where Brooks and his men were standing. The men were dumbfounded at the closeness of the shooting. What started out with only a few machine guns firing, quickly blossomed into the noise of a full-scale battle. The sharp crack of the large caliber tank guns resounded loudly in the still morning air, mixed-in with the unmistakable sound of the 20mm anti-aircraft guns that the Germans also used against infantry. They were infantry shredders as nasty as the big .50 cal.

While the infantry hunted down and destroyed the anti-tank guns, the Shermans engaged what armor the under strength German battalion had on hand: four Wirbelwind, anti-aircraft tanks mounting a quad, 20mm gun system, and six Pz III tanks. The Wirbelwinds were very effective against infantry. Against Shermans, these lightly armored vehicles didn't stand a chance.

Sergeant Brooks, however, wasn't aware of these happenings. His only concern was that a battle was slowly moving east, right towards him and his men. Jackson had estimated German troop strength at around 200 men, but his estimate was wrong. There was over 300 Germans in the forest west of the road. Brooks was in a quandary. With the Germans retreating right at him, he had to figure out which direction he was going to take in order to keep from getting shot up by both sides. The explosions from the mortar rounds, the tank rounds, and bazooka fire was extremely thunderous, and added to this thunderous sound was the snap-crackling of small arms fire from both sides.

Although the Germans held a slight advantage due to cover and concealment, the superior firepower of the Americans was slowly but steadily pushing the enemy east. Forty minutes into the battle, American infantry were engaging the bunkers Jackson had previously run across. Although the forest was too dense for armored movement, the M9 bazookas and satchel charges were destroying the bunkers just as well.

The under strength German Battalion was stretched out from north to south for over 1,200 yards. Without their armor and anti-tank guns to help support their defense, they were slowly but steadily losing the battle. Uncle Sam's infantry was moving through the forest, while the armored units moved south down the canopied road, trying desperately to cut off the retreating Germans.

When the battle started, Sergeant Brooks had decided to head north, but his squad didn't like that decision. Although they followed his orders, they made it known to him that they didn't like running from a fight. After walking another fifty or sixty yards, Sergeant Brooks decided he didn't like leaving a fight either, so he turned his men around and they headed towards the shooting.

When the squad reached the east shoulder of the road, they stopped, and Brooks deployed his men. Covering the lane, they waited for the enemy to appear. Jackson, in the meantime, had moved north, hoping to see the American units coming south down the road. When he spotted a Greyhound armored car, followed by two Sherman tanks heading his way, he immediately put the definition of excited to shame.

Immediate firing erupted where the squad was deployed, but by the time Jackson got back to his friends, the little firefight was over. There were six Germans lying dead on the road, and one of them was carrying a panzerschreck, a very deadly anti-tank weapon.

The armored car and the two Shermans pulled up just short of the dead and came to a stop. A couple of minutes later two more armored cars and four Sherman tanks passed by the other three vehicles stopped on the side of the road, and continued to head south. They had only moved about forty or fifty yards south of the squad when they started firing into the woods. The pointblank shooting procured the desired results, and a dazed and battered group of German soldiers cautiously filtered out of the trees and onto the road with their hands in the air. The immediate enemy was surrendering. Two hours and thirty minutes after the battle began, it ended. Well over 200 Germans had surrendered to the American force.

The defeated troops were rounded up and moved onto the road where they were searched and formed up into columns with their hands on top of their heads. In the meantime, Sergeant Brooks and his men had emerged from their positions on the east side of the road and were happily talking to the newly arriving GI's.

Hundreds of American, government-issues were now crossing the road and continuing east through the trees with the Allied armored vehicles following the road to the south. Nobody in the squad was prepared to believe that their mission had finally ended. That fact hadn't sunk in yet, but what was even more surprising and exciting for the squad to see was the American army this far south and east of St. Lo. An almost overwhelming sight to behold.

Another unexpected surprise was the arrival of a colonel who was sent to debrief Sergeant Brooks and his men. However, this debriefing turned out to be a wasted effort for the colonel. First of all, the colonel had never heard of the Special Tactical Force. As much as he tried to get that information from Sergeant Brooks, he was stymied every time because the sergeant refused to answer his questions. This refusal, of course, agitated the colonel more than just a little a bit. He was not used to a sergeant first class refusing to answer his questions, so steam began to trickle out of his ears and nose. Nothing thick, just little tendrils, angrily rising into the sky.

This Sergeant First Class Brooks even went so far as to tell the colonel that he needed to get in touch with a Colonel Martin or Major Thomas at the Special Tactical Force headquarters. "What the devil is a Special Tactical Force? How do I get in touch with this Colonel Martin?" the colonel kept asking.

Sergeant First Class Alfred Brooks continued to answer the colonel with a smile on his face. "That information, sir," he said repeatedly, "is classified."

The colonel stared at Sergeant First Class Alfred Brooks for another minute, then shook his head, and muttered his disgust. Heading for his jeep, he looked over his shoulder and shouted back at a smiling warrior. "You need to take a shower. You smell like cow piss."

Still smelling, Sergeant First Class Alfred Brooks just smiled, nodded, and waved...goodbye.

By the middle of September, the Allies had taken Antwerp, liberated most of Belgium, Luxembourg, and almost all of France. The only reason the Allies didn't head straight into Germany was that they ran out of fuel and were forced to halt. Because almost all of Europe west of Germany had been liberated, Sergeant Brooks and all those in the Special Tactical

Force, including Colonel Martin, Major Thomas, and Captain Shane were now out of a job for the moment.

Sometime around the first week in November, 1st squad, 1st platoon, Baker Company was on its way north to meet up with 5th Battalion somewhere near Luxembourg. With winter just around the corner, the Allies prepared to weather the cold until spring arrived and the assault on Germany could begin in earnest.

Chapter 27

At dawn, on the 14th of December, 1944, an American squad was sent east through the Ardennes Forest on a recon foray behind German lines. One day out, and one day back. The squad chosen for this mission was 1st squad, 1st platoon, Baker Company. They were given this assignment because of their many experiences with similar situations.

"What's up, Al?"

Sergeant Brooks was wearing a somewhat disgusted expression on his face when he replied. "Battalion seems to think the Krauts are up to something, so Major Thomas has ordered us to go out and find the ghosts everyone keeps seeing in the fog. We're to report back by the 16th. Form up the squad, Alex. We're about to earn our pay."

Now, a day and a half later, 1st squad was about five miles east of battalion headquarters. *It's cold, wet, and I'm miserable. Damn! What happened to the desert?* Without a doubt, Sergeant Brooks was not at all happy with his present situation. The snow had been falling off and on for two days in a row, and no one in the squad could remember anymore what it felt like to be warm and dry. Beanpole wasn't smiling either. No one was. The temperature was just too damn cold to move any facial muscles. Something else that had Sergeant Brooks equally disgusted was the strong hints the clouds were showing. *More snow again, and soon. Great. Just what we need, more damn snow!*

First squad had been out on patrol in the Ardennes Forest since the 14th of December. Walking through the Ardennes was exhausting. The men's exertions left thick clouds of white breath streaming back each time they exhaled, like steam coming out of a locomotive's pressure release stack. In some places, they struggled through knee-deep snow that turned their pant-legs into portable freezers. Trudging through the Ardennes in zero-degree weather was no fun at all, and their feet let them know about it every painful step they took.

On their second day, the day they were to head back to report their findings, the squad was still out and about and still looking for ghosts. Around 1500 hours, Corporal Sims quietly emerged from the sifting snow and shadows, looking around for something. Finally spotting what he was searching for, he immediately set a course for his platoon sergeant.

Sergeant Brooks was squatting down with his butt resting on his right heel, waiting for Sims' report. "Al, I think there's something out there. I believe I heard someone banging on steel."

Hesitating for a moment, Sergeant Brooks looked up at Corporal Sims and said, "Alex, headquarters has you spooked. Look around. What do you see? Nothing. You see nothing but snow, trees, and us. It's empty. Listen? Do you hear that? All you hear is silence. Corporal Sims, you remind me of my old grandmother."

Carefully, Brooks took one last look around before he stood up. "Okay, Grandma, show me what you heard."

Slowly, cautiously, the squad moved east again. The whole situation was spooky. The absolute stillness of the forest and the fact they were now behind German lines put everyone on edge. Focused, ready, and alert, the men continued to move east despite their uneasiness. About twenty minutes into their trek, Sergeant Brooks heard a sound and immediately stopped to listen, waiting for the noise to re-occur. What he had heard was definitely metal banging on steel.

"Corporal Sims," ordered Brooks. "Take Avery and Todd with you and try to slip around to the right. Watch out for observation posts and scouts. Find out what's banging around. I think we might have found the Major's ghosts."

Sergeant Brooks watched his three men silently disappear into the sifting snow and shadows. *Well, now. Maybe Major Thomas is right. Maybe there is something going on.* His abrupt change of thought disturbed him. *SHAEF thinks the Germans are finished, and they're just digging in for the winter.*

Without warning, a cold knot of fear grabbed at his stomach. Startled, and taken aback by his previous observation, Brooks cast a more thoughtful look at the weather conditions, and another, even more intriguing notion immediately followed the last one. *What if the Germans are not digging in*? *What if they have something else in mind*?

Trudging through the trees in the snow, crouched over, was hard on the back, but the men had no choice. If they were spotted by the Germans, they were dead men. Cautiously, they crept closer until they crested a small rise.

~ ~ ~

Major Jake Thomas, formerly the executive officer of the disbanded Special Tactical Force, was anxiously pacing the floor at 5th Battalion HQ, his new command. He had a worried expression on his face when he asked, "Jack, am I getting spooked or just getting old? Why do I feel like something terrible is about to happen?"

"I don't know, sir," replied Captain Shane, the major's executive officer. "It seems kind of quiet to me. What makes you think something's up, sir?"

"I don't know. I can't explain it. Just a feeling I have."

~ ~ ~

Lying on his belly, Corporal Sims was staring at a scene that had him deeply concerned. "Look at all that damn, armor. Where'd the Germans come up with this many tanks? Hanky, go get Sergeant Brooks. I'm sure he'll want to see this. Be careful. Don't let anybody spot you."

Crawling back deeper into the trees, Private Todd circled around to where Sergeant Brooks was waiting. Upon arriving, he whispered his report. "The Germans have a large concentration of tanks and infantry just over that rise. All kinds. Tigers, Mark lV's. Looks to me like they're gearing up for something we're not going to like, Sarge. Lots of armor and infantry. Sims and Avery are still watching up ahead."

Pausing for only a second, Brooks nodded to Todd and said, "Show me." Then he turned to another of his men, "Corporal Baker, take Jackson and Lemons around to the left and see what you can find out. Be careful. If the Germans have something planned, they'll have people out hunting for people like us."

~ ~ ~

Lying just below the crest of a tree covered slope, Brooks gazed across the body of a dead German scout, and a chill that had nothing to do with the cold went down his back. After a sudden shudder, he dropped further below the crest before he turned to his men and said, "We'll keep an eye on the Krauts until the sun goes down. When it's dark enough we'll head back. I don't like the looks of this, Alex. Get an armor count."

After his men reported their findings, Sergeant Brooks had to see for himself. What he was staring at had him pulling hard on his ear. "Where in the world did the Germans come up with this many tanks? Are they planning a major attack?"

"I don't know," whispered Corporal Sims. "There is a bunch of them, though. With all this cloud cover, maybe they're thinking of trying something."

Letting out a deep sigh, Sergeant Brooks continued to stare at the enemy tanks for a moment before he turned and said, "You just keep on being that old lady, Alex. I like that. Good nose."

~ ~ ~

First squad was still moving west two hours after leaving their hillside perch behind. Concerned over what he had witnessed, Brooks was deep in thought, wondering about the intel he and his men had gathered. *Shit. The Krauts look like they're about to hit us hard. SS mixed with Wehrmacht troops? They're not forming up just to stand around in the snow. Not those guys. They're up to something*! Not feeling good about the situation, he studied his surroundings and the weather conditions more intensely while he and his men continued trudging westward. His next thought had him muttering to himself, somewhat disgusted, and pulling hard on his ear. "I sure hope Division takes this intel seriously. G-2 will probably write the report off as another ghost story. Those bastards can't get anything right."

Major Thomas was pacing the floor, waiting for Sergeant Brooks and his men to return. The rumblings he kept hearing off in the distance had him concerned, so he cranked up his field-phone to let Division know what was going on in his sector. "General, if the Germans are well below strength, then why is there so much vehicular noise coming from behind their lines? Have you stood outside and listened? It appears our under-strength enemy is not so under-strength. Just go outside and listen, sir."

"Major, the Germans are running their vehicles back and forth across their lines to give us the impression they are stronger than they actually are. Relax, Jake. The Germans won't be coming anytime soon."

Division headquarters, despite higher command's reassurances, was also worried. They were asking questions of their own about what was going on east of Allied lines. SHAEF, however, was still pointing at all of the intelligence and estimated reports and standing firmly by their conclusions. "The idea is impossible. The Germans don't have the manpower or the fuel to mount any kind of an offensive. Especially in this weather. Hell, people, the Krauts barely have enough gas to keep their lanterns going. They have to scrounge around the countryside just to gather enough fuel for recon forays."

Sergeant Brooks was a bit angry and swore at himself for having to leave the radio back at battalion. The situation was definitely important enough to report immediately. *Damn. Where's the desert when I need it? What the hell is that rumbling*? A sudden chill hit him when he realized what the rumbling was. Yelling at his men, he shouted, "Run you, bastards. Head for that hill. The Krauts are coming right up our asses." The hill the squad was running for was about sixty yards away.

~ ~ ~

On the morning of December 16, 1944, Major Thomas, upon hearing the shrieks of artillery rounds, woke up from a sound sleep and looked up. *Why are the Germans shelling us at this time*? *Hell its 5:00 a.m. What's going on here*? Expecting only the usual ten-minute barrage, the bombardment continued on for fifteen minutes and then twenty minutes. After forty minutes, Major Thomas called in all of his commanders and issued a call to arms followed immediately by orders to prepare for a German attack.

Without warning, the phones started ringing off the hooks, and the radios were singing. All hell had broken loose.

Then silence commanded the switchboards as the phone lines were being cut by the artillery barrage. Reports had been coming in all along the entire Ardennes front. Hundreds of tanks and thousands of infantry were just pouring through the lines. The Germans were on the attack in strength, and the Americans were unprepared for it. The quiet Ardennes ghost front was not so quiet anymore.

First squad was still burrowed under the snow, behind the trees, on the west side of the hill. In shock, most were shaking their heads, stunned at the numbers that passed by them. "Jesus, Alex! Where did they all come from?"

Chapter 28

In his command bunker, located just west of a small German town, Major Thomas was just astounded at the ferocity of the barrage. It seemed that every artillery piece the enemy owned was being used. The barrage was amazing, and at the same time, devastating. Behind this wall of raining steel followed the German infantry, with their Tiger tanks, Panthers, and other assorted fighting vehicles, eager for battle.

From the west side of the hill, Sergeant Brooks watched while hundreds of German armored units and thousands of German infantry troops passed by him. He didn't need to remind his men about making any sudden moves or noises. They were trapped behind a Nazi juggernaut with no place to go. The only option they had at the moment was to wait until the enemy passed, and hope they could make it back to Allied lines without being killed. His next thought stopped him cold. *Allied lines? Where will our lines be after the Germans are through hitting us?*

At battalion HQ, Major Thomas was looking at his map of the area and was beginning to formulate some theories concerning the German attack. Before he could delve deeper into his ideas, he was interrupted from his thoughts. Captain Jack Shane, the battalion XO, came running into the command bunker shouting for everyone to evacuate. "The Germans have broken through our lines!" he warned, "They're about fifty yards from the command bunker with Tigers in the lead!"

Tiger tanks weighing in at over 50 tons had frontal armor of over 100mm thick. They could be knocked out only by hitting either the side or the rear. Three of these beasts were coming down the pike towards the command bunker, followed by scores of infantry in support.

The attack was brutal. Along with the chaos of battle, there were bright flashes and sharp, loud cracks as tank guns fired, mixed-in with the smaller noise of machine gun and small arms fire. The incessant screams of the wounded and dying were heart-wrenching to those with a conscience. *Damn*, thought Major Thomas. *Who in the hell dropped this ball*? Staring around at all the pandemonium and violent death, he shook his head while he moved west. *If there is a God, I sure hope he chooses our side.*

~ ~ ~

The men of 1st squad lay on the side of the hill, behind the trees, listening to the artillery barrage and thinking *those poor bastards on the receiving end of that shit can't be very happy right now*. Looking at his watch, Brooks noticed the time: 6:30 a.m., but there was no sign of the sun. "I guess," he muttered to himself, "it's not going to warm up today."

Everyone in 1st squad was concerned about the changed situation. They turned to look at their platoon sergeant after Hanky asked, "What the hell do we do? Where do we go now, Sarge?" After contemplating the two questions for a couple of moments, Sergeant Brooks issued his orders. "Corporal Sims, form up the squad. I want an ammo and ration check. We move out in fifteen minutes."

The squad began their trek west, with Corporal Sims about thirty yards to the rear. They were nervous, apprehensive, and very much aware of their location. Caught out in the snow with only shelter-half's for cover and no fire was not a pleasant situation to be in. Not behind enemy lines.

Major Thomas' orders for command were only two weeks old when he was forced to withdraw to the west to avoid capture. Setting up roadblocks appeared to be the only way to slow the German onslaught, at least, long enough to give the other units time to dig in and fight back. Scores of soldiers with as much equipment as they could carry set out ahead of the enemy, alternating between running and walking, trying to get some distance between themselves and the onrushing Germans, so they could set up their barricades and strong points. The time was 9:00 a.m., on December 16, 1944. Hell had opened its gates, and the result was not a heartwarming experience.

~ ~ ~

The snow Sergeant Brooks thought would come had finally begun, and within a few minutes, it was coming down hard. The snowfall was so thick Brooks was compelled to call in his flankers. The scouts were forced to go out to extreme visual and wait in place for Sergeant Brooks and the rest of the squad to catch up before starting the whole process all over again. The effort wasted a lot of time, but it kept them from running unexpectedly into the Germans. Getting back to Allied lines was going to be a very long and tough road to travel.

After about an hour, Brooks called a halt. "All right, ladies, check your weapons. Clear the bolts. You don't want to find the action frozen at the wrong time." After a twenty-minute rest and a ration break, 1st squad started out again. They still had six hours of daylight left, plenty of time to find some shelter before nightfall. What they needed was a place where they could have a fire and not be seen. "Damn! This cold weather sure makes the bones hurt," said Sergeant Brooks.

Corporal Sims laughed before he responded. "And you call *me* an old lady?"

Brooks and Sims had been together since basic training and had become very close friends. When the time came for joking everyone could see their friendship. When it came time to be a soldier, however, they went by the book. Whatever Brooks wanted done, Sims did it with no hesitation whatsoever. Their very lives and the lives of those under their command depended on their exact co-operation.

Two hours of daylight still remained when one of the scouts appeared, ghost-like, out of the hard falling snow; it was Jackson. He came to report to Sergeant Brooks that a small structure had been found about a quarter mile to the right of the route they were taking. "It's roomy enough for the whole squad, Sarge. If we cover the holes with mud," said the scout, "we might be able to build a fire and not be seen."

"Okay, beanpole. Take us there," said Brooks.

After traipsing through the snow for about fifteen minutes, they were all inside and out of the storm, snug as bugs in a shed, but according to Sergeant Brooks, it was still colder than a witch's breath inside. "Let's plug up those holes and see about a fire," said Brooks.

With the thought of a warm fire urging them on, the entire squad went outside and plugged the holes with everything and anything they could find. After about thirty minutes of freezing and covering holes, Brooks went inside and started a fire, with everyone still outside, and checking for any light showing. No light escaped.

Each man was set to stand a two-hour watch, including Sergeant Brooks. Within an hour after the fire was going, all but the guard, Brooks, and Sims were asleep, and no one was eating. When they had gone out on patrol, they had taken rations for only three days, and now food had become another problem. No telling where they would get more once the last of their rations was gone.

Sometime around 2:00 a.m., the men of 1st squad woke up, and one by one, felt a rumble. The wind was howling towards the east, so they couldn't hear anything. A few seconds later, they were looking at each other trying to recognize it. "Is the wind causing that rumble?" asked Private Brown. That question was answered when Jackson came bursting in, whispering, "A Mark IV and some infantry are coming right towards us."

Everything outside was so blurred from the blowing snowfall, no one could see more than ten feet in any direction. Brooks was hoping that the Germans would miss seeing their warm little shelter, but he didn't hold his breath on that possibility.

They could now hear the tank coming closer, and they cringed. The rumbling grew stronger as the tank moved closer, and they could feel it through the wooden-planked floor. Their only other escape route was a window located on the back side of the structure, and it was boarded up. After removing the boards, everyone was ordered out through the window, so they wouldn't be trapped inside.

Once outside, Brooks quickly deployed his men in a skirmish line. His aim was to try and kill the infantry first and, with luck, disable the tank. Maybe with Baker, he could distract the Germans long enough to do just that. Set them at ease and then ambush them.

The Germans discovered the shelter shortly after the Americans had vacated it. Brooks heard them yelling back and forth and thought maybe if Baker called out to them, they might come over to investigate. Being that the Americans were about five miles behind enemy lines, they probably wouldn't believe that their adversary was so close to them. Sergeant Brooks whispered to Baker, "Tell them you're hurt and that you need help fast before you freeze to death." Baker nodded before he crawled a few feet away and then called out in German.

All yelling by the enemy stopped when they heard Baker's voice. They called back asking him what he was doing out in the storm at this hour of the morning, and the corporal responded by shouting, "I was out hunting earlier and broke my leg in a fall. This is as far as I was able to go. Please help! I am freezing!"

The men of 1st squad could almost picture the Germans looking at each other, peering through the snow, trying to locate Baker. *It's going to work*, thought Sergeant Brooks, and he was excited. One of the enemy warriors yelled to Baker to keep on talking so they could locate him and help him. Corporal Baker was scrunched down in the snow, freezing, shivering, waiting, and wanting to kill his enemy so he could get back inside the shelter and build another fire to get warm. The tank, in the meantime, had pulled up close to the shelter, and the crew had dismounted to check the inside. They were also cold and wanted a fire.

Baker silently moved ever so slowly away from the shelter, drawing the Germans further out. The enemy squad walking towards him was unaware of the predicament they had just placed themselves in. Brooks was kneeling about ten feet away from Baker when he spotted the Germans. Through the blowing snow, he watched and held his breath, thinking, *just a little closer. Just a little closer*. He was eager to get the ball rolling so he could get back inside and get warm.

The squad was poised, waiting for Brooks to begin the action, but when their sergeant started shooting, they were taken by surprise from the unexpected suddenness of the gunfire. They immediately recovered, however, and very quickly laid down a withering fire. Within the time it took to draw three more breaths, all ten of the Germans were dead. When the last one fell, Brooks immediately yelled for the squad to go after the tank, only to discover that the tank was empty, and the crew had fled into the blowing snow.

"Damn, that was close," said Brooks. "Who knows how to drive a tank? Corporal Baker, see what you can do to get this big bastard going. Corporal Sims, take Lemons and Jackson and go find that tank crew. I don't want them reporting to their brass what just happened here. No prisoners, Corporal. Can't afford to have them tagging along. The rest of you go back inside and get another fire going. Warm the place up. It's cold out here."

Baker's failure to start the tank was immediate. "I think we need to wait until daylight to figure out how to crank this thing up. My eyes are freezing shut."

"All right, Baker," said Brooks. "Let's get inside where it's warmer."

After a thirty-minute hunt, the three men entered the shed through the only door, and they looked half frozen, but they were smiling brightly. "We got 'em," said Lemons. "They were SS. Master race, hell! Didn't put up much of a fight at all." Then Sam paused for a moment before he asked, "How do you think our guys are doing, Sarge?"

"I don't know, Sam," said Brooks. "I'm trying not to think about it. Right now, we have to worry about us and how we're going to get out of the mess we're in." After a short pause, Brooks nodded and continued, "I'll take first watch," he said. "Green you're next, then you Snow. Todd you come after Snow. Stony, you're the last in line. By then, there should be light enough to try and start that tank again. This time, Baker, take a flashlight with you since you can read German. The rest of you guys get some sleep."

The notion that Major Thomas might be right about his hunch never entered the platoon sergeant's mind until he saw for himself the massive forces that had passed before him.

How in the world am I going to get these men back without getting them killed or captured?

All through the 17th of December, 1st squad stayed at their little shelter. Baker managed to get the Mark IV running and had moved it around behind the structure and into some trees to keep it out of sight. With the snow coming down hard, the tank was soon covered with a soft, white blanket, making it hard to spot from more than twenty feet away. Sergeant Brooks had decided to wait until the next morning before resuming their trek back to Allied lines. His theory was that any Germans lurking about would probably not think anything about seeing one of their tanks moving west. The thought was a hopeful one.

~ ~ ~

Under a dark, cloud covered morning, Major Thomas and what was left of his men were wearily trudging westward, hoping to find some kind of organized resistance. They still had a river to cross before reaching friendly troops. The Our River. They had managed to stall the German column that had broken through their lines, but that was all they were able to do. Their efforts, though energetic, had only slightly slowed the enemy down, and now those same Americans were on the run. Had they remained where they were, they would have been captured or killed.

The major knew it was only a matter of time before the Germans were on the move again. By then, any stragglers would've rejoined the main force, ready to continue on. Major Thomas looked around before he shook his head and said, "What a crock. What a load of shit. Five days ago, all was peaceful and quiet. Now we're running for our lives from the Germans and fighting the weather at the same time. How crazy is that?"

"Who are you talking to, sir?"

Chapter 29

Around 8:00 a.m. on the morning of December 18, Sergeant Brooks mounted his men in and on the enemy tank. Since dawn, they had used the couple of hours before full daylight to familiarize themselves with the workings of the tank. Corporal Baker went over everything until the men started interrupting him. "Yeah, yeah, we know, Sir Charles. You've already showed us that three different times."

The plan was to drive the tank until it ran out of fuel and then use the onboard ammo to try to destroy it. Sergeant Brooks wanted to get as close to Allied lines as possible before abandoning the tank.

By the 19th of December, the Germans had pushed the Americans back from about three or four miles east of the Our River to anywhere from one to five miles west of the river, all the way to the outskirts of St. Vith, about twelve miles behind where their lines used to be. Even though the Germans needed the road junctions at Bastogne, they were not as important as the road junctions of St. Vith. The Allied commanders, not knowing what the intention of the German offensive was, were soon to realize that if the Germans controlled either of these road junctions, they would be hard to stop.

The sounds of the battles taking place were heard by the squad. Judging by the intensity of the fighting, some major skirmishes were indeed being fought. Who was winning was foremost on their minds, and they were worried. After what they had witnessed, coupled with what they were hearing, the situation didn't look good for the Americans.

Following the tracks of the scouts was becoming more and more difficult with each passing minute. The snow was coming down harder and thicker and was rapidly covering their tracks, so Brooks was forced to send some men ahead to act as an in-between lifeline to follow. Lack of decent vision wasn't the only problem. The sun was on its way down, so it was time to think about a safe place to stop, preferably under some cover.

Moving behind enemy lines was exhausting and time consuming. Constantly being on the alert drains the energy and mentally fatigues the men involved. Sergeant Brooks was aware of this threat, and was constantly on the alert, watching his men for these signs of weakness. About an hour before darkness settled in, he called a halt. They stopped just inside a small patch of woods. The night was going to be long one. Fireless, cold, and miserable.

~ ~ ~

Major Thomas looked tired and disgusted while he watched his enemy pass unhindered. His roadblocks didn't hold up the Germans for very long at all. Most of his men were either captured or killed, and it seemed as though for nothing. *What a waste.* His longtime friend and XO, Captain Jack Shane, was dead, and there was nothing he could do about it. *How did this happen*? he wondered. Cut off from any help, he shook with anger and frustration. There was absolutely nothing he could do anymore except try to reach friendly units.

~ ~ ~

"I think it's going to get really tough staying hidden from the Germans," said Corporal Sims. "I saw signs of a lot of troops up ahead. I think we're catching up to their stragglers."

Sergeant Brooks turned to Corporal Baker and said, "Take one of the scouts with you and see what you can find out. Jackson would probably be the best man for the job. He's a better sneaker then Sam. I wouldn't doubt that boy can track a fly in a snowstorm. See if you can get close enough to hear what the Krauts are saying, but don't get stupid and get caught. Give it about an hour before you leave. And Chuck. Be very careful."

Corporal Baker looked at his sergeant and smiled before he replied. "Sarge, I'm always careful. You already know that." All Brooks could do was force a smile back and nod. The situation his men were in was serious. Even more so was the burden of responsibility, which he felt was his alone. He was responsible for the safety of the men under his command, and he suffered the weight of it. They were also his friends. Another burden added to his already sagging shoulders.

~ ~ ~

An hour after sundown, Baker and Jackson started out on their foray. Sergeant Brooks gave out his last minute instructions to the two men just before they disappeared into the snowy night.

Brooks stood where he was, staring at the swirling snow and their disappearing backs, before he turned towards Corporal Sims and said, “Man, I sure hope they don’t get caught. Could get kind of hairy for us if they are. The Germans will definitely come looking for us, of that I have no doubt. I’m surprised they haven’t sent out any patrols to locate any of our units they’ve overrun. We’ve sure been lucky. I sure hope our luck still holds out.”

~ ~ ~

Corporal Baker and Private Jackson had been walking for what seemed like hours. Beanpole had been looking at something, but what he was studying didn’t register right away. Then it hit him, *Germans*! What he was puzzling over was the silhouette of an enemy sentry’s elbow sticking out while he leaned up against a tree, smoking a cigarette. Signaling Baker, they both dropped to the ground and froze where they were.

After his heart had calmed down a bit, Baker tapped Jackson on the shoulder and whispered, “Let’s wait until they change sentries before we do anything. After they change the guard, you can sneak up on him and kill him. We’ll have an avenue of escape if we run into trouble.”

The stand of trees the two Americans were slinking through were dark and shadowy, making it difficult to see anything past a few feet. *If that sentry hadn’t of been smoking, we would’ve walked right into him.* Swearing at himself and absolutely chilled by the close call, Baker turned to the scout and whispered, “Damn, that was close. Pay attention next time, or you’ll get us both killed.”

“Very funny, Corporal,” replied the Arizona beanpole. “I noticed you didn’t even know he was there until I signaled you to hit the ground.”

Smiling at his friend's comment, Baker said, "Shh, cowboy. You'll wake the dead."

The two men stayed where they were for over an hour before they were rewarded for their patience. An officer and a private appeared out of the shadows and walked to where the sentry was. The men talked in hushed tones for a few minutes before the officer and the relieved sentry left, and the snowy night was soft and still once more.

After what seemed like forever, Baker and Jackson, slowly and quietly, inched their way towards the sentry, who was completely unaware of what was about to happen. Silently, they drew closer and closer to him, praying that nothing would give them away. They didn't look directly at their enemy while they inched their way forward; both were afraid he would look their way, and then a lot of bullets would start flying.

Twenty minutes of slinking went by before the sentry was silenced. Jackson performed the task because he was quieter then Baker. "Now comes the hard part," whispered Baker. "We have to sneak in close enough to hear what those Krauts are saying. You, lead. I'll be right behind you."

After a few minutes, they heard faint voices, but they were still too far away to distinguish any words. The closer they advanced the more on edge they became. Jackson signaled a halt to point out to Baker what appeared to be a command vehicle. Searching around to make sure nobody was looking their way, the corporal motioned for Jackson to head that way. "Take a roundabout route to avoid being spotted," he ordered.

Moving to within about thirty or forty feet of the command vehicle, they came to an abrupt halt. Standing not more than ten feet away and almost blending in perfectly with a tall spruce, was an officer talking to someone who appeared to be a higher-ranking officer. The two men had their backs to the two Americans, so they didn't notice them lying on the ground behind them.

After a while, the two officers started talking about the next day's upcoming reunion with their division. The two Americans were afraid to move, scared to death that if they did they might be heard, so they stayed where they were, praying for the officers not to turn around, and at the same time, they hoped and prayed that no one approached them.

Hours later, Baker and Jackson were on their way back to where the squad was waiting. The trip took them far less time to get back, and they were soon talking to Sergeant Brooks about what they saw and heard. Baker gave the report. "The units that are in front of us are elements of a Volksgrenadier division. They're waiting for something or someone to arrive so they can move out and catch up to their division."

"That's all they talked about?"

"No, Sarge. They talked mostly about their families. From what I gathered, the two officers grew up in the same town, so they knew each other's families."

"Hmm. Any mention of when they're leaving?"

"Yeah. If whatever they're waiting for arrives, they'll be leaving in about 3 hours."

Sergeant Brooks pulled on his ear for a moment or two before he voiced his thoughts. "We can't keep driving this tank all over the place without eventually being discovered by the Germans. If they discover it's us, our day will end real fast. We can't even destroy the damn thing without giving away our position. Be a waste of time to disable it. The Krauts will just repair the damn thing and put it back into circulation. Damn! All right you two. Get out there and find us some trees to hide in."

About two hours after the report, Brooks called a halt in a small stand of trees to await the end of an upcoming day.

~ ~ ~

"Al. Wake up," whispered Sims. "I hear voices over by those trees."

Having just woke up, Brooks lay beneath the trees where they had stopped earlier that morning. He was listening for the voices Corporal Sims thought he had heard. *Damn it's cold,* he thought. *Colder than a witch's breath.* Then he heard it. Sure enough, it was voices, and they were coming their way. "Alex," whispered Brooks. "Wake 'em up now and be quiet about it. Company's coming."

Within seconds, everyone was instantly awake, and fear had a mean grip on everybody's insides. "Skirmish line, quietly now, and stay below the snow bank! Move it." Within a matter of moments everybody was in place, praying that their weapons would not fail them, that they would fire when needed.

"Hold your fire, boys, and wait for my command," ordered Brooks. "Jackson? Can you see how many there are?"

Completely unexpected, and without warning, Sergeant Brooks received his answer. "Many cold palefaces in white coats." Quiet snickers immediately erupted.

Lying motionless, Brooks stared in Jackson's direction for a moment before he muttered, "Damn you, Jackson. Always a smartass."

On the enemy came. Their voices carried across the snow-covered ground. German voices, and they were getting closer and closer. Jackson quietly moved next to Sergeant Brooks and said, "I think there's only a squad, maybe about ten or twelve men." Then he pointed out something else. "Look at 'em, Sarge. Their attention is on that Mark IV. I don't think they know we're here."

"Looks that way, beanpole. Pass the word," ordered Brooks. "Whoever has grenades get 'em ready, but don't use 'em until I say to. I want to save 'em if we can."

The enemy was only about sixty yards away, but that was still too far.

"Let 'em get closer," whispered Brooks. "I want them dead to rights. No chance whatsoever of surviving."

Closer and closer the enemy trudged, completely oblivious to their danger. They were walking through their own backyard without a second thought. There were no enemies on their back porch, so they were not worried. Now, they were sixty feet away and still coming. Forty feet, thirty feet. All of a sudden, and without warning, gunfire erupted, and it decimated the surprised Germans.

Brooks nodded, and everybody stood up, firing as one. In a matter of seconds, every enemy soldier was lying dead on the ground, and the short battle was over. Sergeant Brooks immediately jumped up and ordered, "Search for food, and then let's get the hell out of here! Let's go! Move it, people!"

Within minutes, the squad was well away from where the firefight had taken place and moving east until they changed direction and turned south, stepping out at a good pace. Nobody wanted to be around when the Germans discovered what had happened.

A little over an hour after the firefight, a German halftrack, en route to pick up an infantry squad, found their dead comrades. Word was immediately sent out that there were enemy troops on the loose behind their lines. The alert filtered around command until it arrived on the desk of the commander of the clean-up crews.

Chapter 30

The sight was spectacular. The Mark IV gun turret went flying thirty feet into the air, and the blast was almost loud enough to be heard in Berlin.

After the firefight, Brooks moved his men due south. Coming to a small stand of trees, he decided to remove the tank they had commandeered from the German order of battle, forever. Standing in the trees and looking at their dirty work, Brooks smiled before he pointed north and said, "Follow me, boys."

They headed north at a brisk pace while the snow fell all around them. No complaints were voiced by anyone this time. Everybody was smiling because the falling snow would cover their tracks. Anyone who might be looking for them would have no idea which direction they were taking.

Having relieved the dead of their cold weather coats and rations, the Americans had enough food for maybe two more days. Getting back to Allied lines would be difficult at best, but Brooks, having been in similar situations, was somewhat confident that they would somehow reach friendly lines this time as well. What he didn't know was how many of his men would still be with him when they did make it back. Coming from the west were the intense sounds of the battles being fought. Along with the lightning like flashes of the artillery being fired, they were all reminders of how serious a situation he and his men were in.

Talking to his men during a brief halt, Brooks said, "We've been lucky. No doubt about it. We've been behind enemy lines for three days now, and we've only stumbled into two small fights. So far, nobody has been injured. We still have ammo and food. What we need to do from now on is to avoid any and all contact. Stay away from fights and out think the Germans. We'll head north for a ways to try and throw off any pursuit, then turn west, and sneak through the German lines. Keep your eyes and ears open at all times. Baker, get Jackson and

Lemons out front with you. Todd, I want you and Avery on the flanks again. We move out in five minutes."

~ ~ ~

Within an hour after they had the fire going again, Major Thomas and his miscellaneous assortment of troops were warming up nicely. Most of their clothes were finally dry except for a few socks steaming nicely beside the fire. Their Our River crossing turned out to be a coldly shocking experience, and the adventure of a lifetime. The swim across the river was painful, and the water was so freezing cold, they were struggling to breathe every inch of the way, but they all made it across in one piece. "Who has any food?" asked Major Thomas.

A 2nd lieutenant named Simmons answered the major and said, "I have some k-rats. Anybody else?" Six others added their rations to the growing pile of food stocks. Even so, there was only enough rations to last the eight men for two days, if they ate once a day. "I believe gentlemen," said the major, "it's time to eat."

Lieutenant Jacobs was Sergeant Brooks' platoon leader during the fighting in North Africa. Just before the mission to Clervella, Jacobs was given command of Charlie Company, 5th Battalion, and Lieutenant Jack Shane took Jacob's place as platoon leader for 1st platoon, Baker Company, 5th Battalion. Major Thomas turned to him and said, "Lieutenant Jacobs, you set up the watch. Two people, one at either end of the curve. You and I will take the first watch. The rest of you eat and then get some sleep. We need to be out of here before 0400 hours."

Having moved back another forty yards from the road into a deep hollow they had found, the rest of the men curled up with what extra clothing they had and were soon fast asleep beside the small fire. Major Thomas and Lieutenant Jacobs took the first watch.

While they were moving down the slope they heard footsteps approaching. Hunkering down, they waited. As dark as it was, their only concern was the dull reflection of firelight dancing around behind them. The footsteps were getting closer, and they were sounding cautious, as if somebody was trying real hard not to be heard. "You stay here, Lieutenant, while I find out who's sneaking up on us."

Being as quiet as possible, the major moved towards the sound of the footsteps. Ever so slowly, he inched his way forward, his .45 automatic ready for instant use. Stopping abruptly, he hunkered down and waited, listening for the footsteps to begin again. Thirty seconds, a minute, two minutes, and nothing. There was absolutely no sound other than the sound of battle. Even all the insects had quit their buzzing.

Listening for breathing, Major Thomas was just about to shift his weight when the footsteps started again. He almost jumped out of his skin. *Those steps sound right beside me*! Sweat started pouring down his face, and his stomach was all knotted up. Turning his head slowly towards the sound, he found himself looking up the bore of a rifle. The fear and shock of what was happening was coursing through his body like a raging fever. Slowly raising his head higher, he saw the coldest pair of eyes he had ever looked into. Not knowing what else to do, he just sat there, staring at the bloodied face, and the cold, menacing eyes staring down at him.

"Major? Is that you?"

Gulping, and with almost no voice, the major asked, "Who are you?"

"It's me," answered the man. "Sergeant Cane, sir."

For two full heart-throbbing breaths, Major Thomas could not move. The fear and shock of what had just happened was quickly wearing off, but he was still unable to move. "Dan. Damn it all, man. You just scared three weeks of shit out of me. You're fired!" Still shaking his head, he said, "Damn, you're fired."

Finally able to stand up, Major Thomas motioned for Lieutenant Jacobs to come on down. By the time Jacobs had reached the two men, the major's color had returned to its normal shade, and he had quit shaking. The three men stood looking at each other, grinning and gripping each other's hands until Major Thomas reminded Jacobs that they still had the first watch.

The road made a hairpin curve around the hill Major Thomas and his men were located on. Lieutenant Jacobs took the east end of the curve while Major Thomas and Sergeant Cane handled the west end. "Dan, what happened to you and the rest of the men after we were split up at the roadblock?" asked the major.

"Everything," replied Cane. "There were Krauts everywhere we went. They killed a lot of our guys at the roadblock, sir. Those they didn't kill they captured. I could see the Germans rounding up our men. Me, Shorty, and a few others finally managed to get away, but the Krauts caught up to us again. Shorty's men were killed a couple days ago. Davis and the last of his squad were killed yesterday."

Shaking his head at the memory, Sergeant Cane paused for a moment before he continued. Tears, anger, revenge, all of it, appeared on his face when he said, "Shorty and me were hit this morning. I got burned on the side of my head. That one hurt. Shorty took one in the chest. When I went down Shorty landed on top of me. The Krauts came and stood by while he bled out. They never once tried to help either of us. They just stood there watching and laughing. When they left, they never looked back. I was unable to move and was bleeding like a stuck pig, so I guess they thought I'd bleed out like Shorty did. Sir, if you don't mind, I'd like head on out and kill some Kraut bastards on my own. I wanna settle some things for Shorty and the guys."

Nodding sympathetically, the major replied. "No, Dan, I need you to stay with us. We need to stick together for the men. I understand what you want to do and why, but I really need you here with us. Okay?"

"Good enough, sir," replied Sergeant Cane. "I'll hang around, but don't expect me to like it."

"Don't worry, Dan. I know exactly how you feel. I don't like it either."

The next hour and a half passed by so quickly that Thomas was surprised when his relief arrived. Turning to Sergeant Cane, he said, "Let's head for the fire and get warm. When was the last time you ate something?"

"Uh, maybe a couple days ago, sir."

"You're in luck, Sergeant. Follow me."

After a few steps, Major Thomas looked over at Sergeant Cane and said, "Dan, it sure is good to see you in one piece. Jack got killed at the roadblock, so I guess that makes you Baker Company's new CO."

~ ~ ~

The SS major was standing smartly at attention while his commanding officer, Colonel Walther Marcs, briefly outlined his assignment. "I have received several reports stating that an enemy unit is operating behind our lines, killing our soldiers, and destroying our equipment. I want you to hunt these men down and kill them all. No prisoners. Do you understand, Herr Major?"

"Yes, Herr Colonel," he replied. "May I look at the intelligence reports, sir?"

Nodding towards a folder lying on his desk, the colonel said, "Yes, Major. Here they are. Study them well."

Searching through the report, the major asked, "When do you want me to leave?"

"In three hours," replied the colonel.

The major's response was almost immediate. Clicking his heels together, he saluted at the same time he shouted, "Heil, Hitler," and then he left the room.

~ ~ ~

Having spent the last several hours studying the reports, Major Paul Schmidt thought he had a pretty good idea of what he was up against. Over forty soldiers killed, four halftracks and one panzer destroyed, and no signs of any enemy dead or wounded. *The English have problems of their own, so they must be American. Elite and highly trained tells me they must be Rangers, or maybe even airborne. I will have mg 42's mounted on the Schutzenpanzerwagens. That will provide me with some additional firepower*. Then he noticed what he had taken earlier as an ink-spill was actually a smeared side-note. Looking closely at the blurred writing, he only read through a couple of words before his eyes narrowed and a long forgotten memory appeared. A memory concerning France, the French resistance, and a very clever American sergeant. *Hmm.*

~ ~ ~

Not knowing how infamous he and his squad had become, Sergeant Brooks signaled his men to move out, going due north. The snow had stopped falling where they were walking, but it was still damn cold. The temperature was even colder trudging through the woods. Brooks' plan was to move north for a day or so and then turn west. His hope was they would luck out, sneak past the Germans, and reach their own lines. *Man, just think, hot chow, hot coffee and a warm tent, and rest...*Seconds later, he was shaking his head, disgusted with himself. *Daydreaming is for civilians and fools. I gotta quit that shit*!

~ ~ ~

Five hours after departing headquarters, Major Schmidt and his mechanized detachment arrived at his enemy's last known location, the dismembered hulk that used to be a Pz IV. Upon arriving, Schmidt immediately dismounted his men from the halftracks, and quickly had them looking around for any clues as to which direction the Americans took after they had destroyed the tank. His thoughts, however, were not centered around his assignment. He was thinking ahead, after he killed the culprits. His arrogant hope, once he returned victorious, was a promotion to colonel. He was tired of taking orders from a has-been old fool. Colonel Marcs was in his 50's, and going nowhere. Major Schmidt was just into his 30's. He still had plenty of time to connive his way to a General's rank.

Thinking, this mission could be his chance, Major Schmidt pushed his men hard. He was an arrogant and selfish commander, so he didn't think twice about pushing his men until they dropped.

Standing off, about a hundred yards away, one of his sergeants was frantically waving his arms as if he had found something. Schmidt hurried over to where the sergeant was standing to find out what all the excitement was about. When he arrived, he noticed a satisfied smile on his sergeant's face, for in his sergeant's hand was an American candy bar wrapper from a U.S. ration box. Looking back towards the burned-out tank, Schmidt smiled for the first time since receiving his orders. Thinking out loud, he said, "I've got you now."

Walking back to the halftracks, he was trying to figure out the best way to handle the situation. Signaling for his men to mount up, the major climbed into his halftrack, pointed due north, and off they went.

Chapter 31

Thomas' detachment was slowly catching up to the rear of the attacking Germans, and the major was concerned. All of the men, were. They were hiding in some trees on the west side of the Our River, and the situation had turned extremely dangerous. Shivering uncontrollably, Major Thomas explained the situation to his men. "We're getting closer to the Germans," he said. "We need to be extra careful in everything we do from here on out. Remember, men. We're still surrounded by the Krauts, so keep it quiet." After a short pause, he nodded to his troops and whispered, "Okay, people, let's go. Move out." Turning his attention to his sergeant, he whispered, "Don't you ever sneak up on me like that again. You're liable to get shot the next time." Cane smiled and said nothing. He just nodded his response.

Nine people were in the group. Four were from 5th Battalion, Major Thomas' command. The rest were displaced troops who units were almost annihilated when the Germans first hit their lines. Out of those nine, only six carried weapons. They had four M1's, one M1 carbine, and Major Thomas' .45 pistol, so firefights were out of the question. Following the road, but off to the side, the nine men of the Thomas detachment crept forward, and with hearts pounding almost out of control, they inched their way towards what they were hoping were friendly lines.

They had been walking for almost an hour when Private Johnny Adams, another addition to the Thomas group, emerged from out of the shadows. "What's wrong, Private?" asked the major.

"Private Adams, sir. The Germans are up ahead, but I don't know how many."

Looking at the private, the major asked, "Do you think we can get below the road and sneak by them?"

"Well, sir, it's possible. If we can get past those two Germans up ahead, then I think we can sneak by the rest."

Major Thomas moved the men back about fifty yards and then thought the situation over. When he was through contemplating, he turned to Private Adams and asked, "Have you ever had to kill someone up close with a knife before?"

"No, sir," replied Adams. "I don't think I've ever killed anybody. I've only been here two weeks, sir. I'm scared to death, Major."

"We all are, son, but we have a job to do. Do you think you can do it?" asked the major.

"I honestly don't know, sir," said Adams.

Major Thomas looked over at Sergeant Cane and asked, "Dan, who do you want to go with you to take out those two Germans up ahead?"

Looking around at the men gathered around, he turned to the major and said, "I think I'll take Decker with me. He's good with a knife. When do you want us to go?"

Remembering the scalping incident, Major Thomas said, "Decker, huh. That name sounds familiar. Does he still have his hair?" Not waiting for an answer, he nodded and replied to Sergeant Cane's inquiry. "I guess now is as good a time as any. Let's move closer before you strike. Private, you go with Sergeant Cane and show him where the two Germans are."

"Sir?" asked Cane. "We might want to wait to see if they change guards. If we can hit them after a relief, we'll have a little more time to sneak further away."

"Yes. You're right. Good idea." Turning his attention back to the young soldier, Major Thomas said, "Private, I need you to sneak back to where you can watch those two guards. As soon as they're relieved, sneak back here and tell us. Can you do that?"

"Yes, sir," replied Adams.

"What time is it?" asked Thomas.

"It's, uh, 2100 hours, sir," replied Adams.

"Okay, son. Get going and be careful." Turning to the rest of his men, Major Thomas said, "Now we wait."

~ ~ ~

About noon, on the fourth day of the German attack, Corporal Sims came running up from the rear of the squad, signaling for everyone to get down. Within a heartbeat, everybody was lying bellies-first in the snow. Sims crawled up to Sergeant Brooks and whispered, “German halftracks. Three of them, maybe a mile or so off to our right.”

Looking to his right, Brooks could barely make out three dots moving in the same direction as they were. Looking at the vehicles, he whispered to Sims. “Move the men back into the trees, and keep them out of sight. We’re holding here for a while.”

Staying where he was, Brooks continued to watch the halftracks while he was deep in thought. *There’s nothing in that direction for miles.*

Thinking about the Mark IV tank they had destroyed, he wondered if maybe the Germans were out looking for him and his men. Signaling for Sims to come join him, he continued to watch what the halftracks were doing. When Sims arrived by his side, Brooks turned to him and said, “I think they’re looking for us. There’s nothing out here for miles, so why would they be out there and going in the same direction we are? How many men can one of those things carry?”

Sims looked at his platoon sergeant and said, “About ten, not counting the driver and maybe a co-driver.”

“Damn,” said Brooks. “That means about thirty men. We definitely can’t handle thirty of the bastards. We’re just going to have to out think ‘em. Crawl back and get an exact ammo count for all weapons. I want to know how much ammo each weapon has left.”

“Got it,” said Sims, and then he was gone.

Damn Germans. What the hell are they doing way out here? Startled, Sergeant Brooks watched the halftracks change direction. They made a ninety-degree turn to the left and were heading straight for him. “Ah, hell,” he muttered. “They are looking for us. Damn!” Crawling quickly to where his men waited, he ordered the squad to move deeper into the trees. After they had crawled about thirty yards or so, he ordered them back onto their feet, and immediately, they double-timed it even deeper into the evergreens. Not liking the changed situation, Brooks was pulling at his ear, and contemplating deeply. *If they are looking for us, how in the world did they figure out which direction we took? It was snowing really hard when we left, so the snow should've covered all of our tracks.*

~ ~ ~

Standing in the machine gun cupola, Major Schmidt looked at the surrounding countryside while he tried to guess where the Americans had gone. There were stands of trees everywhere. *Which one do I search first*? Glancing off to his left, he thought he saw movement over by one of the larger stands. Shouting down to his driver, he ordered him to turn left and head for the distraction. The other vehicles, seeing their command track turn, followed suit. When they arrived at the edge of the trees just a few minutes later, Major Schmidt dismounted his men and said, "We'll bivouac here for the night."

Brooks had moved the squad deeper into the evergreens, but they still heard the halftracks when they pulled up and stopped at the edge of the tree line. Looking around at his men, he decided to find out for sure what was going on. "Beanpole!"

~ ~ ~

Jackson and Baker had been watching the Germans for the last couple of hours and located all of the sentries thanks to a shift change. As dark as the shadows were, getting close to any officers shouldn't be too hard. With luck, they should be able to get the information Sergeant Brooks was looking for.

Spotting a couple of men off by themselves, beanpole noticed what appeared to be plenty of gold braid adorning one of their peaked caps, and they were talking to each other. Deciding to take a chance, he signaled Baker to follow, so they crept closer to the German officers, stopping only when they were about ten to fifteen feet away, just in time to hear some startling news.

"Finding that candy bar wrapper on the ground yesterday was pure luck, Captain. It pointed out the direction they chose. Now, all we have to do is search all of the wooded areas until we find them. Remember, Captain. They are on foot we are not. We can move a lot faster than they can. Make sure everything is in order and check with the guards and then get some rest. Good night, Captain." With that said, Major Schmidt headed for his tent and a well-deserved, full night's sleep.

Jackson was getting ready to turn and head back to camp, but something-a shadow of movement, a small sound, a sudden hunch. Whatever it was made him freeze. Upon seeing Jackson tense up, Baker didn't budge either. Next, the corporal heard breathing coming from behind them and knew immediately what had stopped the scout from moving. For what seemed like hours, neither of them moved a muscle.

The enemy soldier standing behind Baker and Jackson couldn't see them, but something about the shadow he was staring at didn't appear quite right, and he was bothered by the distraction. The shadow on the snow was cast by two large standing spruce evergreens. A natural occurrence, but it still troubled him. After a couple of minutes, he moved off a ways, but he continued to watch the shadow Baker and Jackson were hiding in. The two scouts stayed where they were, not moving at all. After a while, the enemy soldier left, but the two men still refused to move. Another hour passed before they finally got up the nerve to move out and head back to where Brooks and the others were waiting for them.

Sometime around 2300 hours, the two men emerged out of the whispering snow and startled everyone. Brooks just happened to glance up, and there was Jackson with Baker just behind him. Taken by surprise, once again, he was shaking his head and whispering, "Damn you, Jackson. Warn a fellow before you sneak up on him like that. You almost gave me a heart attack."

Baker didn't take long in spreading the bad news. Brooks sat thinking for a few minutes then he looked at Sims and said, "We move out in five minutes. Pack it up. Excellent job. I owe you guys a round of drinks when we get back." The two men grinned. Coming from Brooks, the statement was high praise. Compliments like that one were almost unheard of.

The next morning, Major Schmidt was staring just past the very spot where he and the captain had stood talking the night before. Deeply embedded in the snow, between two twenty-foot evergreens, were the outlines of a couple of bodies, not more than ten feet away. Looking back at the soldier who had confessed to his lack of due-diligence, Major Schmidt was dumbfounded and greatly agitated. "How in the hell did you let this happen?" shouted Schmidt. "Look at that," he shouted again. "Look! There! You see? They were right under your very nose, and you let them get away scot-free. If I didn't need every man here I would shoot you myself right where you stand." Then he did. *Crack*!

Turning to face his men, he shouted out, "This is what will happen to you if you fail me!" After a really tough struggle, he forced himself to calm down. Calling all of his officers together, he gave them their orders.

During the next several hours, the Germans scoured every square inch of an estimated twenty-acre stretch of forest with a fine-tooth comb. They found nothing. Having divided up the forest into small sections, they searched the first area with no results. Moving their investigation to the second sector, they came up empty handed there as well. After several more hours, the results were the same. Nothing. Finally thinking that the search was taking too long, Schmidt called for one of his lieutenants.

Lieutenant Hauptman ran up to his commanding officer and snapped a salute. Standing at attention, he waited for Schmidt to speak. "Lieutenant, I want you to take ten men and a halftrack, and go along the outside perimeter of these trees. Keep your eyes open for any sign of enemy troops. If you find something call me on the radio. Now, get going."

"Yes, Herr Major. Right away, sir." The lieutenant snapped another salute and off he went. After collecting his ten men, he headed for the nearest halftrack, and minutes later, they were gone, searching for any telltale signs of their elusive foe.

Chapter 32

Waiting for well over an hour, Major Thomas was a little concerned. *I hope Adams is okay*. Lying on a slope, below the road, the small group of Americans was lost in their own thoughts as they waited for any news from the young soldier.

"Look, Major! Something's wrong with Adams," said Cane. The major immediately scrambled up the side of the slope, and had just reached the spot where Private Adams was struggling to stand when the kid dropped to the road in a sitting position. When the major got to him he found the boy covered in blood and going into shock. "Cane, he's hurt," whispered Thomas, but Corporal Cane was already kneeling beside the major.

Adams was shaking uncontrollably when he whispered, "Got 'em sir. You better get going." After having said that, he slowly slumped over onto his side and was dead. Shocked, the two men just stared down at Private Adams while tears trickled down their cheeks. "Damn," said Major Thomas. Letting out a deep sigh, he looked over at Sergeant Cane and said, "Get the men moving, Dan, but stay below the road." Looking down at the dead boy, he shook his head, saddened that another young life had been taken. "Damn! Damn this war and the people who started it!"

Behind enemy lines and scared to death of being captured, the men under Thomas' command took their time and managed to travel half a mile before stopping for a short breather. Taking out his compass, Major Thomas looked at it to get his bearings, pointed due west and said, "This way men," and started walking slowly and quietly towards American lines. The time was 0300 hours.

The conditions were still pitch black two hours later, when Sergeant Cane threw up his fist, signaling for everybody to drop. Crawling up beside Cane, the major asked him what was wrong.

"Troops up ahead, sir," answered Cane, "but I don't know who's they are."

"I guess we better go have a look, then," said the major.

"No, sir," said Cane. "I'll go myself. You stay here, sir."

Major Thomas looked at Cane and asked, "Is that an order, Sergeant?"

"Yes, it is. Stay put ... sir."

Half an hour later, and with the darkness beginning to lighten up, Sergeant Cane returned. He went straight to the major to report. "I think they're on our team, sir," reported Cane. "I got as close as I could. The uniforms look like ours, and I didn't hear anyone speaking German."

"It looks like we made it, Dan," said the major. "Damn, what a relief."

"Sir, let me go back just to make sure."

After what seemed like forever, but it couldn't have been more than ten, maybe fifteen minutes, Sergeant Cane appeared along with a captain. They walked over to where Major Thomas was sitting and sat down beside him.

Major Thomas nodded to the captain and said, "Man, are we glad to see you. Lead us to the coffee, Captain. We'll be right behind you."

~ ~ ~

Thinking of what Jackson and Baker had told him, Sergeant Brooks muttered angrily to himself. "A damn candy wrapper of all things. Hell!"

The morning of December 23 heralded, not only that bad news, but also more snow, which started falling before full light. At first, it wasn't much, but by noon it was really coming down hard.

After hearing about the candy bar wrapper, Brooks moved his men farther west to another stand of trees, and there they waited while he figured out what to do next. *Damn. This Kraut bastard seems to be a very determined cuss.* Corporal Sims, however, interrupted his train of thought with some very interesting news. "Al, the Krauts are using a track to scout along the perimeter of that bunch of trees we just vacated. What do you think?"

Brooks paused for only a brief moment, and then his head jerked up. Looking straight at Sims, he said, "Let's go. We're moving out." However, instead of running from the enemy, Brooks was leading his men north, towards the lone halftrack. A plan was already formulating in his mind. "If we can convince the Krauts to leave their track, we might be able to ambush the bastards and steal it. If not, then we'll be no worse off then what we are right now. We'll just have a few less troops to worry about. What do you think, Alex? Dismounted, they'll be a lot easier to handle."

Sims nodded and said, "Why don't we use Baker again? With him shouting and one of us yelling back, that might be enough to draw the Krauts out of their shell."

"Could be," said Brooks. "Let's push that thought around and see what we can come up with."

~ ~ ~

The enemy halftrack slowly ground its way along the outside perimeter of the trees, leaving a deep, clear trail through the still falling snow. Lieutenant Hauptman was standing in the machine gun cupola looking for any signs of the Americans. Ordering his driver to stop, he shouted for his men to dismount. After everybody had vacated the vehicle, he split his men into pairs and sent them searching just inside the trees. *This is stupid,* he thought. *The Americans are long gone by now. What a waste of time.*

Sergeant Brooks was watching his enemy dismount the track and thought he saw a better way to ruin their day. "Sims," he whispered. "See if Jackson and Baker can get around behind that track and take it over quietly without alerting the Krauts. If they can manage that, maybe we can get the rest of those bastards in a cross-fire and kill them with their own gun."

Sims talked the idea over with the two men, and they didn't take long to say, yes. Jackson was definitely excited about the idea, especially the sneaking around, part. Looking wide-eyed at Corporal Sims, the little beanpole said, "What an opportunity. I get to slap another insult on the SS again. Crap on the ground! Hell, yes, I'll do it, Corporal!"

Whispering to his men, Brooks said, "New plan, gentlemen. Here it is."

Fifteen minutes after the quick briefing and with all of his men in place, Sergeant Brooks gave the go-ahead signal for Jackson and Baker to move out. The two men took about thirty minutes to get into position for their part in the plan, and then the beanpole was unleashed. Smiling, Baker nodded at Jackson and said, "Go get 'em, cowboy."

~ ~ ~

Lieutenant Hauptman was standing in the machine gun cupola, looking towards the trees when he felt a sharp prick at the base of his nape, and then a dirty hand covered his mouth. A whispered "freeze" in his own language sent chills of fear rushing down his spine. *The Americans*!

A whispered voice followed next, ordering him to climb out from behind the machine gun and not make a sound. He complied, all the while staring at the man speaking his native language and the American uniform he was wearing. Not liking what he was looking at, the lieutenant made a motion as if to spit on Baker, but Jackson's knife was a shade faster.

Momentarily disrupted from his intention, the SS lieutenant felt a sharp prick and nothing else until he felt the blood dripping down his chest. Touching the right side of his face, he immediately winced from the stinging pain and then from the shock of realization. His face had been laid open along the entire length of his jaw line, and all he felt was a prick. When he looked over at Jackson, the little beanpole from Arizona stared right back at him, daring him to argue the point. Abruptly, the lieutenant's face went pale, and fear immediately had a death grip on his insides.

Baker was trying not to laugh at the officer when he ordered the driver out of the vehicle with his hands up. "Your lieutenant will be wearing a new smile below his chin if you try anything stupid." Doing what he was told, the driver came out of the rear of the vehicle with his hands in the air. Straightening up, he stared into the grinning faces of the two Americans. Both were nothing to sneeze at. They were barely five-foot-eight. Soaking wet might make them heavier than most burlap sacks, but that idea hadn't been tried out yet.

These are the elite soldiers we are hunting? They look more like little boys, than soldiers. That was the driver's first thought until he gazed into their eyes. All that he could see, looked cold and menacing, without humor, and without fear. He saw all that in those two pair of eyes, and the sight sent chills down his spine. An immediate shudder went through him, and his first thought changed dramatically. *I hope all the American soldiers are not like these two.*

~ ~ ~

Major Schmidt was fuming at the lack of progress being made, so he was pacing back and forth, and slapping his leg with his baton. *The day is almost gone, and still no sign of the Americans. Where did they go? Lieutenant Hauptman hasn't called in to report a sighting yet, so he has failed to locate the Americans as well.*

Having left several men to guard the halftracks, Schmidt had moved deeper into the forest with the rest of his men in order to motivate them, to put the fear of him into them. After another fruitless search, he called to his men and ordered everyone back to the bivouac area for the night.

They had been walking for about twenty minutes and were getting close to their camp. Night was falling, so they were barely able to see their vehicles. Without warning, one of his halftracks burst into flames. Schmidt just stopped. Staring at the burning vehicle, he cringed when the second halftrack also went up in flames. Looking in shocked disbelief, he stood frozen in-place, while he watched his military career burn up along with his vehicles.

A few minutes later, he was standing next to his flaming vehicles and thinking, *well, at least I know where the Americans are. Now, all we have to do is follow the vehicle tracks.* Disgusted, he ordered his troops to fall in, and they started following their last halftrack through the falling snow.

~ ~ ~

About an hour and a half earlier... "Hey Sarge," called Todd. "Does this thing have any heat?"

"We'll find out soon enough. Baker, since you read Kraut, you're now the new driver. All right people, let's go. Everybody get in. Next stop, we blow up the other two tracks."

As they neared the other two tracks about an hour later, Brooks was surprised to find only three men guarding them. *This ought to be easy,* he thought.

When the halftrack pulled up to the other two German tracks, the three guards, thinking nothing odd about it, approached to within a couple of yards of the commandeered vehicle. Much to their surprise, up through the machine gun cupola popped an American soldier, and out through the backend came more enemy troops. The three guards, realizing there was nothing they could do, put their weapons on the ground and raised their hands in the air.

Sergeant Brooks was watching through the trees when the first track burst into flames and saw nothing. When the second track burst into flames, he ordered his men back inside the stolen vehicle so they could leave. Another glance before they pulled away rewarded him with the sight of a German officer and about twenty men just standing there, watching them. The utter shock and disbelief of the changed situation was revealed by the soldiers' postures and the expressions on their faces. They were so astonished at their abrupt change of fortune that the thought of shooting at their retreating adversary took a couple of minutes to enter their minds. By then, it was too late to do anything other than stand where they were.

Chapter 33

As Brooks and his men were leaving, he took the commandeered machine gun and put about 20 to 30 rounds into the engine block of each burning vehicle just to make sure they stayed where they were. Then he waved good-bye to an angry enemy who was held at bay by one of their own machine guns.

"Sarge, did we really have to kill all those Germans back where we got this thing?" asked Avery.

"Yes, Private Avery. We had no other choice. Besides, their orders were to find us and kill us all. Why, Jase, I have no idea. As it stands, though, it's kill or be killed. No mercy. The black flag is their idea, so don't hesitate, Private. They won't."

~ ~ ~

Major Schmidt was thinking about their present situation and knew he couldn't return to headquarters now. Not without completing his mission. If he did, he would be disgraced and his career ruined. Complete this mission or die trying was the only option left open to him.

Calling a halt, he realized it was getting too dark to continue, so he ordered his men to stop where they were for the night. With just a little over twenty men left, he had to be very careful. He couldn't afford to lose any more before he had a chance to close in on the Americans.

Hate was a burning fire that consumed him with a vengeance. Currently, his only desire was to destroy the enemy that had come so close to ruining his career and ending his life. He stood by himself, shaking with rage at the picture of the burning halftracks; his halftracks, and of the insolent Americans waving to him as they drove off in *his* vehicle, images that wouldn't leave him alone. "I will have my revenge," he muttered quietly into the cold, silent evening.

~ ~ ~

Not knowing how many miles they had traveled, Sergeant Brooks figured that he had a good head start on the Germans, so he started thinking about when they should destroy the track they had commandeered. *Maybe in another couple of hours. That ought to put a little more distance between us and those goons.* "Alex, tell Baker to watch the bumps and wake me in a couple of hours. That ought to do it. We can destroy the track then."

"Okay, Al."

Darkness had closed in on them, and despite the bumpy ride, most everybody in the squad was fast asleep. Only Sims, Baker, and Jackson were awake. Baker and Jackson were telling and retelling each other what they had done earlier that day. Corporal Sims had nothing better to do, so he sat and listened to them talking and laughing while a smile played across his face.

Out of nowhere, there was a loud whoosh, followed by an even louder explosion, and a shuddering lurch later, the halftrack came to a grinding halt, the engine shattered by an anti-tank round through the engine block. Men started pouring out of the back of the track even as it burned. Baker was the last one out and his jacket was on fire. Jackson, seeing that Baker was flaming up, shoved him down into the snow and put out the fire.

Brooks signaled everyone to follow him, and they immediately sprinted to cover, running bent over, towards a small stand of trees. When they reached the trees, Brooks spread his men out, and then waited in the darkness while he tried to figure out what had just happened.

A good ten minutes went by before he noticed what appeared to be a lone person trying to inch his way to the burning track. Signaling his men to get ready, Brooks kept watching the area around the burning halftrack where he thought he had seen somebody. Movement off to his right caught his eye, and slowly, so as not to make any sudden moves that would catch someone else's eye, he turned his head to the right to see what had caught his attention.

Nothing was moving out there anymore. Now Brooks was worried. *Who the hell is out there?* "Pass the word," whispered Brooks. "Jackson on me, now."

In the time it took to light a cigarette, the Arizona scout was lying down beside Brooks. "We need to know who is out there. You up for it?"

"Yes, sir, Sarge," whispered Jackson.

Staring at the pain-in-the-ass wearing Uncle Sam's uniform, Brooks shoved his helmet to the back of his head and muttered, "Shit," absolutely amazed. Studying his scout for a moment longer, he slapped Jackson's helmet and said, "How many times have you called me, sir? I swear beanpole. One of these days, the right Kraut is going to come along, and I'm going to hand you straight over to him. Hell, I've even been saving up my money to pay the bastard in case he won't take you for free." Brooks didn't notice the scout leaving. One second he was there, and the next he was gone.

Beanpole didn't take long to find out who was out there. Within minutes, six men, along with Jackson, were walking towards Sergeant Brooks. Amazed at what he saw, he stood up and headed towards Jackson and the others. When the men came together, one corporal turned to Brooks and asked, "Where in the hell did you pick this guy up from? One minute we're trying to figure out where you disappeared to, and the next minute, I find his knife at my throat. Jesus! We never heard a thing."

Laughing, Brooks introduced himself and Jackson, and then they all moved into the trees to get under cover and meet the rest of the men. When they were hidden by the trees, Brooks turned to the newly acquired staff sergeant and made the introductions. Before the handshakes ended, the staff sergeant turned to Sergeant Brooks and asked, "How come you're driving that German halftrack?"

"It's a long story," replied Brooks. "We were getting ready to destroy it anyway. You just saved us the effort. How did you get way out here, of all places?"

"Got overrun by the Germans when they hit our lines. The only way to get away from them was to head in this direction, so here we are," replied Staff Sergeant Miller.

"Well, we can talk about that mess later. We've got a pissed off SS major on our tails with orders to kill us where we stand. We need to keep moving, or he'll catch up with us. He's got more men than we do, and I imagine he's really pissed off at us right about now."

Major Schmidt was indeed greatly agitated at the Americans. To prove it, he was willing to kill his own men in order to get the chance to stand over his dead and dying enemy and shoot each one in the head at close range. The weather, however, didn't care about his personal ambitions. A prayer was sent to the Almighty, and that evening, a miracle occurred. The sky started clearing up, and by the early morning, the snow had stopped all together. At dawn, on December 24, 1944, the morning woke up to a rising sun and a cloudless blue sky.

~ ~ ~

Even though Schmidt's detachment had several fires going, they had slept fitfully. With no barriers to contain the heat, only what body parts were close to the fires actually got any sustained warmth.

Major Schmidt's anger from the previous night had not dissipated any at all. In fact, it was on the rise, thanks to the cold weather conditions he was forced to endure, and his frustration at the changed situation. Also, his first involvement with Sergeant Brooks was beginning to haunt him. In his nightmare chase across France, he had lost almost his entire force from an ambush Brooks had unleashed on his troops. A captain at the time, Schmidt barely escaped with his life when that catastrophe occurred.

While his men were eating their food, Schmidt walked out beyond the trees to scan the horizon. Lost to his thoughts, he spent several minutes shivering and staring at the black smoke on the horizon before it registered in his brain. Then it grabbed his full attention. Immediately, he was fully awake and screaming for his men to form up and move out. Either it was his halftrack burning, or the Americans had destroyed another German vehicle. In either case, Schmidt was convinced that where that smoke was he would find the Americans close by.

~ ~ ~

As the Germans drew nearer to the smoke, they became more cautious. Moving closer to the tree line, they tried to blend in with the darker shades of the shadows. They had been walking most of the morning, and it seemed as though no progress was being made until they reached the crest of a slight rise. Several hundred feet away was the halftrack, still burning, and still pouring out the black smoke they had seen earlier that morning. Having only twenty-three men left, including himself, Major Schmidt divided his men into four squads.

Leaving one team below the rise with one of the two MG 42's they had salvaged, he took the rest of the men back through the trees to converge on the halftrack from the tree-covered side. One squad he sent to cover their rear with the other MG 42 while he kept the other two teams with him. When he had his men in position, he signaled the lieutenant covering from the rise to send his man to check out the burning halftrack.

Schmidt watched from the cover of the trees while the trooper moved cautiously forward and started looking around. After a few minutes, the soldier signaled all clear. Leaving his men in their positions, Schmidt walked over to the halftrack to hear what the scout had to say.

It was obvious from the evidence that some sort of fight had taken place. What was confusing was why. Two groups of men had converged to a spot several feet from the vehicle, and by the looks of the jumbled tracks, they had all headed back towards the trees on friendly terms. No shell casings were lying about which meant no small arms fire, but the vehicle was hit by an anti-tank weapon. Why?

Major Schmidt walked around and looked at the tracks left by the Americans and the other group of men. After studying the problem for a while, he came up with the conclusion that the men he was hunting had met up with another group. That other group had fired on what they thought was an enemy vehicle only to find out it was filled with Americans and not their enemy. That was the only scenario he could come up with explaining why there was no small arms brass lying about. If there had been Germans inside the vehicle, there would have been a firefight and dead bodies left lying on the ground. Only six people walked away from the side the anti-tank fire came from. As far as he knew, the men he was hunting had no anti-tank weapons that he could see.

While he was still contemplating on his theory, one of his NCO's came up to him. When Schmidt acknowledged his presence, the NCO pointed to the west and said "Herr Major. I found the tracks of the Americans, and they are heading west."

Immediately, Schmidt's eyes narrowed almost to slits, and his expression turned vicious. Gazing intently at his sergeant, he said, "Show me." A few minutes later, he was looking down at the tracks and the direction they were heading. Gathering his men, he started them after the Americans

~ ~ ~

Little events were beginning to happen in the west that proved disastrous for the Germans. The fuel dumps they were hoping to capture to fuel their offense were being blown up by the Americans, as the enemy approached them. The few fuel dumps they had already captured could be used only by the capturing units, so a lot of vehicles were about to run out of gas. Also, the weather had cleared up to the point that Allied fighters and bombers were flying again, and they were hitting the German positions with everything they could carry. The towns once surrounded and cutoff, such as Bastogne, were getting all kinds of supplies air-dropped in.

Patton was on the move towards Bastogne with three armored divisions gearing up to attack the German left flank. Thousands of reinforcements were pouring in at the staging areas before being reorganized and sent to the front. The Americans were getting stronger every day while their enemy was growing weaker. The beginning was over for the Germans. They had failed in their mission, thanks the heroic stands of many die-hard American soldiers, slowing down the German attack along the entire axis of advance.

The Germans were starting to feel that rising strength. Resistance from the Americans was stiffening, and some

American units were even audacious enough to attack, stalling the Germans' advance even more. The enemy commanders, veterans of two different brands of warfare, recognized what was happening, and they all came to the same conclusion. Their great offensive in the west was dying out.

Chapter 34

The two senior sergeants were off by themselves, sorting through all of their options. At the moment, Sergeant Brooks was talking. "Look, Sergeant Miller, it's like this. If you want to take your men and leave, that's up to you, I won't stop you. If you decide to stay, you'll follow my orders to the letter."

Pausing for a moment so that his words had time to sink in, Brooks nodded to the sergeant and said, "You spend a little time thinking about it because once you decide to stay, there's no going back. We're leaving in thirty minutes, so you'll need to make a decision by then. If you stay, that gives us sixteen men to their twenty-something. Like I said, think it over before you decide."

Sergeant Miller walked over to his men to talk the situation over for a few minutes, but he wasn't gone long. The quick briefing was first, and it was short: a moment or two to think about the offer was next, followed by an immediate decision ending the conversation. Nodding to his men, he walked over to Brooks and said, "Strength in numbers. You'll probably need us in the long run when that major catches up to you. Besides, we prefer the company. We'll stay with you."

"Good," said Brooks. "Okay, people, pack it up. We're moving out."

While they were leaving, Brooks informed Sergeant Miller how he wanted the men organized. "We'll break the men down into two squads," he said. "Corporal Sims is acting sergeant, so he'll take one squad. You'll take the other squad. Jackson, Baker, Avery, Todd, White, Snow, Stony, and Corporal Sims will be 1st squad. You'll have your men plus Green, Lemons, Brown, and Shift. Sam's as good as Jackson on the scout, but he's not as good a shot. How many Bazooka rounds do you have left?" asked Brooks.

"Four, I think," said Sergeant Miller. "I'll find out." With that said, he went back to check with Corporal Peters. After the quick ammo check, Sergeant Miller returned and reported to Sergeant Brooks that his count had been correct. Several hours later, Brooks called a halt. The sun was going down, so he wanted to find a suitable, defensible location for the night before it got too dark to see. He had a hunch that the enemy major was not far behind.

~ ~ ~

"Captain, get the men moving," said Major Schmidt. "We have a direction, and we have several hours of good daylight left, so let's take advantage of that."

"Yes, Herr Major."

Only five minutes passed before the men were on the move again, heading west. "Captain, in a couple of hours we'll stop for a break," said Schmidt. "I want to keep moving all night with a break about every two hours. I believe we will end up close to the Americans by daylight tomorrow."

"Yes, Herr Major."

By 1900 hours, however, his warriors were dragging their feet, almost ready to collapse to the ground because they were so tired. They had been marching through two feet of slowly melting snow for over twelve hours. One of his sergeant's shook his head and thought, *as tired as we are, and he wants us to go on through the night*? Before he could think more about his dilemma, he was pulled away from his thoughts by Major Schmidt's voice. "Captain, it's time to give the men a break."

The men were so tired they just dropped were they stopped. Nobody ate; they just fell asleep in the snow where they were. The snow had been slowly melting all day so the ground was soggy. Nothing kept them from sleeping.

Instead of waking the men after their two-hour break, Schmidt decided to give them an extra two hours. He was just as tired. Setting no guard, he leaned up against a tree to daydream the time away until he was ready to wake his men. His last thought before he fell asleep was his promotion to colonel. Snoring strongly, he was dead to the world.

~ ~ ~

Jumping to his feet, startled and confused, Major Schmidt realized he'd fallen into a deep sleep, and so had his men. Because they were so tired, he had to kick everybody awake.

"Get up, you bastards," he screamed. "They'll get away. Let's go. Now. On your feet. Move it!"

Slowly, his soldiers got to their feet. Their clumsiness wasn't a good sign. Along with being stiff from the cold, they were also shaking from it, so they took a few minutes to get stirring, much to Major Schmidt's irritation. "Eat while you march, damn it. Let's go." With that order given, Kampfgruppe Schmidt started off again on their search to find the Americans.

~ ~ ~

Brooks had sent Private Jackson on ahead to try and find a good place to stop. About forty minutes passed before the scout materialized out of the darkness with a smile on his face. "Damn you, Jackson. If that Kraut following us doesn't shoot you, I will," whispered Brooks. "What did you find?"

Jackson turned and started walking away before he said, "Follow me, Sarge."

Shaking his head, half in anger and half in amazement, Brooks muttered, "Lead on," and trudged off after Jackson. After walking for about ten minutes Brooks came to a quick, three-step halt and stood staring in amazement at a small hollow with a fire burning. The rest of the squad, however, didn't take the time to stop and gaze at the fire. They brushed by Sergeant Brooks without hesitation and, within seconds, they were standing next to the wondrous heat, and voicing their pleasure.

Taking another look at his surroundings, Brooks pulled at his ear for a moment before he turned to Jackson and said, "Damn, beanpole. You did it again. I couldn't see that fire until I was almost on top of it." Smiling and rubbing his palms together, Brooks winked at Jackson and muttered, "Ah, to be warm again!"

As the dawn approached, Brooks and his men were already on the move. They were out in the open and currently traveling spread out, in a loose wedge formation. They could see off into the distance another small stand of trees, but it would be awhile before they reached them.

~ ~ ~

Major Schmidt and his men were moving along the edge of the woods that Brooks' detachment had just left an hour before. Calling a halt, he sent several of his men deeper into the trees to look for any sign of the Americans. Cold, wet, and exhausted, the rest of his men just collapsed to the ground and instantly fell asleep. However, twenty minutes was all the sleep they were getting for the moment. Schmidt had them on move again. His scouts had found where Brooks and his men had bivouacked for the night. They were closing in on the Americans, and Schmidt's excitement was rising. Pushing his men harder, he was hoping to catch the Americans before the sun set. He could hardly contain his eagerness.

Major Schmidt was looking off into the distance, hoping beyond measure to spot the Americans. All thoughts of luck had gone out of the door the day he watched his vehicles go up in flames. Now, he no longer prayed for it. Then his heart skipped a beat. "THERE," he muttered softly. "There they are." Calling for his men to move faster, Schmidt was raring to close with the Americans before they reached the trees they were heading for.

Private Lemons was looking back the way they had come. He thought he saw a lot of silhouettes moving around behind them, but he wasn't sure. Whistling, he caught the attention of Corporal Sims to get a second opinion. Sam pointed back at the stand of trees they recently departed, and sure enough, he was right. He could see them plainly. Sims nodded and immediately ran forward to inform Sergeant Brooks of the sighting.

"They've caught up to us, Al. What do you want to do?"

Brooks stared at Corporal Sims for a moment before he nodded to himself and came to a decision. With anger leading the charge, he turned to Sims and said, "I think it's time to end this right here and now." Turning to face the Germans, Brooks issued out his orders.

Without cover, the men were spread out wide on the snow-covered ground. They had their backs to the trees they had been moving towards, but they were still a long way off from the tree line. Looking back, they could see their refuge off in the distance. Staring out across the snowy landscape, their breaths were like white clouds rising into the cold, crisp air while they waited tensely for the Germans to close the distance. "Jackson. You think you could hit one of them from here?" asked Brooks.

"Maybe," replied Jackson. "You want me to try?"

"Yes," said Brooks. "See what you can do."

Watching his enemy drop to the ground, Schmidt's excitement grew by leaps and bounds. *I have you now, you bastards.* Staring out at the Americans, he shouted out his order. "Kill them all where they lay. They have killed our comrades. Show them no mercy."

Schmidt spread his men out, and they started moving towards the Americans. All thoughts and feelings of being exhausted were gone. The imminence of battle and the rush of adrenaline had removed it all. They were going into battle against a very elusive enemy, a very worthy and experienced adversary.

The Germans were almost to the point of hitting the ground and low-crawling the rest of the way when one of their men grunted, let out a sigh, and collapsed to the ground, unmoving. Then they heard the shot.

Chapter 35

Brooks watched while Jackson adjusted his sights. When he was ready, beanpole snuggled into a more comfortable position, took a breath, and slowly exhaled as he squeezed off the shot. When Brooks saw the German topple to the ground, he turned to Jackson and said, "Damn, beanpole. That was good shooting." Smiling, he shouted out, "That's one down."

Immediately dropping to the ground, Schmidt's men opened fire on the Americans until their commander yelled to cease fire, "You're wasting ammo," shouted Schmidt. "We have to get closer, so start crawling!"

Brooks called out to his men, "Hold your fire until I give the command! Let 'em get closer. Sergeant Miller, move your men back about fifty yards or so. When you get there, let me know." When Sergeant Miller reached his new position, he alerted Brooks, who turned his head and immediately shouted at Corporal Sims. "Move your squad back, Alex. We'll leap-frog our way to the trees."

The Germans were still too far away to launch any kind of a rushing attack without losing all of their men. By moving towards the trees this way, Brooks hoped to keep his enemy at a safe distance and still reach the tree line in time to deploy his men properly.

Major Schmidt was watching what was going on and instantly understood what Brooks was trying to do. Swearing vehemently, he shouted at his men. He had to get closer so he could concentrate all of his firepower against the fleeing Americans. With limited ammo, they couldn't afford to waste any on long distance shooting. "If the Americans get into those trees, we will lose them again! Do not let them reach those trees, or there will be hell to pay!"

Low on ammo and with no re-supply available, the Germans had to be very careful: they had to make every shot count. "Lieutenant Grueber, I want you to take eight men, and on my command, I want you to sprint forward about twenty meters and then drop. Captain, take four men and a machine-gun and move off to the left about thirty meters or so. You'll cover Lieutenant Grueber when he makes his dash forward. Sergeant Manstein, take six men and move to the right about twenty meters. When Lieutenant Grueber hits the ground, I want you to sprint forward about the same distance and then hit the ground. We will use sprint and drop tactics until we can close with the enemy. I will keep the other four men and the other machine gun with me to help cover your advance."

Having received their orders, Schmidt's men moved to their positions and waited for the order to move forward. Watching his men disperse to their starting points, Schmidt was thinking ahead. His confidence rose, and so did his arrogant attitude. He was already visualizing his promotion to colonel. Signals from all of his junior commanders told him it was time to put his plan into action. By the time Schmidt had his men in position, the Americans had moved back about sixty to seventy yards.

While Sergeant Miller was moving further back again, Brooks was watching the Germans. Staring out at his enemy, he watched a group of enemy soldiers jump up from the ground and sprint forward a little ways before they dropped to the ground. No sooner had the first group dropped than another group popped up and did the same thing. Smiling, Brooks thought, *well now. I guess Jackson's shooting didn't impress anyone. Maybe it's time to remind them again.*

When the two larger groups were about forty meters ahead of the covering machine gunners, Major Schmidt signaled Captain Schnelling that it was their turn to move forward.

At the same time Schnelling started forward, Major Schmidt's crew made their move as well. The two covering squads dropped to the ground at almost the same time. Nobody had fired any shots during their movements, so Schmidt signaled the largest group to go again. Just as they started their sprint, one of the men let out a grunt and fell face first into the muddy snow, and then they heard the shot. "Damn!" shouted Schmidt. That's two men down and we're still out of range."

"Hell, Jackson. You have eagle eyes," said Brooks. "Down goes another one, boys!"

Sergeant Miller smiled and said, "Man, am I glad you're on our side and not theirs. Can you do that again?"

"I think so," replied Jackson.

"Okay, everybody," said Brooks. "If they want to play those games, so can we. Sims, when I give you the signal, you get up and haul ass about thirty yards and then drop. Miller, when he hits the ground you get up and do the same. Jackson, you stay here with me and drop any German who tries to shoot at 'em."

This leapfrog battle went on for several hours until Brooks and his men finally reached the small wooded area they had been trying for. During those hours, Jackson had managed to kill two more Germans. As each enemy soldier fell, a very loud cheer rose from the Americans, and it could be heard drifting across the snow-covered ground by the SS major and his men, a taunting jeer that deeply infuriated both the major and his remaining troops.

When Schmidt saw that his enemy had reached the trees, he stopped the movement of his men. There was no sense in going up against a well-covered and concealed opponent with him and his troops so openly exposed. *Well,* he thought. *First blood goes to the Americans. Tomorrow will be a different story.*

Waiting for darkness to fall so they could creep up on the Americans without being seen, Major Schmidt took stock of his own situation. He had started out with over thirty men, three halftracks, and all the firepower he needed to get the job done. Now, he was confronted with the fact that not only had he lost more than a third of his men, but he had also lost all three of his halftracks, and not one of the Americans were dead. To add fuel to his anger, the Americans had out maneuvered him every step of the way. That was a hard slap to the face that could be satisfied only with the blood of the American dead all over his hands. He smiled when he remembered his orders. "Leave none alive."

Brooks knew that as soon as it got dark the Germans would start creeping up on him, so he decided to let his men get some sleep during the two hours of daylight still remaining. When the sun went down they would be moving out.

Sergeant Brooks sent Jackson and Lemons out to scout in different directions with orders to find a suitable defensive position they could fight from. Brooks knew they had been extremely lucky so far. They had limited ammo, no machine guns, and only light automatic weapons. What was needed was to lure the enemy into an ambush and eliminate all of them.

When the men of kampfgruppe Schmidt stopped fighting, their weariness immediately took over. With two hours of daylight still remaining Major Schmidt let his men sleep where they were. Not wanting to fall asleep himself, he smoked cigarette after cigarette until his throat burned, which also helped to keep him awake. His main concern was after the sun went down. *Will the Americans leave, or will they try and set up an ambush, expecting me to come after them*?

Not knowing if his enemy had left the trees or which direction they would take if they did made it next to impossible for Schmidt to set up an ambush of his own. With three men dead that left him with only twenty, which meant that the two antagonists were just about even in that respect. However, with his two MG 42's, he had long range covering fire, which gave him a slight advantage over his adversary. As the sun was going down, so were the major's eyelids. Before long, not a single German soldier remained awake.

~ ~ ~

Jackson was the first to return. Off to the southwest, he had found a dry creek bed that offered some cover and concealment, but no high ground worthy of the title and very limited ambush possibilities. Brooks was still waiting for Lemons to return to find out what he had uncovered.

The sun was just dropping below the horizon when Sam finally appeared out of the shadows. Going straight to Brooks, he told him that he had found nothing suitable. After hearing what both men had to report, Brooks had a choice to make. *Do we stay here and let the Germans close in on us, or do we leave and head towards that dry creek bed*? Then another thought occurred him. *Or do we go hunting Germans tonight*? "Jackson," he whispered. "Got something for you. Are you interested?"

"Sure," replied Jackson. "What is it?"

"I want you to find out where those Germans are and leave them a message."

While the SS troops of Major Schmidt were playing their cat and mouse games with Sergeant Brooks, the battles in the west were still raging. On the 23rd of December, the weather had cleared enough that the Allied air force was able to fly minor sorties against German positions. The 24th of December gave the Allies beautiful skies, and they took full advantage of them. The major sorties flown against German positions were doing their damage, tearing up the enemy and ruining their attack schedule even more. The 26th of December heralded even better news. Patton had at last punched a hole through the left flank of the German forces surrounding Bastogne, finally ending that siege.

Allied supply drops were in full swing, and so were troop movements. The Americans had stopped the German offensive dead in its tracks, and now they were gearing up to push the enemy back into Germany.

The German commanders were calling for a retreat, but Hitler refused. The tide of battle had turned. The enemy, not achieving their goals, were going on the defensive everywhere along their lines. The Americans, having stopped the Germans cold, had begun their counter attack, something that neither Major Schmidt nor Sergeant Brooks knew or even cared, about. Their only concern at the moment was defeating the other before the other did the same to them.

~ ~ ~

Having tried three different approaches, Jackson was unable to infiltrate the German line without getting caught. Major Schmidt still remembered his first infiltration, so he took pains to make sure the little scout failed on his next attempt, and he was successful in his endeavor. However, not all of what the scout set out to do was a failure. He did notice that the Germans were preparing to move out.

Hearing Jackson's report on his failed infiltration, Brooks took his helmet off and rubbed his head before he said, "Damn! This Kraut is a determined cuss. Let's go, people. We're moving to that dry creek bed. We'll fight 'em from there."

~ ~ ~

Major Schmidt woke up to another cold and damp early morning and, in turn, woke up his troops. When Jackson had tried his infiltration, they were awake, fully alert, and waiting, but that didn't keep the scout from snooping around their perimeter. Besides discovering his enemy's preparations, he also noticed the two MG 42 machine guns they were carrying. Those guns could bring down a whole lot of pain on Brooks and his men if they were successful in bringing those babies to bear.

Sometime around 0200 hours on Christmas morning, Brooks had his men ready and positioned along the creek bed. Every third person stayed awake, with the shifts changing about every two hours. All was still quiet. Brooks, having been awake for the last thirty-six hours, was finally getting some sleep, and his buddy, Corporal Sims, made sure nobody disturbed him.

Earlier, Sergeant Brooks had sent out Jackson and Lemons to keep track of the German's progress. After an hour, Jackson sent Lemons back with word that the Germans had not left the wooded area yet. To all appearances, they were still searching for a direction. Jackson reported back to Brooks just before the crack of dawn.

~ ~ ~

Shortly after sunrise, the Germans were heading southwest. They had found some indications as to the direction the Americans had taken, so they tightened up their belts and set out to kill the Americans. Around 1000 hours, they were spotted by the Arizona beanpole.

Sergeant Brooks had decided to let the Germans get close until he and his men were spotted. To Brooks, this situation was ending now. Either the Germans left the field of battle victorious, or the Americans would leave triumphant.

Sergeant Brooks was through running. He was tired of the whole mess and tired of that damned SS major.

"Hold your fire, boys. Don't shoot until I give the command," said Brooks. "I want them real close."

The creek stretched north and south. Starting just inside the trees, it meandered crookedly in a southerly direction until it ended near a clump of bushes, a good seventy yards away. The dry watercourse was also filled to the brim with snow, so the creek bed was un-recognizable in most stretches. The trees were just sixty feet behind and to the right of where Brooks and his men were waiting.

Major Schmidt was watching the tree line, and searching for his enemy, so he didn't pay much attention to the small ridgeline angling off to his right. The reverse side wasn't tall enough to hide a body, and he didn't recognize the white, German overcoats lining the creek bed or the Americans wearing them. The mounds of snow behind the low ridgeline didn't concern him. His only thought concerning the berm was that it afforded him cover in case his enemy started shooting. With his men spread out in a skirmish line, they slowly advanced towards the trees.

~ ~ ~

Wanting to see what was going on, Brooks had to force himself to stay down. He didn't want to spring the trap too early by popping his head up at the wrong time. He could hear the enemy approaching, sloshing through the soggy ground with every step they took. Tensely, the Americans waited while the minutes passed. Creeping closer, the Germans continued splashing their way towards their objective until Brooks thought he had them dead to rights. Then he signaled for his men to stand up and open fire.

Major Schmidt and his men were about fifteen feet from the small berm line to their right, and still watching the trees when the Americans jumped up. Hit in the flank and looking towards the wrong danger, the Germans were hammered with small arms fire. Major Schmidt was shot three times before he could even think to hit the ground, and not a single enemy soldier fired a round. The ambush was so completely surprising to the Germans that they were decimated before they had time to react. They were expecting the attack to come from the trees, so they were prepared for that eventuality. Their eyes were looking elsewhere at the wrong time, and to all appearances, the area to their right looked devoid of any ambush possibilities.

Surveying the results of his plan, Brooks walked over to the SS major and stood looking down at him. Almost immediately, Brooks recognized him, and instantly, he remembered the harrowing chase through France when his dying enemy now lying at his feet first tried to kill him.

The major was still alive, but not for long. Calling for Baker, Brooks was curious as to why the man was so hell-bent on killing him and his men. Bending down on one knee, Brooks looked at him and asked, “Why?” When Baker had translated the question to the major, he looked up at Sergeant Brooks and said, “Because you are the enemy. I almost got you again.” With that said, SS Major Paul Schmidt let out one last gasp before he died.

Immediately after the major spent his last breath, Sergeant Brooks stood up, looked around, and then issued an order. “Search the Germans for anything we can use. Food, ammo, maps, and don’t forget about those two MG 42’s. They just might come in handy later on.”

After a thorough search for anything useful, they set out, heading west with their newfound items, smiling the big smile. They had enough food to last them for several more days, and their latest victory had them stepping out lively. “Hey, boys,” shouted Brooks. “Merry Christmas.” Grinning from ear to ear, the men rejoiced in the knowledge that they no longer had to concern themselves with that damn SS major and his men. The action was a perfectly executed ambush, and they were proud of the outcome. Not one enemy soldier was able to get off a shot. They had time only to look and die.

Chapter 36

What in the world did I do to deserve this kind of bad luck? wondered Major Thomas. Walking beside the major with his head bandaged and his right arm in a sling, Sergeant Cane was thinking the same thing.

En route to their next assignment, they had unexpectedly run into the enemy. They were considerably outnumbered, and the situation didn't look promising, so Sergeant Cane suggested to his commanding officer that he swap his shirt with a dead sergeant just in case they were captured. Cane was afraid the pinholes on his commander's collar from wearing brass might give him away. If the Germans found out he was an officer, they would immediately isolate him from the rest of the men and probably send him off to some headquarters to be tortured and interrogated. Cane was having a heck of a time remembering not to call him major or sir. He really had to watch himself on that score.

Walking east, somewhere between St Vith and Bastogne, the column of Allied prisoners being escorted by their enemy was a cold, wet, miserable, and dejected group of people. The war for them had ended. They were on their way to Germany as POW's. Not a very pleasant turn of events for these Americans.

After about a day and a half of trudging through the mud, snow, and water, the prisoners were coming up on the town of Winterspelt, not too far from the major's old stomping grounds. Here the Germans called a halt. Only about thirty or so prisoners remained from the original fifty that were captured. The others were officers, and they were taken away a couple of hours after Major Thomas was taken prisoner. There was no doubt in anyone's mind that they were being interrogated or, even worse, being tortured for any information the Germans could get out of them.

Sergeant Cane was like a shadow to Thomas and wouldn't leave his side. The two had been together since North Africa.

Their charge to war began less than twelve months before when the major was a 1st lieutenant, commanding Cane's company. They had been through many battles together and had managed to survive every one of them. A new fight was about to begin for the two men, and they only had each other to count on. A brother-like relationship was developing between them on their journey through captivity, and Sergeant Cane was taking it seriously.

Not knowing how far into Germany the two men were going or what was going to happen to them once they got there began to wear on both men. They started moving off by themselves when a halt was called, never mingling with the other prisoners. They very rarely talked above a whisper, and when one of the other prisoners approached, they walked away. That move was Sergeant Cane's idea. Only he knew the major was a major, and he wanted to keep it that way. No inadvertent slip-ups by one of the prisoners if they kept to themselves.

By evening of the next day, the fact was hitting home with everybody. The time indeed was going to be very long before they saw their families and friends again, if they ever did. The Germans were taking their prisoners somewhere near a town called Prüm, situated less than twenty miles north of Bitburg, where there was a POW camp located nearby.

~ ~ ~

Sergeant Brooks and his men were moving slowly and carefully in a westerly direction. Because they were starting to encounter more and more villages and homes, they had to be extra careful that no one saw them. With all of the Allied bombing and strafing going on, there were also a lot of burned-out farmhouses dotting the countryside, along with a lot of angry German citizens. If anyone spotted them, Brooks had no doubt they would call the authorities immediately and, quite possibly, help the authorities track them down. They would be the hunted again, a prospect nobody was looking forward to.

Spotting a burned-out farmhouse, Brooks sent Jackson and Lemons ahead to scout it out. When they returned, they reported it all clear and safe to occupy. Once they were in the farmhouse, they noticed it had a basement, which meant they could have a fire without being spotted. Posting his guards, Brooks then called for an inventory of everything on hand.

They had seventeen, white, German cold weather overcoats, ten potato mashers, (German long-handled grenades), five American grenades, the SS major's 9mm pistol and ammo that Brooks had kept to remind him of what they had gone through, two MG 42 light machine guns with about four hundred rounds each, their own small arms, and one Bazooka with four rounds, plus enough food left for all of them for another three days. The map that Brooks had confiscated from the dead SS major made it easier for them to sneak past all of the little hamlets they encountered.

Walking over to where Brooks was squatting on one knee, Corporal Sims asked him where they were. Smiling, Brooks pulled out the captured map and pointed to the spot. "Here, just south of Prüm."

"How in the hell did we get so deep into Germany?" asked Sims.

Shivering, Brooks looked at his corporal and said, "With all the direction changes we've made and the fact that we were running for our lives, we got turned around a few times. I'd be willing to bet that our abrupt direction changes are what drove that SS major crazy the most. One day we're heading away from Germany, and the next day, we're heading back deeper into Kraut-land. Must have been a real nightmare for him trying to figure out what our next move was going to be."

~ ~ ~

Night had fallen, and it was bitterly cold. Christmas had come and gone, but it wasn't much of a Christmas to Sergeant Cane and Major Thomas. They were heading straight back into Germany, for God knows how long and with no hope whatsoever of anything good happening to them.

Major Thomas wondered if anybody even knew he was missing. All the colonel said was get to *this* unit and report to *that* colonel to do *this* job with no written orders, specifying where he was supposed to be. With a sigh, he resigned himself to the fact that there was absolutely nobody who knew where he and Sergeant Cane were, let alone whether they were even alive or not. The night was going to be a long, cold, stretch of misery for both men.

An hour after sunrise, on the 28th of December, the German guards woke up their prisoners and fed them cold rations. As soon as the Germans were finished eating, they herded the prisoners together, whether they were still eating, or not, and started them marching east again, deeper into Germany. What the prisoners didn't know was that when they reached the town of Weissenhof, they would be loaded onto trucks for the remainder of their journey to their new home, a German POW camp.

A loud roaring noise came first, then the bullets were flying all around, and everybody was running, trying to get off the road and behind some kind of cover. Allied fighter planes were everywhere, strafing anything and everything that looked like the enemy. Soldiers on both sides were dying from the sudden hail of bullets, and then the planes were gone. They had disappeared into the distance, leaving behind the dead and dying scattered everywhere. What medics the Germans had on hand went from soldier to soldier regardless of whose uniform they were wearing.

Sergeant Cane and Major Thomas had been lucky enough to be standing next to a bombed-out building with some of the walls still intact. They jumped behind one of the walls just before the bullets hit where they had just been. "Damn, that was close," said Thomas. Cane nodded in agreement while his face very quickly turned pale.

When the confusion was over, the prisoners were put to work moving the wounded and dead out of the way. Thirty minutes was all the time that chore took, and then they were on the march again, arriving at their destination sometime around 1800 hours that evening. Bone-weary, and just too tired to think about food, they entered Weissenhof, Germany, a dejected group of Americans. A few minutes after arriving, they were quickly herded off to a basement in one of the bombed out buildings where they were to spend the night before heading out in the morning on the last leg of their journey.

At 0700 hours on the morning of December 29, the prisoners were fed cold rations again, moved to the center of town, and loaded onto trucks to continue their journey eastward. Only about twenty-five prisoners were left, so they were loaded onto two trucks. Space was cramped on the vehicles, but the Germans didn't care. Five motorcycles with sidecars guarded the trucks.

Two motorcycles followed behind each truck, with one leading the prisoner convoy. Sitting in each sidecar was a soldier carrying a sub-machine gun, so escape was very unlikely with all that firepower guarding the prisoners. By 0830, the prisoners were on their way east to their new digs where they would spend the remainder of the war, however long that might be.

~ ~ ~

While they were lying in a ditch, taking a break by the side of a road, Sergeant Brooks watched two trucks and some motorcycles pull off to the side and come to a stop on the gently sloping shoulder, about three or four hundred feet from where he and his men were resting. Much to his surprise, Brooks witnessed two groups of uniformed soldiers jump down off the back of the trucks and rush into the field beside the road to relieve themselves. Only two eye-blinks passed before he recognized the uniforms, and he was pulling hard at his ear. *Damn*! He already knew what was about to greet him. Turning to look at his men, he could see by their expressions what they had in mind. Shaking his head at them, he whispered, "We can't let anybody know we're here if we want to get back to our lines in one piece."

The little beanpole from Arizona stared at the prisoners for a moment longer before he turned to face his platoon sergeant and said, "Sarge, they're Americans. They're our men. We can't let them rot in a lousy German POW camp. It's just not right." Again, Brooks shook his head, and again, he received the same argument as before.

Within a couple of minutes, the prisoners were herded back onto the trucks. Once more, Brooks was privy to the disapproving looks his men were giving him while they re-stated their previous argument. His surrender was apparent when he finally turned to Corporal Peters and asked, "Can you take out the lead truck with that Bazooka and not kill the passengers?"

"Yeah, Sarge. Piece of cake," answered Peters. "When the truck reaches that telephone pole, I'll put one right through its engine block. Load me up quickly, and I'll take out the other one before they can slam on the brakes. The rest of you guys can have the motorcycles."

Chuckling softly, Brooks shook his head and said, "Okay. It's your plan."

After putting Corporal Peters out of harm's way so that everyone was clear of the back blast from the Bazooka, Brooks designated which of the Germans to shoot first. With that chore out of the way, Brooks fixed his gaze on the lead truck and waited for the ambush to begin.

~ ~ ~

As soon as the last prisoner was loaded into the trucks, the motorcade pulled out onto the roadway and continued their journey northeast. They had barely reached traveling speed when their world collided with hell.

The lead truck was almost to the pole when Brooks tapped Peters on the shoulder, and immediately, the corporal rose up, took aim, and pulled the trigger. Perfect shot, right through the engine compartment. Private Waters was already in the process of quickly reloading the Bazooka while the rest of the men started firing on their respective targets. The lead truck, after being hit, veered off the road and onto the slanted shoulder and slowly toppled over onto its side, spilling some of the prisoners out of the back end. Another whoosh was followed almost immediately by a loud boom, and the second truck came to a shuddering halt.

When the first truck was hit, the driver on the lead motorcycle turned back to see what had just happened. However, before the motorcycle crew had any time to react, they were shot to pieces. The motorcycle and sidecar continued moving forward, rapidly accelerating until it rammed into the front of the truck that had just fallen onto its side and exploded from the impact.

Only one of the two motorcycles following the lead truck managed to avoid running into the back of the truck it was following, and they were closest to the ditch the men were hiding in. That motorcycle crew also died before they could react.

The motorcycle that ran into the back of the lead truck had no chance to swerve out of the way, and both riders died from broken necks when they rammed into the solid-steel frame of the truck bed. The two motorcycles following the second truck were a bit luckier. They had time to avoid a collision with the truck they were following, but in doing so, exposed themselves to a withering fire from the roadside ditch. They never once saw who was shooting at them. All in all, the attack was another successful, pop-and-bang ambush, and the victors had emerged unhurt again.

Even before the smoke and dust had begun to settle, Brooks and his men were running over to the trucks to help the freshly freed prisoners who were starting to mill about, confused and thoroughly bewildered over the strange occurrence. While some of his men gathered weapons and ammo, Brooks was using the rest to gather up their newly acquired charges and get the hell out of Dodge. Brooks now had about forty men. After checking both trucks and the motorcycles, they got the hell out of there.

Of the twenty-five or so men who had been in the trucks, only about five or six were limping. However, no one had escaped unscathed. All of them had bumps and bruises somewhere on their bodies. Those who were uninjured helped the injured, and very quickly, they were on the move, trying desperately to get as far from the burning trucks as they could before the enemy arrived at the scene. Brooks looked at all of the men he now had under his command and pulled at his ear. *How in the hell am I going to keep all these men hidden and still reach our lines in one piece*?

~ ~ ~

Marching west, Sergeant Brooks was out in front leading his men when he felt a tap on his shoulder. With all of the excitement going on, nobody had time to do any talking while they made their escape. When he turned to look at who was doing the tapping, he almost stopped walking when he noticed the tapper was his battalion commander, Major Thomas. Then he spotted Sergeant Cane. Smiling, he said to the major, "Damn, sir, you were right. The Germans are about to attack us." All three men laughed at the comment while they shook each other's hands. "It sure is good to see you, sir. Dan. I see you're barely staying out of trouble."

Returning the chuckle, Dan replied, "Some kind of war, isn't it?"

"Yes. It surely is," said Brooks. "You look like hell!" And he did. Sergeant Cane's uniform was still bloodstained, despite his earlier swim across the Our River. His head wound kept breaking open from his exertions.

With sunset still three hours away, Brooks pushed the men harder, trying to increase the distance from the burning trucks and any pursuit the enemy might mount. Currently moving north, he had deviously changed direction during their westward march, hoping that anyone searching for them would think they were still heading due-west and trying to get through to Allied lines as quickly as possible. Sam and beanpole spent hours covering up their multi-layered direction change. The platoon sergeant's idea was to get behind anyone searching for them and follow the hunting hounds while they cleared a path to freedom. Looking up at the sky, Brooks closed his eyes and silently prayed for more snow.

While they walked, Sergeant Brooks and Major Thomas spent the rest of the day going over what had happened after the Germans attacked and ended the de-briefing with the recent rescue by Brooks and his men. The major also left Sergeant Brooks in charge, a decision he had no problem making. He knew all about the classified missions Brooks had been sent on, information that less than a handful was privy to. He also understood that if they were to make it back to friendly forces successfully, Brooks was the man to lead them there. The major's decision was based on what the sergeant and his squad had accomplished under some very extraordinary circumstances during their tenure with the

Special Tactical Force. First squad had to contend with an Arizona beanpole as well as the Germans.

~ ~ ~

Brooks stopped the men when they entered a small stand of trees they had spotted earlier. Calling a halt, he could see that everybody was tired. They had put a considerable distance between themselves and the burning trucks, so Brooks figured they could afford to stop for a couple of hours. Calling to Jackson, he said, “Take Baker and head back to see what’s going on. Find out if anybody’s following us. Two hours out and two hours back should do it. Be careful, you guys. They’re on to us, again.”

~ ~ ~

Standing at attention, Colonel Walther Marcs was listening to the ravings of his commanding officer. A veteran of the eastern front, Colonel Marcs was transferred west after he lost 80% of his battalion. His skills as a panzer commander were less than tolerated by the likes of General Guderian and other acknowledged panzer leaders. He remembered how he felt when he was relieved of his command. He could hear and see his general’s anger and the fear of losing another command was strong and it settled in the pit of his stomach. “Over twenty five POW’s have escaped and are on the loose in western Germany. Twelve of our soldiers have been killed, and we don’t know yet who is killing us! Where is Major Schmidt? Why hasn’t he reported in? Have you even heard from him, yet?”

“No, Herr General. I haven’t heard anything from Major Schmidt,” replied Colonel Marcs.

“What are you doing about it, Colonel?” asked the general.

“I am sending out a kampfgruppe, with light armor support. They will find out what happened to Major Schmidt and hunt down the escaped prisoners.”

“Very good, Colonel,” replied the general. “Just to make sure they complete their mission successfully, I want you to lead the charge. Do I make myself clear, Colonel Marcs?”

“Yes, Herr General. I will be leaving at dawn.”

General Günter gazed angrily at his colonel before he nodded slightly in response. Then arrogantly, he turned and left the room. The colonel's hand was still outstretched from his salute when the general abruptly turned his back and left, leaving it un-answered.

~ ~ ~

With no fires going, the men were getting colder. While Brooks took stock of the men and equipment he now had, he was forced to change the way he was handling the situation. He currently had over forty men with him, so moving across his enemy's home turf during daylight hours was out of the question. They had to start traveling at night and hide during the day. This change of plans had Brooks pulling at his ear, but it couldn't be helped. He had too many men. They'd stick out like freshly broken noses.

Once again, Brooks was forced to divide his men up, so he re-organized his troops, creating four squads. Sergeant Cane, Sergeant Miller, Corporal Sims, and Corporal Peters were acting squad leaders. Corporal Baker, Private Jackson, and Private Lemons were assigned as roving scouts, with Jackson as lead pathfinder.

Out of the twenty-five new men, only eighteen had weapons, and those were the weapons they had confiscated from the dead guards, along with what ammo the enemy had on them. Six more potato mashers were added to the fifteen grenades they already had.

The two MG 42's were divided up between four of the new men. The food the guards had on them wouldn't last but a day, so now food was once again a problem. After receiving the all-clear from Jackson and Baker, Brooks felt that it was time to move out. Putting the three scouts out in front about fifty yards or so, they continued north.

~ ~ ~

Jackson sent Lemons back to report that everything was all clear about every fifteen minutes, just to ease his sergeant's mind. Once again, the men of 1st squad were smiling. Brooks, however, despite his smile, was still shaking his head when he said, "Damn, beanpole. You're going to run poor Sam to death if you keep this up. Hell, he looks an inch shorter already! Only send him back when you see the enemy, not when it's all clear." The time was 0300 hours on the morning of December 30.

Looking at the pre-dawn light reminded Brooks that it was time to find a hole to hide in. Thirty minutes later, Lemons came to him with news that Jackson had found a small stand of trees about a mile ahead. "He wants to know if you wish to hide in those trees," said Sam. Staring at his number two pain in the ass, Brooks replied, "Yes. And, Sam, you go back and tell Private Jackson that if he doesn't watch it, I'll have him out scouting in his birthday suit." Chuckling, Brooks passed the word down. "We stop for the day in thirty minutes."

Chapter 37

Colonel Marcs had arrived at the scene of the escape several hours ahead of the bulk of his battalion. His early arrival gave him time to look around the area before his other units had a chance to churn up the ground with all of their tracked vehicles.

Looking at the still-smoldering trucks from the driver's side, he noticed that they had been hit by anti-tank fire. Well-placed anti-tank fire. *Hmm. Maybe a shoulder fired weapon? Certainly not a towed gun. Takes too much time to reload and re-locate a quickly moving target. There's not much distance between the two trucks, so the action must have been fast. Too quick for a towed gun. One round right through the engine compartment on each of the two trucks. That's pretty accurate shooting*.

Walking over to the motorcycles, Colonel Marcs glanced around, trying to visualize what had taken place. While he was studying the scene, he noticed a drainage ditch off to his ten-o-clock. Looking at the trucks and then back at the ditch, he thought he knew where the anti-tank fire had come from. With that idea floating around in his head, he walked over to it and immediately spotted small arms brass all along its length for at least thirty or forty feet. Staring down at the shell-casings, it was obvious that a lot of men were hiding in the ditch. The evidence pointed to a startling fact that removed any remaining doubt he had about who the perpetrators were.

Studying the scene of the attack, he tried to piece together what might've taken place. Searching the ditch, he found no traces of blood anywhere, so that told him the attackers had escaped without injury. Staring down at the shell-casings, he came to the conclusion that whoever devised the ambush was very well trained.

Still thinking, he muttered to himself. "Either they reloaded that anti-tank weapon really fast, or there were two of them." *Hmm. Both trucks were hit in just about the same places*. He also noticed that whoever had attacked the convoy had stripped the guards of their weapons and overcoats. Nothing else was taken. *This was a well-executed ambush. No rebel-rousers could do this much damage and escape unharmed, so they must be soldiers. I wonder if these are the same people I sent Major Schmidt after. If they are, then maybe Major Schmidt and his men are dead.* "An interesting thought," he muttered to himself.

Colonel Marcs ordered his men to move the dead off to the side of the road and had their bodies covered. Once his investigation was over, he turned his men out, searching for signs of what direction the prisoners had taken. That information was fast in coming. Forty men can churn up a soggy ground in no time, especially if they were in a hurry.

Two hours after he concluded his investigation, three of the Pz lll light tanks, and one of the two companies he had added to his order of battle finally arrived. The two companies were a late addition after he re-evaluated his conclusions concerning Major Schmidt. Over forty men dead, three halftracks destroyed, and no enemy bodies? Somebody knew what they were doing, so the colonel wasn't taking any chances.

A battalion sized unit on paper, his kampfgruppe looked large and impressive, but in reality, it was barely the size of an under-strength company, consisting of about 150 men, and his assigned motor vehicles: four Pz III's, fourteen halftracks, and five trucks, carrying extra fuel. However, the weapons they carried still hit hard, despite the unit's small size. Plenty of firepower for what he needed.

The Pz III was Germany's main battle tank during the invasions of Poland and France, firing a 37mm round. That role ended for the Pz III when Germany invaded Soviet Russia and was introduced to the thicker skinned T-34, Russian tank that fired a 76mm round. That wake-up-call cost the Germans over 600 tanks before they finally won that engagement. Now, the Pz III was nothing more than a light, scout tank compared to the new monstrosities ravaging the battlefields.

Captain Otto Busché jumped down from his Pz III and quickly walked over to where Colonel Marcs was standing.

Coming to attention, he raised his hand in salute and shouted, "Heil Hitler!" Colonel Marcs returned the salute and then glared at his captain. His expression was unmistakable. "Why did it take you so long to arrive, Captain Busché?"

Captain Busché bowed to his commander and said, "Herr Colonel. Since the weather has cleared, Allied airplanes have been everywhere. I lost two halftracks earlier today, and three of my men were killed. I arrived as quickly as I could, Herr Colonel."

One of the tank commanders walked up to the two officers and stopped at attention. When the colonel looked his way, he said, "Colonel Marcs. I just received word that the rest of the kampfgruppe will arrive in about ninety minutes. They were held up by air attacks."

Disgusted, Colonel Marcs looked at the two men for a moment, then shook his head, and walked away.

~ ~ ~

Hearing a dull droning sound, Sergeant Brooks glanced over at Jackson with a questioning look on his face. Jackson, not recognizing the sound either, shrugged his shoulders. Abruptly, his eyes opened wide when he realized they were hearing a light airplane buzzing around. "COVER!" whispered Jackson. Immediately, everybody hugged a tree and froze. A few anxious minutes passed before the airplane turned north and left the area. Running to the edge of the tree line, Brooks was just in time to see a Fieseler Storch, reconnaissance plane, flying north and disappearing into the distance.

Immediately gathering his men together, he said, "Gentlemen, thanks to our little rescue operation yesterday, we might have really stirred up the hornets this time. That was a recon plane that just flew overhead, and it's my guess they were looking for us. Damn! We just finished a fight with a fanatic that just wouldn't quit, and now ... damn Krauts! Brown, did your leg twitch again?"

~ ~ ~

The gathering of forces was complete. The third company and the last Pz lll arrived about the same time. The only trouble with their late arrival was the sun was going down, so they couldn't coordinate with Luftwaffe air reconnaissance.

Calling all of his officers and NCOs together, Colonel Marcs outlined his plans for the mission at hand. “Captain Busché, you’ll take your company, along with two Pz lll’s, and head northwest to this position just south of Prum, where you will stop and wait for further orders.”

“Captain von Schorn, you will start from here in the morning and take your company west until you reach this point, southwest of Bitburg, and there, you will also stop to await further orders. You, Captain Deil, will proceed with me on a southwesterly course with the two remaining Pz lll’s in support. I will co-ordinate the search from Trier.”

Pausing for a moment, he waited for the information to sink in before he continued. Captain Busché didn’t appear too thrilled with his assignment. “I am sending you to these locations to be ready to move at a minute’s notice. With air reconnaissance, we can cover more ground, so when we spot them, you won’t have to waste time rushing frantically to cut them off from escape. You will already be ahead of the enemy and in position. All we’ll have to do is set our intercept course and converge on them. We will have them surrounded by morning. Then we flush them out of hiding.”

Tapping his finger at a location on the map, he said, “We are mobile, gentlemen; our enemy is not. Remember that fact. We can travel thirty kilometers in one hour, while our enemy will take at least a day to march the same distance. By morning, gentlemen, our enemy will be somewhere in the center of our positions. Captain Busché, you will be the one to slam the door shut on our trap. You have your orders. We move out in six hours, so get some sleep. Once we start, there will be very little rest until we capture and kill what we are after. See to your commands. You are dismissed.”

Six hours after their briefing ended, the kampfgruppe was on the move. Using the stars to navigate, they headed for their assigned positions. With sunrise due to arrive in just a few hours, they had to be at their assigned start positions before daylight broke the horizon.

~ ~ ~

While the sun was setting on the evening of December 30, Sergeant Brooks was preparing to move out. When all the preparations were completed, the men took twenty minutes to eat before they started out. An hour after sunset, they were marching in columns of two with Jackson, Baker, and Lemons on point.

The night was dark, and cold. Nobody was talking. They were too concerned about breaking the eggshells they felt they were walking on, and everybody was on edge. Alert for any sound or movement, they stared into the night, straining to hear anything that would indicate their enemy was close by. They had about eight to ten hours of darkness left, just barely enough time to find another hole to hide in.

~ ~ ~

By the time the sun came up on the morning of December 31, the Germans were in position and awaiting further orders. With the rising sun also rose the reconnaissance plane sent by the Luftwaffe to help Colonel Marcs find his elusive prisoners.

The unit Colonel Marcs was riding along with was still on the move when the sun rose, and they were still heading southwest six hours later, thanks to the thoroughness of their commanding officer. All during the previous night, the colonel had ordered them to stop and investigate every burned-out building they came across just to make sure nobody was hiding in them. The spot-checks wasted a lot of time, but the searches couldn't be helped. Any structure large enough to hold more than two people was a potential hiding place.

From where Captain Busché's company was positioned to where the colonel was currently located covered a distance of over twenty miles. By the time he arrived at his destination, that distance had risen to well over thirty miles. The colonel had also received his radio reports from both companies stating that they were ready and waiting for dawn to arrive. So far, everything was going according to plan. His units were in place, and all that needed to be done was for him to get to his position. Then the hunt could begin.

~ ~ ~

The night of December 30 was crisp and cold when they left their old digs. Brooks and his men were moving quietly through the countryside, listening to the roar of vehicles roaming about in the distance. The sound was coming from two or three different directions, and Brooks didn't like any of it. Changing course, he decided to move a little more to the southwest, more towards the lower corner of Luxembourg, just a two-day jaunt from their present position.

After another hour of walking, Sergeant Brooks called a halt for a short breather. They could still hear the vehicles moving through the night, and nobody felt good about the situation. Already on edge, the night movements by the vehicles put the anxiety of capture back into their hearts.

Not liking the feeling of dread that was slowly creeping up on him, Brooks called in two of his scouts. After giving out his instructions, he nodded and said, "Be careful out there. Don't be gone more than an hour one way. If you can't locate anything in that amount of time, come on back. We'll be in those shadows right over there."

~ ~ ~

Lemons reported back with bad news about two and a half hours after he left. He didn't find anything. "I did hear what sounded like a lot of vehicles moving northwest. Couldn't tell how many, though."

Staring at his scout for a moment, Brooks didn't know what to say at first. Then, nodding to himself, he placed his hand on Sam's shoulder and said, "Thanks, Sam. That was a very enlightening report. I'm glad we have your good ears to hear things we can't."

Smiling like a patient teacher, Sam shook his head and said, "No, Sarge. You got it wrong again. You're still too monotone when you crack one. Relax. You'll catch on one day."

Fifteen minutes later, beanpole once again scared the daylights out of Brooks by tapping him on the shoulder, when a second before, there was nobody behind him. Startled, the first words out of Brooks' mouth were, "Damn you, Jackson," followed almost immediately by, "I would've shot you if I could've heard you!"

Jackson smiled and said, "I have to keep you sharp and on your toes, don't I, Sarge?"

After pushing his helmet to the back of his head, Brooks whispered angrily, "What did you find out, you little sneak?"

"I didn't get close enough to see anything, but I sure heard enough to know that what's on our left is more than what that SS major threw at us. I heard some trucks and a lot of tracks."

Thinking about what he just heard, Brooks pulled at his ear and swore. "Damn Krauts! Let's go, people," he said. "We have some serious trouble coming our way in the next day or two, and we need to get out of here fast. All right, you sneak thieves," he whispered, "get out front where you belong. Jackson, I need you to find a good place to hide, a real good place. We have five hours, men, so let's go."

Twenty minutes after leaving, Lemons reported back that all was clear up ahead. "Have you heard anything from Jackson, yet?" asked Brooks.

"No, Sarge. Not a thing," replied Sam.

Muttering to himself, Brooks said, "We're running out of time and darkness, here. Damn! Where in the hell is beanpole, anyway?"

The early morning was beginning to brighten up when Jackson finally did appear. Pointing to his right, he said, "Sarge, there's a small undercut about sixty-feet deep in the side of that hill over there. It'll keep us out of sight for a while. It's in a small ravine just beyond that rise."

The morning of December 31, had risen on schedule, and it brought a bitterly cold day along with it. The snow, however, had failed to arrive, and Sergeant Brooks was pulling at his ear while he searched around for absolutely nothing. Frustrated and completely baffled, he had no idea on how to escape their dire situation. They were deep inside Germany with half of the German Army blocking their way to freedom. Between two to three hundred thousand enemy troops stood in their path. All they had to do was sneak their way through them. Nodding to himself, Brooks accepted what was thrown at him, then he turned to the beanpole and said, "Okay. Show us."

By the time the sun was fully awake, Brooks and his men were safe inside their new digs. However, before they could put anything down, Brooks issued out an order. "Cover all weapons and metal items. No reflections, people. Until we can figure out how to camouflage this place so nobody can see it, we're going to have to hide everything under some of those coats. We're staying here for a day or two. If those bastards are looking for us, then let them run ragged trying to find fresh signs. Damn! What the hell happened to the snow?"

"What's wrong with you, Al? I thought you were worried about where the desert disappeared to? Are you running a fever?"

As stern-faced as he could manage, Brooks turned to the speaker and replied, "We don't need the desert anymore, Alex. We need the snow. Damn, it's cold."

Disgusted, Corporal Sims shook his head and stared at his platoon sergeant for a moment before he responded. "Yeah, right. Today you're looking for more snow. Tomorrow, you'll be screaming, "What the hell happened to the desert?""

"Shut up, Alex. I'm sure the Krauts are still looking for a used hood ornament. You don't qualify as a new one anymore."

~ ~ ~

While Sergeant Brooks and his men were getting acquainted with their new digs, Colonel Marcs was still traveling towards his destination, a position just five miles northwest of Trier, a German town located on the east bank of the Mosel River about five-miles east of the Luxembourg border. From there, he planned to direct the actions of the other two companies.

Off in the distance and coming closer, was the reconnaissance airplane sent to help him locate their lost prisoners. When the plane was overhead, Colonel Marcs waved his arm, and the plane responded by dipping its wing. Establishing radio contact a minute or so later, Colonel Marcs and the pilot discussed their ideas for a few minutes in order to conduct their search more effectively.

By noon on the 31st, Colonel Marcs had reached a position just a little north and west of his original destination. The manhunt was just about to begin. All the pieces were in place, and all he had to do now was flush the game out of hiding.

~ ~ ~

Hearing the dull drone of a search plane, Brooks knew, without a doubt, that they were definitely being hunted. He could no longer hear the sounds of the vehicles moving around, so whoever it was must have reached his destination.

Debating on whether or not to move out weighed heavily on his mind. His desire to get back to Allied lines was almost overwhelming, but Brooks also knew that to move now could result in consequences he didn't want to happen. He had no idea what his enemy's plans were.

Without that knowledge, no movement was possible without the grave risk of being discovered. Shrugging his shoulders, he thought, *I guess the best thing to do would be to sit tight and let the scouts keep track of the Krauts*.

Walking over to where Jackson was sitting, Brooks sat down beside him and explained to him what he had in mind. Spreading out the map that he had taken off of the dead major, he went over what he thought were the probable plans of the Germans.

Pointing on the map at the possible locations of the vehicles they had heard the night before, he looked over at Jackson and said, "Look. Sam said he heard vehicles somewhere near here. That's north of us. You said you heard a large concentration of trucks and tracks moving southwest of us. There was also some movement I lost track of right about here." Pointing at a different location, he said, "And guess where we are? We're caught smack-dab between your group and Sam's group."

Taking a moment to study the freshly drawn lines on the map, Jackson pulled at his chinstrap for a moment before he said, "There must be another unit somewhere behind us. You said you lost track of similar movement south of us. What if they didn't have as far to travel? Maybe you lost track of that other unit because they stopped. Look at this, Sarge. If there is something behind us, then they've set this up like an animal hunt. If they have units behind us, then those units are the chasers driving us to these guys, up here."

After their little strategy session was over, Jackson said, "If we're going to be stuck here for a while, maybe Sam and I should set up some animal snares and catch some small stuff. I used to do that all the time when I was growing up. The only problem after catching them is cooking what we catch. With no fire, we'd have to eat it raw."

Brooks stared at the beanpole for a good, *long* moment, and his look of revulsion was unmistakable. Disgusted, Sergeant Brooks shook his head and muttered, "Only you would come up with something like that, Jackson. Okay, beanpole. Let's try it now while we still have something decent to eat." Turning to address the men, he said, "Everybody, get as far back under this overhang as you can and get some sleep. Movement catches the eye, so if we don't wonder around, they can't spot us."

Their new hideout was actually a wedge-shaped crevice about forty-feet wide that stretched deep inside for about fifty feet before the ceiling height diminished sharply until it was just two feet. Despite the closeness, the low ceiling height was still roomier than a ship's bunk.

Chapter 38

The battles that were still raging in the west had been continuous for almost three weeks. The Germans held a slight edge in the beginning, but their time had come and gone, and the tide of battle had turned sharply against them. The spearhead of the Sixth SS Panzer Army had been stopped cold and then cut off from its supplies when the Americans cut across their rear and recaptured the town of Stavelot. Stymied and without fuel, Kampfgruppe Peiper, the spearhead of the Sixth SS Panzer Army, was forced to break through the American lines and head towards their own lines on foot, leaving behind their vehicles and tanks.

When the first of the year arrived, along with it, came a new hope, a fresh breath of new vigor. The Germans had been completely stopped and were currently fighting a defensive battle. The initiative had indeed changed. Now, on the attack themselves, the Americans were forcing the German armies to conduct a fighting withdrawal, and without fuel, they too were forced to leave most of their armor behind. All of these events were unknown to Colonel Marcs and Sergeant Brooks. They had their own little war going on, and what was happening in the west, would have no bearing whatsoever as to the outcome of their confrontation.

~ ~ ~

After giving Jackson the go ahead to set up his snares, Brooks had decided that the best course to take at the moment was to stay put. As Jackson put it, and with his best western drawl, "Palefaces always leave tracks easy enough to follow even at a dead run, so let the white-coats wear themselves out searching for ghosts."

As long as we don't move around, we won't be leaving any evidence for the Germans to find. That sounds simple enough, thought Brooks, *but what happens when he does catch something in his little traps. What will we do then? Will we be able to eat what he catches raw*? "Yuck!"

With everybody asleep or lying down, Brooks, Jackson, and Lemons were the only men moving about. Jackson was setting up his snares to the south while Lemons set his to the north, doubling their chances of catching something. "Damn, what a war," said Brooks. With that said he went further back into the cave to try and get some sleep. Twenty minutes after Brooks fell asleep, Jackson and Lemons returned to the cave and sat down to discuss where their snares were located. After they were finished debriefing each other, they both went to the back of the cave looking for a place to sleep.

~ ~ ~

Ravenously hungry for the chase to begin, Captain von Schorn finally received the call he had been waiting for. Turning to his men, he gave the order to move out, and the hunt was underway. Their plan was to have their quarry within the next couple of days. The colonel's schema suited Eric von Schorn just fine, and he was dead set on ending the mission as quickly as possible. After just a few hours, he was already tired of the cold, wet, and miserable conditions he was forced to endure.

Having seen what forty pairs of boots can do to a wet and soggy ground and the path they left behind, made it easy for him to follow his enemy. Confident and then overconfident, he sent two men out from each platoon to scout ahead. Starting at the scene of the escape, their orders were to look for any change in direction. Taking for granted his scouts would uncover any route changes, he didn't back up their search with extra eyes. Despite their thoroughness, his scouts still lost track of the Americans.

The German scouts missed what the Americans were doing until it was too late to figure out *when* they had lost them. They weren't expecting their foe to leave their line of march, two at a time, during their escape west. The Americans had slipped cleanly away from their enemy and had moved north, back towards Prum until Captain Busché's rumbling around forced another direction change.

Captain von Schorn was constantly in radio contact with his forward scouts as well as his platoon leaders and Colonel Marcs. He was not about to fail in his mission. He was ranging out from his troops as far as a mile, riding in his Puma armored car and hoping to draw some kind of a response from the Americans. His mission was the most important part of the plan. He was the menace, meant to drive the Americans from their hole and herd them into the jaws of the trap.

~ ~ ~

Captain Busché was a die-hard Nazi and a very dedicated SS officer. He was also next in line to command the battalion since Major Schmidt was presumed dead. None of his men really cared for him that much, but they did fear him, and that was okay with Busché as long as they did what they were told.

His men knew he had connections with the SS high command, and that knowledge by itself was part of their fear, but the main reason for their fear came from the fact that Busché was just plain mean. Because of his high connections, he was able to get away with a lot of incidents that other officers couldn't, like the time he shot one of his NCO's for balking at an order he had given him. Or when he almost beat a private senseless for not moving fast enough. There were other occasions that were deviously shoved under the table, so to speak. Captain Busché was also a very ambitious and self-serving man who didn't mind climbing up the ladder of success using someone else's back.

~ ~ ~

Brooks heard the plane as it receded off into the distance. Looking out from under cover, he noticed the plane was heading east. "Good," he said. "He must be heading back to his airfield." Hearing a noise off to the south, he spotted Jackson walking towards him, but because the sun was going down and was partially in his eyes, it was difficult for him to see the scout clearly. As Jackson moved closer, Brooks noticed that he was happy about something. Holding up his hands, the scout had a big grin on his face. Then Brooks spotted what beanpole was carrying. Four rabbits. "Look, Sarge," he said. "The traps worked!"

"I suppose now you expect us to eat those damn things raw, don't you?" asked Brooks; his face had sour written all over it. Another ten minutes passed before Sam returned with three rabbits in his hands. He too was smiling. Shaking his head, Brooks walked away.

"Hey, Sarge. Maybe if we could rig up some kind of a blind back in that corner we might be able to build a small fire to cook with. It may take a while to cook these things, but I think it could be done."

After repeated attempts, they finally managed to build a blind that blocked the light from the small fire Jackson had built. Lemons immediately shoved some of their catch over the open flames, while Jackson went out about a half a mile or so to see if they could be detected. After spending about thirty minutes roaming around, he finally headed back. Sergeant Brooks was really worried about the fire and the aroma from the cooking rabbits until Jackson arrived and reported, "We're in luck, Sarge. I couldn't see anything of the fire, and I didn't start smelling the rabbit until I was about twenty yards from the hideout."

Brooks let out a big sigh and finally started to relax. Chuckling and shaking his head, he looked at Jackson and said, "I sure am glad I didn't have to eat those things raw. Damn, what a mess that would've been!"

When the smell of the cooking rabbit reached their noses, the snoring men instantly awoke, their heads turning in the direction of the aroma even before their eyes were open. "Damn. What's that smell? Are we back home?" asked Major Thomas.

"Rabbit, sir," replied Brooks.

"Really? Jackson and Lemons actually caught something?" asked Major Thomas.

Smiling, Sergeant Brooks replied, "Seven to be exact, sir. And we don't have to eat 'em raw either. Rabbit's hot, sir. Better get some before it's gone."

After Jackson and Lemons had removed the rabbits from the snares, they reset the snares with the intentions of going back in the morning to see if they had caught anymore. The fact was obvious that seven rabbits wouldn't feed forty people, so the two scouts were going to have to set a lot more snares then what they already had out. They knew their idea wouldn't last forever, but they only needed their scheme to work for about three or four days.

Scrounging around, the two scouts had gathered enough wood to last them for several days. The fires they built were so small they could almost put them into a pair of cupped hands. Brooks had decided to build the fire only about a half an hour before the sun went down in order to lose the smoke in the shadowy clouds of a closing day. At the same time, they had to cook quickly what meat they had before the fire was extinguished for the night. They would be cold the rest of the night, but to Brooks, no fire was better than freezing to death in a POW camp.

As the sun rose up into the sky, so did the reconnaissance plane. Another dawn had arrived. Stretching and shivering, Brooks whispered to his men, "Happy New Year." Then he chided himself for whispering as if the airplane could hear him if he talked too loud. The day was January 1, 1945, and, brother, was it cold.

Chapter 39

The morning was bitter cold when the men of Kampfgruppe Marcs woke up on January 1. During their sleep, a foot of new snow had dropped onto the still soggy ground, hiding the consequences of a freeze that had set in during the previous late evening. Parked in six inches of melting snow the night before, the ice had to be chipped away from the tracks before the vehicles could be moved. When all of the vehicles were free of the frozen ground, the men finished up their preparations for the day's march.

On the radio with the reconnaissance plane flying overhead, Colonel Marcs was giving out his instructions for the morning's hunt. Captain Busché had been given his orders earlier, so he was already underway.

Most of the men in Busché's unit were walking, searching the surrounding area, looking for their elusive quarry. Only Busché and the tank crews were riding. Spread out wide, they covered a front of over two miles. Heading in a southwesterly direction at leisurely pace, their orders were to keep the escaped prisoners from reaching Luxembourg. Their final destination was Arlon, a town in Belgium, just 45 miles from Prum. Unintentionally, his company was heading straight for a point about a mile north of the wedge-shaped crevasse Brooks and his men were hiding in.

Captain Busché was riding in the commander's hatch, absentmindedly thinking while he stared down at the main gun on the Pz lllB. *This little tank should be in a toy store, not fighting in a war. We should be using Pz lV's or Pz V's instead.* Calling Colonel Marcs on the radio he informed his commander that he was passing just below Arzfeld. "Do you want me to halt?" asked Busché.

"Let me find out where Captain von Schorn is. In the mean-time keep moving," replied the colonel. "I'll call you right back."

"Yes, Herr Colonel."

A few minutes went by before Captain Busché received a radio transmission from his commander. "Stop where you are, Captain. Set up a forward base, and wait there for further orders."

"Yes, Herr Colonel."

~ ~ ~

Captain von Schorn was only about seven or eight miles from the Americans, but he was completely unaware of this fact. No one in the kampfgruppe knew exactly where their enemy was thanks to beanpole's brilliant idea. After von Schorn's scouts finally realized they had lost the Americans, they also discovered they had destroyed all traces of their enemy's passing. Currently, Captain von Schorn's orders were to continue on for another hour before halting and setting up his own forward supply base.

Nodding to himself in anticipation, Colonel Marcs muttered his next thought out loud as he headed for his tent. "Tomorrow, we should run into the Americans. With Captain Busché already in position, there will be no problem sealing the trap."

~ ~ ~

Just before midnight, Brooks nodded to Jackson and received a return nod. Smiling until his cheeks were well hidden, the Arizona scout rose to his feet and said, "I'll be back before dawn," and then he was gone. However, despite what everybody else thought, Brooks was worried, and still troubled over his decision to stay in the undercut instead of hightailing it towards friendly troops. The next day would show if he was right or wrong.

Looking at all of his men, Brooks was wondering just how many would still be alive in the next 24 hours. *So far, we've been lucky. No one's been killed, and the wounds have been light*. Taking another look around the cut, he shuddered at the thought of being trapped against stone walls, with hundreds of misshaped enemy bullets ricocheting off the sides and ripping into flesh instead of punching through, leaving a clean hole. *If they find us tomorrow, we're in deep shit*.

Standing at the mouth of the cut, he was lost in thought until he felt little spots of cold on his neck and hands. Looking up, he noticed that it was snowing. He stood still, watching it fall, wondering how long it would last. Within a few minutes, he was smiling brightly. The snow was falling so hard he couldn't see anything past ten feet. *Well, what do you know?* he thought. *We just might make it after all. I sure hope Jackson's all right. He's still got a few hours left before dawn. I sure hope he makes it back in one piece. I really like that kid.* Looking out into the darkness one last time, he slowly turned away and went back into the cave to think more about his decision to stay.

~ ~ ~

After Jackson left the cave, he turned due north for about two miles, and then he turned east. Using a slow and steady, ground eating pace, he moved towards where he figured the enemy camp was. When he had run for what he thought were a couple of miles, he slowed to a walk. *It wouldn't be good to run into the Germans now,* he thought. *I'm supposed to sneak over to where their camp is, not introduce myself.*

The Arizona scout had been walking for about an hour when he heard what sounded like a mess pan banging. Instantly, he was on the ground, and waiting to hear the sound again. Another clang resounded off to his right, so he turned, looked in the direction of the disturbance, and immediately spotted lights glowing faintly in the distance. Moving towards the lights, he was smiling and deviously thinking, *they're not very smart banging things around and having so many lights showing. Maybe they don't realize just how close they are to us.*

Moving closer, he noticed some vehicles. He was still too far away to see what they were, so he moved even closer until he was about sixty yards from them. Moving so the light was directly behind the vehicles, he discovered that they were halftracks, and there were a lot of them.

Not wanting to get any closer for fear of being discovered, he continued to watch the camp. After a few minutes, he moved back about sixty yards and then headed south across the front of the encampment. He wanted to see how big it was. After an hour of crawling, he stopped. Not more than a stone's throw away was a large tent.

Searching the area for anyone near the tent, Jackson decided to investigate. Crawling south, past the canvas structure, he put the lights directly behind it, so he would be in the shadows.

When he was forty or fifty feet away, he stopped. He could see silhouettes moving around in the tent, but he couldn't see who it was. Looking around to make sure nobody was coming, he edged a little closer until he was about twenty feet away, and then he paused. Glancing around, he was surprised at his discovery: the encampment was actually very large.

He was about to leave and head back to the cave when somebody came out of the tent. The man called out in German, but Jackson couldn't understand what he was saying. The enemy soldier was standing in the light, so it was easy for the scout to see the man's gold braided peaked cap. *Hmm. This guy must be an officer. Nuts. Where's Baker when I need him*?

When another man approached the officer, he saluted the peaked cap and came to attention. Only a moment passed before the scout heard the other man being called captain. Although he didn't know a lick of his enemy's language, he did know what the word captain in German was. The captain saluting the other officer first indicated that the man wearing the peaked cap was a senior officer, perhaps a major or possibly a colonel. Certainly, no general would be traipsing around the countryside in such miserable conditions. Not for this kind of a mission.

After a couple of minutes, the captain saluted again and left. The major, or whatever he was, turned to his left to look unintentionally in the direction of the cave, and as he did so, Jackson spotted the SS runes on his collar. *Nuts*! *More SS skunks chasing us. Crap on the ground. Sergeant Brooks will want to know about this*.

Jackson waited where he was until the officer went back into his tent. Not liking what he had discovered, the scout continued to study the encampment for a few minutes longer. By the time he was ready to head back, the snow was coming down again. Ever so cautiously, he backed away until he felt he could get up without being seen, and then he stood up and started his slow and steady, ground eating pace back to the cave. While he was running, he noticed that the snow was coming down even harder. *Good,* he thought. *No tracks.* His journey back to the undercut took him the rest of the night, and his report after he arrived back at the cave had Sergeant Brooks pulling at his ear again.

Chapter 40

When Colonel Marcs stepped out of his tent after a restless night's sleep, he gazed out at a world wrapped in white. Two feet of new snow had fallen, and it was still coming down. Surveying the countryside, he thought to himself, *if they were on the move last night then their tracks are well covered by now*. After that disappointing thought, he called the airfield to get a status report, and again, he was ready to kick at the ground.

Talking to the pilot, he was informed that almost three feet of snow had fallen on the runways, delaying the recon flight's departure by several hours. Their maintenance equipment had broken down as well, so they were going to have to clear it the old-fashioned way, using a lot of men with shovels. Even though what the pilot told him had brought bad news, Colonel Marcs still had to laugh. He could just picture 40 men huffing and puffing while they struggled to clear the knee-deep snow off the runway.

~ ~ ~

The sun was back at war with the clouds on the morning of January 2, and its fight was a losing cause. Jackson had arrived at the undercut just as the sun had started its battle with the clouds. When he found Sergeant Brooks in the back of the cave, the snow was still falling, but not very hard. "Damn you, Jackson," whispered Brooks, "I am going to shoot you by mistake on purpose if you keep sneaking up on me like that."

This time, the Arizona beanpole wasn't smiling when he whispered back. "Sarge, judging by the size of that camp and the number of halftracks I spotted, I figure it's at least a company sized unit. I also noticed an armored car. I think it was a Puma, and they're SS. I was able to get close enough to hear two SS officers talking, but I couldn't understand what they were saying."

Absolutely astonished, Brooks could only stare down at the Apache scout for a moment or two. Then he pushed his helmet to the back of his head and said, “Damn it all. How do you get away with that shit? You sneak right up next to the bastards and they still don’t see you. What else did you find out, you little sneak-thief?”

The snow was coming down harder by the time Jackson had finished his report. Then he expressed his opinion. “I don’t think we should move around in the snow during the day, Sarge. I think the Germans might be able to spot our tracks from the air. It’ll be safer if Sam and I wait until after the sun goes down before we check on the snares. It looks like more snow tonight, so we should be safe checking on the snares after sundown.”

Nodding, Sergeant Brooks agreed with his scout. “Yeah, you’re probably right.” Then his next thought had him pulling at his ear again. *Damn. Those SS bastards are hunting us again. A company size unit. Hell! That means there’s at least a battalion of those bastards hunting us, now. We must’ve stirred up the big-man’s hornet’s nest this time.* Waking up his squad leaders and Major Thomas, he immediately held a powwow, to inform them of the changed situation.

Jackson was looking out at the falling snow and noticed that the weather conditions didn’t appear to be changing. All indications pointed at a continuing snowfall, so he went to Brooks and informed him of his plans to check the snares while it was still snowing. Twenty minutes later, it was still snowing when the two scouts returned. When they arrived back at the cave they were carrying twelve rabbits and four quail. Brooks nodded and smiled after he was informed about their catch. *Nice little haul this time.*

~ ~ ~

By noon the snow had stopped falling. In the meantime, Colonel Marcs had been pacing around in his tent, cursing the weather and the delays the weather conditions had forced on him, until he received the phone call he had been waiting for. “Colonel Marcs, the runway has been cleared enough for me to take off. I will be arriving over your location in about forty minutes." When the airplane appeared overhead, Marcs ordered von Schorn to move out.

While the pilot was flying over a wooded area about four or five miles in front of von Schorn's forces, he noticed a shadow that looked like it might be a cave or just what it appeared to be, a shadow. Flying lower, the pilot still had difficulty identifying what he was looking at, so he radioed Colonel Marcs and informed him of what he had spotted and what his thoughts were. Immediately, Colonel Marcs turned to von Schorn and ordered him to send a couple of his scouts forward to investigate the sighting. Excitement showed again on the colonel's face and it was contagious. Even Captain von Schorn was motivated by his commander's expression.

~ ~ ~

After Jackson and Lemons had returned from checking on the snares, Brooks gathered all of the men together and changed the game plan. "More SS bastards are on our tail. According to Jackson, we could be facing at least 300 men, and they have light armor support. If they catch us here, we'll be chewed to pieces. The bullets will ricochet off of the walls, and we'll be shredded meat in no time. It's snowing, so our tracks will be covered. We need to vacate the premises, now. We're leaving this deathtrap, so gear-up."

Brooks had some of his men rig some decoys by stuffing several of the German overcoats with leaves and anything else they could find. Using thin straight branches for the arms, they used single, wrist-thick branches for the bodies, and wedged them between the slanted ceiling and the cave floor, keeping the dummies in an upright position as if they were live men standing in place. While they were building their fake men, Sam and beanpole were putting their own idea together.

When the men had finished with their ploy, they placed American helmets on the decoys where the heads would be and moved them back into the shadows where they could barely be seen. Then beanpole and Sam put the finishing touches to their platoon sergeant's idea with an idea of their own. When all of the preparations were completed, Brooks said, "Let's go," and they all moved out, heading due west.

A little over an hour after Brooks and his men had departed their digs, the snow started slowing down, and by noon, it had quit altogether. About forty minutes after the snow had stopped, they heard the dull drone of an airplane approaching the cave area. They were in a thick evergreen forest and figured that if they couldn't see the airplane, then the airplane couldn't see them, but they still stopped moving and hugged the trees just the same. "Damn," whispered Brooks. "It looks like we got out of there just in time."

"Shit, Al. What the hell are you whispering for?" whispered Sergeant Cane.

"I don't know, Dan," replied Brooks. "I guess they can't hear us way up there, can they?" After circling for a few minutes, the airplane turned east and flew away. Brooks waited a couple of minutes to make sure the airplane had actually left, and then whispered again for the men to move out.

~ ~ ~

Colonel Marcs was talking to Captain von Schorn when the radio came alive. He had to calm the man down before he could understand what the soldier was trying to say. Listening to his scout, the colonel's posture stiffened, and he became very alert, concentrating intently on what the soldier was saying. When the conversation was over, he turned to von Schorn and said, "We have them. There's a cave up ahead, and the Americans are still in it. One of our men reports that he has spotted what appears to be several soldiers wearing American helmets standing back in the shadows of a cave. Damn, damn, damn. We have them, Captain."

Contacting his other two commanders, he ordered them to close in on the location of the cave. If they arrived at the scene first, they were not to do anything other than wait for further orders.

Captain Busché shook his head after hearing the order to close in on the cave and immediately thought, *if you think I am going to wait for you, you're wrong. This is the opportunity of a lifetime. Once I take care of the Americans, you will be bowing to me. This will be the break that will catapult my career towards the top.* Sensing a change in

Busché's, demeanor, his men knew something was about to happen, and they cringed.

Captain Deil was the first to arrive near the cave. Using field glasses, he searched inside of it and recognized what appeared to be figures standing in the shadows. However, what he was looking at had him somewhat confused. He had spotted the silhouettes, but they didn't appear to be moving about. *Do they not see us*? Baffled, he decided to follow his orders and wait for Colonel Marcs to arrive. While he waited, he went ahead and deployed his men for the attack, excited that this mission was about over.

~ ~ ~

It wasn't long after the plane left that Sergeant Brooks and his men heard the roar of ominous trouble on the move. A lot of vehicles were roaming about. "Crap on the ground, Sarge," said Jackson. "You sure called that one right. It sounds like the whole German army is out there."

Letting out a sigh of relief, Brooks felt a whole lot better about his decision to move. *I wonder if those decoys are working*. "Jackson. You, Baker and Lemons get on point," he said. "I want to make sure we don't run into any stray Germans up ahead."

Other than the roar of battle far to their west, the forest was quiet. The only sound they heard was the crunching of the snow under their boots and the background noises of vehicles moving about. Fog was all around them, so it was hard to see more than twenty or thirty feet ahead sometimes. Private Lemons reported back to Sergeant Brooks every few minutes, just to make sure the men didn't get lost. After they had been trudging through the freshly fallen snow for about 40 minutes, Brooks finally called a halt for a much needed break.

Leaving Baker and Lemons where they were, Jackson slipped away because he never passed on an opportunity to sneak up on Brooks. It was a game he had started playing shortly after arriving in North Africa.

Jackson hunkered down behind a tree, not far from the men, and waited for Brooks to show himself. A couple of minutes passed before he finally spotted Brooks heading for a tree to relieve himself. Trying not to laugh and give himself away, the Arizona scout crept up on the unsuspecting sergeant, who was completely unaware of his pending surprise. Just as Brooks was about to begin his session, the beanpole stood up and blurted out, "You're going to kill that tree if you piss on it!" At the same time Jackson blurted out his words, they heard his idea back at the cave open up.

Such an uproar of weapons' fire erupted following beanpole's idea that everybody thought they had come under fire. People were diving for cover all over the place. Brooks, in the meantime, had almost pee'd all over himself when he jumped about two or three feet in the air because of beanpole's shout. And despite what was happening in the background, Jackson was rolling on the ground and laughing so hard he couldn't breathe. Sergeant Brooks, however, wasn't looking for the crap on the ground, this time. He was trying to find his heart.

Chapter 41

Colonel Marcs and Captain von Schorn were still over thirty minutes away from the cave when Captain Busché arrived at Deil's position. Busché jumped down from his Pz lll and walked over to where Captain Deil was standing. Deil, being the subordinate, saluted as Busché walked up to him. Returning the salute, Busché asked him what the situation was and where the Americans were hiding. Pointing to the cave, Deil gave his report. "It's hard to see them, sir. They're standing back in the shadows, but I definitely recognize their helmets. I believe it's them, sir."

Busché took the binoculars from Deil and scanned the cave until he noticed a strange looking shadow. Then his attention sharpened. Turning to two of Deil's men, he ordered them to advance on the cave until they reached a tall snow bank, where they were ordered to stop about 200 feet from the cave mouth. When the two men arrived at the snow bank, Deil turned to remind the senior captain of their commander's orders, but was interrupted when the shadowy men in the cave started shooting.

One of the two men sent to the snow bank had noticed something odd lying on the ground. When he took a step towards the strange sight, he felt something tug at his right ankle, so he looked down and immediately heard a series of whipping sounds. Looking up, he was just in time to watch the last of the whipping branches jerk back into place. Then he saw the white string tied to some of the branches, and immediately, beanpole and Sam's idea exploded into action, sending ninety, 9mm bullets from three captured MP40 submachine guns tied to poles inside of the cave, hammering the two men standing behind the snow bank. They were holed many times before they fell to the ground.

Seconds later, the late afternoon was shattered once again. This time, however, the disturbance was caused by return fire when the Germans opened up with every weapon they possessed, firing at the cave that was shooting at them. After a couple minutes, Busché called for a cease-fire. The cave and everything in it was just hammered by the hell that was unleashed when the Germans started shooting at it, but the cave wasn't bleeding. Only rock chips fell to the ground.

After the shooting stopped, Captain Busché glanced menacingly at Captain Deil and then told him to wait where he was. Turning, the senior captain started walking to the cave to gloat over the destruction wrought on the Americans. His walk took him a few minutes, but he was finally standing at the mouth of the cut. When he had reached a spot just a few feet short of the undercut, he stopped dead in his tracks. Instead of finding dead Americans splattered all over the walls, all he found were bullet riddled German overcoats, shot-up American helmets, and three MP40 submachine guns lying on the ground, with string still attached to the trigger and handle, holding the triggers, pulled to the stops. Stunned, he could only stand at the mouth of the cave as the enormity of the situation overwhelmed him.

Desperately, he searched every inch of the cave only to find absolutely nothing more than the bullet riddled German overcoats, shot-up American helmets, and the three MP40 submachine guns that were still lying on the ground. Even after his frantic search, the reality of the situation had not changed at all, and panic put a cold knot of fear in the pit of his stomach. *This can't be*? *Where are the Americans*? Then, realizing that he had disobeyed a direct order from a superior officer, an SS officer to boot, he started falling apart.

Not thinking straight, he headed back to Captain Deil. When he arrived beside Deil, he turned to his junior captain and said, "All of the Americans are dead, so we should start heading back to meet up with Colonel Marcs to tell him the good news."

Looking at Captain Busché, Deil was surprised to see that his captain's face was looking a bit ashen, and his hands were shaking, an observation that had the junior captain smiling behind his neutral expression. *I guess the sight of all those dead Americans and all the blood and guts must have gotten to him. Hmm,* he thought. *Our fearless captain sickens at the sight of blood.*

Colonel Marcs was still about twenty minutes away from the cave when the firing erupted. Standing in the commander's hatch, he was furious. He had given strict orders not to do anything until he got there. He had wanted to give the Americans a chance to surrender before he ordered them shot. "Wait until I find out which bastard disobeyed my orders," he screamed. "I will make him wish he'd never been born. Push the pedal to the floor, corporal. Get me to that cave right, now!"

Inside the armored car, Captain von Schorn smiled to himself, happy that he wasn't at the cave with the other two captains. He had seen Colonel Marcs agitated before, but never had he observed him as angry as he was at the moment. *I wouldn't want to be in the shoes of the person who just disobeyed his orders. Under any conditions.*

Deil and Busché were only ten minutes away from the cave when they ran into Colonel Marcs. Captain Deil instantly noticed that his colonel was extremely agitated, so he tried not to smile when he dismounted his armored car and approached his commanding officer. Not wanting Deil to talk first, Busché ordered the driver of the Pz lll to head over to the colonel's Puma, so that he could talk to Colonel Marcs first.

Looking from Deil to Busché, Marcs climbed out of the Puma, followed by Captain von Schorn. After departing the vehicle, the two men stood beside the armored car, waiting for the other two captains to approach. When they arrived, Colonel Marcs stood still and glared at his two captains for a good long moment until he could no longer hold back his anger. "What the hell happened? Why did you open fire? Why did you disobey a direct order?"

When Deil tried to speak, Busché interrupted him and started with his own explanation of what happened. Deil didn't say another word. He just turned his body a little to the right and remained silent. *Let Busché seal his own fate*, he thought. *It's his ass in a sling, not mine. I had to follow the orders given by a superior officer.*

Busché was the senior officer on the scene, so Deil had to follow his orders. When the senior captain was finished with his explanation, Colonel Marcs turned to Deil. Knowing the position his junior captain was in, he decided not to interrogate him. Instead, he looked back at Busché and said, "Show me the Americans. Now!"

"No, Herr Colonel," replied Busché. "I am not going back there."

Shocked at the refusal, Colonel Marcs lost control and started yelling. "You are an SS officer, and you will obey my orders, or I will have you arrested right here and now."

"You will arrest no one!" shouted Busché, and he grabbed for his pistol, forgetting that his holster was buttoned down.

Captain Deil still remembered how Busché looked on his return from the cave. Even then, he had sensed something was wrong with his commander, that something just wasn't right, so he had turned his body slightly away from Busché during the captain's explanation and unbuttoned the flap on his holster.

Captain von Schorn had noticed Deil's action, but he hesitated about a minute or so before he reluctantly followed suit. After un-buttoning his holster, his arm hung limply by his side for only a moment before Busché started grabbing for his pistol. However, by the time the disconcerted captain had freed his gun from its holster, his success was too late. Deil and von Schorn were already emptying their guns into his chest, killing him instantly.

Colonel Marcs stood where he was, astonished at the sudden explosion of violent death in front of him. Both Deil and von Schorn stared down at Captain Busché's bullet riddled body, not believing that they had just killed a fellow officer. Everyone from the two companies who had gathered around the four officers were shocked and confused, milling about, and just absolutely astounded over what they had witnessed. In the meantime, the rest of von Schorn's men had started arriving.

When the whole battalion was gathered together, the men were informed that Captain Busché had tried to kill their commanding officer. Although the colonel was still shaken by the incident, he didn't let the distraction interfere with his assignment. First company was currently without a commander, so he called all of his officers together to remedy the situation. Lieutenant Joseph Warner was the most senior light-officer left in the company, so he was named first company's new commander. "Don't let me down, Lieutenant," said Colonel Marcs.

Standing proudly at attention, the lieutenant replied, "I won't, Herr Colonel!"

Once he had finished re-arranging the chain of command, Marcs listened to Deil explain what had happened at the cave. After hearing the report, Colonel Marcs decided to go to the cave and see for himself, wanting to understand why Captain Busché had acted the way he did.

Escorted by Captain Deil and two squads, he left orders for the rest of the battalion to set up camp while he headed for the cave. When they reached Deil's previous position, his captain pointed out where all of his men were situated at the time of the attack. Once the colonel had all the information that his captain could provide him with, he headed for the cave.

The jaunt took them a couple of minutes to reach the undercut. Standing at the mouth of the wedge-shaped hideout, both officers were speechless. Instead of the blood and torn body parts they had expected to find, all they saw was exactly what Captain Busché had seen, *a lot* of rock fragments, bullet riddled German overcoats, shot-up American helmets, and three MP40's lying on the ground. *Dummies, damn it*! *Just decoys*! *The Americans have made fools of us all, and they have escaped, as well*!

Absolutely astonished, all Colonel Marcs could do at the moment was slap at his leg with his baton and stare at an incredibly ingenious ploy. Quite a few moments of incredulous silence passed before Colonel Marcs finally left the cut with Deil following. Gathering up the men, they went back to where the battalion had made camp.

Chapter 42

Over thirty minutes passed before Jackson could look at Sergeant Brooks without laughing again. After everyone heard about the surprise he had laid on Brooks, they all fell over laughing, including Sergeant Brooks.

As Brooks' detachment was enjoying their roughshod humor session, they heard some shots off in the distance. The shooting sounded a lot like pistol shots, but they weren't sure. They didn't stay to find out either. Grinning, Brooks said to Jackson while they were moving west, "That was good, beanpole. A nice payback for your court martial. But don't think you can do that again because I'll be watching for you from here on out. Next time, I'm gonna shoot your ass, before I smile." Nodding at Jackson, Brooks said, "Now, you three. Get back on point before I decide to drop-kick you there."

~ ~ ~

"Damn, it's cold," whispered Brooks. Calling a fifteen-minute halt after a forty-minute jaunt, he wanted to look at the map again to see if there was any place nearby that might have some bombed out buildings they could stop at. An abandoned basement would be the perfect place to build a fire and get warm. What he discovered, though, had him pulling at his ear again. "Damn," he said. "Wouldn't you know it? Nothing within miles of us. All right, you three. Get back on point." With no towns nearby, he ordered his men to move out, heading west.

Jackson walked up to his platoon sergeant about an hour later. The smile on his face gave hint that everyone was about to become warmer. Sure enough, he had found a deep ravine about a half a mile from their present position, and he was wanting to get back. "Follow me, guys," he said. "Sam and Chuck are waiting at the fire. It's hot, Sarge. You better get to it before it's gone."

Brooks stared at his scout for a moment before he shook his head and muttered to himself. "Damn you, Jackson. Lead on." Amazed, his mind was a jumble of confusing chaos and Jackson was in the forefront of that hectic mess in his head. *Damn his hide anyway. Two years with that little runt and I'm still putting up with his bullshit*. His last thought had him smiling.

~ ~ ~

Sitting in one of the big tents, Colonel Marcs was looking over his maps. *Now, we have to start our search again*, he thought. Muttering out loud to himself, he was still amazed at the ruse. "Damn, what an idea. And they got away scot-free. I'll have to figure out where they disappeared to before they can make a clean escape. I almost had them! Damn, that was a brilliant ploy!" His next thought, however, had him slapping his leg with his baton. The situation had changed once more, and he wasn't happy about the new problem he was currently faced with. *I'd better get that recon plane back out here tomorrow. The Americans have a good head start on us, so I'll need it to help us track them down. Damn*! *I'll have to split up my forces again*!

Gathering all of his officers together, he issued a call for dinner to formulate a plan of action concerning their second attempt to capture and kill the Americans. After they had finished eating, and the theoretical discussion was over, Colonel Marcs got down to business. "The Americans have at least a good day's head start on us. If they're in that pine forest, then we're going to have a tough time finding them. The trees are going to slow down our vehicles and take away our speed advantage. There are a couple of roads, here and here, that I think might be useful, but don't get used to them. We'll probably be forced to end this chase on foot. Look here."

Colonel Marcs pointed to a spot on the map just a few miles ahead of their current location where a single dirt road separated into two dirt roads, splitting a large stand of trees into thirds. His theory was that the fleeing Americans were hiding in the middle stand of trees.

"We will break up into companies again. You, Captain von Schorn, will take the left fork. Captain Deil, you'll take the right fork. Both of you will leave at first light, so it would be wise to make sure your radios are still in good working order.

Also, you had better re-supply tonight before you leave. I have the fuel trucks already en route. They'll be here in about three hours."

Turning to Lieutenant Warner, he said, "Lieutenant you are the most inexperienced of my commanders, so I will be traveling with you. I hope you don't mind." Not waiting for an answer, he turned to Captain von Schorn and said, "I am commandeering your Puma until I can arrange to have another one sent to us," and without waiting for his captain's reply, he faced all of his officers and asked, "Do you have any questions?" When he received no response, he said, "Good! See to your commands, gentlemen, and good luck." After the briefing ended, he left the officers' mess tent and went to bed.

~ ~ ~

On the morning of January 3, 1945, the men in Brooks' detachment woke up and discovered a light snow falling. Once again, the sun was losing its battle with the clouds.

"It's colder than a witch's breath," whispered Brooks. Still shivering from the cold, he nodded and said, "Take a look around, gentlemen. We are halfway to freedom. We're in Luxembourg. We crossed over the border about an hour before we stopped."

Looking at his men shivering along with him, Brooks broke into a smile before he turned serious again and said, "We'll stick to the trees from now on. Using the trees may be slower, but it'll be a lot safer. Jackson, I want you out front about 150 yards. Baker, you stay about 50 yards behind Jackson and keep in sight of him." An affirmative nod from Baker allowed Brooks to continue. "Lemons, you keep both Baker and me in sight and stay alert. The Krauts are everywhere. Okay, people, let's move out. Two columns and keep it tight. I don't want to lose anyone."

Knowing what his enemy's orders were, Brooks knew that their only chance for survival was to make it back to Allied lines. To do that, they had to keep moving and stay one or two steps ahead of their enemy's planning.

~ ~ ~

Sergeant Brooks was looking at his scout when the signal to drop was given. Within seconds, everyone was lying bellies-first in the snow, and it was cold and wet where they were lying. Crawling to where Lemons was crouching, Brooks asked what was wrong. Sam shrugged his shoulders and whispered, "I don't know, Sarge. Baker hit the ground, and then he signaled for me to do the same."

"Okay," whispered Brooks. "We stay put."

Crawling back to Major Thomas, he explained the situation. When Brooks was finished with his report, he said, "We'll wait here until I hear back from Jackson, sir."

"Sounds good, Al," whispered the major. Then the major smiled and whispered words of wisdom that Sergeant Brooks wasn't expecting. "This is your show, Sergeant Brooks. You do this better than I do, so have at it, *sir*."

Before Brooks could respond to the colonel's, sir, he spotted Jackson running bent over, through the trees. When the scout reached Baker, he tapped him on the shoulder and nodded for him to follow. Grabbing Sam along the way, he quickly reported to Sergeant Brooks. Whispering, he said, "A German patrol is just up ahead, and they're coming this way."

"How many?" asked Brooks.

"Maybe ten or fifteen," replied the scout.

Signaling for his men to get up, Brooks pointed to their left and they moved out. As they were leaving the area, Brooks put a finger to his lips to indicate absolute silence. When he had moved his men about 200 yards from their previous position, he turned to Jackson and whispered, "Sneak back and keep an eye on that Kraut patrol. See what they're up to and then report back. Don't get caught, beanpole, or I'm coming after you."

Smiling deviously, the scout waved and said, "Yes, sir, Sarge," and then he was gone from sight before Brooks could finish loading his anger. *Damn! He has to be doing that intentionally. That little shit. Maybe another court-martial will cheer him up. Hmm. Where's the colonel when I need him?*

~ ~ ~

Hunkered down in some bushes, Jackson watched silently while the enemy patrol passed his position, completely unaware that an Arizona beanpole was watching them from just a few feet away. The German troops were armed with submachine guns and StG 44 assault rifles, and they looked like they knew how to use them. *These goons are after something*, thought Jackson.

Watching the Germans, he also noticed that they were occasionally looking towards the ground as though searching for something or maybe tracks. A chill more powerful than what the cold could throw at him went up his back until he involuntarily shuddered, and then the chill was gone. *How did they catch up to us so fast*? he wondered. Still hunkered down in the bushes, he waited until the Germans had disappeared into the distance. Then he waited another ten minutes before he made his way back to Brooks.

When Sergeant Brooks spotted Jackson slinking towards him through the softly falling snow, he didn't like the look on his scout's face. Beanpole wasn't smiling like he usually was when he returned from a scout. When he reached Brooks, Jackson quickly whispered his report. "There's a bunch of Germans ahead of us, and I think they're looking for us."

Staring at his scout for a moment or two, Sergeant Brooks stood up from his squat and started pacing, somewhat floored by the report. "Damn," he whispered. "How did they catch up to us so fast?" Turning to Jackson, he issued his order. "Follow that patrol to see what they're up to and then report back. I'll see you in a couple of hours. Be careful out there, beanpole. Don't make me come after you."

Nodding, the beanpole answered, "Yes, sir, Sarge," and then he was gone.

"Shit," whispered Brooks. "That little bird turd!" Then he shook his head, worried about that little bird turd. *Be careful out there, beanpole*.

After Jackson had departed, Brooks turned to Lemons and said, "Not a word, Sam. Don't say anything." Then he swept his arm in an arc to show his other pain in the ass where he wanted him to search. "Go out about a mile then make a semi-circle sweep of the area in front of us and around our right, then report back to me with what you find out." A nod from Sam was enough for Brooks, so he turned to the rest of his men and issued out his orders.

With Jackson and Lemons both gone, Brooks felt blind as a bat. He had come to rely on them as both his eyes and his ears. Now, with the two of them gone for what could be hours, he felt unsafe and exposed. Thinking about the pissing tree, he shook his head and smiled to himself. *That little scoundrel.*

Preparing for the worst, he spread his men out behind whatever cover they could find. He also posted guards in all directions, about fifty yards out from the rest of the men, with instructions that if they spotted the enemy, they were to immediately return and report the sighting. With that chore completed, there was nothing left to do, but wait for Jackson and Lemons to return. *Damn! I hate waiting.*

~ ~ ~

Jackson scurried around for over an hour before he found the enemy patrol again. When he located them, they were taking a break, so he hunkered down behind a tree and waited. Because it was so cold, he had to breathe into his jacket to try and dissipate his white breath. However, he didn't have to perform that life-saving procedure for very long. Just a couple of minutes after crouching down to begin his wait, the Germans stood up and started off again.

Staying about sixty or seventy yards behind the enemy patrol, the Arizona scout was able to keep them in sight and also keep out of their sight. Several times, he was forced to hug a tree because one of the Germans turned around and looked along their backtrail to see if they were being followed. The action wasn't because they thought someone was following them. They were just going through the motions of a second-nature routine, a habit created by war.

Why does it have to be so cold? thought Jackson. *Why do people fight wars during the coldest times of the year*? *Hell, my people were smart. They only fought during the warm months.*

Startled, he looked around and realized that he had lost sight of the patrol. Creeping forward, he scanned through the trees trying to find them. When he couldn't find them, he went back to where they took their break and started following their tracks from there. After a couple of minutes, he discovered where he had lost his enemy, so he continued to follow the new trail until he noticed a freshly broken branch, about waist-high. It was still swinging lightly back and forth. Moving on, his focus was unexpectedly interrupted by a smile inducing thought.

While he was moving towards his enemy, he was thinking back on the little surprise he had handed out to his platoon sergeant. Wondering how he was going to top his latest prank, he wasn't thinking about what he was supposed to be doing. Instead, he almost stumbled himself into captivity without any help from the Germans. Looking up for instinct's sake, he discovered that he was just one step away from breaking cover and walking onto a dirt road...and joining hands with the enemy he was searching for.

Cautiously, he inched his way back into deeper cover and quietly dropped to the ground. A couple of eye-blinks later, he was crawling further away from the road and the Germans. "You damn fool," he muttered to himself. "That was a stupid thing to do." After he was finished scolding himself, he stayed hidden until the fear of almost being captured had left him.

After he had calmed down, Jackson moved towards the road. This time, however, he was fully aware of what he was doing. When he felt he was close enough to the edge of the trees, he scanned the area for any signs of the enemy. For ten or fifteen minutes, he watched the trees and the surrounding area for any movement, but saw nothing. Moving deeper onto the trees, he sat down to contemplate all that he had uncovered. *They're Wehrmacht troops, so maybe they don't know we're here. Maybe they haven't heard about us, yet*, he thought. *They don't appear to be looking for us, so they're probably just on a patrol, walking a perimeter beat.* "Interesting," he whispered.

Looking up at the sky, he took the time to be around mid-afternoon. *Crap on the ground,* he thought. *I've been out for over three hours*. Shaking his head, he started walking in the direction his enemy had taken, but stayed about sixty yards inside the trees. Using the road, the Germans appeared to be heading back towards Brooks, so the 18 year-old scout from Arizona decided to try and catch up with them to see exactly what they were up to.

About twenty minutes into his idea, he spotted the Germans through the trees, but they weren't walking anymore. In fact, they were just standing around, looking east towards the hiding Americans. *What are they looking at*? thought Jackson. When he heard the sound of a vehicle approaching, he hit the ground behind a tree.

Peering around the tree, he watched an armored car pull up to the patrol, but before it came to a complete stop, the commander's hatch opened, and an officer's head appeared and then his shoulders. After departing the armored car, the officer walked over to the patrol and stopped in front of a sergeant. When the salutes and greetings were over, the two men conversed for a few minutes, with the officer doing most of the talking.

Jackson couldn't see the man's face, but he thought him to be at least a captain. After talking to the NCO for about ten minutes, the officer turned to his right, fully facing Jackson and the evergreen forest, contemplating while he stared at the trees. Then he turned and headed back to the armored car. Only a couple of minutes passed before the armored car had turned itself around and was heading back in the direction it came from.

Jackson stayed where he was, watching the armored car disappear from sight, and he was just absolutely amazed. *Crap on the ground*! *I saw you standing in front of your tent, not too long ago,* he thought. His next eye-opener had him shaking his head and not liking what he discovered. "He's not a captain," he muttered to himself. "He's a colonel." *Nuts*! *They're at it again*! *Don't these guys ever give up*? *Crap on the ground*! *I better get back to Sergeant Brooks with this bit of news*.

After the colonel left, the enemy patrol continued on, moving east towards the Americans. Curiosity and a tinge of fear for his friends got the better of Jackson, so he decided to follow the Germans to see exactly what their intentions were. Following the patrol was easy. With them using the road, all he had to do was stay far enough back in the trees where he couldn't be seen. Just like a walk in the park to the scout.

Later in the day, sometime around late afternoon, Jackson watched a truck pull in behind the patrol, and come to a stop. Within minutes, the Germans had clambered into the back of the vehicle, urging the driver to step on it. "Private! Get this truck turned around and get us back to camp. It's cold as hell out here. Step on it!" A few minutes later, the truck was on its way back to camp, moving west, away from Jackson and even farther away from the hiding, Americans. The scout could hear his enemy celebrating their imminent return to warmth, but he couldn't understand what they were saying.

Surveying the area for a few minutes longer, the Arizona scout turned and headed back to Brooks. The somewhat good news he was carrying also gave birth to a devilish expression. They were still surrounded, but there wasn't an enemy soldier within five miles of them. Smiling deviously, he was interrupted from his machinations when he caught a slight movement out of the corner of his right eye. Instantly, he was on the ground and moving away. Because he thought he had been spotted, he wanted to get far from the area as quickly as possible. After moving about thirty yards or so to his right, he glanced around, but didn't see anybody.

Waiting in the shadows, he remained still, but his heart couldn't: it was pounding about fifty beats a second until he spotted movement again off to his left, about thirty yards away. Watching for the disturbance, his eyes narrowed for a couple of seconds before he started smiling.

Looking around, the scout found a small rock, and rising to his knees, he threw it at the shadow that shouldn't have moved. He heard a dull impact, so he knew the rock had flown true and had hit its mark. His next move was to drop back down to the ground and circle around behind his target. Knowing that what he had hit was human, he started smiling again. *If it had been an animal it would have run away after it got hit.* After the rock hit its mark, all movement had ceased.

Twenty minutes of cat and mouse slinking with the shadow elapsed before the beanpole was almost directly behind his objective, about twenty or so yards away, and he was trying desperately hard not to laugh. A moment later, he spotted Lemons again, and before another breath could be taken, he was on his way back to Sergeant Brooks. The scout was more than halfway back to the detachment when Sam finally realized that he had been out-foxed once more. Standing up, he whispered to himself, "Damn! He did it again!" Disgusted, he checked his carbine to see if a bullet was chambered before he headed back to where the men were waiting, knowing full well that Jackson was probably already there.

Five hours had gone by since Jackson had left. Getting worried, Brooks decided that if his scout wasn't back by sundown, he was going to send Lemons after him. Sam was on his way after Jackson when beanpole spotted him. Even before Sam could stand up and swear at him, the little scout from Arizona had disappeared and was quietly slinking his way behind his platoon sergeant, waiting for Brooks to realize someone was behind him.

Brooks, however, had no clue as to what was about to happen. Sitting down with his back resting against a tree, he was busy gazing around, looking at his men, searching for any signs of distress or indications that the men were ready to call it quits, but he didn't see any. Instead, what he did see had him puzzled. The men were looking at him with an I-didn't-steal-the-cookies expression on their faces.

Still trying to figure out what was going on with his men, he heard someone coming. Thinking it was Jackson, he looked up, ready to verbally beat him to death, and then maybe shoot him a couple of times for taking so long, but as it turned out, it was Lemons, and Sam didn't look so happy. In fact, he looked straight towards Brooks with a disgusted look on his face and started to say something, but instead, changed his mind and walked away, shaking his head. *Now where in the world did that look come from*? thought Brooks.

A little disturbed by look he received from Private Lemons, Brooks was staring at his men again, trying to figure out what the hell was going on. Glancing up, he noticed the major's expression, and it had him baffled, *What gives*? he wondered. Gazing at the major's eyes, he also realized that the major wasn't actually looking at him, like maybe his eyes were focused on something just above his head. Already a bit irritated, he once again, looked at each of his men. This time, however, their expressions were sheepish grins.

Greatly agitated, Brooks tried to jump to his feet to bring his full wrath to bear, but he was immediately jerked back down to the ground, instead. Somewhat confused, he tried again to quickly rise to his feet, and still, he was slammed back to the ground. Thoroughly bewildered, he just starred at his men until his eyes narrowed, then the steam came pouring out. His men were rolling on the ground and laughing so hard they had to cover their mouths with their hands, and they were ready to piss in their pants. Even Sam was on the ground laughing.

Reaching behind his back, Brooks discovered that he had been tied to a tree root. *JACKSON!* Searching around, he discovered the Arizona beanpole sitting on his heels. He carried such a devious expression on his face that Brooks immediately burst out laughing. He could do nothing else. "Damn you, Jackson," he whispered.

Sergeant Brooks was laughing so hard he was forced to cover his mouth with his hand, which made it very difficult for him to whisper out his wrath at the scout. "If I didn't need you so much, I'd shoot you right where you sit." Still laughing so hard he hurt, Brooks thought, *damn. I'm glad that kid made it back safely*. And while he was splitting his guts laughing, he was looking around at his men, and a disturbing notion hit him. *Damn*! *If that kid gets killed, I'm going to lose this whole bunch*. It was a very unsettling thought, and it had Brooks worried.

After all of the fun and mouth-covered laughter had died down, Jackson began his tale, and everyone was listening. "That patrol was Wehrmacht, Sarge, and I don't think they know how close we are to them. From what I could see, they were searching for something, but I have no clue as to what they're looking for unless it's us."

Sergeant Brooks stared at Jackson for a couple of eye-blinks before he raised his hand and stopped the scout from continuing. "You said, know. You think they know we're here?"

Before Sergeant Brooks could continue, Jackson interrupted him. Looking his platoon sergeant dead in the eye, he said, "An armored car pulled up next to the German patrol that I was following, and an SS colonel climbed down from it and had a discussion with the NCO in charge. He was talking to the squad leader of that patrol I was following. The conversation lasted about five or ten minutes. What they said I have no idea, but the colonel got into the armored car and drove back in the same direction he came from...east. That colonel is the same SS officer I saw standing in front of that tent. You remember, the night you sent me to find out if there was a unit directly east of us, and how big it was. Sarge, the SS unit that attacked the cave is commanded by that same colonel I saw in front of the tent that night, and he is the same man who climbed out of that armored car this afternoon."

Absolutely taken aback, Sergeant Brooks just stared at Jackson. He didn't know what to say at first. He was speechless. Searching all around thoroughly bewildered, he pulled at his ear until he looked at Sergeant Cane, and said, "Damn, Dan. Did you kick Fritz in the ass again? Those SS bastards are after us again!"

When the men started laughing, Brooks stood statue still and stared at them. He couldn't believe what he was hearing. They were just told that the same SS goons who had been trying to kill them over the last several days were back at it again, and their only reaction was laughter. "Well, Sarge," said Jackson. "I guess those SS boys don't scare us anymore."

Not knowing how to respond, Brooks paused for a moment before he said, "I guess not."

~ ~ ~

Colonel Marcs spotted the patrol that Jackson was following and decided to find out if they had come across any Americans heading west. Walking over to the NCO in charge, he asked, "How long have you been patrolling this area, Sergeant?"

"Four days, Herr Colonel, and we haven't seen anyone but ourselves in those four days. Why do you ask? Is something wrong?"

Not answering the question, Colonel Marcs asked one of his own. "Where is your headquarters located?"

Pointing across the road to the colonel's left, he said, "About a mile and a half that way, Herr Colonel."

Just before he left, he told the NCO to be on the lookout for about thirty to forty Americans heading west. "They are escaped POW's, and they have already murdered over sixty of our men. If you see them," he said, "kill them. Don't try to capture them. They refuse to surrender to anyone."

Deciding to scout out the road for himself, Colonel Marcs chose the left fork and traveled almost ten miles before he spotted the patrol Jackson was following. After his conversation with the NCO, he was convinced that the Americans had not yet arrived at the patrol's location. *Good,* he thought. *Now, I know where to start our search, and where to place the other two companies. Hiding thirty or forty men from a determined search is hard to do, but they have eluded us at almost every turn. How are they able to do this*? Staring off into the distance, he tried to put himself in his enemy's position, to try and figure out what their next move was going to be, but he failed.

Chapter 43

Not long after their well-deserved laughing session was over, Brooks' detachment was on the move again. Traveling west through a thick evergreen forest, they trudged along in a two-column formation, with the men spaced at five-foot intervals. The three scouts covered the front, while Sergeant Cane covered the rear. With the added protection of the flankers, Brooks felt it was quite unlikely that they would be taken by surprise.

Sergeant Brooks had a lot of confidence in his men. They had been in combat together from the beginning and had grown into an extremely efficient fighting unit. Veteran warriors and very worthy opponents, they carried many victories and successfully accomplished missions tied to their belts. Especially, first squad, first platoon. They were the best of his best, and they were leading the procession, riding shotgun for the platoon of men he was commanding. Blazing trail for first squad was his scouts, and there were none better in anyone's army. No. Sergeant Brooks wasn't worried about surprises. His only concern was the fanatical SS colonel and what his orders were.

About an hour after leaving their tension-release antics behind, Jackson reported back with news that another patrol was wandering around in the area. "Damn," whispered Brooks. "If these guys are roaming about, then there must be more of them, up ahead." Before he could say anything else, Jackson interrupted him. "Sarge? There's no one north of us. It's all clear." Immediately turning to his other two scouts, Brooks said, "Sam, Baker, you two go with Jackson and keep our path clear. Head north, people. Move out. We'll wait 'em out, and then we head west again."

While the men were waiting for the Germans to pass, Brooks ordered Jackson to scout to the west just to make sure there was nothing in front of them. The sun had set hours before, so the men were uncomfortable waiting in the dark with frozen mist falling on them. Hearing the roar of vehicles coming towards them was equally disturbing to Brooks, especially when they shut down. Then he really began to worry. The lack of motors running also hinted that his enemy might be dismounting from their vehicles, and he didn't like that scenario any better.

Sometime around 2300 hours, Jackson made his appearance. Slinking quietly through the falling mist, he didn't try to surprise his platoon sergeant this time. Instead, he went straight to Brooks and reported what he had uncovered. "Sarge, were surrounded again, and they're close. I found a company of Germans straight in front of us. When I tried to go around them on the right, I ran into a dirt road and another camp about fifty yards north and to the right of the road. We have roads on both sides of us, Sarge."

Pausing for a moment, he waited for Sergeant Brooks to ask his questions, but only silence followed his words, so he continued. "When that colonel was talking to the squad leader, I think he asked him a question because the squad leader pointed south after the colonel said something. Maybe his headquarters is south of us. If that's the case, then we're standing smack-dab in the middle of a battalion of German infantry. I think we can zig zag past these guys before that colonel discovers our whereabouts, but we're going to have to be real quiet. That means no laughing, Sarge."

Staring down at the beanpole, Brooks could only shake his head, a gesture that had become a habit with first squad and its leader. Most of their head shaking was caused by amazement. "How do you get away with that shit?" asked Brooks.

"What shit, Sarge?" asked Jackson.

Glaring down at his scout, Brooks felt like he was about to step into something really thick. Shrugging his shoulders, he said, "Sneaking up on people without anyone knowing about it."

That devious expression Jackson sometimes carried around was back in full force when the Arizona beanpole answered his platoon sergeant's question. "I don't know, Sarge," he whispered. "You're the one with all the experience."

Immediately, quiet snickers erupted, and the major had to pinch his nose hard to keep from laughing out loud. Welcome to the Brooks club.

Whispering harshly, Brooks was shaking his head, again, when he said, "Damn you, Jackson. One of these days you're going to set your ass on the toe of my boot, and I'm going to be laughing as I watch you sail through the air. Crap on the ground! I can't even pay the Kraut bastards to take you off my hands. What's a guy to do?"

Still snickering, first squad offered many original ideas until Brooks waved them off. Pushing his helmet to the back of his head, and thoroughly astonished, he turned back to Jackson and asked, "I take it you already have something in mind?"

His devious expression no longer visible, the scout replied, "We can't take everyone at once, so I was thinking that Sam and I could take four men each and sneak between the camps. Once we get past them, one of us can come back and get the next four. We'll have to sneak through their encampments this way until everybody gets through. There's just too many of us. We'll make too much noise with all of us going at once."

Brooks asked him if there were any more Germans lurking about after they got through the camps. The answer he received was about what he had expected. "I don't know," whispered Jackson. "I didn't get that far."

Nodding to his scout, Brooks whispered back, "I guess we have to get past these Krauts first before we can do anything else. Okay, Jackson. Sounds like a plan to me. Start whenever you're ready."

"Sarge, I think either you or the major should be in the first group so there's somebody in command on the other side," said the scout.

Not paying attention to his scout's expression Brooks whispered back, "Good idea, Jackson." Then he looked over at Major Thomas and said, "Why don't you go first, Major?"

Nodding to Brooks, Major Thomas answered. "Yes, Sergeant Brooks, an excellent idea. I'll go with the first bunch. Thank you, sir."

Absolutely taken aback, Brooks stared at his commanding officer for a moment or two before he nodded and said, “Right, sir. Keep it up, Jake. You’re wearing stripes now, sir. I can mistake you for a sergeant and dent your helmet without going to Leavenworth. Then he turned back to Jackson. “Keep away from the major. You’re a bad influence on him, beanpole.”

~ ~ ~

A light fog had been moving in since early evening, and by the time Jackson had divided the men up into four-man teams, the fog had become so thick no one could see past twenty feet. Just before starting out, Jackson once again cautioned everyone to keep very quiet, or they would end up very dead.

Sergeant Brooks stayed with the rest of the men and waited for Jackson and Lemons to return. Sam had gone with the first batch to see where they had to go before he led his own group. Jackson knew the lay of the land better than anyone, so he was leading the charge.

On the second trip, Jackson took Baker in case they needed his language skills to get them out of trouble, and then he decided to take Baker along on all of the trips for that same reason. On one of their jaunts, just as they were passing one of the German outposts, Hanky tripped over a hiding tree root, lost his balance, and fell, dropping his rifle on the ground. Instantly they were challenged by the enemy. Jackson was ready to attack the outpost, but Baker put a hand on his shoulder to stop him, and then he whispered harshly in German. “Shut up, you dumb ass. There might be Americans around!”

“What are you doing out here?” asked the startled soldier.

“Making sure the Americans don’t sneak up on you and cut your throat,” replied Baker.

“Okay,” said the jittery soldier, “but be a little quieter next time. This fog makes me nervous.”

Smiling, Baker winked at beanpole before he replied. “Sure,” and the Americans quietly moved on. Jackson walked over to Sir Charles, lightly slapped his shoulder, and whispered, “Thanks.”

By 0200 hours, only half of the men had made it to where Major Thomas and the rest were waiting. The fog was so thick that the scouts were only taking one group at a time instead of two. Jackson was in the lead while Sam brought up the rear.

When 0400 hours arrived on the morning of January 5, there was only one group left, and Sergeant Brooks was in that group. Just as they were about to leave, they heard somebody whispering in German. Brooks signaled, and they all hit the ground, praying that they wouldn't be discovered. After the enemy, had move off out of hearing, Brooks signaled and the men got up.

Jackson was in the lead followed by Brooks and then Baker, with the rest of the men between Baker and Sam. They were sneaking past the last German outpost when out of the fog stepped two German soldiers walking right towards them. Absolutely astonished, the two enemies abruptly stopped walking and stood staring at each other from about four feet away. Beanpole was the first to react. He moved so quickly that his actions caught both sides by surprise.

Immediately attacking his closest adversary, Jackson pulled out his hunting knife from where he kept it strapped to his chest and slashed his closest opponent's throat before anyone could react. Again, before anyone could think to do anything, he thrust his knife through the second German's forehead with such force that it penetrated all the way to the hilt. Quickly removing his knife from the dead soldier, the Arizona scout stood crouching, knife extended, ready to do damage to his next enemy, but there were none in sight.

After the first soldier fell to the ground gagging, Brooks jumped onto him and put his hand over his mouth, trying to quiet the man's choking. Staring at the two dead men, nobody moved a muscle or even took a breath. Many tense heartbeats went by while they waited, hoping there were no more adversaries to deal with. Their hearts were thumping so hard in their chests that each man thought the Germans must surely hear them. Several minutes passed and still no one showed. Everybody started breathing again.

His face pale, Sergeant Brooks stared at Jackson for a couple of moments before he shook his head and whispered,

"Damn, beanpole. You just saved our asses with that little stunt you pulled."

The action had happened so fast that everyone was in shock. Afraid to speak and looking fearfully pale himself, the scout just stared at Sergeant Brooks and tried to smile, but he couldn't quite pull it off. Then he heard Sir Charles whisper, "Nice job, cowboy. Chalk another one up for the Indians. That was sweet!"

Still shaking from the adrenalin rush, they headed off again, moving with extreme caution. The surprise encounter took more than a few minutes to get over, and the adrenalin was still pumping strong. Walking into their enemy like they did put the fear of capture right back into their hearts that night; it was an unsavory sensation. A very slow hour later, they made it to where Major Thomas and the rest of the men were hiding.

After taking several minutes to calm down, Jackson and Lemons took off again, splitting up to scour the area to see if there were any enemy slinkers roaming about. Just before dawn, they returned and reported that there were no Germans in the area for at least two miles. The men were no longer surrounded, but they were still in a lot of danger. Gathering up his troops, Brooks led them west, trying to distance him and his men from the enemy encampment. He was walking beside Major Thomas when they started out. Noticing how pale his sergeant was, Major Thomas asked him what had happened.

Sergeant Brooks nodded to himself; he was still astonished at the outcome of their most recent encounter. *Damn that Jackson.* Then he turned his head to gaze at Major Thomas and took several more steps before he answered. "That little man out in front just saved all of our asses, sir," he said. "That's what happened."

~ ~ ~

Colonel Marcs was cursing the fog because it meant that the reconnaissance plane couldn't be used. The only option left to him couldn't be helped as well. Without his high-in-the sky, spotter, he was forced to search through the trees on foot.

He had sent his armored car along with Captain Deil's forces, so he was walking with Lieutenant Warner and his men. Spread out in a wide skirmish line, they were advancing towards Captain von Schorn's position. The time was 0700 hours on the 5th of January, and it was a very cold, wet, and foggy morning. After several hours of miserable conditions, the fog began to dissipate and visibility began to improve.

Around noon, the scouts from Lieutenant Warner's platoon stumbled into Captain von Schorn's scouts, but they hadn't stumbled across any Wehrmacht troops, yet. They were located about six miles further to the west. When Colonel Marcs heard about the contact, he immediately radioed the northern group to find out if they had seen the Americans. "No, Herr Colonel," replied Captain Deil. "We have not seen anyone."

Frustrated again, Marcs ordered Captain Deil to bring up all of his men and to hold a position where the road began curving to the southwest. Having been ordered to leave his vehicles behind, he understood why when his company arrived at their new location. About a half a mile from where he stood the road ended, and a vast expanse of forest stood before them.

~ ~ ~

On the same morning, and about the same time, one of the Wehrmacht soldiers stumbled over the two dead men Jackson had killed earlier. Within minutes after the alarm sounded, the entire battalion was on the alert and manning their positions. After the dust of excitement had settled, the battalion commander gathered all of his officers together and held a confab in his tent. Nobody knew who had killed their men, or why, but the mortal wounds of their dead told them all they needed to know. War is hell and merciless to souls.

The battalion commander's first thought was resistance fighters. However, upon further investigation, they discovered a pack of Lucky Strike cigarettes squashed into the ground by an American combat boot just a couple of feet from where the two men were found. Within a few short minutes, two fifteen-man patrols from each of the three companies were sent out to search the woods for any sign of the killers of their comrades.

About two hundred yards in front of the center encampment, they found where a large group of people had stayed for a while before they left the area, moving west. Sending the patrols out in that direction, the battalion commander was hoping to find whoever had killed his soldiers. Five hours passed before the first runner from the patrols reported back to the battalion commander. "We have lost their trail, Herr Colonel. They were still heading west when their tracks ended."

Chapter 44

Watching Jackson through the trees, Brooks was looking at him, and pulling at his ear. Remembering the first time he had ever laid eyes on him, he was amazed at the transformation that had taken place with the little man. Not taller than 5' 7" his hundred and twenty pounds of weight was finally without the addition of rocks in his pockets. Despite his small size, however, the Arizona scout was a deadly and dangerous foe to tangle with. His dead enemies could attest to that fact, if they were still breathing.

"Can I take a look at that map again?" asked Jackson.

"Sure thing," said Brooks.

Concentrating on the map for a few minutes, Jackson looked up to face his platoon sergeant, his expression serious. Looking back down at the map, he said, "We're not going to make it, are we, Sarge?"

Chuckling, Brooks gazed at his scout and said, "Sure we are, and you're going to lead us there. Hell, beanpole," he said, "we're only about ten miles from Bastogne right now. I bet if we head southwest for a couple of miles, we'll end up well below the town, and that SS colonel will miss us because he's thinking we're heading straight for it. We'll give him the slip and be home in no time." Patting his scout on the shoulder, Brooks stood up and said, "Fifteen minutes are up, gentlemen. Time to go."

Private Lemons was just arriving back from his little venture eastward when he heard the order to move out. Walking up to Sergeant Brooks, he quickly gave his report. "The Germans are on our tail again, Sarge. I spotted them less than a mile behind us. They were stopping for some reason, but I didn't stick around to find out. I thought it more important to warn you."

Brooks checked his M1 to make sure a bullet was in the chamber before he nodded to Lemons and said, "Good job, Sam. You were right to come back and warn us." Looking at the rest of his men, he issued his orders. "All right, people. You heard the man. Put it into high gear and let's get the hell out of here. The Krauts are almost within rock throwing range. Sam, you and Baker get on point. Dan, take Stony and cover the rear. Hanky, you and Avery get out on the flanks where you belong. Let's go people. The Krauts are about to crash our party."

Turning to face Jackson, he said, "Keep an eye on those Krauts for me. See you in a couple of hours.

Late in the afternoon, sometime around 1600 hours, Sergeant Brooks called a halt. Sam had stumbled across a dry creek bed devoid of snow, so Brooks had his men stop for a couple of hours for a much needed sleep-break. Looking at his men and then back along his backtrail, he started wondering. *Only ten miles to go and we still have a bunch of Germans on our ass.* He didn't like the idea of his enemy being so close, but before he could think more on the subject, he was interrupted by a strange noise. Hearing his stomach growl reminded him that they had run out of food the day before. *Great*, he thought. *We're going to get caught because the Krauts can hear our stomachs growling*.

Interrupting his thoughts, and not knowing why, he had an abrupt urge to turn around, and there was Jackson...and he was smiling again. Brooks nodded to himself and thought, *damn. It's about time. I thought I lost you after you killed those two Krauts. I guess you're over it, now.*

Still smiling, the scout informed his platoon sergeant that the Germans seemed a bit confused. "I think they lost our trail, Sarge. They're scratching their heads and moving east, back towards their camp."

"Good," said Brooks. "We'll post some guards and let the rest of the men sleep."

After the guards were posted, Brooks leaned his back up against a tree and was soon fast asleep.

~ ~ ~

Confused and disoriented, Brooks found himself standing in a loose, company formation with his men. Looking around, he felt that something about the scene wasn't right. Hearing footsteps off to his left, he turned his head to see who was walking towards him, and immediately, fear shot through him with the force of a raging river. Marching towards him was the same SS colonel he and his men were trying to evade. Brooks tried to force himself to run, but he was unable to. He even yelled for his men to run, but they didn't respond to his yells. All he could do was watch the SS troopers form up into a skirmish line just twenty feet in front of him.

Hearing the crunch of footsteps again, he turned to his right and watched the colonel move to a position just to the right of his squad, his pistol gripped in his hand. *Damn*! *They're going to shoot us*! he shouted. Still unable to run, he just stood there, waiting. Looking at the enemy colonel, Brooks noticed that he was smiling. Then the colonel shouted, "Fire."

Brooks woke up yelling, "NO!" and threw a vicious haymaker at Jackson. If not for the scout's quick reflexes he would have been lights out upon impact. Staying out of range, Jackson chuckled and said, "Crap on the ground, Sarge. Don't you think you should share?"

"*Huh*?" Greatly confused, Brooks looked around until he spotted the man behind the voice. It was Jackson. He was showing off his pearly-whites with so much gusto that his cheeks went into hiding. Slowly, sanity began to return to Brooks. Looking around, he muttered, "Damn! That was one hell of a dream!" Then he remembered what his scout had said. "Share what?"

Still smiling proudly, the Arizona beanpole pointed to the ground. Brooks looked to where he was pointing, and lying at his feet was a stag. It wasn't much bigger than a large dog, but to the men it looked as big as an elephant. "I couldn't find any Germans anywhere, so we should be able to light a small fire to cook this thing."

Amazed, once again, Brooks looked up at his scout for a moment before he asked, "How in the hell did you manage to kill that thing without telling everybody about it?"

Laughing softly, the Arizona scout said, "Death from above, Sarge. I jumped on top of it from a tree limb. It never knew I was around."

After Jackson had his small fire going, they spent the next several hours cooking the stag because of the small fire. What meat they ended up with wasn't much for the forty or so men, but everyone had a taste, which was the main thing. After the cooking was concluded they buried the fire, the ashes, and everything not eaten from the stag, some fifty yards away, leaving no traces of their meager feast.

Posting his guards again, Brooks had decided to give his men an additional two hours of sleep. Not knowing the strength of the Germans west of them, the Americans were going to have to take their time and *slink* their way through during the daylight hours.

From out of nowhere, something that had eluded Brooks for most of the day all of a sudden entered his mind. *Why is he carrying that stick*?

Jackson had been carrying a stick throughout most of the day. Brooks also noticed a piece of string hanging out of the scout's back pocket. Quickly looking behind his back, he was happy to notice that he wasn't tied to anything.

Watching his scout for a moment, Jackson looked just like a kid searching for something close to trouble. He had been wandering around all day, and like his first revelation, Brooks was just now realizing what his scout had been doing. *What the hell is he looking for*? Then his expression changed sharply. Softly, Brooks called out, "Hey, beanpole? Are you still looking for the crap on the ground?"

Immediately, Sam cracked up laughing so hard he couldn't say anything for a couple of moments. After he calmed down a bit he turned to Brooks and said, "Damn, Sarge. You cracked a good one! I knew you'd get the hang of it one day."

~ ~ ~

Two days later, shortly after midnight on the 7th of January, Sergeant Brooks went to wake up Jackson. As he reached down to shake his scout awake, he noticed there was a grin on his face, but the scout's eyes were still closed. And still, he was startled when the smiling face spoke up, "You walk harder than an elephant, Sarge," said Jackson. Immediately, Brooks' heart was pounding so hard he could see his shirt moving. "Damn you, Jackson! Where's that Kraut colonel when I need him? Damn! All right you little heathen. It's time for you to get up and earn your keep."

~ ~ ~

Pacing around and angry at himself, Colonel Marcs was more than a bit irritated at the lack of progress being made in their search. He had overestimated his men's ability to move fast through the forest, and he had underestimated the time it would take them to catch up to the Americans. Visibility was still acceptable although there was a light fog covering the forest. He was also beginning to understand the difficulties the Americans were going through just to stay ahead of his men, as well as the fact that, with all of the fighting his enemy had been engaged in, they had come through it apparently still in one piece. Respect for his enemy was beginning to loom in the colonel's mind.

The time was well after midnight when Colonel Marcs reached the command post of Major Dietz. One of the colonel's sergeants had discovered the Wehrmacht encampment and informed his commander about the contact. After all the pleasantries were finished, Colonel Marcs came to the point. "Major, my sergeant tells me that you had a run-in with the Americans we are hunting. Tell me about it."

After the hour-long report was concluded, Colonel Marcs sent one of Lieutenant Warner's platoons on ahead to continue the pursuit while the rest of the battalion remained behind, waiting for him to finish with Major Dietz.

The argument following the report was a relatively short one. Heated, but short. The colonel had tried his hardest to enlist the major's help in his search, but his attempt ended in failure. Major Dietz politely and repeatedly refused because of his orders until Colonel Marcs threw his hands up in defeat and stormed out of the tent. Not even the major's commanders would give their permission to help.

On his way back to Lieutenant Warner, Colonel Marcs was slapping his right leg with his baton, greatly frustrated. *Germany is in a fight for survival, yet these army fools refuse to help me find the enemy*! *The Americans are our enemies, so why are these idiots refusing to help*? He had no answer to his question, but at least he knew about where the Americans were.

Chapter 45

The eruption of exploding trees was loud in the early morning stillness. January 7, had arrived, bringing a bitterly cold temperature with it, and the trees were paying the price. The temperature was so cold the tree sap froze and expanded, bursting the tree from the inside out.

The sounds of the battles raging in the west were getting closer, and Colonel Marcs couldn't help but wonder about what was happening. Rumors were flying around that the great German offensive in the west was not going well. There were also stories floating among the troops that the German armies fighting in the west were starting to retreat east towards Germany because their attacks had failed. Although the stories bothered him, they were not his problem. His only concern was the escaping prisoners. They were his only mission, and he wasn't letting anything interfere with his plans.

SS Lieutenant Karl Metz and his platoon had left the battalion shortly after arriving at the Wehrmacht encampment. His orders were to find and, if possible, delay the escaping Americans. This mission was his first independent combat command, and he was determined not to fail.

Using six-man squads, he deployed four squads for the search, all the men he had. Three were formed into a two-up-one-back skirmish line with about fifteen feet of separation between each man. His last squad was in line about fifty yards in front, serving as point guard, with about forty feet separating each man.

Looking at his men, he was shocked at how depleted his platoon was. He could remember a time when the platoon stood 40 strong, but now it wasn't so strong anymore. Only 25 remained. The entire battalion was in the same shape. Out of 600 men, the battalion could only deploy 150 battle-worthy soldiers, and they were all with Colonel Marcs.

Lieutenant Metz was unaware of his colonel's second deployment, so he didn't know that an additional platoon was dispatched with the same mission orders. The second platoon left about an hour after he did.

Stopping for a break two hours into their trek, the men of the Metz platoon waited in the cold while their commander tried to figure out where they were.

SS Lieutenant Paul Hauser was an experienced field officer. He had cut his teeth on the eastern front, spending seven long months in combat before receiving his wounds. He was wounded twice. His second wound was in the right leg and had left him with a slight limp. He was unable to return to his duties in the east, so he was transferred west and ended up under Colonel Marcs' command. The colonel needed an experienced platoon leader, so he chose the wounded officer despite his leg injury. He was also senior to Lieutenant Metz.

Lieutenant Hauser had deployed two of his squads in a wide wedge formation, about sixty feet apart and walking abreast. In front of and to the left of the two squads was another squad, positioned about fifty yards in front and about thirty yards to the left of the formation, while a fourth squad was in the same position to the right of the formation. He also had about 25 men.

Lieutenant Hauser knew about Lieutenant Metz being out in front of him because he was informed about the move. Although Lieutenant Metz had some combat experience under his belt, he didn't have Hauser's caliber of experience. While each Lieutenant had their own combat experiences, neither one of them had ever fought against U.S. troops before. They were about to learn from a new form of combat soldier, Private initiative.

Lieutenant Metz was two hours ahead of Colonel Marcs and one hour ahead of Lieutenant Hauser. If trouble erupted, he was on his own for the first hour.

~ ~ ~

Smiling triumphantly, the Arizona scout said, "I figure you just ate part of my keep, Sarge. I thought I earned it by bringing home the bacon?"

No one could keep a straight face, including Brooks. "No, beanpole. That was for yesterday. You're breathing the air of another day, so find us more keep. We need the rest, so we're going to stay for a while. Besides, I like it here."

"Wow. You're such a tyrant," said Jackson. Immediately, everyone was shaking his head and trying not to laugh. So was Sergeant Brooks.

Leaning down, the scout grabbed his M1 carbine and slung it over his left shoulder. Then, he bent over, picked his stick up off the ground, turned, nodded to Sergeant Brooks, and very quickly disappeared from sight, leaving everyone wondering about his stick.

~ ~ ~

After getting his bearings, Lieutenant Metz ordered the platoon to move out, the time was around 0400 hours. They were closing in on the Americans, but the lieutenant was unaware of the fact.

There wasn't much snow on the ground where the Metz platoon was walking, just little spots here and there, but the conditions were still miserable, and almost unbearable. The early morning was cold and damp, and it penetrated to the bone. Shivering greatly, and struggling to move forward, the men were not as alert as they should have been, and because of their lack of attention, they lost sight of their platoon leader.

~ ~ ~

Jackson had been out scouting their backtrail for about thirty minutes when he finally found what he had been searching for. The hunt had started two days prior, and it was just about over. He was looking for straight, dead sticks about two and a half feet long and about the thickness of his middle finger. Finding a treasure trove of what he was looking for under a high towering oak, he chose the best and ended up with four that would do just fine. Looking around for some place to sit, he spotted a downed tree with plenty of cover still on the branches, so he ambled on over and sat down.

After he sat down, he pulled a tiny spool of army-green thread out of his right breast pocket and placed it beside him on the fallen tree. Reaching into his butt-pack, he pulled out a leather pouch containing a few quail feathers that he had remembered to save and put them down by the thread.

Using his hunting knife, he patiently shaped each stick into an arrow, cutting the grooves for the quail feathers and putting a point on it. After he cut a notch for the bowstring, he tightly wrapped several layers of thread just below the notch to help keep it from splitting. Then he sliced the quail feathers down the middle and put each half in a groove he had cut for that purpose. When the feathers were in place, he took the thread and tied them down snug.

Reaching into his butt-pack again, he pulled out four M1 shell casings and a tapered piece of steel rod about three-quarters of an inch thick and six inches long. Using the steel rod, he pushed it into the casing mouth until the brass casing split its sides, like a pealed banana. Breaking off the larger pieces, he shaped them into blades, using a small pair of pliers he always kept in his butt-pack. Bearing down hard, he forcefully embedded them deep into the shaft, creating a deadly, homemade, bladed arrow.

When he was completely finished with his arrows, he inspected them again just to make sure he had done everything correctly. Satisfied, he took out his bowstring, which he had made out of parachute cord, and strung his bow. He had sliced open the cord and pulled out the inner string. When he braided them together, he came up with a nice sturdy bowstring. Looking at his handy work, he started smiling.

Putting all of the little stuff back into his butt-pack, he stood up to move on, but he stopped cold when he heard someone cough. *Crap on the ground,* and in an instant, he was ducking behind the downed tree. His heart was pounding so hard that he could feel the ground shake. *Crap on the ground. Where did that cough come from*? Fear had a mean grip on his stomach, and despite the cold temperature, he started sweating.

~ ~ ~

Lieutenant Metz and his men were about 200 feet from Jackson when the lieutenant swallowed wrong and ended up coughing. He had reached for his canteen to get a drink of water, but he had difficulty freeing the container, so he was forced to stop to remedy the situation. In the mean-time, everyone else, still freezing and shivering, had continued on, mindlessly putting one foot in front of the other until they pulled ahead of their platoon leader, leaving him about ten yards to their rear.

Lieutenant Metz was looking back at his canteen pouch, and this time, he was having trouble holstering it. Out of nowhere, something caught his eye, so he looked up just in time to see the arrow a split second before it entered his head just above his right eye. None of his men heard anything, so they just kept on walking.

~ ~ ~

After the cough, Jackson didn't know if he had been seen or not when he dropped to the ground behind his perch, so he waited a couple of minutes before he circled around behind the Germans. He wanted to see how many troops they were facing and thought it would be safer counting heads from their rear instead of in their visual range, at least, until he could gather his thoughts enough to come up with something diabolically dangerous.

While he was hunkering down behind their line, he noticed that one of the men had stopped to take a drink. Watching him for a minute or so, the scout was surprised to discover that the man was an officer and that he was having trouble with his equipment. *What is he doing*?

Jackson continued to watch the officer until the man struggled to put his canteen back into his pouch, and still, his men paid no attention to him. None of them were looking back. Smiling, the Arizona scout notched an arrow and let it fly.

As soon as the arrow struck its target, Jackson moved deeper into cover, using every advantage the trees gave him to keep out of sight. Sneaking quietly north for about a minute or so before turning west, he paralleled the German's line of march until he found their extreme right. Before he could do more than find their flank, one of them turned around and stopped. Immediately realizing that something was wrong, the trooper sounded the alert.

Cautiously searching their surroundings, the Germans couldn't locate their platoon leader, so they headed back through the trees to where they had last seen him. After a couple of minutes of searching, they found him. They discovered him lying on his side, dead. What really shook them up was the crude arrow sticking out of his head and the fact that they had heard nothing.

Standing behind a tree, Jackson watched the Germans gather around their fallen platoon leader. Crouched behind a huge spruce about thirty yards away, Jackson was studying his enemy with intense interest. *They look a bit confused. Why are they just standing around*? Searching the scene, he spotted a lone man and immediately thought, *I wonder if he's their platoon sergeant*. The soldier was standing a little apart from the rest of the men, and warily searching the trees.

Studying the man for a moment, the scout nodded, and a smile formed on his face while he notched another arrow. Whispering to himself he said, "I bet he is."

Still hiding behind the spruce, he watched the arrow fly straight and true. It entered the man's arm between his left shoulder and elbow and pinned both of his arms to his sides. It was a killing shot, but this time, the Germans heard the body hit the ground. When they turned to see what the commotion was, they quickly discovered that another one of their men was dead, another commander. They were shocked. The way their sergeant's arms were pinned disturbed them even more.

Immediately, they searched the trees with their eyes. Milling around, and with their weapons gripped tightly in their hands, they were nervous and scared to death. Both of their leaders were dead, leaving only a corporal in command. They appeared as though ready to panic, and fear was the motivator.

Jackson could see his enemy moving nervously about. They were jumping at the slightest noise, and not even the corporal could calm them down. He could hear someone whispering out orders, but he couldn't identify who it was. Then he spotted the whisperer, and he had his back to the scout.

~ ~ ~

Lieutenant Hauser had just started his men moving when they heard the shots. They took a moment or two to get the direction, and then they started running towards the sound of the shooting. After about fifteen minutes, however, they slowed to a walk because the firing had stopped, but they kept on moving forward anyway. Only a few minutes passed before they heard a lot of people running towards them, so Hauser readied his men for combat.

When Lieutenant Hauser spotted who was running towards them, he was absolutely shocked. He couldn't believe that Lieutenant Metz's platoon was running scared and without their weapons. Immediately, he tried to rally the running troops. His experiences on the eastern front had put a steel rod in his spine, and that knowledge told him what to do in a panic situation, but even he couldn't stop them from running. When the last man had run out of sight, Hauser deployed his men for battle. He knew about where his enemy was, so there was no need to continue the search. In his mind, the prey had been located, so all that remained was running it down.

Colonel Marcs and the rest of the battalion had been on the move for several hours when they heard gunfire off in the distance. *Lieutenant Metz has found the Americans. Good*! *Now we'll finally finish them off.* Orders immediately went out and 100 men began their advance northwest, with Colonel Marcs snapping at their heels. "We have found the Americans. One of our platoons is already firing on them. Get a move on, damn it!" *Who the hell put these trees in my way*?

Chapter 46

Everyone stopped where they were when they all heard the shots. Brooks immediately turned to the major and asked, "Where's Jackson? Those shots were close!" Seconds later, he was looking around for a good defensive position just in case they had to fight.

The firing lasted for almost ten minutes before it stopped. Worried, Brooks gave the order, and the men dug in and prepared for battle. Still concerned because of the shooting, he turned to Sam, ready to send him out after Jackson, but was stopped cold. Surprised once again, he watched his scout materialize out of the drifting fog, without a sound, just four feet from him. Immediately, he recalled their nightmare fight at the chateau, and he shuddered. Staring at Jackson, he noticed that his scout looked about the same as he did back then. Like a roaming shark. Deadly and dangerous.

"Well? What was all that shooting about?" asked Brooks.

Jackson turned to his platoon sergeant and said, "We need to leave, Sarge. Now! We have to get out of here fast!"

Brooks didn't even flinch. He just turned his head and issued his orders. "Baker, you and Sam get on point and head us southwest. We're going to cut below Bastogne and try to throw that colonel off track."

While they were walking, Brooks noticed what Jackson was carrying clinched tightly in his left hand. What really caught his attention, though, were the arrows. Blood had soaked into the freshly scraped shafts, making the homemade arrows look even more sinister and deadly.

Towards the late afternoon, Brooks called a halt. They had been on the move for almost eight hours straight without a break, and the men needed to rest. Jackson was still walking beside his platoon sergeant, but he wasn't saying anything. He was feeling guilty over his bow, kills. They were too easy to make, and that fact bothered him.

After a twenty-minute breather, they were on the move again. Baker and Lemons were back out on point with Jackson covering the rear. Brooks was pulling at his ear and swearing at himself for having stayed put those two days, but the men had really needed the rest. Now, because they had stopped for so long, their enemy had somehow caught up to them. He had no idea how far back the Germans were, but he had no intention of letting them get any closer.

~ ~ ~

Lieutenant Hauser had picked four of his best men and sent them ahead to locate where the fight took place. After the scouts left, he continued with his advance northwest, trying to catch up with the Americans before they could disappear again. Ten minutes into their advance, he ordered a double time march, which lasted about ten minutes before he slowed his men down to a fast walk.

Alternating between running and walking for ten minutes each stretch was beginning to wear out his men. However, forty minutes into their run-walk march, they met the scout who was sent back to guide them to where the fight took place. After another twenty minutes of double-timing it, Hauser's men, huffing and puffing, finally arrived at the scene. Coming to a halt, they stood voiceless like stone statues as they stared down at their dead comrades. Hungering for vengeance, they turned to face their commander and awaited his order.

According to his scouts, it appeared as though only Lieutenant Metz's men had done the shooting. The scouts had scoured the area out to about sixty yards in a complete circle and found no evidence of an enemy anywhere. They didn't find any small arms brass anywhere else, except where the rifles of their comrades lay on the ground. The scouts also pointed out to Hauser, the four dead men, and where they had been hit. The wounds had not been made by bullets.

Lieutenant Hauser walked off a little ways to ponder about what had transpired before he turned and called to his platoon sergeant. "Sergeant Krause," he shouted. "Send a runner back to find Colonel Marcs and guide him here."

~ ~ ~

Colonel Marcs was extremely annoyed at the slow progress they were making, but he realized that the thickness of the forest was the problem, not his men. Nevertheless, he pushed his men relentlessly, harshly, and without letup.

The conditions were cold, wet and almost intolerable, but Colonel Marcs was struggling right along with his men, contending with everything they were forced to endure right along beside them. Watching their commander take the same punishment that they had to deal with surprised a lot of his men. In fact, they were beginning to enjoy watching their fifty-year old colonel shiver and stink like mud with the rest of them. After his two-hour journey, Colonel Marcs was standing beside Lieutenant Hauser.

Staring around at nothing in particular, Marcs couldn't believe what he had heard from Lieutenant Hauser. *What would cause over twenty veteran soldiers to run away like frightened children*? Looking at the evidence, he pondered the question for over an hour while his men rested. When the hour was up, he deployed his men for their final push to capture the Americans.

Captain von Schorn's company was on the left, forming up into a wedge formation. Captain Deil was on the right with his two platoons, and they were ready and waiting. Lieutenant Warner's company had only one platoon left, so his men were positioned in front, on point, about a hundred yards ahead of the battalion.

Three men from each platoon were sent out to act as scouts. Their orders were to cover the front and protect their flanks. With a three to one advantage the colonel wasn't worried about an ambush. Forty men against his more than 125 put that fear to bed. He was more concerned about them getting away.

~ ~ ~

Brooks called another halt around 2100 hours, and everybody collapsed where they were. "Okay, gentlemen. You have two hours, and then we head out again." Within minutes almost all were asleep.

Major Thomas called Brooks over and said, "We seem to have run out of map, Sergeant."

Smiling, Brooks looked at the map and said, "Well then, sir, I guess we wing it." Taking another look at his surroundings, Sergeant Brooks nodded and continued. "It appears that the trees are thinning out a little bit, sir. I think we're getting close to the Belgium-Luxembourg, border. As soon as we cross into Belgium, we'll head due south. We're sure to run into Arlon or someplace close to there. Let's talk about this after we sleep, sir."

Nodding in agreement, the major said, "Good idea, Al." With those words still echoing in their minds, the two men followed everyone else and were soon adding their snoring to the symphony of noise.

~ ~ ~

"Go away, Mom. I don't have any school today, remember? It's Saturday for Pete's sake!"

"Hey, Sarge," whispered Jackson. "We slept too long."

Brooks was up in a flash. "Damn! Boy, am I glad *you* woke up in time. Get 'em up quick. We've gotta get out of here, pronto."

Midnight had arrived on the 8th of January, and nothing concerning the elements had improved. The night was windy and still bitterly cold. Without proper cold weather gear, they were at the mercy of a merciless Mother Nature. While Jackson was helping his platoon sergeant wake everyone up, he informed Brooks that he had been able to make ten more arrows. Smiling sadly the scout said, "I would have made more except I ran out of quail feathers."

Nodding for no reason in the world, Sergeant Brooks replied, "Well, remember to pick some up the next time we're near a store. There's got to be somebody around who's got nothing better to do. Who knows? Selling quail feathers might turn out to be a pretty good business venture."

"Come, Sarge," said the scout. "We're in Europe. Nobody here wants feathers when they can eat cheese and drink wine, instead." The nonsense conversation continued on until the escapees were on their way again, stumbling along, not quite awake yet. An hour passed before they came across a startling discovery. "Look! Over to the right. I see some lights." Sergeant Brooks immediately looked to the right and sure enough there were lights showing. Vehicle headlights. “Damn. How did they get out here so fast?” Before he could swear again, the vehicles turned to the right and disappeared into the distance. Brooks let out a quiet sigh and thought, *shit. That was too close.*

Sergeant Brooks was just about to send Private Hanky back to get Jackson, but he didn’t get past the thought. Beanpole emerged out of the darkness and scared the hell out of his platoon sergeant, again. “Sarge, we got Germans behind us,” he said.

“How many?” asked Brooks.

“I counted ten,” said Jackson.”

“How far apart are they? I mean, can you take ‘em out one at a time with that thing?” asked Brooks.

“Well,” said the scout. “I might be able to get one or two of them before they notice something’s wrong,”

“Not good,” replied Sergeant Brooks. “We have to get ‘em all, or they’ll warn the others. How far back are they?” asked Brooks.

“Two, maybe three hundred yards.” said the scout.

“Go back and check their flanks to see if there’s any more of them floating around.”

“I already did that, Sarge. These guys are the bottom rung of the ladder. All the other lookouts are north of them.”

“Good,” said Brooks. “We’ll ambush the bastards.” Then his scout’s words finally hit home. Brooks stood floored, again, staring down at the Arizona scout, and once more, he was shaking his head and wondering, *how does he get away with that shit*?

Sergeant Brooks kept his men moving while he tried to formulate a suitable plan of attack. Thinking about what Jackson had said, had him pondering over his next move. *If these guys are the bottom of the pile, then they have no idea where we’re at. If we eliminate their bottom rung, we might be able to slip away cleanly*. “Jackson, where are they headed?” asked Brooks.

“Right at us, Sarge,” replied the scout.

Nodding, Brooks came up with a plan. “Go get Baker. Quickly, now. I think I have an idea. Sir Charles is about to become a German again.”

Chapter 47

The time was 0145 hours, on the 8th of January, and the early morning cold had everyone shivering. Tense breaths rose whitely into the brisk morning air, while they waited for the fun to begin, but no one was happy. The wind had died out, yet the crisp late-night was bitterly cold by the time Sergeant Brooks had all of his men in place, and still, they were not happy. To Sergeant Brooks, however, their discomfort wasn't a concern. The time had arrived for Baker and Jackson to do their part.

The lone German scout was moving west, searching for the Americans; and he had no idea that he was the center of his enemy's attention. His orders were simple: find the Americans and report back. He thought he was the stalker, but that notion turned out to be an illusion.

Jackson had his bow ready, and he was crouching down to silhouette his enemy against the skyline. Where they were hunkering down, the forest canopy wasn't as thick as what they were used to so some light was getting through the trees. They couldn't see their boots when they looked down, but looking up from the ground was a different story altogether.

Searching for the Americans, the German scout heard a whispered, "Hey" in his own language and turned to investigate. The darkness didn't allow him to see more than three or four feet ahead, so he was having trouble penetrating the darker shadows with his eyes. A strange noise caught his attention for a brief moment, just before the arrow entered his head.

While Baker and Jackson were stalking their enemies, the rest of the men were waiting to do their parts, but nothing was happening. After waiting for what seemed like hours, they were getting worried. Out of a windless early morning, Corporal Sims felt a slight breeze hit him on his left side and turned that way and almost jumped out of his skin, leaving behind a number of strange noises. "Damn, beanpole. Tell someone you're coming, next time. Jesus. I think I dumped a load." Jackson was sitting beside him, and he was grinning mightily. Seeing the scout's expression told Sims that they had been waiting to spring their ambush for nothing. Shaking his head, Sims gathered his men and headed back to the rendezvous where Brooks had the rest of the men waiting.

~ ~ ~

Colonel Marcs was talking to Lieutenant Warner when he noticed some movement off to his left. Turning, he noticed several soldiers were running towards him. They were with Sergeant Krause and several of his men, and they were excited about something. Sergeant Krause stopped in front of the colonel and saluted, but before Colonel Marcs could return the salute, Krause blurted out, "We found Corporal Heppner's squad, and they are all dead, Herr Colonel."

"What?" exclaimed Marcs. "Where?"

"About thirty minutes from here," replied Krause. And they have the same wounds as Lieutenant Metz's men. Before anybody else could say anything, they spotted several more soldiers running towards them, and they were also excited about something.

Lieutenant Hauser and a couple of his scouts halted in front of Colonel Marcs. Struggling to breathe, they tried to talk, but they couldn't get the words out. After they had finally caught their wind enough to speak, an excited Lieutenant Hauser shouted, "We found them, Herr Colonel. They are about a mile south of us, and they are heading southwest!"

After sending Jackson up ahead to help scout out the area, Brooks had no eyes on his rear. Because he was so tired, he had forgotten to cover his ass. The Americans were only a few minutes out of cover when one of the enemy scouts noticed their silhouettes walking southwest towards Arlon. Because no one was covering their rear, the Americans were totally unaware that they had been spotted by their enemy.

~ ~ ~

The fleeing Americans had finally reached a small stand of trees they had been shooting for just as the sun poked its head above the horizon. The three scouts met Brooks in the trees and reported that they had stumbled onto a town.

Beanpole said, "I think the sign read "Ettelbruck" or something like it. It's a real small town from the looks of it."

"Did you see anything?" asked Brooks.

"No. I couldn't see anything. I was still too far away from it," replied the scout. That was as far as the conversation went. Catching a slight movement out of the corner of his eye, Jackson urgently whispered, "Down!"

Brooks looked over at Jackson to find out what he had seen, but the scout just shrugged his shoulders, not certain of what he had spotted. "I thought I caught some movement in those trees we just left," he said, "but I can't be sure."

Deep in thought, Brooks pulled at his ear while he stared across the frozen countryside towards his enemy. *Unbelievable. I guess I always knew this would happen. Running around in that thick forest, there was always that hope, a chance that we could make it. Now, we're more or less in the open, and daylight has arrived, and the enemy can see our every move.* Inhaling deeply, Sergeant Brooks nodded to himself and then he turned to his men and said, "Damn, boys. We sure gave the Krauts a good chase, didn't we?"

"What? Are you kidding? Crap on the ground!" whispered Jackson. "They got us right where we want 'em, don't they, Sarge?"

Somewhat taken aback, Brooks stared at his scout for a moment before he asked, "What in the hell are you talking about, Jackson? That's a battalion out there, beanpole. They have us out numbered at least eight to one."

"Well, not really, interrupted Cane. Not the way I see it. With Baker, Lemons, and Jackson, I figure that puts us about dead even. Yeah. Not only that, look at Hanky. He's itching to show those Krauts his medical expertise. I hear he's been practicing up on his surgery. He knows how to amputate, now."

"What's your point, Sergeant Cane?"

"I'm not running another step, Al. You know I hate to run. I told you that in North Africa, but no, you had me running up and down hills the whole time, and you've been running me to death ever since. I hate running."

"Alex?"

"No sweat off my nose, Al. Good a place as any to die. We're not in Kraut-land, so why not here?"

Staring around at his men, Brooks studied them for a couple of moments, gauging their expressions, and they were all pretty much the same. Then the beanpole from Arizona spoke up. "Well then," he said softly, his eyes looking cold and menacing. "That just about says it all. What's the problem, Sarge?"

~ ~ ~

Forty minutes after spotting their enemy, the Germans marched into view. "Look, Al. They've cleared the woods and they're moving straight for us. They know we're here."

"Yeah, Dan," said Brooks. "I believe you're right. Hell. I guess there's no fooling them this time. We don't have enough overcoats, and beanpole's out of string!"

Colonel Marcs had expected the Americans to try and out run them, but they didn't seem to be taking that road. The Americans looked as though they were going to stand and fight. *How stupid*, he thought. *They're severely outnumbered and out gunned. What in the hell are they thinking*?

Marcs deployed one company in a skirmish line and had them advance on the American position, with the other two companies on the wings in a box wedge formation. He didn't think that he was going to need his other two companies.

Colonel Marcs was walking behind his units, somewhere in the center, ready help whichever unit needed his immediate attention. Thinking to himself, the scenario unfolding reminded him of those old movies he used to watch at the theater. The red coats and the blue coats, all lined up in formation with their muzzle loading, single shot muskets, marching towards each other to do battle. While this thought was going through his mind, his soldiers started dying.

~ ~ ~

Sergeant Brooks was nodding happily after the first rounds were fired. "Do you see what they're doing, Major?" he asked.

"Yes," replied Major Thomas. "It appears that the colonel is secretly on our side. Look. He's marching his men like little tin soldiers so we can kill them all before they get here."

Cautioning his men, Brooks was laughing when he said, "Pick your targets gentlemen, and don't waste any ammo. The colonel is obliging us just like the British did. When they get closer, we'll open up with their own machine guns."

Twenty minutes after the start of battle, five Americans had fallen, and Corporal Sims was bleeding from an arm wound. "Damn it, Al! Will you get the hell away from me? I'm fine. Go find your own place to shoot from." However, despite the light humor, their situation was still dire. The Germans had closed some distance, and they were getting dangerously closer, so Brooks decided that it was time to fall back to their last-stand position. Jackson had found the only suitable place close enough for the men to reach: a dried up creek bed.

Brooks had the two MG 42's open up with their long range covering fire while the men were retreating to the creek bed. The sound of ripping linen greeted the advancing Germans when the MG42's started shooting. Firing 1,000 rounds per minute, the sound produced resembled a sheet being forcefully ripped apart. The men of Kampfgruppe Marcs instantly recognized the sound of their own machine gun, and they cringed and immediately hit the ground.

Brooks moved the injured out first because they needed help to get to the creek bed. In his mind, that position was as far as they were going. The wounded couldn't go any further without assistance, and besides, the area behind the dry watercourse was devoid of any cover for almost 100 yards. He knew they had lost the race, but there was still a lot of the enemy left to kill before the end, an outcome that didn't favor the Americans.

When all of the wounded had been moved to the creek bed, the MG 42's were next so they could cover the withdraw of 1st squad, who had remained behind to cover the full retreat. Brooks was now down to less than twenty-five uninjured men. Just before he and the rest of the men left the small stand of trees they were in, he noticed a lot of Germans lying on the ground, and they were not moving.

Using the trees as a shield, the retreating Americans quickly made it to the creek bed. When they arrived, Brooks ordered the men to dig in, deepening the dry streambed to help keep the wounded out of harm's way. The Germans still hadn't reached the back edge of the trees the Americans had just vacated, which gave Brooks' detachment a little more time with their excavation duties.

Looking around at the men lining the streambed, Brooks noticed that most of 1st squad was missing from the firing line. Turning back to gaze across the open field separating them from the trees they had just left, he spotted several bodies before he noticed Private Todd's helmet lying on the ground about forty feet away. Then he saw his body. After the strafing incident in North Africa, Hanky had painted a white star on the top of his helmet so the Allied fighter pilots would know that he was an American. "Damn Krauts," muttered Brooks. All of a sudden, tears trickled down his cheeks when he realized that his best friend was dead. Abruptly and without any warning, a loud roaring noise was heard, and out of nowhere, machine gun fire.

Sergeant Brooks looked out and then up just in time to watch a squadron of five P47 Thunderbolts let loose with their machine guns and light up the enemy, knocking bodies through the air, lifeless and broken. The P47's left as soon as the Germans entered the trees the Americans had just vacated, but the Thunderbolts didn't go far. Circling overhead, they waited for another opportunity to rip into their enemy again.

Two quad-fifty, anti-aircraft machine gun halftracks came rushing up from the rear, heading for the creek bed where the wounded were, hammering away at the Germans, trying to keep them at bay while three ambulances pulled up to evacuate the wounded. That was all the reinforcements Sergeant Brooks had time to spot.

Hearing a shrill screech coming from his left, Brooks was startled to see that his men were leaving the creek bed and charging the Germans, and that Jackson was leading them. Caught up in the excitement, Sergeant Brooks found himself charging right alongside of the beanpole. When they reached the trees they had just retreated from, they slowed down to a walk and started stalking their enemy. Jackson was out of ammo, so he had his bow strung with one arrow ready to fly, and he was searching the trees, looking for his enemy.

What was left of the attacking Germans was being pushed out of the trees by Brooks and his men. The Germans were still fighting with spirit, but the tide of battle had turned sharply against them. When Lieutenant Hauser's men saw him fall to the ground with a piece of stick protruding from his head, they started casting nervous glances around, searching for the shooter. They also started dying faster because of the fearful distraction beanpole created. Another German soldier fell with a piece of stick protruding from his chest, and then the enemy warriors watched Captain Deil take an arrow through the throat. They noticed where it came from, and the distraction cost them their lives as well.

After Captain Deil had taken an arrow in the throat, that left only one officer still alive. Colonel Marcs.

The sound of the battle intensified when reinforcements finally caught up to the fight. Two platoons of American infantry were the first to arrive and they hit the Germans in the flank, but Colonel Marcs' troops held their ground against the repeated attacks by the Americans. Keeping their enemy at bay the Germans fought hard until disaster unexpectedly struck the kampfgruppe.

Standing in the shadows, along the fringe of the battle, Jackson was about ninety feet from Colonel Marcs, facing the colonel's back, but he was unaware of whose back he was facing. His last arrow was already notched, and all he was waiting for was a suitable target. Then the back turned around, and the beanpole spotted Colonel Marcs and recognized him immediately. Staring intently at his enemy, Jackson drew back the arrow and muttered, "This is for Sam." Then he let the arrow fly.

Colonel Marcs stared at Jackson for a moment or two, only recognizing him as the enemy. Fascinated at what was unfolding, he watched the American draw back the arrow. Then it dawned on him; he was looking at the weapon that had caused all those strange wounds on his men. With that realization, he brought up his 9mm pistol and tried to shoot

Jackson, but before he could pull the trigger, he was hit in the forehead by an arrow shot by an Arizona beanpole.

When the Germans realized that their colonel was dead, they stopped fighting and laid their weapons on the ground, calling it quits. A few minutes later, Jackson found Sergeant Brooks lying on the ground with a large hole in his leg. Besides Jackson and Baker, Brooks was the only other member of 1st squad who was still alive. First squad had been decimated when they stayed behind to cover the retreat.

While Brooks was being loaded onto a stretcher, he noticed Jackson wondering around the battlefield, in search of more of his friends. He had something in his hand, and it appeared to be dripping. Then he watched Jackson stop and immediately drop to his knees before he leaned over until his head touched the ground. The scout had found who he was searching for.

Still thinking about what Jackson was carrying, Sergeant Brooks was astounded when he realized it was a scalp. Searching around to see whom it had belonged to, he noticed a man lying on the ground off to the side, with an odd shaped wound on the top of his head. Ordering the stretcher-bearers to amble on over, he wasn't surprised to find that the scalped man was none other than Colonel Marcs.

Following Jackson with his eyes again, Brooks couldn't believe they had finally made it to safety. Shaking his head and with tears rolling down his cheeks, Brooks gazed at the Apache scout for a moment before he muttered reverently to himself, "Damn you, Jackson!"

Thank you for reading.

Please review this book. Reviews help others find Absolutely Amazing eBooks and inspire us to keep providing these marvelous tales.

If you would like to be put on our email list to receive updates on new releases, contests, and promotions, please go to AbsolutelyAmazingEbooks.com and sign up.

Acknowledgements

Edited by Adele Brinkley; with pen in hand.

Technical Advisors; First Lieutenant Thomas Edward Clary, U.S. Army Corps of Engineers; Viet Nam War. First Lieutenant Raymond Darwyn Clary, U.S. Army Air Force; World War II.

A special word of thanks to
Mr. William R. Burkett, Jr.

Thank you, sir, for your amazing endorsement. The whole world now knows the kindness you bestowed on me. After I read through your words several times, shocked and thrilled to death, I was forced to pinch my nose until it hurt just to keep from shouting out and scaring my wife to death. Thank you, Mr. Burkett. Thank you for your generous support.

- J. Allen Clary.

About the Author

J. Allen Clary is currently writing books and enjoying life. He has created 21 stories in just a little over five years, with 10 of them finished. A motorcyclist until death parks his bike, he currently and forever resides at home with his wife of 36 years, along with four cats and two dogs. His oldest son works in theater, building stages. His youngest son is a U.S. Navy veteran.

AbsolutelyAmazingEbooks.com
or AA-eBooks.com

www.ingramcontent.com/pod-product-compliance
Lightning Source LLC
Chambersburg PA
CBHW060928030726
47503CB00003B/510